Praise for

C.E. MURPHY

and her The Walker Papers series

"The breakneck pace keeps things moving...
helping make this one of the most involving and
entertaining new supernatural mystery series in an
increasingly crowded field."
—*LOCUS* on *Thunderbird Falls*

"Fans of Jim Butcher's Dresden Files novels and
the works of urban fantasists Charles de Lint and
Tanya Huff should enjoy this fantasy/mystery's cosmic
elements. A good choice."
—*Library Journal* on *Thunderbird Falls*

"A swift pace, a good mystery, a likeable protagonist,
magic, danger—*Urban Shaman* has them in spades."
—Jim Butcher, author of the bestselling
The Dresden Files series

"C.E. Murphy has written a spellbinding and
enthralling urban fantasy in the tradition of
Tanya Huff and Mercedes Lackey."
—*The Best Reviews* on *Urban Shaman*

"Tightly plotted and nicely paced, Murphy's latest has a
world in which ancient and modern magic fuse almost
seamlessly....Fans of urban fantasy are sure to enjoy this
first book in what looks to be an exciting new series."
—*Romantic Times BOOKreviews* on *Urban Shaman*
[nominee for Reviewer's Choice Best Modern Fantasy]

C.E. MURPHY

COYOTE DREAMS

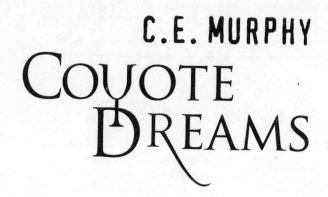

LUNA™
www.LUNA-Books.com

COYOTE DREAMS

ISBN-13: 978-0-373-80272-2
ISBN-10:   0-373-80272-2

Copyright © 2007 by C.E. Murphy

This edition published by arrangement with Harlequin Books S.A.

® and TM are trademarks of Harlequin Books S.A., used under license.
Trademarks indicated with ® are registered in the United States Patent
and Trademark Office, the Canadian Trade Marks Office and in other
countries.

www.LUNA-Books.com

Most especially, I want to say thank you to my husband, Ted. The kernel of this series was his, and I quite literally wouldn't be here without him. I love you, hon. Let's hope there are lots of Walker Papers to celebrate in the future.

Thanks are also due to cover artist Hugh Syme; my editor, Mary-Theresa Hussey; and my agent, Jennifer Jackson; as well as my usual suspects, particularly Silkie, who once more went beyond the call of duty in doing unpaid research and catching my embarrassing spelling errors.

For Ted,
because I wouldn't be here without him

CHAPTER ONE

Tuesday, July 5, 8:58 a.m.

Someone had driven a tire iron into my skull. I could tell, because centered in my left temple was a vast throbbing pain that could only come from desperate injury. It felt like there were a thousand vicious gnomes leaping up and down on the iron, trying to increase the size of the hole in my head. I had the idea that once it was split open far enough, they would run down the length of metal and dive into the soft, gooey gray matter of my brain and have themselves a little gnomish pool party.

Neither of my eyes would open. I fumbled a hand up to poke at them and encountered sufficient goo that I took a moment to consider the possibility that the gnomes were already in my head, had overfilled it and were now flowing out my sinuses and tear ducts. It wasn't a pretty thought.

Then again, nothing could be a pretty thought when someone'd smashed a tire iron into my head.

I rolled my fingers across my eyelashes, trying to work
some of the ook out of them. My heart was beating like a
rabbit on speed, except when it paused with an alarming
little arrhythmia that made me start hyperventilating. I
hoped I was dying, because anything else seemed anticlimactic with all that going on. Besides, I had some experience with dying. It was kind of old hat, and so far it hadn't
stuck.

Unlike my eyes. I physically pried one open with my
fingers. The red numbers on my alarm clock jumped into it
and stabbed it with white-hot pokers. I whimpered and let
it close again, wondering why the hell I was in my bed, if I
was dying. Usually I found myself dying in more exotic locations, like diners or city parks.

A whisper of memory drifted through my brain in search
of something to attach itself to. The department's Fourth of
July picnic had been the day before. I'd attended, feeling
saucy and cute in a pair of jeans shorts and a tank top. I'm
five foot eleven and a half. *Cute* and I are not generally on
speaking terms, so the feeling had been a novel one and I'd
been enjoying it. The outfit had shown off a rare tan and the
fact that I'd lost twelve pounds in the past few months, and
I'd gotten several compliments. Those were as rare as me
rubbing elbows with *cute,* so it'd been a good day.

Which did nothing to explain how it had ended with a tire
iron separating the bones of my cranium. I walked my fingers
over the left side of my head, cautiously. My fingers encountered hair too short to be tangled, but no tools of a mechanic's
trade. I pressed my hand against my temple, admiring how

nice and cool it felt against the splitting headache, and the memory found something to attach itself to.

Morrison. My boss. Smiling fatuously down at a petite redhead in Daisy Mae shorts that hugged her va-va-va-voom curves. Right about then somebody'd offered me a beer, and it'd sounded like an awfully good idea. I tried to close my eyes in a pained squint, but I'd never gotten them open, so I only wrinkled them and felt crusty goo crinkle around my lashes.

The only other thing I remember clearly was a bunch of guys from the shop swooping down on me as they—each— bore a fifth of Johnnie Walker. With my last name being Walker, they figured me and Johnnie must be cousins and that gave me a leg up on them. I was pretty sure my leg up had turned into a slide down the slow painful descent of hangover hell.

I gave up on rubbing my eyes and prodding my head, and instead flopped my arm out to the side with a heartfelt grunt.

Unfortunately, the grunt wasn't mine.

It turned out my eyes were willing to come open after all, with sufficient force behind the attempt. I wasn't sure I had eyelashes left after the agony of ripping through loaded-up sleep, but at least the subsequent tears did something to wash away some of the goop. I was out of bed and halfway across the room with a slipper in hand, ready to fling it like the deadly weapon it wasn't, when I noticed I wasn't wearing any clothes.

Neither was the blurry-eyed guy who'd grunted when I'd smacked him. At least not on his upper half. He pushed up on his elbows while I scrubbed at my eyes with my free hand. I'd gone to sleep with my contacts in, which partly explained why

there was such a lot of gunk in my lashes, but I didn't believe
what my twenty-twenty vision was telling me. I was pretty
certain the goo had to be impairing it somehow, because—

—because *damn, sister!*

"Easy on the eyes" didn't cover it. He was so easy on the
eyes that they just sort of rolled right off him as precursor
to a girl turning into a puddle of—

All right, there was way too much goo going on in my
morning. "Who the hell are you?" I demanded, then coughed.
I sounded like I'd been on a three-day drunk. In my defense,
I knew it wasn't more than a one-night drunk, but Jesus.

"Mark," he said in a sleepy, good-natured sort of rumble,
and grinned at me. "Who're you?"

"What're you *doing* here?" I asked instead of answering.
He arched one eyebrow and looked my naked self over, then
lifted the covers a few inches to inspect his own lower half.

"I'd say I'm havin' a real good night." He grinned again
and flopped back onto my bed, arms folded behind his head.
His hair was this amazing color between blond and brown,
not dishwater, but glimmering with shadows and streaks of
light. His folded-back arms displayed smoothly muscular
triceps. Who ever heard of someone having noticeably beautiful triceps, for heaven's sake? The puff of hair in his armpits
was, at least, an ordinary brown and not waxed away. That
would've been more than I could handle.

"So who're you?" he asked again, pleasantly. More than
pleasantly. More like the cat who'd stolen the cream, eaten
the canary and then knocked the dog out of the sunbeam
so he could loll in it undisturbed.

For a moment I was tempted to open the curtains so I
could see if he'd stretch out and expose his belly to the

morning sunlight. God should be so good as to give every woman such a view once in her life.

The thing was—well, there were many things. Many, many things and all of them led back to me being unable to think of the last time I'd done something so astoundingly stupid.

No, that wasn't true. I knew exactly the last time I'd done something so astoundingly stupid. I'd been fifteen, and I'd have hoped the intervening thirteen years of experience would be enough to keep me from doing it again. Only I hadn't been shitface drunk then, and if the God who was kind enough to provide the gorgeous man in my bed was genuinely kind, there wouldn't be the same consequences there'd been then.

The *point* was, Mark was so far out of my league it wasn't even funny. I didn't think I'd said that out loud until he pushed up on an elbow again and looked me over a second time before saying, "I beg to differ," in a mildly affronted tone. Then curiosity clearly got the better of him as he sat all the way up, drawing his knees up and looping his arms around them as he squinted at me. He had a tattoo on his right shoulder, a butterfly whose colors were so bright it had to be new. His biceps were magnificent. He had smooth sleek muscle where most people didn't even have flab. It was like he took up more space than he really ought to.

Which, in my experience, suggested he probably wasn't human.

I didn't realize I'd said *that* out loud, either, until he threw his head back and laughed, then scooted around on my bed like he belonged there, giving me a curious grin. "What *is* your name?"

"Joanne," I finally answered. "Joanne Walker. SPD," I added faintly, for no evident reason. Maybe I thought announcing I worked for the police department would provide me with some kind of physical shielding.

It struck me that clothes would be a lot more effective in that arena. Still clutching my slipper as a weapon, I scampered for the bathroom and pulled my rarely used robe off the door.

"I'm pleased to make your acquaintance, Joanne Walker," he called after me. I stuck my head out the door incredulously.

"Is that what you call it?"

"What should I call it?" He shrugged, a beautiful movement like glass flowing. "I'm gettin' a kinda freaked-out vibe from you, ma'am. You want I should vacate the premises?"

"I want you should tell me you had rubbers in your wallet and you don't anymore, and that you've got a nice clean blood test in your hip pocket. I'll think about the rest of it after that." I retreated into the bathroom again and poked through the garbage nervously. Funny what strikes a girl as relieving in the midst of mental crisis. Having a naked guy whose name I barely knew in my bed would normally be more than enough reason to come apart at the seams, but oh no. Give me a little evidence of safe sex despite drunken revelry and it seemed I could handle the naked guy.

Pity there was no such evidence. Despite that, my hind brain announced it wouldn't half mind handling the naked guy. More than once. Which, in fact, I could only presume that I had.

Augh.

"Sorry," he said. "Still got three in my wallet."

Three. I stopped poking around in the garbage to stare though the wall at him. "Confident, aren't you?"

I heard a grin come into his drawl: "Looks like I got cause, ma'am. I had five to begin with," he added cheerfully. I lurched to the door so I could stare at him more effectively. I'd developed some unusual skills lately, but X-ray vision hadn't been one of them.

"Are you serious?"

"No," he said, still cheerfully. "Sorry, ma'am."

Jesus. I didn't remember the last time I got laid, or more accurately, I remembered in exquisite, precise detail, and now it appeared I'd missed an all-nighter of action thanks to way, way too much whiskey in the jar. That was wrong on so many levels I didn't even know where to begin.

"Stop calling me ma'am." For some reason I found the ma'aming kind of charming, and I wasn't sure I wanted to be charmed. I wasn't sure what I wanted at all. All my base impulses were to throw the guy out and hide under the bed until it all went away. It'd been an approach to life that had worked pretty well until recently, but a couple of weeks ago it'd become violently clear that the ostrich strategy wasn't going to cut it anymore. *Violently* was the key word: there were two people dead because I'd refused to step up to the plate when I should have. So much as I wanted to take my slipper and drive Mitch out of my apartment with it, I kind of thought maybe I should do something adult and sensible, like own up to my great, huge, flaming mistake and try to cope.

The tire iron reasserted its presence in my skull. I groaned and grabbed my head, trying to focus on a cool, silver-blue flutter of power that typically resided beneath my breast-bone. A hangover, in a mechanic's parlance, was essentially an overheated engine—dehydration in any form fit nicely into that analogy—and helping someone recover from de-hydration was in my bag of tricks. I called on that power, for once selfishly glad to have access to it.

Absolutely nothing happened.

No, that wasn't true. Reluctance happened, a feeling I'd encountered once before, when I tried healing a knife cut on my cheek. That cut had left a scar when being stabbed through the chest by a four foot sword hadn't: my newly-awakened power's way of announcing that it thought some things should be acknowledged and dealt with on a purely human level.

Apparently hangovers fell into that category, too.

I whimpered and dared peek at myself in the mirror while I got a glass of water and fumbled for aspirin. Aside from the sleepy eyes, I didn't look nearly as awful as I thought I should. In fact, between the tan, the mussy hair and what could reasonably be called a rosy, satisfied glow, I actually looked sort of hot. As in sexy, not overheated, the latter of which being how I'd normally use the word. The robe was even this nice soft mossy green that played up the hazel in my eyes.

Mitch or Matt or Mark or whatever the hell his name was, appeared in the reflection behind me. He'd put his jeans on and left the top buttons undone, which was possibly more distracting than him being naked. My eyes just sort of slid right down his torso and fixated at that little flat bit of belly before more interesting things got started.

"Don't suppose you've got any more of those?" he asked in a woeful little-boy voice. I flinched, slammed the aspirin with a gulp of water and handed him the mug without rinsing it or refilling it. Ordinarily I'd think that was gross, but under the circumstances, being squeamish about swapping a few bodily fluids seemed hypocritical. Matt seemed to feel the same way, because he took the cup without comment and put out his other hand for some aspirin. I dropped two in his palm and he popped them, then sagged against the bathroom wall with a groan and extended the mug again. "More," he pleaded, putting enough pathos into the croaked word that I erupted a startled giggle. He gave me an adorable wan grin in return and I got him some more water, then took the cup back and drank another fourteen ounces myself. When I was done I felt like my equilibrium had been restored, which I knew perfectly well was a big fat lie, but I planned to run with it, anyway.

"So." I leaned on the counter and looked at his reflection behind me. He was taller than I was by at least three inches. I couldn't remember having ever slept with somebody who was taller than me before.

For that matter, I still couldn't.

My brain went *augh* again and I squinched my face up. Mike's reflection made concerned eyebrows at me. "So," he echoed, as if it might smooth my features out again. It worked, because I forced my own eyebrows up to make myself stop squinting.

"What was your name again?"

"Mark."

"Mark. Right." I pressed my lips together, staring at our reflections. He looked sort of woeful and cute and headachy, and throwing him out seemed kind of like kicking a puppy. "I don't suppose you can cook, Mark."

He gave me a big bright grin in the mirror. "Just tell me where the kitchen is."

* * *

The problem with my kitchen was it didn't have anything to cook in it. Mark slapped around the linoleum floor barefoot and cast me looks of unmitigated dismay as he opened cupboards that would do Old Mother Hubbard proud. His butterfly shifted subtly with the play of muscle in his shoulder, as if it might wing away from his skin. I watched it and mumbled, "There are toaster waffles in the freezer."

It was the best I could do. I had no raw ingredients in my apartment; the only reason there were eggs was my weakness for fried-egg sandwiches. That was as close to cooking as I got. The rest of it was frozen dinners and canned soup. Even the frozen dinners were a real step up for me. A year ago it'd been all about the macaroni and cheese. Since then I'd met a seventy-three-year-old man whose physique put mine to shame, so I'd started making an effort to eat meals that at least came supplied with a serving of vegetables. The seventy-three-year-old looked pleased, then started nagging me about my sodium intake. I couldn't win.

"How can you have that body and nothing but junk food in your cupboards?" Mark asked when he'd finished looking behind every door in the kitchen. I looked down at my terry-cloth-clad self and wrinkled my forehead.

"That body?" I knew I'd lost some weight, but the way he said it you'd think I was a cover model. "I walk a lot at work," I added lamely. "Beat cop."

"It's not nice to beat cops," he said, mock-severely. I blinked, and a smile swam into place. At least if I was picking guys up in fits of drunken idiocy, they were not only handsome, but also even mildly clever.

Speaking of which. "How, um. I mean, who, um. I mean, um." Okay, only one of us got the Mildly Clever Badge for the morning, and it sure wasn't me.

"Barb Bragg is my sister," he volunteered, somehow managing to translate my garbled question into something coherent. "Redhead? Yea tall?" He made a gesture around five and a half feet from the floor, and took a frying pan out of my cupboard. "She's got some buddies in the North Precinct and got invited along to the barbeque. I tagged along. Never could resist a woman in uniform."

I stared at his shoulders. Nice wide world-supporting shoulders that tapered into a narrow waist and hips that— "I wasn't in uniform," I muttered. He flashed a grin over his shoulder at me. His teeth were very slightly crooked. It was the only thing that saved him from sheer perfection. He couldn't possibly be real, although my dreams weren't usually this good. "Are you actually real?"

"Guess I can't resist a woman out of uniform, either. Least-ways not when she can out-arm-wrestle me." He did a double take at me. "Am I real? I dunno. Did you want an after-party drunken philosophy answer, or just my driver's license?"

"The license would be great." I was pretty sure the average godling or demon or monster under the bed didn't carry one, although I hadn't thought to ask any of the ones I'd met. I'd try to remember, next time. Mark arched an eyebrow, then took his wallet out of his back pocket and tossed it to me.

I opened it and pulled out an Arizona state driver's license that had a relievingly bad picture of Mark, along with his birth date—he was two years younger than me—and an organ donor's stamp. A knot I didn't know was there untied beneath my heart. I could look up his license number at the precinct, but the fact that he even had ID was an awfully good start. I put it away and let out a fwoosh of air. "Did I really beat you arm wrestling? You must've been really shit-faced." My biceps weren't sore and I was sure I didn't have the upper-body strength to match his smooth muscles in a fair fight.

Not sore seemed rather important there for a moment, but Mark laughed, which was surprisingly distracting. He looked even brighter and prettier when he laughed, just all-around sparkling with geniality. I kind of liked it.

"Either that or I know what hill to die on." In the time it'd taken me to peruse his ID, he'd taken over my kitchen, and now appeared to be making omelets. I hadn't known I had omelet fixings, but he was managing. Omelets with chili and cheese, no less. And toast. He'd even taken a can of orange juice out of the freezer. Maybe I needed to get drunk and pick guys up more often. I'd never managed to get such a babe to sluff around my kitchen half naked when I'd tried sober dating. Not that I'd done that for a while, either.

"Your sister," I said. "She wouldn't be the one in the Daisy Mae shorts, would she?"

"That's her, yep. A million pounds of punch packed into a teeny-weeny body. Cute, isn't she?"

I knew there was some kind of enormous cosmic irony going on here, but I put my head down on the table, held my breath and hoped, just for a moment, that it would all go away.

Instead, the doorbell rang.

CHAPTER TWO

"Want me to get that?" Mark asked easily. Maybe he was ac-customed to waking up in strange women's beds as a matter of course and had a certain protocol about it all. Me, I wasn't accustomed to that sort of thing at all, and leaped out of my chair with a yelped "No!" The chair banged into the wall and I ran for the door as if Mark might disregard my reply and whisk himself off to open it. The smell of omelets cooking made my stomach rumble impatiently as I unlocked the door and pulled it open to find a big old man with bushy eyebrows looking at me quizzically.

"Nice robe. You ain't cookin' an old man breakfast, are you? 'Cause I brought doughnuts. Besides, I know how you cook."

I clutched the collar of my robe closed, feeling like a fifties housewife. "Uh. Gary. Uh. Hi. What're you—ah, shit!" God, my prowess with the language was stunning today. I was an embarrassment to the diploma laying claim to a B.A. in

English lying somewhere in my apartment. "Gary, I, uh, forgot."

He squinted down at me, gray eyes curious. Gary Muldoon was the most solid, real-looking person I'd ever met in my life, and at seventy-three he still had the build of the linebacker he'd been in college. But there was a bit of tiredness in the Hemingway wrinkles, and he was moving slower than he had when I met him, thanks to a heart attack a few weeks earlier.

A heart attack that was my fault, something I couldn't forget. Even the memory made a nervous flutter in my stomach.

It wasn't your usual butterflies. It was the way I perceived the power that had awoken in me seven months earlier, when catching sight of a fleeing woman through an airplane window had triggered a series of what I considered to be re-markably unfortunate events. Finding the woman had resulted, more or less directly, in getting a sword stuffed through my lungs. While I was busy dying, a snide coyote dropped by my psyche and gave me the option to survive the skewering—as a shaman. A healer, one with Great Things in store for me.

If I'd known then what I know now…

All right, I'd have made the same decision, because nobody wants to die at twenty-six if there's a choice in the matter. But I didn't want to be a shaman. The whole idea that there was a magic-filled alternative to our world made my skin itch. I like rational, sensible explanations for things: that was part of why I was a mechanic by trade. Or had been, anyway. Vehicle diagnostics were simple and straightforward. Follow a certain set of steps and the vehicle runs better. *Et voilà*. Normal.

Having an insistent, fluttery coil of power centered right below my sternum, impatient to be used to right the world, is not normal. And that bubble was what shivered in me every time I saw Gary, partly because he was still healing, and partly because his illness really had been my fault.

I'd spent most of the past six months ignoring my power as best I could. It turned out that had been a massive error in judgment. Among other things, it let a very nasty person induce a heart attack in my closest friend so I'd be distracted while the world went to hell in a handbasket. It had worked extremely well.

I was capable of learning from my mistakes. After six months of strenuous denial, I finally realized I was going to have to suck it up and learn to use this power, because otherwise I was going to be used and taken advantage of. Worse, my friends were in danger, and that, if nothing else, was enough to convince me to pull my head out of my ass.

I put my hand over Gary's heart. A little thread of glee burst free from that coil of power inside me, silver-blue light splashing up my arm, under the skin, as if it followed the blood vessels. It probably did. Through that spatter of power I could feel the steady, comforting strength of an ancient tortoise, sharing its spirit—and, I hoped, its longevity—with Gary. It was the one thing I'd done right recently, bringing a totem animal back to help heal my friend.

The tortoise accepted my offering of vitality, though I got a sense of amusement from it as I worked through my favorite analogy: cars. To me, patching up a heart that'd had an attack was like changing out bald tires. They were worn and tired, just like an attack made the heart, but you couldn't just switch out one heart for another. I liked the idea of working from the inside, like I could slip a new tire around the hub and slowly inflate it, strengthening the old muscle with newer healthy cells. Every time I saw Gary I threw a little of that idea into him, trying to help fix the damage I'd allowed to be done. I expected his next annual checkup to determine he had the heart of a twenty-five-year-old.

"How could you forget?" he demanded as I let my hand fall again. "We been doin' this every day for the past ten days, Jo. And your eggs are gonna burn."

"What's 'this'?" Mark came out of the kitchen, all full of tenor good cheer. "Crap, Joanne, are you seeing somebody? I'm sorry if I screwed—oh." He got a good look at Gary and evidently categorized him as too old. That was new. Half the people I knew were convinced I was involved in a lusty May-December romance.

"The eggs aren't going to burn," Mark added with a broad grin, and offered his hand to Gary. "I'm Mark."

I wrinkled up my face, afraid to look at Gary, but one eye peeped open, unable to look away, either.

He'd all but dropped his teeth, jaw long and eyes googly. He was staring at Mark, but somehow managed to encompass me in that stare, making me squirm. I felt like a teenager caught necking with her boyfriend. Gary put his hand out and shook Mark's without winding his jaw back up, and Mark gave him another broad smile. "You Joanne's dad?"

"No!" Gary and I said at the same time. Mark's eyebrows went up and he rocked back on his heels a bit. "Just a friend," I muttered. Gary transferred his googly-eyed stare to me, and it was a lot worse than when he'd managed to pull off gaping at me without actually looking directly at me. I squirmed again. "I, um, yesterday was the department picnic, and, um…"

Gary handed the box of doughnuts to Mark and said, in his best deep-voiced dangerous rumble, "Could you excuse us a minute, son?"

Mark retreated to the kitchen while I gave Gary a steely-eyed look of my own, hoping to head him off at the pass. "'Son'? Women get 'dame' and 'broad' and 'lady,' and he gets 'son'?"

"It's part of my charm," Gary muttered, then scowled enormously at me. "You okay, Jo?" There was no reprimand in his voice at all, just a hell of a lot of concern.

My mouth bypassed my brain entirely and said, for no reason I was willing to admit to, "Morrison was flirting with this redhead." To my huge irritation, that clearly made sense, because Gary's expression landed between understanding and sympathy, with a good dose of wryness thrown in. I said "Shit," and stomped into the kitchen. Gary closed the door behind himself and followed me.

"Hungry?" Mark asked genially. "Plenty where this came from." He lifted the frying pan and then slid its omelet onto a plate that already had two slices of buttered toast on it. I was in the presence of culinary genius. Gary eyed me, eyed Mark, and shrugged.

"I could eat. 'Cept you sure you want to eat, Jo? You know it'll ground you." He put on a solicitous tone, but

underneath it I heard: *don't eat anything, we got work to do.*
Gary had been there, quite literally standing over me, when
my powers woke up. Frankly, he handled the entire thing a
lot better than I ever had. I was, he'd told me more than
once, the most interesting thing that'd happened to him in
the three years since his wife had died, and he wasn't going
to miss out on any of it. I wasn't at all sure I liked being an
interesting thing. It was like the proverbial Chinese curse,
may you live in interesting times. I'd far rather live in really,
really boring times. Especially since much of the interesting part seemed to be directly focused on trying to make me
dead. Boring was good.

With this in mind, I took the plate like a lifer in prison,
hunching myself over it protectively. "Right now I need
some serious grounding."

"What are you," Mark said, "some kind of electrician or
something? I thought you were a cop." He brought a glass
of orange juice to the table and gave me a quirky little grin
that went a fair way toward melting my knees, even if I both
knew better and was sitting down, anyway. Nobody ever said
knee-melting only worked on the vertical.

I managed to mutter, "Thanks," and tried giving Gary the
hairy eyeball to shut him up, but he answered Mark with
such blasé cheer I knew he was ignoring me on purpose.

"Not that kinda grounding. Spiritual grounding. Food
anchors your soul to your body, makes it a lot harder to go
spirit questing. Jo here's a shaman." He said it all casual-like,
but his gray eyes were sharp and judging as Mark went back
to the stove to make another omelet. Me, I just sank down
into my chair until my nose practically touched the eggs,

and shoveled as many bites into my mouth as I could before Gary took notice of me again.

"No shit," Mark said curiously. "Like a medicine man? What exactly does a shaman do, anyway?" He grinned, bright and open. "Get hooked up with some peyote, maybe?"

My stomach contracted around the food I'd eaten. I un-hunched from over the plate and Mark noticed, speaking a little more quickly, as if he was afraid I'd cut him off. Which was exactly what I'd been going to do, so I couldn't exactly blame him.

"No, no, look, I'm sorry, I'm kidding. Bad joke, sorry." He sounded like he meant it, expression all fussed as he looked at me. "I just never met a shaman before. Guess I don't know what to say. Mom says her grandad was Navajo—"

"What," Gary said, "not a Cherokee princess? I thought those came standard these days."

I shot him a look. I actually *was* part Cherokee, although not through remote ancestors. My father'd grown up in Qualla Boundary and I'd gone to high school there. There were a lot of people there who legitimately could claim Cherokee blood, but most of them weren't royalty. Mostly it seemed like people from much further away than the Carolinas—or Oklahoma—had managed to land themselves the royal blood. It was like the U.S. version of being de-scended from Cleopatra.

Mark only laughed. The guy was nine kinds of casual. Maybe he did this for a living, like the kid in *Six Degrees of Separation*. Never mind his health or my peace of mind. It seemed like I shouldn't trust him.

I'd start not trusting him as soon as I was done eating breakfast. I hunched over it again, hoping Gary wouldn't notice.

"Nah. I guess my family came over from England in the early nineteenth century and settled in the southwest during one of the land rushes. Never had a chance to hook up with Cherokee royalty."

"Just Navajo."

"Well, she never said he was royalty." Mark slid me a wink and a bit of an "Overprotective, isn't he?" look. I avoided Gary's eyes and stuffed a too-large piece of omelet into my mouth. "Anyway, whether he was or not, that's like the total of my familiarity with Indian culture."

"Native American," Gary said in a tone that sounded remarkably like one I'd employed on him some months earlier, when he'd called me Indian. Mark had the grace to turn red around his jawline and lift his hands in apology.

"Native American. Sorry. Maybe you can tell me about it sometime, Joanne. I'd like to hear about it."

So he was good-looking, but he was bonkers. Anybody who was that agreeable about the possibility of magic woo-woo stuff in people he'd just met pretty much had to be. I knew I shouldn't trust him. At least my friends at the police department had gotten mixed up in my séance-thing back in January because they knew me and wanted to help, not because they were buying into a whole big weird world of Other out there.

Gary grunted, a small noise that I couldn't interpret as pleased or displeased, and saved me from responding by saying, "Not now. We got work to do."

"Sure," Mark said easily. "Some other time. I don't want to get in the way."

I inhaled a chili bean and started coughing, then washed cough and bean down with a long swig of orange juice. The acidity made my nose sting, and the whole combination made my eyes water, which let me open my eyes all the way. Overall I called it a win and stuffed an entire half slice of toast into my mouth before anybody could expect me to say anything. I didn't see why I should. Gary and Mark seemed to be getting on just fine.

The doorbell rang.

My social life was not such that the doorbell rang twice in one week, much less twice in five minutes. I stuck my head out, turtle-like, over my omelet, surprise keeping me in the pose for a few seconds. Then, afraid Gary would dump my food if I left it unguarded, I clutched the plate and went to answer the door.

A leggy blond woman and a six-year-old girl stood outside it. The girl noticed neither the bathrobe nor the plate of food I held and squealed, "Ossifer Walker!" before leaping up into my arms with the confidence of a child who'd never been dropped.

Chili-cheese omelet went flying over the door, the rug and the girl as I fumbled the plate while catching her. Her mother looked completely dismayed. "I am so sorry. I thought—it was this morning, wasn't it? Tuesday, nine-fifteen? We were going to have a tour of the station?"

"Oh, God." I juggled the girl around until she was sitting on my hip, and gave her a falsely bright smile that she didn't seem to see through. "Hi, Ashley. You look nice and healthy. Are you keeping hydrated?"

"Yes," she announced, pleased with knowing the word. "I drink six glasses of water a day." She held up all ten fingers, demonstratively, and my fakey smile turned into a real grin.

"Good for you. Um, Ashley? We've got chili all over ourselves. We should probably get cleaned up."

"Do we hafta?"

"Yes," her mother and I said together, and I put Ashley down. I'd encountered her a few weeks earlier, the victim of heat stroke. My power had refused to let me ignore it that time, and once her core temperature was stabilized I'd sent her to the hospital. She'd come away from it with the idea that I was some kind of hero, and that she wanted to grow up to be a "peace ossifer," just like me. "I'm sorry," I said to her mother. Allison. Allison and Ashley Hampton. Just the names sounded like they belonged somewhere a lot ritzier than a college apartment turned permanent abode. "I completely spaced it. If you're not in a time crunch I can get cleaned up and—"

"Wow," Ashley said dreamily. I wrinkled up my face and looked over my shoulder. Mark, in all his half-naked glory, was leaning in the doorway to the kitchen, grinning. See, when a six-year-old notices that a guy's gorgeous, you know it's not just your overactive imagination telling you he is.

"Breakfast, ladies?" He was going to use all the food in my house. "We've got omelets and doughnuts."

"Mommy!" Ashley crowed. "Can I have a doughnut pllleaaaase?"

"You already had breakfast, Ashley," Allison said automatically. Ashley wriggled all over.

"I know, but pllleaaaaase?"

"Come on in." A sense of the absurd was blooming over me, forming a stupid amused smile on my face. "Join the party. Mark can feed you," I said, like that was perfectly normal, "and I'll get dressed and we can go to the station." I ushered Allison Hampton into the apartment, leaned on the door and waited for another shoe to drop.

The phone rang, and I laughed out loud. Everyone peered at me curiously as I made my way over chili-stained carpet to pick it up. "Grand Central Station."

"This is Phoebe," a woman said. "You've been a total flake the last two weeks, so I'm calling to remind you about your—"

"Fencing lesson," I said with a groan that sounded like a laugh even to me. "I know this is going to shock you, but—"

"You forgot." Phoebe sounded smug. "That's why I'm calling. If you're not here in—" I could imagine her looking at her watch in the pause "—twenty-three minutes," she went on, "I'm going to come kick your tall skinny ass up and down the Ave. I will never make a fencer of you if you don't come to practice, Joanne."

"You sound like my mother," I said, except she didn't, because not only did my mother have an Irish accent, but she'd also dumped me with my father when I was three months old, so I'd never had the pleasure, or lack thereof, of being lectured by her. At least, not until after she was dead, which was some more of that lack of normality that I didn't like about my life. Nonetheless, Phoebe sounded like what I imagined mothers to sound like.

"Twenty-two minutes, Joanne."

"I can't make it," I said with a shrug. Ashley, in the background, squealed with delight. I looked into the kitchen to see Mark flipping an omelet, like he was a real chef or something. "I've got company," I added, although Phoebe knew me well enough she'd never believe it.

"It's nine in the morning. How can you have company? You're always saying you have no life."

I held the phone out toward the kitchen. "Everyone please say hello to Phoebe."

A chorus of hellos swept over me and I put the phone back to my ear. "See?"

"All right," Phoebe said in a no-nonsense voice, "but we're going out clubbing tonight so you can tell me what this is all about."

"Clubbing," I echoed. "What, like cavemen?"

"You're the only person I know who might really mean that. Clubbing as in dance clubbing, after dinner."

"I see. Are you threatening me into social activities?"

"Yes. And if you say no I'll beat you up."

I grinned. "Assuming I ever come to another lesson so you can." I'd taken up fencing after a sword-bearing god had skewered me. Shaman lessons, those freaked me out. Fencing lessons, those were basically normal. Even I could see the pattern developing. "Okay," I said, heading off Phoebe's splutters. "Tonight. We'll do something. I promise."

"See you at eight," she said in a tone that brooked no compromise, and hung up.

The doorbell rang. I turned around and gaped at it. Gary came out of the kitchen, looking as astonished as I did. "I can't imagine," I said before he asked, and went back to the door to answer it for the third time that morning.

"Walker." Captain Michael Morrison of the Seattle Police Department stood on my doorstep, looking less like a super-hero and more like a sunburned, unhappy man than usual. His shirtsleeves were rolled up and the collar of his shirt was loose, neither of which I could remember ever seeing on him before. Even dressed down, he was enough snazzier than me that he took in my moss-green robe and messy hair with a single scathing glance. "Get dressed. Holliday's in a coma."

CHAPTER THREE

My hangover returned with a vengeance, a brand-new tire iron slamming into my brain along with Morrison's words. For a moment my vision doubled, so there were two tense-looking Morrisons looming over me. I checked the impulse to stand on my toes so Morrison's shod state didn't make him marginally taller than me. Normally we looked each other in the eye, the same height right down to the last half inch.

"What? I just saw him last night. He was fine. What are you talking about? Is Mel okay?" I backed out of the door even as I asked questions, letting Morrison into my apartment.

"Hail, hail, the gang's all here," Gary said from the kitchen doorway. Morrison didn't quite do a double take at the old man, but it was a near thing, his lips thinning and nostrils flaring. "Mr. Muldoon." Morrison was one of those who thought I had Something Going On with Gary. He transferred his attention back to me, expression saying both, "I knew it," and at the same time clearly wondering why I wasn't dressed and ready to go yet. "Melinda Holliday called me this morning to inform me Detective Holliday wouldn't be in. Sometime after midnight last night he fell into a sleep that he can't be woken from. She's all right," he added a little more gently. "Upset, but all right."

Panic clutched my heart in quick pulses. Billy Holliday was one of my oldest friends at the department, a big man whose unfortunate name had prompted him to a cross-dressing quirk. At least, that was my theory. I'd never been brave enough, or maybe rude enough, to ask outright why he did it.

Oddly, that wasn't the thing he got ridden about at work. People had adapted to the nail polish and the occasional appearance in a brightly colored sundress, possibly because Billy's biceps were bigger than most people's heads, but also because he was a hell of a detective, and the truth was most people didn't give a damn what kind of oddnesses you were into if you were good at your job.

That, and he had another quirk that seemed safer to pick on. Billy Holliday was a True Believer when it came to the world of the paranormal. He made Mulder look like a skeptic, and when my universe turned upside down, he was the first one to support me, despite the ration of shit I'd given him for years. I didn't deserve friends that good.

"He was fine last night," I repeated. "What happened?" *Close mouth, Joanne, and engage brain.* I pressed my lips shut, inhaled deeply through my nose, and said, "I'll get dressed. Did Mel want me there?"

Morrison gave me a sour look and followed me to my bedroom door. I could see the tension in his shoulders as he folded his arms and leaned on the wall, ostentatiously turning his gaze toward the living room. I hesitated, then left the door open, since Morrison clearly intended to keep having a conversation while I was getting dressed. "I—"

"Joanne, will someone else be—oh, Captain Morrison." Mark's question overrode Morrison's answer, and I wished, just briefly, that I was still in the living room so I could see Morrison's expression. "Mark Bragg," Mark said cheerfully. I had never heard anybody so cheerful in the morning. Especially someone whom I thought should be suffering from the same kind of brain-pounding headache that I was. He had, after all, shared in the aspirin I'd taken. Maybe his had worked better. "We met yesterday afternoon at the picnic," he went on. "Barbara Bragg's my sister."

"Sure," Morrison said in such a controlled voice I winced to hear it. "I remember. Nice to see you again, Mark."

"Mommy, it's a peace captain!" I heard Ashley come tearing out of the kitchen and looked toward the door in time to see her skid to a stop about six inches from Morrison, beaming up at him. "Hullo! I'm Ashley! Ossifer Walker is going to show me her school! I mean her work." She wrinkled up her face until her nose looked like a button at the midst of a bunch, then smoothed it out again to smile adoringly at my boss. Her mother came out of the kitchen after her, offering a smile with a hint of apology for Ashley's enthusiasm.

Morrison couldn't take it anymore and shot me an incredulous look through my bedroom door. Fortunately for both of us I'd at least pulled on a pair of pants and had managed to get a bra in place. "Did I come at a bad time,

Walker?" Sarcasm abounded so mildly that I wasn't sure anyone else heard it.

"No, sir." I was standing in my own bedroom half dressed calling a man sir. It really seemed like I ought to at least get laid, if I was doing that.

Then Mark stepped into view, his jeans still falling off his hips, and I remembered that all appearances indicated I had. Dammit. "Why don't you go ahead and make everybody else some breakfast, Mark," I muttered. "Since everyone's here and all. Morrison and I have to go." I pulled a white T-shirt on because I knew it would set off my tan and went to crouch in the doorway so I could talk to Ashley.

"We're going to have to reschedule, Ashley. This is my boss, Captain Morrison, and I have to go with him this morning."

Disappointment flooded the kid's face, although at the same time she shot a conniving look at Morrison. "Maybe I could come with you!" All the guile was gone from her expression by the time she started speaking, big blue eyes full of hope and charm. I choked on a laugh. Even Morrison cracked a grin, proving he wasn't entirely immune to feminine wiles.

But his voice was very serious as he answered, "'Fraid not, Ashley." He crouched, too, so our knees knocked together, and gave Ashley all the respect due an adult. "Officer Walker and I have to take care of some police business by ourselves. But when Officer Walker gets the chance to reschedule and bring you to the station, come by my office and I'll see if I can't scare up a case for you to work on, all right?"

I thought the girl was going to lift right off the floor from so much delight and pride. "Okay!" She darted back to her mother to say, "Captain Morrison's going to make me a police ossifer, Mommy! With a case for my own! I'm going to be a peace captain when I grow up!"

"I'm sure you will be, Ashley," Allison Hampton said with the fond patience of a parent who heard at least a half-dozen different *when I grow ups* a day.

Morrison put his hands on his thighs and pushed himself upright, a quiet hint of a smile on his mouth. I looked up at him for a few seconds, trying to hide my own half smile.

I liked to think of Morrison as my personal bane of existence, the end-all and be-all of rigidity and things I didn't like about cops. We shared a years-old antagonistic relationship that stemmed from me knowing a lot more about cars than he did—although honestly, I still couldn't comprehend how someone could possibly mistake a Mustang for a Corvette—and which had developed into long-running habitual disagreement on any given topic. But the truth was I respected my captain, and he regularly pulled off little coups like the one with Ashley that made it clear to me that he deserved the captaincy he held, even if he didn't know a damned thing about cars.

I took my gaze away from Morrison and caught Gary looking at me with the faintest smirk in the world. He wiped it off so fast I knew I'd read it correctly, making me hunch my shoulders and scowl as I straightened out of my crouch.

"I'm sorry," I said to everybody in general, except Morrison. "I've got to go. Gary, I'll call you when I'm done."

Gary's bushy gray eyebrows shot up. "You mean I ain't goin' with you?"

"No." Morrison bristled so much I suspected Gary'd asked just to get a rise out of him. "You're not."

I couldn't get the cabbie to meet my eyes and confirm his intentions, though. Instead, Gary gave Morrison a toothy white smile and asked, "Then who's gonna drum her under?"

Every hair on my body stood up, until I felt like a spooked cat. Morrison's expression went tight, as if he'd been caught out. I thought he probably had been. Gary's smile stayed toothy. I found myself staring at the floor, feeling like looking at one or the other would be playing favorites in some kind of weird male rivalry thing that I didn't understand.

"I will," Morrison said. He didn't sound happy about it, and cold lay down all over my arms and spine. I started to say, "I'm not sure that's a good idea, Captain," but he fixed me with a gimlet glare.

"It'll be fine, Walker. Where's your drum?"

I was pretty sure being drummed under by somebody with Morrison's temperament and opinion about my abilities—which were pretty much on par with my own—wasn't really fine, but Allison was looking at me curiously, and I very much didn't want to get into it with her there. I jerked a thumb over my shoulder. "In there. On the dresser."

Morrison walked into my bedroom like he'd done it a hundred times, while I gave Ashley and Allison another apologetic smile. "Monday and Tuesdays are my days off. We could reschedule for next we-eek?" My voice broke on the last word as I *felt* Morrison pick my drum up, a startling gentle caress that ran over my stomach like he was brushing the instrument's surface. Warmth spread through me, up and down, and I put my hand on the door frame for balance as I looked back at my captain.

He held the drum like it was valuable, which it was. An elder in Qualla Boundary had made it for me, the only thing I'd even been given in my life that was unique and for me alone. It had a raven dyed into the soft deer leather, its wings sheltering a rattlesnake and a wolf. The stick that went with it had a knotted leather end and a rabbit-fur end that was dyed raspberry red. It meant more to me than any other possession I'd ever owned. Gary usually drummed for me, when I needed its music to go into a healing trance.

Gary picking up my drum had never given me a visceral thrill that made me consider locking myself in my bedroom with him. I swallowed on a surprisingly dry throat and Morrison looked up, expression so mild it was neutral. Either he wasn't getting the same kind of thrill I was from him handling the drum, or he was hiding it very well. I bet on the former and swallowed again, turning back to Ashley and Allison. "Would that be okay?" My voice croaked, but no one seemed to notice.

Allison nodded and Ashley bounced up and down in enthusiastic agreement. That in hand, I looked beyond them at Mark. I had no idea what to say to Mark. I desperately didn't want Mark to still be here when I came home. I'd be happier if Mark had never been there at all, but unless I could turn back time, that didn't seem a likely scenario. I had a horror of going near him, for fear he'd try something unforgivably intimate, like kissing me goodbye. I'd have to break his lovely nose.

"Make sure the door's locked when you leave," I said after a few seconds. It seemed to cover all bases: it said I expected him to be gone, and I thought it didn't leave room for Morrison to infer that Mark had a key to my apartment, which "Lock the door when you leave" might have.

Not that I cared what Morrison thought of my love life.

I slid a pair of sandals on and went out the door before anybody could say anything else.

Morrison followed on my heels, his gaze making the skin between my shoulder blades itch. He didn't say anything, which was worse by far than questions. Even, "You had a party and didn't invite me?" would have been nice. Something I could snap back at and therefore restore my shattered equilibrium. But Morrison wasn't obliging me, no doubt on the warped logic that my personal life wasn't his business. Never mind that if he said one word, that's exactly what I'd tell him. That wasn't the point, dammit.

"Mel asked for me?" I asked again, as much to shut my thoughts up as to break the silence. We cornered at a landing—I lived on the fifth floor in the same apartment building I'd been in since college—and I shot a cautious glance over my shoulder at the captain. He looked like he'd bitten into a sour grapefruit, not, once I thought about it, that I'd ever encountered a genuinely sweet one.

"No."

"So what're you doing here?" Somewhere in the midst of the sentence I figured it out and wished I hadn't asked, because it meant Morrison had to answer.

"You're supposed to have a knack for fixing this kind of problem," he growled, and I wished some more I hadn't asked. It hadn't been all that long ago that Morrison and I had shared a healthy disrespect for the whole concept of other worlds and mystical healing and things like magic. That it was all malarkey had been the one thing we agreed on.

Empirical evidence had changed my stance, even if I'd spent most of the time since then resisting it with every fiber of my being. Morrison had been treated to an overwhelming load of first and secondhand proof that ranged from watching me come back from the dead to Billy Holliday's house being all but destroyed by a demon I'd unleashed on Seattle. He was not a man to disbelieve his own eyes, but it was possible he hated it even more than I did.

But he was also too smart and too good a police captain not to use the assets he had available. If Billy was suffering from an inexplicable medical condition, then Joanne Walker, Reluctant Shaman, was the right person to come to. Whether Morrison liked it or not, he was putting his faith in the esoteric abilities I'd proved to have. I didn't deserve his trust.

And I hoped he wasn't making a mistake. Two weeks of crash-course training—much of which had been spent desperately searching for my spirit guide, who'd disappeared during that whole demon incident—was likely to be worth diddly. I was still working on instinct, which had turned out to be a messy way of life.

"That thing with Ashley," I said, too loudly and too abruptly. "Is that how you ended up wanting to be a cop? Somebody gave you the time of day when you were a kid?" We hit the July sunlight as I asked the question, me squinting against it as I forged into the parking lot. Morrison caught up with me in two steps and cast me a sideways look that said he knew I was changing the subject and it was just fine with him.

"You think there had to be some kind of life-changing event that made me want to be a police officer? Just because it's not your cup of tea, Walker…"

"It's just that I never met a guy so obsessed with growing up to be a cop he couldn't take time to learn the difference between a Mustang and a Corvette." I reached the Mustang in question and strode around to the driver's side while Morrison shot me a look of horror.

"We are not taking your muscle car, Walker. I'm driving."

"I hate other people driving, and you always drive when we go somewhere together." Crime scenes and funerals. Morrison knew how to show a girl a good time. "I bet you've never even ridden in a Mustang before, and besides, Morrison, I mean, come on, give me a break. Your car sucks."

He looked affronted. "It's got the highest safety ranking in its class. And the back end of yours is bashed in."

"Like I said." I jangled my keys at him, exasperated. "Look, you can drive yourself if you want, but I'm taking Petite. Come on. Live a little, *mon capitán.*" I leaned forward to put my hand on Petite's purple roof and murmured, "It's okay, baby. You're not bashed in. Just a little dinged up. It's not that he doesn't like you. He just doesn't know you like I do." Honestly, Morrison was right. Petite's rear end was smashed up, ugly but not disabling, due to having fallen down a fissure opened up by an earthquake. That wouldn't be so bad, except I'd caused the earthquake.

Okay, it would have sucked every bit as much, but being

the epicenter of a world-shattering event that racked my car up made it just that much worse. Petite had survived, and her calm steel soul wasn't concerned about the depleted bank account that had already paid for one vehicular disaster this year. She was sure I'd make her as beautiful as she'd once been, and she was right. I whispered that promise as if she could hear me, and patted her roof a second time.

"Walker, your relationship with your vehicle is pathological." Morrison glanced down the parking lot at his staid Toyota Avalon and sighed. I beamed and unlocked Petite's door, giving her another pat as I swung into the driver's seat.

"See?" I said as I unlocked the passenger door for my boss. "Nobody can resist you, baby. Not even the Mighty Morrison."

"The what?" I'd never seen anybody look so awkward getting into a car before. Morrison sat down in the leather seat as if he was afraid it might bite him, and put the drum carefully into the back. "Walker, does this thing even have safety belts?"

"Click it or ticket, sir," I quipped. "I put them in myself. Just for you. Even though she's a classic and strictly speaking I didn't have to." I pulled my own seat belt on and waited for Morrison to get his on before adding, "I figure anything that goes a hundred and fifty oughta have 'em, after all."

Morrison turned pale. I grinned and pulled out of the parking lot too fast, feeling pretty chipper despite the hangover, Billy's condition and Mark.

CHAPTER FOUR

Once upon a time, the antiseptic smell of hospitals gave me sneezing fits every time I went in one. The past month I'd been in and out of them often enough that the sneezing had reduced itself to just feeling like somebody'd stuffed plugs up my nose, making my eyes tingle and water. It wasn't much of an improvement, and I really wanted to just not have to go into hospitals at all anymore.

The universe was supremely indifferent to what I wanted. I rubbed my nose and followed Morrison up to an ordinary hospital room, not the intensive-care unit I was expecting. Billy Holliday was, by all appearances, sleeping comfortably in a bed that looked too small for his barrel-chested frame. There was an oxygen sensor on one finger, and monitors I couldn't identify beeped in the background. He looked fine.

His wife, on the other hand, looked like hell. I'd only seen

Melinda Holliday look less than lovely once previously, during the demon-in-her-kitchen episode a couple of weeks earlier, but the one-two punch seemed to have taken the spark out of her. Her dark hair was in a listless ponytail, olive skin drawn and pale and she wasn't dressed to disguise early signs of pregnancy. Since I'd been admonished not to mention she was pregnant for several weeks yet, I knew she was worried: Mel wasn't the kind of woman who would accidentally dress badly, or let show something she wanted kept private.

Morrison stopped in the doorway and let me go in ahead of him. Or maybe he made me go in ahead of him, but either way, I went in as he hung back in the door frame. Mel looked up and blatant relief swept her expression, tears bright in her brown eyes. "Joanie. Michael said he'd get you on his way over. I'm so glad you're here." She got herself around the bed and over to hug me as she spoke, while I stumbled over the idea of someone calling Morrison by his given name. I knew he had one, of course, but it was the mental equivalent of Babe Ruth saying, "Hiya, King!" to King Edward of England.

I wasn't sure who would find it more appalling that I was putting Morrison on the same pedestal as British royalty: Morrison, or the English. Fortunately, it was a thought that would never escape the confines of my mind.

"It's gonna be okay," I said to the top of Melinda's head. "Billy's going to be fine. What happened?"

Mel extracted herself from the hug, stepping back with her chin lifted, a way of instigating control over her emotions. "I don't know. He just wouldn't wake up this morning. The doctors said his vitals are strong and he seems to be in REM sleep, but he just won't wake up."

"I'll do what I can, Mel. I'm not all that good at this." I sat down at Billy's side, trying not to gnaw on my lower lip.

"You'll help him." She went back to her seat on the other side of the bed, taking Billy's hand. I bit my lip after all and looked over my shoulder at Morrison.

He leaned in the door frame, arms folded across his chest as he stared at me so intently I felt a blush crawling up my cheeks. My drum dangled from his fingertips, against his ribs, like he'd forgotten it was there, though I was certain he hadn't. He was waiting for something, and I knew both what and why. I almost couldn't blame him.

Morrison had never actually been present when I'd tried healing someone before, though he'd been in the vicinity and had seen the evidence of success after the fact. Proof didn't make him happy about my talents, and I could feel discomfort rolling off him in waves. It wasn't any especial attunement to emotion or altered states of being that let me feel it, either, just his glower and the tightness of his shoulders.

"Mel could drum me under," I offered. It wasn't what he wanted to hear—he wanted to be told none of this was necessary—but it was the best I could do. By getting me here he'd already pushed well past the boundaries of what he considered reasonable behavior. It wasn't the first time he'd forced his own hand into asking what my esoteric gifts might be able to come up with, but it was the first time he'd found himself playing an actively supporting role.

I had complete and total sympathy with the not wanting to be there for it. I'd have checked out myself, if I could've, although that impulse was slowly being replaced by a grim determination to just get this shamanism thing right. A wash of regret burbled through me, leaving weary sadness behind. "You don't have to do this, Captain."

"Yeah, I do." Morrison shoved off the doorjamb, making it creak. I startled at his contrary agreement, then found myself staring at the man.

I tended to think I was Morrison's size because I was Morrison's height, but seeing him framed in the doorway reminded me why I also tended to think of him as an aging superhero. The summer heat had taken some of the extra flesh he'd been carrying from around his middle, so the aging part seemed to slip away, leaving just the hero behind. His hair needed cutting, which was the sort of thing I rarely noticed on myself, much less anyone else, but the marginally longer length played up silver streaks that in turn emphasized just how damned blue his eyes were. I wished, very abruptly, that we were at the office and he was in his usual two-piece suit instead of shirtsleeves, so I'd just see my boss, instead of a man.

I turned back to Billy with my shoulders hunched, just in time to catch Melinda's pursed-lip look of curiosity before she schooled it into neutrality. My shoulders went higher, and Morrison came up behind me, dragging a chair to the foot of Billy's bed. I heard the door click shut as he sat down, the drum held awkwardly but carefully in one hand. "Heartbeat rhythm, right?"

I looked back at him and he shrugged. "People talk, Walker. Especially about you."

Millipedes stampeded up and down my spine, leaving me

with shivers and a bump of nausea in my stomach. "I wish you hadn't said that." I knew on some level that people talked about me. It was clear from the way offices or the garage beneath the station would get quiet when I came in, and from how guys I'd once considered friends wouldn't quite look at me anymore. Having it said out loud, though, was a lot different from knowing it.

Morrison, bless his sensitive soul, said, "Too bad," and knocked a heartbeat thump into my drum.

The world lit up as if a few thousand angels had dropped by for afternoon tea. Gold splattered my vision, fading to lens flares of white and peach before clarity reasserted itself.

And what clarity it was, going far beyond the normal solidity of day-to-day life. A second sight descended over mine, giving the room, the sunlight in the window, the three people with me, everything, a depth that made normal vision seem weak and meaningless. Even the hospital walls glowed with purpose, vibrant green telling me they held their place as a hall of healing and took pride in that. Dust motes in the air glittered like star stuff, and I knew that if I got up to look out the window, there would be neon-bright colors flooding the streets, purposeful vitality making up all the aspects of the world. Every time I looked around me with the second sight, a part of me wanted to never let it go. Doing so ached inside of me, as if the overblown beauty visible through a layer of magic was how everything ought to be seen. Like I was cutting myself off from something important, when I looked at things with an ordinary woman's vision.

I'd never really seen Morrison through these eyes, though

I'd felt his colors a few times, deep blues and purples that spoke of reassurance and confidence about his place in the world. Looking at him now, I could see red tingeing the edges of his aura, confirming his irritation in participating in this—*charade* wasn't the right word, and not even he thought so. *Escapade*. It was only that, though: irritation. There was no deep coil of red through his colors, nothing that poisoned his drumming against what I wanted to accomplish with Billy. As I watched, discoloration roiled through, shading blue toward a sickly green and purples into murky reds. He couldn't have said *Get on with it, Walker,* any more clearly if he'd spoken aloud. My shoulders flinched back and I looked across the bed at Mel.

Sunlight from the window behind her was captured in her hair, streams of fire that helped lighten an orange-streaked yellow aura that lay flat against her skin. That wasn't right: when I'd last seen Mel's colors, they'd danced and swirled around her, even in the midst of a very bad situation. That they were dulled and drained now worried me. I reached across Billy to take her hand.

Power poured into me, unrelenting as a river delta. I blinked twice, each blink bringing my second sight deeper into Melinda's aura, until I could see what she was doing. A ball of sunlight was collected over her heart, drawing all her surface colors down into it. Orange and yellow ran against the flow of blood, pulling in from her skin to become ever-more intense as it neared her heart. Once there, she pushed it outward, toward Billy. Billy'd made a similar offering to me a few months earlier, lending his strength to my own so I could try to defeat a banshee before it killed again.

But the life force Melinda was pouring into her husband wasn't helping him stay alive. I kept one hand over Melinda's and put the other over Billy's heart, turning my focus down to him. His colors were fuchsia and orange, oddly complementary to Melinda's, and I could *feel* that they were locked up tight, kept in the psychic equivalent of a strongbox. A trickle escaped, but not to keep his heart beating and mind functioning. It felt as if it was being drained, a pinhole leak that something was feeding from. The thinnest fraction of that was allowed to divert and keep him alive, like a vampire that knew perfectly well it would die if its food source did.

Right now, though, Billy wasn't providing the real food source. Melinda's sunshine strength was being swallowed whole by lethargic blackness that had a heavier feeling to it than death. Death held a remoteness to it, a star-spangled void that didn't carry burdens; but the darkness that held Billy felt like sleep. It was laden with dreams and portent, pressing down like night paralysis, as if it wanted something. Death, in my experience, didn't want. It just took.

"Melinda." I wasn't quite sure I was talking out loud, but she looked up, dark eyes shining with too little light. "Mel, you have to stop it," I said quietly. "You're exhausting yourself, and if you keep doing this it'll be bad for the baby." I could see the baby's cheerful rose-colored glow, still safe from the power drain Melinda was putting on herself, but with the way she shed energy, it was a matter of time before the baby started to suffer. "You have to stop. You're not helping Billy by doing this. You're helping whatever's done this to him."

Disbelief, then rage, flashed in Melinda's eyes before the

stream of power cut off so sharply I felt blinded for a moment. I lifted a hand to my eyes, shaking my head, and mumbled, "You're going to have to teach me how to do that. Jesus."

She gave me a very faint smile. "Later." Melinda, like Billy, was not only comfortable with the world of the paranormal, but had sought it out. She'd told me once she and Billy had met at a paranormal activities conference, and that her grandmother had been a *bruja,* a witch. I would have snorted up my sleeve at such an admission a year ago, but as my life had grown increasingly weird, I'd discovered a couple of things. One was that more people than I'd have ever imagined believed in a mystical world that complemented our own.

The other was that I was desperately grateful for those friends who didn't think I was insane, especially when I'd been less than generous in my opinions about their sanity before my own world had turned upside down.

"Morrison?" I was half afraid to turn my head to look at the captain. My grip on second sight was usually so tenuous that moving my physical body while trying to hold on to it was a work of vast concentration.

On the other hand, when Morrison had begun the drumbeat, something abnormal had happened. It usually took at least a breath or two before I could slide into another state of consciousness. I generally had to wrestle with deliberate acceptance, with *choosing,* to exit what I was learning to think of as the Middle World, and I always had to struggle to hold on to the shaky ability to see auras and energies. I did not slam into double vision and healing trances with no time to blink. Maybe I was getting better at this.

Or maybe it had something to do with Morrison.

I made myself look at him instead of pursuing that thought. He hadn't stopped drumming, although he looked far more uncomfortable with it than Gary ever had. A twinge of unhappiness sailed through me as I wished it *was* Gary doing the drumming. His enthusiasm for whatever weird shit I was about to get myself, and him, into, somehow made it easier. "Think you can keep that up for about fifteen minutes?"

Morrison's mouth pulled into a sour twist. "Pretty sure I can handle it. If I start getting carpal tunnel I'll let Melinda pick it up."

I stuck my tongue out, feeling more like an e-mail emoticon expressing exasperation than a person making a face at my boss. Morrison looked completely taken aback, which I found surprisingly satisfying. I went with the victory and turned back to Billy. "Give me fifteen minutes, and then stop. I should wake right up."

"And if you don't?"

Visceral memory shot through me, the warmth of Morrison's hand on my shoulder just before a monster from another realm of reality had eaten me for lunch. The touch had saved my life, although Morrison sure as hell didn't know that, and I really didn't like thinking about it.

"Then put your hand on my bare skin," I muttered. Mel, whose hand I still held, lifted our hands, and then her eyebrows. I glanced up long enough to meet her gaze, then looked away, remembering Phoebe's insistence that she'd shaken me repeatedly, trying to wake me, but that I'd flinched back into wakefulness the instant my boss touched me.

"It has to be Morrison." I could barely hear myself through the mumbles, and try as I might I didn't miss Melinda's slow smile or the glance she gave the police captain at the end of the bed. I sighed and straightened my spine, trying to concentrate on the drumbeat and nothing else. I wasn't sure where to begin with bringing Billy out of his sleep, but sitting around feeling embarrassed that I had a cru—

The door behind me banged open, preventing me, thankfully, from finishing that thought, and an incredulous voice demanded, "What in the hell is going on in here?"

CHAPTER FIVE

Next time I get handed an exciting new power set, I want it to include a Spidey sense that warns me of oncoming danger. Or, in this case, oncoming doctors. I yanked my hands away from Billy like a guilty pickpocket. Morrison stopped drumming, and true to my word, my second sight fell away in a rush. Disorientation buzzed over me and I shoved to my feet, wondering why normality felt so wrong. I saw Melinda come to her feet, too, but the doctor was scowling at Morrison. "What," he demanded again, "the hell is going on in here?"

That offended me on all kinds of levels. First off, any questions about what was going on ought to have been addressed to Melinda, as the ill man's spouse. Second, while Morrison did have the drum, and I could see how that made him the instigator in the doctor's eyes, I was the one who'd been doing the laying-on of hands. I might not like my powers, but I wasn't by God going to let somebody else get blamed for them. Especially not Morrison, who'd taken enough on the chin this morning.

Third, the guy simply hit all my arrogant-prick medical-professional buttons. He stalked across the room in his white doctor's coat and put his hand out for the drum. A heavy ring with a yellow stone glittered on his hand, making the gesture all the more imperious and insulting. I thrust myself between him and Morrison like a knife, glowering. Morrison's chair scraped on the floor as he pushed it back, but to my surprise, he didn't stand.

The doctor looked up his nose at me. I had at least two inches on him, so he couldn't, try as he might, look down his nose at me. I gave him my very best, politest, most friendly, cheerful smile, and the wonderful thing was, I genuinely meant it. It was one of those rare, beautiful moments when I really loved every inch of my nearly six foot height, not to mention the shoulders and arms that came with spending a lifetime working on cars. I might've been slender next to my boss, but I wasn't exactly a waif, and once in a while looming over officious jerks in an imposing manner was incredibly satisfying. "I'm sorry, Doctor, is something wrong?"

His nostrils flared and he backed up a step. I showed tremendous restraint and didn't follow him. His expression suggested he'd stepped back of his own free will so he could see me better. My neighbor's cat got that same kind of expression when he fell off the windowsill: *I wanted to be on the floor.* I smiled some more.

"This is Mrs. Holliday. Oh, you've met," I said into the

sour face of acknowledgment he made, and before he could actually get a word in edgewise. "So I'm sure you understand that whatever's going on in here is happening with her approval, which makes it, let me see, what's the phrase I'm looking for here. Oh, yeah. None of your goddamned business."

He inhaled. I pointed a finger at him and he coughed on his words. "Does it appear to you that anyone in this room is providing illegal medical advice, or in fact trying to remove Mr. Holliday from the hospital's expert care?"

He inhaled again. I thought if I could keep him doing this for a few minutes, he might just puff up and blow away like a hot air balloon. It was worth a shot, so I carried on full bore. "I didn't think so. I'm sure you're familiar with the idea of positive thoughts and prayer shoring up the ill, Doctor, even if you don't subscribe to its usefulness yourself." His nose pinched again and I smiled less pleasantly this time. "That's what I thought. But you'd hardly deny the family and friends of an ill man the chance to surround him with those thoughts and prayers, would you? I didn't think so." Somewhere in the middle of that I started walking toward him, and he started backing up. By the time I got to the end, I was smiling so hard it hurt, and he was on the wrong side of the door that I closed in his face. I turned back to Melinda and Morrison, triumph writ large in my expression.

"That," Melinda said, "was Bill's older brother."

It turned out ritual suicide wasn't an option while hanging out in a friend's hospital room. Morrison wouldn't even let me crawl under Billy's bed and hide in humiliation. Billy's brother—who, now that I knew was his brother, did bear some resemblance to him, in a shrunken-down, weasly kind of way—gave me the world's flattest look and then ignored me wholesale when he came back into the room. I not only couldn't blame him, I was sort of grateful.

Bradley Holliday had driven up from Spokane the moment his shift at Valley Hospital ended, which was why he wore doctor's whites. On hearing he was from Spokane, I wanted to know any number of things, like why I hadn't known Billy had a brother, if he lived nearby and whether or not Bradley Holliday had ever met a teenage girl named Suzanne Quinley who'd gone to live in Spokane after her parents were brutally murdered. I figured the answers were "You never asked," and "No," respectively, but I wondered, anyway.

I also wondered why my friend Billy, who loved all things paranormal and who had married a woman like himself, had a brother who became livid at a healer's drum in a hospital room.

I sat down on the far side of Billy's bed, making myself as small as possible while I put a hand on his shoulder. It hardly mattered: none of the others were paying any attention to me, but I felt like I needed to be surreptitious, anyway.

The coil of energy flared inside me as I touched Billy's shoulder, impatience sparkling through my skin like champagne. I felt a knot loosen in my shoulder and let my eyes close for a moment, absurdly grateful that the power was responding. It hadn't been a couple of weeks earlier, and although it'd been behaving since then, the idea of failing my friends again made my stomach clench with nausea.

In a way it was helpful to have Brad over there talking intently with Melinda and Morrison. It put less pressure on me to be the performing monkey, and I was uncertain enough about what to do as it was. I did know one thing: pouring my life essence into Billy, like Melinda had tried to do, was right out. She didn't have the healing knack that I did, but that hadn't been the important part of what she'd been offering. She'd been trying to give him the will to live, and Billy wasn't missing that. What I'd felt was more like a siphon draining away what would have normally made him vital.

And siphons were a metaphor I could work with. The idea brought a smile to my lips even as I concentrated on my breathing, unwilling to interrupt and bring attention to myself by asking for my drum. Ideally I would pop by the garden that housed my inner self, invite Billy in and do a little fixer-upper from there. Even more ideally, I'd pop right into Billy's garden and do my work from inside his own head, but the one time I'd fallen into somebody else's garden, it'd been Gary, and I didn't really have much idea of how I'd done it. I suspected I hadn't done it at all, in fact, and that the old man's sense of self had just overwhelmed my newbie attempts to set up his shop in my head. It all meant that realistically, I was going to try slipping inside my garden, drawing Billy's soul closer to mine and pinching off the siphon that was drawing life force out of him. It seemed very straightforward and simple.

Oh, what my life had come to, that such things should seem simple.

A few deep breaths had me drifting, like the clarity Morrison's drumming had brought on was simmering just below the surface, waiting for me to pay attention to it again. My goal this time was an internal journey, not an external one, so there was no lens flare effect or rearrangement of the color spectrum into neons and pulsing life. Instead I slid down a brightly colored rabbit hole, tumbling chaotically through my own mind into a place I didn't recognize at first.

There were familiar elements. The pond with a waterfall feeding it at one end, for example, and the pathways that lay in straight lines through the grounds. But the grass, usually cropped so short I could see dirt between individual blades, had grown up to ankle-deep, and there was a hint of Kentucky blue to its color now. Leaves were fully open on trees that were still tidily trimmed, and a few of the hedges even bore flowers, though I had no idea what kind. The garden had been rectangular and functional last time I'd been in it, but now the far end, away from the waterfall, seemed hazy, as if fog were hiding the possibility of more.

It was almost pretty.

I stood by the pond, rotating slowly and trying to remember when I'd last actually gone inside myself. I'd been looking outward for days, searching for Coyote—my erstwhile spirit guide, who'd stopped speaking to me after I threw him out of a dangerous situation—but I'd been avoiding taking a look at the state of my soul ever since the catastrophe that had cost two people their lives. It seemed unlikely that those events had led to all the blossoming going on around me now.

Of course not, said a snide little voice inside my head. *Because horrible things happening couldn't possibly have any positive aspects, like forcing you to get your act together.*

I really hated that voice. I was almost certain it'd been there before my shamanic powers had been woken up. It was the *almost* part that made me nervous. Sometimes I wanted to ask if other people had snarky little voices that gave them smart-ass commentary on their lives, but I was afraid they'd say no.

Obnoxious little voice or no, I sat down by my pond, trailing my fingers into the water. It struck me suddenly as being a good conduit for reaching Billy, even working into the siphoning of life essence he was experiencing. I could still feel my hand on his shoulder, in a vague, disconnected way, which was interesting. I'd never tried paying attention to my physical body while inside the garden of my mind. Then again, I hadn't really needed to, and now I was trying to build a bridge between myself and my patient. Trying to find a way inside him so we could get the healing process started.

It was my right hand both on his shoulder and sploosh-ing around in my pond. The most peculiar thing was that having two body awarenesses going on at once only sounded strange when I tried putting it into words; it *felt* completely natural. I turned my focus to my fingers, calling up the bubble of power that resided inside me.

It responded as easily as it had before, splashing through me in silver-blue joy at being used. Warmth and glee ran up through my torso and into my arm, washing down the blood vessels just as it had done with Gary, and then poured itself into my pond. The charged water glimmered and shone, quicksilver with life and depth of its own. My consciousness spilled into it, and over Billy's skin, making me aware of his heartbeat, his breathing, first on the surface, and then slowly from within, as if he was permeable and I was water.

I cut the snide little voice off before it could comment, that time. I knew perfectly well the permeation was what I was trying to accomplish, but it didn't make succeeding any less surprising to me. Still, having my brain back-talk at me when I was trying to concentrate couldn't be of any help.

The entire sensation was incredibly subtle, like being brushed by fur so soft I couldn't be sure I'd been touched. It could also have been insanely erotic, and for a moment I was torn between gratitude I was working with Billy and a fantasy about working with Morrison.

God, I wished I would stop thinking things like that. I set my teeth together both literally and figuratively, and concentrated on the idea of permeating my way through flesh and bone and into Billy's psyche, so I could enter the garden of his soul and work my anti-siphoning magic.

For a minute there, I thought it was going to work. I slid through dreams, trying not to look at them, under the unlikely logic that they weren't my business. Traipsing around in people's unconscious minds: my business. Snooping while I'm doing it: not kosher. I had an interesting set of moral boundaries going on there.

But the water metaphor was working, letting me drain down toward his garden. I got the impression that the idea of the garden was something I superimposed on Billy, and that he adapted to because I was the one awake in this scenario. Regardless, it provided the structure I needed, a bright spot at the center of his being, hints of green visible even from my outside vantage point. I exhaled a sigh of relief.

Warm, heavy blackness came down around his garden like a Carolina night, so thick and dark there was nothing left to breathe. There were faint shining prisms in the black, ripples of purple and blue that had the faintest living texture to them when I saw them from the corners of my eyes, and which disappeared entirely when I looked straight at them, too dark to be seen.

My water metaphor held together, leaving me beading against tar, unable to push through the darkness. I gnawed my lower lip, wondering which level of reality I was doing that on, and tried to pull the droplets of myself back together, coalescing into a whole presence lingering within Billy's mind as a semi-welcome guest.

Sleepy, weighty midnight swam around me, trying as hard—harder—than I was to enter that core of Billy's self. It brought slow pressure to bear, something about its presence suggesting it had all the time it needed, and that it would eventually prevail. I, on the other hand, was beginning to think I had a limited window in which to save my friend's life. The sleepy power didn't seem to be interested in acknowledging me, and I couldn't tell if Billy knew I was there. If my water metaphor had failed, there had to be another way. Something more direct, something completely the opposite of what the weight that kept Billy asleep was trying to accomplish.

A needle sounded good. I restructured the idea of my approach without putting too much thought into it, half afraid I'd tip something off if I was too noisy about my intentions. Coyote had told me more than once that the psychic planes were dangerous places, and while I felt relatively safe in the confines of Billy's head, he probably had, too, and now he was stuck in a coma. I made the idea of myself thin, piercing through the uncomprehending darkness with ease as I injected myself toward Billy's garden. One pinprick hole to carry a healing element into the garden. It made sense.

I smacked into a barrier hard enough to make my head ring and landed back in my own body, holding a hand over my eye. "Ow."

"Walker?" Morrison was beside me, his hand hovering over my shoulder. I moved my fingers away from my face, brushing his touch away before it happened.

"I'm okay." My left eye socket hurt. Not like the hangover, which I'd managed to forget about, but as if I'd been smacked with a ball. Or like a needle tip had hit bone instead of forgiving flesh. "I'm all right." I put my hand over my eye again, squinting the other one at Melinda. "Mel, I think I should talk to you." I didn't want to give Brad a significant look, but my squinty eye flashed to him, anyway. "Alone."

Brad exhaled in noisy exasperation. "She's one of your insane friends, isn't she, Melinda?"

"Joanne Walker," Morrison said in clipped tones, "is a police officer under my command. She is here because I asked her to be. If you have a problem with that, Dr. Holliday, you can take it up with me."

I wanted to cheer Morrison or hug him or something equally inappropriate, but my mouth had broken into a wide grin and my tummy was jumping with barely contained jiggles of laughter. "Doc Holliday," I said happily. "I mean, I never got why your parents were cruel enough to call Billy Billy instead of Will or William, but Doc Holliday you did to yourself."

The look Morrison gave me suggested I wasn't helping matters. The look Bradley Holliday gave me suggested he'd heard the joke several thousand times now and it wasn't any funnier than it had been the first time. Me, I didn't care. For one brief, shining moment, life was good. Still grinning, I turned to Melinda, and all my humor fell away at the scared look in her eyes. "Crap," I said quietly, and looked at Brad again. "Can you give me a minute with Mel, please?"

"She'll tell me whatever you tell her," he said pompously. I glanced at Melinda, who shrugged and nodded. I shrugged, too.

"Okay. There's something keeping him asleep. Something that's trying to drain his life energy. You were feeding it with all that pow—" I glanced at Morrison and Brad, shrugged again and modified what I was saying to "—good will you were giving him. I could get through it, but I couldn't get into Billy's psyche. He can take care of himself." I lifted my hand to my eye again, then let it fall. "His own shields kept me out, and they're keeping that thing, whatever it is, from draining him dry, too. I've never had to get through somebody's shields, Mel. I don't know how to do it, but I can learn, and then between me and Billy we'll get that leech off him. It's going to be okay."

Melinda began a nod, taking a quick breath to speak, but Bradley beat her to it with a growled "This is preposterous.

Bill needs medical care, not a quack with a drum and a mouthful of new-age nonsense."

Morrison scowled at me, clearly on Brad Holliday's side of things. I sympathized with them both, which only made everything more complicated. "I'm sorry, Captain. If it was going to be easy, the doctors probably could've woken him up. But I'll figure it out. I really will," I promised, then offered a hopeful smile and added, "Look at it this way. At least nobody's dead."

Morrison's cell phone rang.

CHAPTER SIX

I steepled my palms and fingers together against my mouth, fitted my thumbs under my chin and tried not to throw up. I had the distinct feeling I'd just made the *at least it's not raining* comment on a much nastier scale, and from the tension throbbing in Morrison's temple, he thought I had, too. For a few seconds the only sound in the room was the beeping of Billy's monitors while we all watched Morrison pick up the call.

He tilted his head back and exhaled, shoulders slumping a little before he cast me an indecipherable glance and left the room with an apology on his lips for whoever it was he was talking to. Relief-tinged nausea settled into my bones and I put my head down on my knees and breathed for a minute. If somebody was dead, the look Morrison'd given me wouldn't have been unreadable. I was willing to take small favors where I could get them. A shiver swept over me and I curled my arms around myself more tightly.

Melinda put her hand on my shoulder. "Thank you, Joanie."

I shook my head against my knees. "I didn't do anything."

Brad's disgruntled "You certainly didn't" came across the room in a mutter. Melinda ignored him, squeezing my shoulder.

"You'll find a way to help him," she said with quiet confidence. "And at least I've got something to tell the kids."

"What," Brad snapped, "that their father is being held captive by a psychic whammy? Melinda, you have got to start dealing with the real world here. Bill is in a coma and he may never wake up. These things aren't caused by evil spirits and magic. It's a physical condition and has to be treated with science and medical professionals, not voodoo and snake oil."

I lifted my head to watch him rant, hands steepled against my mouth again. "We're all worried, Dr. Holliday," I said when he was done. "I know you've already lost one sibling." *Careless of him,* my snide little voice said, but I didn't let it out. Brad didn't like me as it was. Joking about dead family wasn't exactly the best way to win friends and influence people. "I hope the doctors can help him. In the meantime, maybe voodoo hoodwinks won't hurt." I could hardly believe I was hearing myself say that. How very far the mighty had fallen.

I stood up and gave Melinda a hug. "I'm going to head home and see if I can scare anything up about sleeping sicknesses and…" I trailed off with a sigh. *And penetrating mental shields* was how the sentence ended, but my coping mechanism had slid out of place, and it just seemed like too much to say right then. "I'll call you as soon as I've got anything, okay?"

"Okay." Mel returned the hug and I heard the argument with Brad start up again as I left the hospital room.

Morrison was folding his phone closed as I came down the hall. "Everything all right, Captain? Who was on the phone?"

He gave me another look I couldn't read. "Everything's fine. Just a friend."

"Tell your friend he's got lousy timing," I said.

"She," Morrison said, then looked like he wished he hadn't. A too-vivid mental picture of Barbara Bragg snagged in my mind and I closed my hands into fists. Morrison noticed and I tried to find something else to do with my hands. "What's going on back there?" Morrison asked just a shade too loudly. I seized on it, grateful for any change of topic.

"Oh, you know." I had something to do with my hands now, gesturing down the hall toward the elevators. Morrison went for the stairs, probably out of sheer contrariness, but I followed him anyway. "Brad's back there trying to convince Mel it's dangerous to let me within fifty yards of his brother, and she's telling him that Billy isn't Caroline, and that everything's going to be all right." My vast psychic powers didn't actually include telepathy, but I figured it was a pretty good guess as to what was going on. Morrison cornered on the stairs and threw a furrow-browed glance back at me.

"Caroline?"

"Their sister. She drowned when Billy was a kid. He told me about it a few months ago." He'd told me considerably more than that, the day after my powers had woken up. Caroline's death and consequent visits had precipitated

Billy's fascination with the paranormal world. He didn't see dead people all the time, the way the kid in the movie did, but he saw them often enough. It was why he'd become a homicide detective: the newly dead were sometimes able to point him toward their killers. I would not in a million years have believed him if I hadn't spent the night before he told me talking to a bunch of dead shamans.

"I didn't know." Morrison pushed an exit door open, letting in brilliant July sunshine. I lifted a hand to protect my eyes as we went out to the parking lot.

"Funny what we don't know about the people we work with." I regretted saying it almost before the words were finished, and Morrison gave me a sharp look that said, as clearly as words might have, No kidding, *Siobhán*. I knotted my fists and muttered, "See what I mean?" at the pavement.

My real name wasn't Joanne Walker. I'd been born Siobhán Walkingstick, names stuck on me by diversely ethnic parents. My father had taken one look at the Gaelic mess *Siobhán* and Anglicized it to Joanne, and I'd abandoned the Cherokee *Walkingstick* the day I graduated high school. Since then I hadn't given much thought to either name, until dead shamans and old gods started calling me by it. I can be a little slow on the uptake, but I got the idea pretty fast that names had power, and my true name wasn't something I wanted bandied about.

So, of course, I'd turned around and told it to Morrison. I'd say I was still trying to work my way through that, but I was more trying to pull the covers over my head and pretend it hadn't happened. Apparently good ol' Captain Morrison wasn't going to let me forget. I wished he would. Regardless of the name printed on my birth certificate,

Siobhán Walkingstick was someone who barely existed. I pushed myself into a jog for a few steps, pulling ahead of the captain as we headed for my car.

Sunlight glittered across her windshield, and for a moment I saw dozens of spiderweb cracks in it, radiating out from a hole that punched nearly all the way through. A surge of panic yanked my stomach downward, but when I blinked the damage was gone. I came up to the car and leaned on the hood, fingers splayed and knuckles popping against the heated metal as I breathed through my teeth. My head dropped between my shoulders, making my neck ache, but I just wanted to touch my Mustang and know she was all right. I could hear the frown and the concern in Morrison's voice as he said, "Walker?"

"Nothing. Thought I saw a crack in the windshield." I had. It just hadn't precisely been Petite's windshield that was cracked. It was, for lack of a better word, my soul. Every flaw I'd ever run away from was imprinted on a sheet of windshield glass, my mechanic-trade influence weighting the way I saw myself. A few times over the past six months some of those cracks had fused, but there were a whole hell of a lot more of them left to heal. I had a pretty good idea of what moment had left the puncture hole, and I wanted to keep as far away from that moment as possible. I didn't like it when my little avoidance techniques threw the whole intertwined mess of my emotional state back in my face.

"…who cracked your windshield," Morrison was saying. I cranked my head up and turned it toward him without comprehension. "I'd pity the poor bastard who cracked your windshield," he repeated.

"Don't. He walked away." My lip curled against the words. Morrison'd been talking about my car, and I was talking about something else entirely. Something I didn't want to talk about, I informed the inside of my head, so if my brain would like to cooperate and pass sentences through it first before they got to my mouth, I'd appreciate it.

Great. Now the snide little voice was me. Not that it wasn't all the time, but this time it was actively me. Lecture given, I shoved off Petite's hood. Morrison got between me and the driver's-side door, not quite touching me, his eyebrows drawn down in concern.

"Walker?"

"Do me a favor, Morrison, and forget I said that, okay?"

"I'm not sure I should."

"Dammit, boss. Please." I turned my face away, looking at the wheel well of the car next to my Mustang. Someone had put hollowed-out, spinning hubcaps on a Subaru station wagon, which seemed a lot like gilding a potato peeler. "It's not what you're thinking, okay?" I said to the Subaru.

"Are you sure?"

I sighed, looking back at Morrison. Sunlight made his eyes a ridiculously clear blue, even as he squinted into it to see me better. "Yeah, Morrison, I'm sure." I didn't want to say the word we were both thinking. It was ugly and scary, and besides, it hadn't happened, despite my horrible phrasing. I edged around it with "Nobody hurt me, I promise. Not physically. And who gets this far in life without some emotional scars, anyway, right?" I even managed to dredge up a crooked little smile, just because Morrison looked so damned concerned. If he'd been someone else—

if I'd been someone else—I'd have put my hand on his cheek and kissed him for fussing. But we were both ourselves, so all I said was, "Okay?"

After a long silence he nodded and stepped back. "All right, Walker. If you say so." He walked around Petite's wrinkled back end while I unlocked my door and climbed into her oven-hot interior to unlock the passenger door. Morrison put the drum in the back again, and I pulled out of the parking lot, concentrating on driving so I didn't have to talk. Morrison didn't push it, and the ride went as it always did when he and I were in a vehicle together: in silence.

I was the one who broke it, as we climbed out of the car back at my apartment building. Morrison nodded as he got out, a dismissal if there ever was one, but I reached across Petite's roof and said, "Captain." He hesitated and curiosity won out, making him turn to look at me again. "Thanks for getting me this morning. I'm sorry I wasn't more help with Billy, and I'm sorry if I made things awkward with his brother."

A faint smile curled the corner of his mouth. "What do you want, Walker?"

I ducked my head and breathed a laugh. "Nothing. I just wanted to say thanks. And…" I made a fist of my hand and bounced it lightly against Petite's roof, twice. "That's all." I met Morrison's eyes with a brief smile and shook my head. "That's all."

He waited a long, long moment before nodding. "You're welcome."

I watched him walk away, wondering just how much research he'd done on me, after I'd confessed Joanne Walker wasn't my real name. I knew he'd done some. I would have, too, in his position. I just didn't know how much. Maybe the flash of concern had been because he knew a lot more about me than I thought anybody west of the Carolinas or north of the Mason-Dixon line did.

Or maybe it was because Morrison was a decent man and I'd chosen unfortunate words at the hospital parking lot.

Either way, I'd just let the best opportunity I might ever have to find out go, throttled by anxiety and my own unwillingness to talk, think or act on my past. Someday I was going to have to turn around and face all of the crap piling up behind me. A lot of people had told me that recently.

It was the first time I'd ever said it to myself, though.

I sighed, thumped Petite's roof again, got my drum and went upstairs to see who was left in my apartment.

Tuesday, July 5, 11:40 a.m.

The answer was an anticlimactic nobody. There was a note from Mark on top of the box of doughnuts Gary'd brought, which said *Maybe we could get to know each other in a less Biblical sense over dinner,* and had a phone number written on it. I crumpled the paper and dropped it in the trash, then got a maple bar out of the doughnut box.

Beneath the maple bar was another note that said *Take his number out of the garbage, you crazy dame, and call him.* I laughed out loud and went to pick up the phone as I crammed half the doughnut into my mouth. It was after eleven, which meant Gary was at work by now, driving his cab. The old man had changed work schedules so he'd be able to play drummer boy for me every morning. I didn't know how I'd ended up with friends that good.

I got Keith, the guy who manned the phones, on the line, and asked him to have Gary call me when he had a chance. I'd sent Keith flowers once for taking a message, and since then his surly mood always took a turn for the cheerful when we talked.

Gary called as I lay on the couch, polishing off a third doughnut and feeling like a bloated warthog. "Did you read the note he left me?" I demanded without saying hello.

"'Course I did. Had ta let myself back in to do it, too. You ate the maple doughnuts, didn't you?" He sounded proud of himself. I laughed and dragged myself off the couch. Talking on the phone always made me want to walk around. That was safe with the kitchen phone, but the one in the bedroom had a cord, and I'd half killed myself with it more than once.

"Yes, I ate the maple doughnuts, and, Gary, how did you let yourself back in? I *know* I haven't given you a key."

"Gotcha an apple fritter, too," Gary said. "An' I wrote down his phone number, so even if you didn't take it outta the garbage like I told you, I'm still gonna leave it lyin' around your apartment."

"I ate it, too. I'd think you were my dating service, except I don't think they're supposed to fatten you up for the kill."

"Three doughnuts ain't gonna fatten you up, Jo. You should give him a call."

"Can't," I said. "Isn't one of those dating-rules things that you're not supposed to call for three days, or something?" There was nothing interesting in the kitchen except more doughnuts, and I couldn't face eating another one just yet. I wandered across the apartment toward my bedroom.

"That's after the first date, Jo, not after you went to bed with the guy."

I winced. "I don't think seventy-three-year-olds are supposed to say things like that, Gary."

"Darlin', this old dog says plenty he ain't supposed to. How's Holliday?"

I winced again and sat down on the edge of my bed, pulling a pillow out from under the neatly arranged covers to hug it against my chest. It smelled like Mark. I thought *augh* again and got up to go stare at myself in the bathroom mirror. "Still sleeping. Something's keeping me from waking him up. I was going to do some research and see what I could find about sleeping sicknesses." The woman in the mirror looked just like she had yesterday. Short black hair, warmly tanned skin, hazel eyes. Scar on her cheek, generous nose scattered with a few freckles, all the same things I expected. I knew her pretty well. She wasn't the kind of woman who got drunk and slept with men she didn't know. Hell. She didn't even sleep with men she did know. Arm wrestling, as Mark had mentioned, now that sounded like my style. I rubbed my biceps absently, still staring at myself in the mirror. He must've gone really easy on me, if I wasn't sore.

Sore.

Something pinged at the back of my mind and I moved to the bathroom doorway, looked toward my bed. "I didn't sleep with him." There was a sort of fluting laugh to my voice, a sound of childish relief. I could all but hear Gary blinking at me.

"What?"

"I didn't sleep with him. I mean, we didn't have sex." I sat down hard in the doorway, my legs no longer eager to hold me. "Jesus."

"You gonna tell me how you came to that conclusion, Jo?" Gary sounded wary. I laughed, the same high sound as before.

"I haven't had sex in ages, Gary. I'd be sore." My heartbeat had jumped up to about a zillion miles an hour, making a lump of sickness that tasted like apple fritter in my throat. I didn't know relief could feel so awful. "I'd be sore and I'd be sticky and I haven't taken a shower this morning and I'm not either of those things and so I didn't have sex with him. Oh, thank God." For some reason I was ice cold and shaking.

There was a profound silence that suggested that old dog saying things he shouldn't or not, I had perhaps overstepped the bounds of friendship with that particular announcement. I was about to apologize when he said, "Kinda glad to hear it, sweetheart. Didn't really seem like your style."

I drew my knees up, still shivering, and shook my head. "Not at all." Then I laughed again, twisting to look back at the bedroom. "He even made the bed."

"You oughta call this guy," Gary said again, with a sort of gentle kindness in the command. "Makes the bed, doesn't take advantage of pretty girls in the bed. Give him a call, Jo. How many guys make the bed?"

"*I* don't make the bed, Gary." I pulled a towel down to wrap it over my legs, trying to ward off the cold of relief. "Maybe I will." I sounded very quiet even to myself. The prospect of calling Mark, if I hadn't slept with him, was considerably more appealing than it had been when I thought I had, and that was its own kind of scary. "Maybe I will, okay? You're pushy."

"Parta my charm," he said, still triumphant. "I gotta fare, Jo. Gotta go. Call the kid."

"I'll talk to you later, Gary." I beeped the phone off and sat there in my bathroom doorway, staring at my bed. It sat there, bedlike, tidy except for the pillow I'd dislodged. No startling attractive men appeared in it. After a minute I took a deep breath and said, "Okay. Just to get you off my back," to Gary, though he was neither there nor likely to believe me if he could hear me. I wasn't entirely sure I believed me. Either way, I got Mark's number out of the garbage and hoped for an answering machine.

To both my delight and dismay, I got one. I straightened with surprise and stuttered out a message, not sure if I wanted any of it to sound like "Call me back."

Right before I said, "So, uh, bye," the phone got snatched up with a clatter and Mark, a trifle breathlessly, said, "Joanne? Hi, sorry, I was in the shower. I heard your voice on the machine. Are you still there?"

I slumped against the door frame. "Yeah. Hi, Mark."

"I didn't think you'd call. Gosh, I'm glad you did."

"Did you really just say gosh?"

A laugh came through the line, somewhere between pleased and embarrassed. "I did. Does that count against me?"

"It's kind of cute," I admitted more honestly than I'd intended to. "Look, Mark, this really isn't a good time. I just wanted to call because, um." Because Gary had told me to. I was twenty-seven years old. I wasn't sure *because somebody told me to* was a legitimate reason for calling a boy. "To say it wasn't a good time."

"Not a good time for what?" he asked, more insightfully than I would've liked. "To talk on the phone or to talk at all? Is this the 'It was a horrible mistake' speech?"

"It was a horrible mistake, or it would've been if we'd had sex, but I'm pretty sure we didn't, so it wasn't. Except I don't bring guys home, so it was."

"We didn't?" Mark, unlike me, sounded sort of disappointed. "Are you sure?"

I couldn't help it. I laughed, even if it was still a sort of shaky sound, and bonked my head against the door frame. "Physical evidence on my part suggests we didn't. Look, I'm sure you're very nice, but frankly, I don't know how to deal with you, and I don't really think I want to have to figure it out." That, again, was rather more honest than I'd intended to be. To my surprise, Mark laughed.

"At least you don't pull your punches. Tell you what. Everything I know about you is you've got a sexy car—"

Anybody who compliments my car earns a special place in my heart. I melted for a moment.

"—and a sexier body—"

"Oh, get real." The thaw was over.

Mark ignored my protest and continued, "You don't cook and you've got a bunch of early-rising friends and you can outdrink half a police department. Now, what do you know about me?"

I pulled the phone away from my ear and peered at it, then sighed and put it back. "You're cute, you cook and for some reason you apparently find me attractive. That's about it." That and he made the bed, which I didn't want to mention, even if it was a point in his favor.

"Right. So that's enough to get a first date on, right?"

"Sure. Wait."

Too late. "I'll see you for dinner tonight, then. Eight?"

"I—"

"Great! We'll go somewhere decent. You can drive." I could almost hear his grin and wink. "See you tonight, Joanne." He hung up before I had a chance to get out of it, and left me gaping at the phone.

CHAPTER SEVEN

Plodding down to the parking lot wasn't taking a shower, and it certainly wasn't the best way to help Billy, but I found myself doing it, anyway, after finally putting the phone back in its cradle. I padded across the lot to the tree I'd parked Petite beneath, popping her trunk and wincing as the wrinkled steel creaked in protest. There hadn't been time or money enough lately to start hammering the dents out. The insurance company still hadn't paid up for the so-reported "act of vandalism" that had taken place back in January. I had full coverage on my baby. I thought the damned insurance company should stop dicking around and give me my money. It wasn't like they even had to pay for a mechanic's work, since I did all my own.

I pulled the jack and toolbox out of Petite's trunk, still not quite thinking about what I was doing, and gave the gas tank cover an extra reassuring pat before I closed the trunk. It was an ongoing apology for having let somebody shoot an arrow through it, part of the same vandalism that'd ripped a twenty-eight-inch hole in her roof. I had no idea what else to call riders of the Wild Hunt taking axes and longbows to her. I didn't think the insurance company would cough up at all if I claimed it was an act of gods.

A minute later I was on my back under the engine, tinkering with hot metal and inhaling the scent of gasoline and oil. Somewhat belatedly I realized I wasn't wearing grubby clothes, and performed a shrug against the warm concrete I lay on. Yet another shirt and jeans relegated to the mechanic pile. I was going to have to go shopping soon.

A vague prickle of guilt set in as I fiddled with bolts. It wasn't Petite that needed work. It was me. My head was spinning. I rarely got drunk. I never brought guys home, even if I had not, at least, actually slept with the one in question. I certainly didn't find myself calling the guy back and agreeing to go out on a date. Well, I wouldn't have thought I did, anyway. It'd never happened before, so apparently it *was* what I'd do in that situation. It still didn't seem like me. I was by nature a much more isolated person than that.

I'd grown up on the road, my father unwilling to settle down for more than a few months. The one time he'd stayed anywhere over a year, a one-night stand he'd had showed up again and dumped a kid on him before flying back to Ireland without so much as an explanation. I'd had a pretty clear idea from a very early age what he was trying to leave behind.

Me.

My earliest memories were of mashing my nose against

the car window, watching other vehicles whip by and calling "Zoom! Zoom!" at them. I loved the leather seats and the tangy scent of old cigarettes, the way the world skimmed by effortlessly and the thrum of power that shook the car as we took interstates and blue roads, always exploring. Dad taught me to read and how to fix cars, the two of us pulled off the road, me holding a flashlight while he bent his dark head over the engine. I got most of my primary school education that way, visiting historical sites and reading books about what had happened there. The one time I remember Dad having any real emotional response to one of those history lessons was at the Battle of Little Bighorn. He never before or after made much comment about it, maybe because although he was as pureblood Indian as you could get, I was only a half blood, but there was a serious undercurrent of *stupid white men* to that particular lesson. The truth is, I'd think anybody who stood there and looked out over the battlefield lands would think *stupid white men,* because even I could tell that no one in his right mind would get in a fight there. But that wasn't really the point, and after that, Dad started teaching me Cherokee. I didn't remember much of it anymore, but there'd been a while when I was seven or eight when it was almost all we spoke.

That was also when we started stopping in small towns for up to a semester at a time, so I could get some proper education. Dad never really understood that I was badly socialized, having only had him for company, or that a white girl—because despite the tan I currently had, my coloring was my mother's: pale skin, green eyes and black hair—who spoke an Indian language wasn't going to fit in. He never had much idea that grades were at different levels all over the country, or that several weeks to a semester was only long enough for me to always be the new kid, not to belong. The older I got, the more I resented it, until I was old enough to enter high school and put my foot down. I told Dad he had to choose a place for us to stay for my whole high school career.

It was like he'd never seen me before. Behind all the years of resentment I had this feeling that at least it was always me and Dad against the world, but the way he looked at me was more like it'd been him on the road alone all that time, and suddenly this young woman had appeared to make demands of him. We went back to North Carolina, where he'd grown up and I'd never been. I spent my high school years in the Eastern Cherokee Nation, fitting in just as poorly as I ever had. Those were the borders I tended to define myself by. When I stretched outside of them, like I'd done with Mark, I found myself turning to the one thing I really knew I could rely on.

Cars. They were my home, my first memories, my comfort foods and smells, and they could take me away from all the things that were wrong with the world. When the going got tough, the tough went shopping, but I went to work on my car.

Concrete and asphalt, even sun-warmed, wasn't exactly the most comfortable bed I'd ever lain on, but it was enough to have me yawning until my eyes watered within half an hour of starting to tinker on Petite's undercarriage. A distant jangle sounded right next to my ear, the wrench sliding from sleepy fingers, but I couldn't convince my hand to grope around for it. Eh, it didn't matter. Nobody was likely to come along and nick my stuff while I was lying right next to it. It wasn't as if I was actually going to take a nap in the parking lot, even if I did feel a bit stretched thin and gooey, like the asphalt was folding itself around me, one big comfy bed.

The sky was the wrong shade of blue. It was a color I knew, hard and pure and unrelenting, but it wasn't the color I was used to. I squinted against it, tracking the sun from the corner of my eye. It, too, was without remorse or gentleness, heat intense enough to redden my skin just from a few minutes' exposure. Weight pressed down on me, both in the dryness of the air and in the inescapable sense that this was one of the more important moments of my life.

Someone put a hand on my shoulder, hotter and drier than the air. I turned to look up—unusual; I wasn't used to looking up at much of anybody—and the scene changed around me.

Hot air became muggy, so full of water I choked on my first breath, tears suddenly blurring my vision. Heat vastly more intense than the air outside radiated at me, a fire built up in the center of a compact mudroom. I was one of four in the room, the other three sitting at cardinal points around the fire. I knelt, blinking against the heat, my hands on my thighs, and felt long hair sticking to my shoulders and back. I had never worn my hair long. My father had, but neither he nor I were patient enough to deal with a child's tangles, and the unfamiliar feeling sent a shudder up my spine. I was not *me*, but I didn't know who I was. Usually in dreams even when I was someone else, I thought I was me; now I felt like the butterfly wondering if he was a man, or maybe the other way around.

I tried to look down, but my head wouldn't respond to my command, neck remaining stiff and my gaze direct and hot on the overwhelming fire. My heart knocked around inside me with a child's excitement that I tried to quell: it wasn't appropriate, no more than the grin that kept wanting to stretch across my face. I needed to be solemn and adult for this, the itchy idea that it would be taken away otherwise skittering over my skin. I knew that wouldn't happen, but I still struggled to be serious about it all. That was what everyone expected, and I didn't want to disappoint them.

Time compressed and ballooned, stretching me across it like taffy until I felt barely attached to my body, a heady swimming sensation that made nausea float in my belly. Voices sang in the background, drums thudding with resolute direction. Sometimes I joined in, singing words I didn't know in a language I didn't recognize. Mostly, though, I let the songs and the heat and the drums sink into my skin, and pull me farther and farther away from my body. That was the purpose: I was there to be guided. Later I would become more active in these rituals, but for now I was the student.

A part of me, far beneath the music and the taffy feeling, said, *so this is how it should have been*, but that didn't make much sense to me as I snapped apart from my body and drifted into a place of absolute quiet blackness.

Oddly enough, I knew where I was. It wasn't the Dead Zone, the starless place between life and death and other worlds, though how I could tell the difference between one utter darkness and another, I wasn't sure. Sparks of life floated through this place, like invisible motes reflected from inside my eyes. I drifted for what felt like a long time, watching them, aware that somewhere behind the bones of my ears, I could still hear the drums beating.

I couldn't remember being so relaxed. The darkness was warm, unlike in the Dead Zone, where it had weight and purpose and chill, even when it wasn't being visited by deadly snake-gods. I could rest here forever, warm and content and safe.

One of the floaties popped into something brighter and more solid, making me chuckle. Last time I'd seen these things, a whole host of them had come tumbling out of the black to rassle for dominance over one another. This time only one creature came, that quick burst of light seeming distant and hopeful. It was a coyote, I could see that, more ethereal than my Coyote and much more playful than the Big Coyote I'd met in the desert. It disappeared, leaving me resting in darkness again, then leaped forward, suddenly far closer.

The fourth time it reappeared, it did so directly in front of me, and looked up with a loll-tongued grin before butting its head against my thigh so hard I felt the ache all the way to the bone. I offered my hand, grinning back at the spirit animal, and it wrapped its long tongue around my wrist, then without warning or pain, began chowing down on my arm.

Surprise ricocheted through me, more out of familiarity and unexpectedness than fear or anger, and I gaped down at the spirit coyote's silver fur and see-through lines as it worked on swallowing me whole. I'd been through this before, though I realized quite suddenly that the person I was in my dream hadn't been. That part of me knew to expect this, but still felt more than a little horror and panic at being had for lunch. I had the peculiar sensation of trying to reassure myself that everything would be okay, and the even more peculiar sensation of not getting through to myself. After a few seconds I realized that for the other part of me, having Coyote eat me *hurt,* and I remembered that being the thunderbird's snack hadn't been a bowl of cherries, either. I was trying to figure out how to get past the pain and offer new reassurances when something nudged my ankle.

I peeled my arm away from my eyes, blinking blearily at legs visible up to slacks-clad knees. The knees bent into a crouch, hands dangling over them as Mark peered down the length of Petite's undercarriage to grin at me. "This your idea of a fancy date, Joanne?"

Tuesday, July 5,.7:53 p.m.

I crunched up several inches, then crashed back down again, having narrowly avoided smashing my head on Petite's engine. "Ma—uh? What're you—what time is it? Jesus!" I flinched up a second time, again just barely missing bashing my head, and rolled to the side, getting out from beneath my car before I did myself serious injury. "Did I fall asleep out here?"

"It's ten to eight," Mark said. "I'm early. Sorry." He stayed in his crouch, still grinning at me while I scrambled to my feet and pushed oily hands through my hair, then swore and rubbed them on my jeans. "Looks like you're not quite ready."

I stared at him wide-eyed, then turned to stare at my Mustang. Concrete wasn't my favorite place to sleep, but concrete beneath a jacked-up vehicle was just asking to get dead. I couldn't place the blame on Petite, but somehow I wanted to, as if she'd lulled me into a potentially deadly nap. "It's eight o'clock?" The location of the sun and the coloring of the sky suggested Mark was not, in fact, lying to me. "Uh. Jesus." I was never at my best right after I'd woken up, but waking up after an all-day snooze in a parking lot was high on a list of Ways to Discombobulate Joanne. I was astonished no one'd called the police or dropped the car on me or stolen my tools. I swung back around to stare at Mark some more, as if doing so would provide some sort of explanation for my behavior.

"You okay?" He looked up at me with the amusement still there, but dampened by genuine concern. "How long've you been out here?"

"Since…like, God, noon. Somewhere like that." I pushed my hand through my hair again, then rubbed the scar on my cheek and felt grease slick across my face. Mark put his hands on his thighs and pushed out of his crouch, grinning again. He wore a maroon button-down that played up the red in his hair and looked soft. I curled my fingers against my face to keep myself from smearing oil all over his clothes, too, and transferred my attention to taking tools out from under my car so I could remove the jack. That was safer than feeling up Mark's shirt.

"I came home to do some work on the car and to think, and…" My heart had started hammering too hard, making a wash of fright climb up my throat. I could believe I might fall asleep under Petite for a few minutes, maybe even an hour or two. But with the sun traveling through the sky and heating up both the day and the car, not to mention leaking light around the mask my elbow'd made, and with people in and out of the parking lot all day—that just wasn't normal. I knotted my hands around the jack and held on, trusting it to not give out and crush me now when it hadn't bothered to all day. "I can't believe I slept out here." My thoughts were still running down those tracks, wash, rinse, repeat. "That hard, all day. It's not…"

"Natural?" There wasn't any teasing in Mark's voice, though he sounded wry. I looked up from the jack, then ratcheted it down, mouth pressed thin. "It'll be okay," he said, sounding a great deal like I had trying to reassure myself within the context of my dream. "Look. I've got reservations for eight-thirty at the Ponti Seafood Grill. You're going to need some food, and I know you don't have anything in your apartment." I heard a smile come into his voice and looked up to see it reflected on his face. "I'm guessing you're not the kind of woman who takes two hours to primp and get ready to go out. Why don't we go up to your apartment, you can clean up and we can go to dinner? I won't keep you long, I swear, but you're going to have to eat one way or another, right?"

I pinched the bridge of my nose. "I don't have anything to wear to Ponti's." Not that there was much dress code anywhere in Seattle—casual wear, hallmark of the Northwest, was accepted anywhere I ever ate—but Mark looked nice, and I didn't have anything between jeans and sweaters and my dress uniform.

A car door banged shut somewhere in the parking lot and Phoebe's voice sailed toward me: "Are you avoiding me, Joanne? You didn't answer your pho—ooh. Hello." The last,

I guessed, wasn't directed at me, as she appeared from down the lot and looked Mark up and down. "Hi. I'm Phoebe." She offered a hand, seizing Mark's forearm in a traditional warrior's grip when he took it. Her expression was delicious, trying to watch both of us at once. "What's up, Joanne?"

I opened my mouth and shut it again. I had managed to double-book the single evening I'd had plans for in months. "Uh. I, uh."

"You have a date," Phoebe surmised, laughter glinting in her eyes. "Is that why you said you couldn't go out tonight? You're not going out in that, are you?" She eyed my jeans and T-shirt with dismay, which didn't seem fair. I'd barely gotten them grease-stained.

"I, uh."

Phoebe turned a very bright grin on Mark and grabbed my upper arm as solidly as she'd taken Mark's. "Twenty minutes," she said. "Give me twenty minutes and you won't recognize her. Joanne, come with me."

"I, uh," I managed one more time, and Phoebe dragged me off to my apartment.

CHAPTER EIGHT

"Start talking," she hissed as soon as we were inside the building door, though it didn't stop her from pulling me up the stairs. "Who is he? Why didn't you say something? He's really cute, Joanne! What were you doing working on your car if you've got a date? What were you doing working on your car if you were supposed to go out with me? My God, it's a good thing I came along. You'd have just worn that, wouldn't you?" The barrage of questions and comments got us up five flights of stairs and into my apartment, where Phoebe let me go and flung her giant black purse onto my couch. "Talk," she repeated. "I want the dirt! No, wait. Go get in the shower." She shed her denim jacket as she spoke, revealing worn hip-hugging jeans and a black sleeveless spandex shirt that said "Hottie" in rhinestones across her breasts.

"I'm in over my head, aren't I?" That was easier than trying to answer any of her zillions of questions.

"You dress fine for slouching off to Bethlehem." Phoebe knocked the front door closed with a toe and leaned on the couch, arms folded. "But for dating you have less dress sense than my dog. Of course you're in over your head. Shower." She pointed imperiously at my bedroom. "Never fear. Phoebe is here. I'll turn you into a heartbreaker."

"I don't want to be a heartbreaker," I said somewhat dizzily, and went to take a shower. Somebody was in control, even if it wasn't me. For the moment I just went with it. My brain didn't seem to have quite woken up yet.

Four minutes of hot water later I felt slightly less fuzzy. The best thing about hair as short as I wore mine was the absolute minimal time frame it took to wash it. Phoebe was in my bedroom when I exited the bathroom wrapped in a towel, her hands on her hips and her expression dismayed as she studied my closet. "I was right," she said dourly. I stuck my jaw out defensively.

"Right about what?"

Phoebe turned on me, thick eyebrows lifted. She very nearly had an eyebrow, rather than eyebrows. It kind of went along with the compact, muscular build she'd gotten from years of fencing. In car terms, she was a Porsche: small, sleek, fast and powerful. In people terms, I was afraid to mention a pair of tweezers in her presence, for fear she'd kick my ass. "You have nothing at all to wear. It's okay." She'd moved her purse to my bed, and now she upended its contents onto the comforter. A glimmering gold thing fell out, then a pair of jeans and a tri-fold leather wallet that had taken a lot of beating. A compact bag fell on top of all of it.

Phoebe pushed the wallet into her back pocket and shook the jeans out. "Put these on."

I clutched my towel and squinted at the jeans. There was something wrong with them. "Are those yours? They're short."

"No, they're not. Either. Not mine and not short. Put them on." She thrust them at me. I edged by her and got some undies out of my dresser first, squirming into them before taking the jeans. I had the distinct impression I was being bulldozed and I'd somehow given tacit permission for that to happen. "What's the gold thing?"

"Get the jeans on first."

"I'm trying. They don't fit. They're too short."

Phoebe inspected my ankles. The jeans hit right where they were supposed to, boot-cut and swinging against my anklebones. "They are not."

"Up *here!*" I pulled the towel up to show her, trying desperately to pull the jeans up. The waistband wouldn't go past my hipbones. My bellybutton was yards above the waistband.

"That's where they're supposed to hit, Joanne."

"Don't be ridiculous." I yanked again, which was certainly uncomfortable, if not in the least productive. I was giving myself an all-around wedgie. Phoebe slapped my hands away from the waistband, zipped the zipper and buttoned the button, then stood back and nodded approvingly.

"Okay, that's good. Shirt now." She handed over the gold glimmery thing. I held it up in dismay.

"This isn't a shirt. It's a piece of gold lamé. With strings."

"Wow. I wouldn't have put money on you knowing what

lamé was. It's a shirt." She took it away from me and tied two of the strings around my neck. "See?"

"I am *not* wearing this in public."

"Yes, you are. C'mon, lose the towel." She tugged it. I squawked and clutched it against my chest.

"Phoebe!"

"*Trust* me, Joanne. Would I lead you astray?"

"Yes." I sighed and unwrapped the towel, feeling put-upon. Phoebe tied another series of strings behind my back, then clucked her tongue.

"Okay. Got any hair gel?"

"Will you have a heart attack if I say yes?"

"No." She sounded far too cheerful, and went into my bathroom to root around. "You don't own *any* makeup?"

"What would I do with it?" I sat on the bed, wondering what I'd gotten myself into. Phoebe clucked again and came back out with a palmful of mousse that she rifled through my hair.

"Close your eyes. And tell me about this guy while I do your makeup." She unzipped the compact bag and dumped its content onto my bed, too: foundation, blush, lipstick, little jars of loose makeup and about fourteen makeup brushes of various sizes. The rest of it I didn't recognize, which made me nervous. "Close your eyes," she ordered again. I did. "Does he have a brother?"

"No," I muttered, "he's got a sister." Wretched petite curvy redheaded Barbara. I could remember her name easily enough. It didn't make sense that it'd taken numerous repetitions for me to remember Mark's.

"That'll do," Phoebe said saucily enough as I opened my eyes. She nearly poked me with a brush and scowled. I closed my eyes again. "Where'd you meet him? How long've you been dating?"

"I just met him last night, Phoebe."

"Ooh, first date. Good thing I'm here. What about Gary?"

My eyes popped open again. "What about him?"

"Does he know you're seeing a younger man, too?"

"I'm not dating Gary! He's seventy-three years old, Phoebe!"

"Uh-huh," she said, full of polite disbelief. "Sure. So's Sean Connery."

I screwed up my face, feeling like words wanted to explode out and not knowing what I was going to say. "Anyway, he thinks I should go out with Mark. That's practically the only reason I am." Somehow that didn't sound like it helped matters any. *"Anyway,"* I repeated, strenuously enough to burst something, "I'm sorry about double-booking. I don't know how that happened. It's—"

"Okay," she said. "It's okay, because I'm going to get all the prurient details afterward. You'll feel too guilty to hold out on me. Open your mouth."

"I hate lipstick."

"I didn't ask. Open your mouth."

I opened my mouth. A moment later Phoebe gave me a tissue to smack on, then pointed me toward the bathroom mirror. "Go on. Go look at yourself."

I eyed her, then got up and went to look.

Even if the mirror hadn't told me so, Mark's expression when we came back out of the bedroom said everything that needed saying. The ridiculous little gold shirt had strings that criss-crossed through half a dozen loops from my shoulder blades to the small of my back, where the shirt stopped entirely. Phoebe's makeup job gave my skin a startling warm golden glow. I'd dug a pair of three-inch strappy gold heels out of the closet, finally glad for the rare bout of shoe lust that had prompted me to buy them years ago. I'd never worn them. Mark did a double-take at my feet when he realized I stood as tall as he did, then developed a slow, astonished smile that made me self-conscious and pleased all at once. Phoebe looked insufferably smug.

"My plan," she told Mark airily, "had been to get Joanne a social life, but she seems to be managing it on her own. I've got a new plan. Now Joanne helps me get a social life. She said you had a sister." Her grin was bright, and Mark laughed.

"I do. Look, I didn't mean to bust in on you two having a night out. Can I make it up somehow? You could come to dinner with us, Phoebe."

"Absolutely not." Phoebe waggled a finger at him. "But if you can get Joanne out to Contour in Pioneer Square for a few hours after dinner, I'll call it even."

"I can't dance, Phoebe," I protested. "I really can't. And this is a fluke. If I need to help you get a social life, you're a disaster."

Phoebe turned the waggling finger on me. "I, personally, am coming off a very bad breakup, which you don't know because we've never really hung out before. So, see, you'll be good for me. It's a whatchacallit, parasitic relationship."

Mark and I said, "Symbiotic," at the same time, and I lifted an eyebrow at him before turning back to Phoebe, curiosity getting the better of me. "When was the breakup?"

"I thought cops didn't know words like *symbiotic*," she

said, grinning. Then she assumed a guilty expression. "Um. A year and a half ago. Anyway, it doesn't matter if you can't dance. Make her come out, anyway, Mark. A very wise man once said, 'Get up and dance, anyway, because nobody else cares if you can't dance.'"

"I'll try," he promised. "Who said that?"

"Dave Barry. It was one of his life lessons. Right after 'Do not take a sleeping pill and a laxative on the same night.' Now go." Phoebe beamed at both of us. "See you guys later."

I left the apartment with Mark, feeling somehow like I was walking half an inch in the air.

I'd hit the earth again by the time we went down five flights of stairs to get to my car. I hadn't been on a date in so long I had absolutely no idea how to conduct myself on one, which didn't go a long way toward creating the casual bantering atmosphere one tends to hope for on a first date. If that's what this qualified as, anyway. I wasn't sure, under the circumstances. Mark, however, was apparently much better at this sort of thing than I was, and put an appreciative hand on Petite's roof as I unlocked her doors. "You did all the work on this yourself, huh? What year is she?"

The way to my heart was through my car. A blind man could see that. Morrison couldn't, but a blind man could.

Morrison was really not the point here. I smiled at Mark and nodded. "Yeah. She's a 1969 Boss 302. There were only about seventeen hundred built, and about half of them are automatics. Someday when I've got a lot more time and money I'm going to convert her to a manual. That's my big dream for her." Mark didn't look glazed over yet, so I went on happily. "She was just a junker in somebody's barn when I found her. They let me take her for the price of hauling her out of there. It's been her and me ever since."

"She's beautiful."

Mark was obviously a genius. I beamed and nattered on about my car all the way down to the restaurant. Unlike Morrison, Mark knew enough about cars to not embarrass himself, and unlike most men, he didn't seem to feel it necessary to try to out-guy me on the topic. I noticed I'd been talking nonstop as we walked into the restaurant, and reined myself in with an effort and a surprisingly easy laugh. "You kind of found my Achilles' heel. Get me started on cars and I can't shut up."

"Nah." Mark waved his hand. "I like hearing what people are passionate about. You learn all kinds of things that way. Everybody's got something they're geeked about."

"Geeked?" I laughed again. "I didn't know *geek* was a verb."

"Sure." Mark actually held my chair for me as I sat down. What fascinating and bizarre behavior the courting male displayed. I wondered if he'd try ordering my dinner for me, too. "I've got this theory," he said as he sat down. "Used to be that being a geek was a bad thing, like being a dork or a nerd, right?"

I put my elbows on the table and folded my fingers under my chin. "Sure."

"Right." He nodded. "But then computers got to be everyday appliances, people needed geeks, and now it's pretty cool to be a geek. And I think the word has adapted. Now you can be a computer geek, a car geek, a cooking geek—"

"Those are called foodies," I interrupted, smiling. Mark

made a face at me and I laughed out loud again. "Sorry. I think I got that word from the Food Network."

"You're not sorry." He didn't look in the slightest bit upset, though, turning his face-making into a laugh of his own. "My point is if you've got a hobby or a job or a passion that you know a lot about, that other people don't, you're that kind of geek, and you get geeked about your topic."

"So *geeked* is a new word for *excited,*" I said. "Were you an English major, Mark?"

His eyebrows quirked. "It shows?"

I made a loose fist and put it out, palm down. Mark, who knew a cue when he saw one, did the same and bonked his knuckles against mine. "Fellow English majors of the world, unite."

"Bad spellers of the world," Mark said, half under his breath, and together we said, "Untie!" Mark's grin went so wide it looked fit to split his face. He put his menu aside—I hadn't even noticed the waiter handing them to us—and said, "Know what really drives me insane? Misused quote marks on signs. 'Big "sale"'," he said, complete with air quotes around "sale." "'Price "reduction"'. 'Lasagna "special"'."

"Oh, my God. Me, too." I actually leaned forward and grabbed his hand in sympathy. He was too good to be true. Not only was he cute and willing to listen to me babble about Petite, but he had the same language issues I did. I wanted one of my very own.

The thought that I could possibly have one of my very own heated my cheeks. Taking him home for a not-repeat of last night's performance suddenly sounded pretty entertaining. For the first time I could remember, the idea made me smile, and I wasn't embarrassed at all to let my English geek get out of hand. "Doesn't it make you just want to stop and fix the signs, or go in and yell at people until they understand that using quotes like that implies sarcasm? That they're saying exactly the opposite of what they mean? '"Rock-bottom prices"'!" Now I did air quotes, too, which was probably good, as it released Mark's hand from my enthusiastic prison. "Or apostrophes. Don't get me started on apostrophes. How hard is it to remember that i-t-apostrophe-s means 'it is,' or 'it has'?"

"True confession time." Mark leaned forward, too, dropping his voice to admit, "I can never remember that one. I always have to think about it."

"But I bet you get it right when you think about it!"

"Well." He sat back with a disparaging wave of his hand that made us both laugh. "Yes." He lifted his menu with a challenging arch of an eyebrow. "First one who finds a typo in the menu wins dessert."

"Oh, you're on." I picked up my menu and started flipping through it, grinning broadly. The waiter appeared at my elbow to ask politely if we wanted wine or appetizers, and Mark and I caught each other giving the other guarded looks. I pursed my lips and glanced sideways at the waiter. "No, thanks," I said.

Mark nodded. "A few more minutes, please."

The waiter slipped discreetly out of view again. "I'm not much of a wine drinker, anyway," I mumbled. Mark gave me a disarming smile.

"More of the sort to go right for the hard stuff, huh?"

I made a laugh that was mostly in my nose and the top

of my mouth, and therefore came out an unattractive wet snort. How delightful. Mark's smile broadened, though, so maybe it wasn't as gross as I thought it'd been. "I'm good with beer. I don't usually drink liquor."

"Does it mess up your—" Mark broke off, caught between winsome curiosity and apology. "Tell me to screw off if it's none of my business, but I'm really curious about what Gary mentioned this morning. Shamanism? You're really into that? Does drinking mess it up?"

For one brief moment I seriously considered killing Gary for opening his big mouth. My inexplicable powers did not strike me as good first-date discussion material. Bitching about the slaughtering of the language, yes; magic powers, no. I sat there looking at Mark for what felt like a very long time indeed, considering whether or not I wanted to answer his questions, and how far I wanted to get into the answers if I did. "No," I said finally. "Drinking just impairs my judgment like it does anybody else's. Um."

"You don't want to talk about it." Mark's smile went all apologetic. "Sorry. It's just…talk about things to get geeked about. Magic. Shamanism. It sounds interesting."

"Does it?" I scratched the back of my neck, looking at my menu. "There's just no real way to talk about it without sounding insane." I glanced up with a shrug. "I mean, honestly, if I went into it, explained what it was all about and said I had magic powers and could affect the weather," which I managed to say without wincing, although it was a trial, "or could heal people, and you said, *yeah, cool, I'm down with that,* frankly, I'd think you were nuts." I did think he was nuts. He'd been far too easy about the whole thing this morning. On the other hand, he asked smart questions about Petite. Maybe a willingness to consider the esoteric was a flaw I could learn to live with. I'd sort of have to, if I ever wanted to have a boyfriend again. Either that or I was going to have to develop a secret identity, and I didn't think I had the body for running around in leather catsuits.

The apology left his expression, curiosity and interest replacing it in a lip-parted half smile. Mark had a very expressive mouth. I thought I could get used to watching it. "Can you?"

"Can I wh—oh." I breathed a laugh and shifted my shoulders, discomfort creeping up and down my spine. "See, I can't answer that. Anything I say, one of us has to be crazy to believe it."

"So." Mark picked up his water glass, swirling ice around, and put it down without sipping. "So you're telling me you're into this thing that you don't expect other people to believe in, and you'd reject them based on their belief?"

I rolled my eyes up, considering that, then shrugged my eyebrows. "Yeah, pretty much. The only reason I believe it is I can't get away from it. I don't expect rational people to buy into the concept of magic going on around them. It's the kind of topic you smile and humor people on, and later go 'Woo, she was a kook, huh?' about."

He tilted his head. "Is that what you do to yourself?"

Maybe I didn't want to get used to watching him after all. I was not accustomed to feeling this much conflict over a guy. I told myself that, and very firmly did not let myself start thinking about my boss. Instead I stared at Mark, then exhaled heavily. "Yeah, basically."

"Huh." Mark quirked an eyebrow. "It must be a difficult dichotomy to be you."

"Sometimes." I shrugged one shoulder. "On the other hand, once in a great while it lands me dates with guys who use *dichotomy* in casual conversation, so it can't be all bad."

"Careful," he said with a quick grin. "I've been known to throw even bigger words around without warning. They misspelled *brulée*, by the way. They've only got one "e" and no accent. You're buying dessert."

"How'd you—I haven't even gotten to the dessert menu yet! No fair!" I went back to perusing the menu, fully aware that Mark had changed the subject deliberately and gracefully to let me off the hook, and grateful for the reprieve.

CHAPTER NINE

A lot of good food and several hours later, it proved that Phoebe was right. No one seemed to care that I was more of a twitchy, spasmodic marionette than a dancer. Impossibly loud music crashing into my bones made me stop caring, too, and consequently there were a couple of times when the woman in the mirror looked like she might know what she was doing out there on the dance floor.

Mark, on the other hand, really did know what he was doing, enough so that I accused him of being gay, which was wildly un-PC of me. He compounded the lack of political correctness by spending the next twenty minutes swishing around the dance floor, until Phoebe and I were leaning on each other and snorting with undignified laughter. I was actually having a fantastically good time when Barbara Bragg showed up.

For one horrible moment I was afraid she'd have Morrison in tow. There were things my constitution could stand, and things it couldn't. My boss at a dance club was one of the latter. In fact, my own presence at a club was almost more than it could take, so compounding it with Morrison's arrival would've just laid me out flat, shattered like so much windshield glass. Mark, blissfully unaware of my mental gymnastics, waved his sister down through a series of complicated hand gestures—which is to say, he pointed at us, then himself—suggested he was with Phoebe and me.

Barbara looked us both up and down, then turned to Mark with a grin. I could hear her over the music, which lent me respect for her lung power, if nothing else, as she bellowed, "You don't get *all* the cute girls, Mark!"

I figured she had to be talking about someone else. I was too tall to be cute, and while Phoebe had great bone structure, I thought the near-unibrow might preclude cuteness. Regardless, Barbara slid an arm around Phoebe's waist, fitting next to her like the proverbial peas in a pod, and grinned broadly at me as she pulled her farther away.

Phoebe looked about a thousand times more relaxed dancing with another woman than I could imagine being with anyone. My reflection was still having fun, but I felt a little thrill of envy spark through me. Barbara Bragg was physically adorable, with a pert, turned-up nose and pixie-cut hair, her big blue eyes full of laughter. I was pretty sure her hair grew out of her head that particular shade of red, too, which I found totally unfair, and I'd never even wanted to be a redhead. It was the principle of the thing. And maybe the way she filled out the frilly sundress she wore, with curves in all the right places. She also had a butterfly tattoo on her left shoulder, matching Mark's in size, color and newness. I didn't know her, but it seemed to suit her: full of life and vibrancy, just like her brother. It wasn't exactly hard to figure out what attracted Morrison to her.

I suddenly felt like a particularly tall and bony stick, and noticed the woman in the mirror didn't look like she was having so much fun anymore. I gave Mark a meaningless smile and shouted, *"Agua,"* before elbowing my way off the dance floor. Being tall and broad-shouldered was good for that, anyway.

I ordered a shot of whiskey before remembering I was driving, then swore and gave it to the guy standing next to me while I flagged down the bartender a second time to get water. The guy looked surprised, then gave me a once-over and a smile that made me feel a little better about being a stick on legs.

A Walking stick. Hah. I was so funny. I said "Shit" under my breath and tightened my fingers around the cold glass the bartender slid at me. A peek over my shoulder told me Phoebe looked very butch dancing with Barb, though really, Phoebe looked butch a lot of the time. I didn't normally think women several inches shorter than me could kick my butt, but I never doubted Phoebe's ability to do so.

"What's up?" Mark said from behind my other shoulder. I startled and almost tipped my glass over, and Mark followed my gaze to Phoebe and Barb. "Oops," he said, the word almost a question. "You and Phoebe?"

The whole world had more faith in my ability to attract romantic partners than I did. I said, "No," and slammed my water as if it was vodka. An ice cube hit me in the tooth. Ow. Mark touched my arm.

"So what's the deal?"

I hate your sister seemed a little extreme as far as answers went. I had no reason at all to hate Mark's sister. Certainly no reason I was willing to listen to myself about, anyway. I swirled ice cubes in the bottom of my glass, put on a deliberate smile and looked over my shoulder at Mark. "Nothing. Nothing," I said more firmly. "Just needed some water. C'mon." I caught his arm and pulled him back onto the dance floor, doing my best to let the music pick me up and sweep me away. Mark slid his arms around me from behind and the soft silk of his shirt brushed my spine, sending an unexpectedly enticing shiver over my skin. I nestled in his arms, closed my eyes and, half a moment later, somebody collided into my chest, completely ruining the moment. I opened my eyes, about to yell, but my objection was cut short as Phoebe gave me a ridiculously abject smile of apology. I rolled my eyes and shouted, "Careful, or I'll take it out on you next time we fence."

"Oh," she yelled back, "so you're planning on coming back to practice?" There was too much noise to carry on a real conversation, so she turned away as she asked, putting her back against me. The top of her head was just above my chin. Barb was in front of her, making a sandwich of the two of us in the middle. I smiled a bit and shook my head, then let my eyes close again. Mark did get all the cute girls, even if one of them was his sister. Ew.

Spotlights swirled through my eyelids, bursting down from above the dance floor in a rainbow of colors. The beat caught me in the small bones of the ear, rather like my drum did, and I detached from my body.

Sound roared incessantly, as powerful as the dance beat, but without its rhythm. Instead it crackled and popped, heat encroaching with every hiss and snap. I opened my eyes, face still tilted upward, and saw a sky of blackness. Not night, not stars, but heavy pressing blackness, the color of sorrow and loneliness. Orange reflected high against that blackness, like city lights glowing against the night, but there was raw intent in this color.

From what I've tasted of desire whispered through my mind, and I lowered my eyes to the horizons, knowing what I would see.

I was wrong.

No. I wasn't wrong. I was just woefully short in my expectations. Fire was all I expected, and it was there, raging on the landscape, but there was more to the world than I thought. Not just empty blackness like the sky, it was built with four mountains that, even scoured by flame, held their colors with resolve. To the east lay a white mountain, gleaming through soot, and to the west a sun-yellow one, defying the orange and red of flame. To the south lay a blue mountain, and to the north black so hard that even fire couldn't diminish it. There was a semi-familiar flatness to all of it, a hint of the Lower World. It tasted of history and of magic, of mythology built up to create reality. Colors here weren't real in the sense that I knew them, and the world had edges defined by those colors and by the mountains.

Between those four borders of the world, fire reigned. Everything burned. I stood at the center of it all, animals and insects fleeing toward me, their panic making my skin itch with growing fear. I saw no people, but I found myself leaning into the wind that fire brought, throwing myself against the destructive onslaught. All the power I could bring to bear, cool and silver-blue, as if it was the antithesis of flame, did nothing to quench it. Tears ran down my cheeks from the heat and I strained into it, gulping in rough breaths as I tried to stop what sure as hell looked like the end of the world.

A gigantic hollow tube settled over me, bringing fresh air with it. Creatures I didn't think could crawl scoured the tube's sides and clambered up, the air and walls thick with them. I couldn't see where they were going, but I went with the masses, scrambling away from devastating heat toward a new world somewhere beyond the sky.

And gasped awake to find myself in the comparatively cool air of a Seattle night, nestled against Mark Bragg's chest. Phoebe and Barb stood close by, faces concerned. "God, Joanne," Mark said as my eyes opened. "Are you okay?"

"You guys didn't…" No. Of course they hadn't seen that. "I had a…" Visions weren't really my thing. Well. Visions hadn't really been my thing up to this point. I had no idea if they were something I'd get on a regular basis from now on or not. If they involved passing out in dance clubs, I hoped they'd be an infrequent visitor to my repertoire. "What happened?" Somebody else talking sounded good.

"You just collapsed," Mark said in bewilderment. "One second we were dancing and you just slithered down to the floor. I picked you up and Barb and Phoebe cleared a path. Are you all right, Joanne?"

I started to lift a hand to rub my cheek, then realized I was still cradled against Mark's chest. He wasn't standing, so most of my weight was really in his lap, but he held me close, like I might be fragile. Since fragile and I had never really been on speaking terms, I felt a little silly, and tried squirming loose. Mark didn't quite let me go, though he relaxed his hold some. "I'm okay," I said. "Really. I just had a little…"

A little psychic escapade. Phoebe'd seen me zone out in the locker room a couple weeks earlier, but I hadn't explained it. Mark, thanks to Gary, knew a little about my shamanism gig. Barb had no idea. None of it made me want to confess to the truth. "I just got dizzy all of a sudden."

Phoebe's hand shot out and grabbed my upper arm. "Oh, my god. You're not pregnant or anything, are you?" The question was filled with equal parts of horror, glee and interest.

Mark, holding me, went very still. My first thought, almost incongruously, was *it might've been easier if even one person had reacted that way*, and my second was that it would not do at all to reach out and throttle my friend. She could not possibly know the demons she stirred up with the question. It felt like it took a long time indeed to pull a sick smile into place and say, "Uh, no, I don't think so, Phoebe. Maybe dinner didn't agree with me."

"You had shrimp in your salad," Mark said hastily. "Maybe that was it." Barb looked between the two of us knowingly, though she kept her mouth shut. That was good. I didn't want to have to punch Morrison's girlfriend in the mouth.

Well. All right, never mind that. "I'm okay," I said after a couple of seconds. "But I think I might call it a night now. It's been kind of a weird day." Between Mark and Billy and unsaid things with Morrison and conking out in the parking lot and having a *date* and—yeah. Weird day.

"I'll drive you," Mark said, and I discovered I felt well enough to say "Like hell" in a relatively mild voice. "Nobody drives Petite but me."

He chuckled. "All right. Guess you're feeling okay, if you're up to arguing about it. Barbie, I'll meet you later, all right? Phoebe, it was nice to meet you."

Barbie?

Mark helped me to my feet, and I had enough sense not to echo his nickname for her out loud. Or snicker at it, which was also high on my list of things to do. I wondered if Morrison knew his new girl was named after a toy.

I had a brief, unpleasant suspicion there was a word for what I was feeling toward Barbara in regards to her relationship with Morrison, and that only small, nasty people let themselves indulge in the emotion described by that word.

Fortunately, nobody ever said I was a good person. Phoebe hugged me, Barb shook my hand and Mark walked me back to Petite very carefully. It'd gotten later than I thought, pressing two in the morning, and the streets were empty as we drove back to my apartment, listening to music too loudly. A few blocks from the building Mark turned the music down and glanced at me. "So what really happened back there?"

I sucked air in through my teeth. "I had a vision." It took a long time to say that.

Mark quirked a smile. "This is killing you, isn't it?"

I hoped not, or that it was only figurative if it was. "Yeah. Look." Apparently that word took so much effort I couldn't say anything again until I'd pulled into my building's parking lot and killed the engine in my usual spot. "Look," I said again, then.

Mark said, "Hang on," and got out of the car. Came around to my door and opened it for me, giving a little half bow as I chuckled and climbed out. He closed the door behind me gently, patted Petite's roof, and then turned his attention to me. "Okay. Now go."

"Why now?"

"Because it's much less awkward to kiss you good night and make an elegant exit after your speech when I'm already on my feet," he said, smiling openly. I stared at him for a few seconds, then laughed.

"Confident, aren't you?"

"Hopeful," he corrected. "So what were you going to say?"

"You know, I really don't know." The heel of my hand went to my breastbone and rubbed there, a nervous habit I hadn't been able to break since getting a sword stuffed through me. "Just…"

"Joanne." Mark lifted a finger, as if he'd put it over my lips but didn't complete the touch. "You seem like a pretty solid person. Obviously this shamanism thing is important to you but you don't want to talk about it, so how about we just leave it at that? You get to where you want to talk, well, I'm kind of hoping I'll be around for that. In the meantime, I won't push and I won't roll my eyes and mutter, 'What a kook,' when you're gone, okay? Does that sound like a good place to work from?"

I felt a disbelieving smile pull at my mouth. "I'm sorry," I said around it. "That sounds pretty great, actually. Maybe too good to be real." I knew people whose too-good-to-be-real early relationships had turned into actually-just-good-enough-to-be-real ones. I knew ones that hadn't turned out, too, of course, but all of a sudden I was feeling hopeful. So he was a kook who was willing to go with my whole magic-filled lifestyle. For somebody like me, that might not be a bad thing. And he knew when not to push it, which for somebody like me was perfect. "Where exactly did you come from?"

"Arizona." He grinned, touched my cheek and ducked his head to steal a brief kiss, as threatened. Then he stepped back with another grin and a wink, and left me smiling idiotically after him as he sauntered off to find his car. Not until he left did I stagger upstairs to collapse in my bed, eyes wide despite a great weariness encroaching on me. I felt peculiarly *normal*, which struck me as all wrong, because nothing in the past twenty-four hours had been normal for me.

Which was a complex thought in and of itself. The last six or seven months, when I'd thought something along those lines, it'd meant old gods and spirit guides and magical things were going on. Right now it meant I'd almost accidentally slept with somebody and had gone out dancing and appeared to have something of a social life. *That* was all wildly abnormal. Billy's illness might've been mystical in nature, but by God if my mind hadn't assimilated that as an ordinary thing that happened in the course of Joanne's life.

I honestly couldn't decide if that was a good sign or not.

Somewhere right around the edge of sleep I could feel an idea of what I should be doing next starting to form. I was afraid to look too closely at it, for fear of sending it scurrying away. A few hours' sleep before work might shake it loose, and in the morning I'd have to tell Phoebe I owed her one. Who could've known that a little R & R was good for the soul? I rolled over, chortling sleepily at myself, and dragged a pillow across the bed to moosh my face into it. It smelled faintly of Mark's after-shave, which made my stomach tighten up, but the vast sleepies had a head start on berating myself with a *what were you thinking* lecture.

I was very nearly asleep when the phone rang.

CHAPTER TEN

Wednesday, July 6, 2:19 a.m.

Panic smashed through me, turning ice water to nausea in my belly. I fell out of bed and grabbed for the phone on the way to the floor, fumbling the receiver and putting it to my ear with shaking hands. "Hello? Jesus. What's wrong? Hello?"

"Joanne?" It was a little boy's voice, so out of place my foggy brain couldn't comprehend it for a moment. "Joanne?" he asked again.

"Yeah, this is—yeah." I rubbed my eyes frantically, trying to wake up. "Who is thi—is this Robert?"

"Yeah." A gulp, precariously near a sob, sounded in the word. "Joanne, Mommy went to sleep like Daddy did. Erik is sick and tried to wake her up and we can't get her to wake up. Can you help us? Please?" Robert was nearly twelve, the quaver in his voice swallowed down in an attempt at adult bravery, but *Mommy* and *Daddy* went a long way toward telling me just how scared he was.

"Everything's going to be okay, Robert. I'll be there as soon as I can. Are your sisters okay?"

"Clara's still sleeping. Me and Jacquie are awake. And Erik keeps saying he's gonna throw up."

"Okay. You guys all get a blanket so you stay warm and keep Erik company in the bathroom so he can throw up in the toilet if he needs to, okay?" I pulled clothes on as I talked, exhaustion burning my eyes. "I'll be there as fast as I can. Just hold tight, Robert. I'll be right there."

"Okay." His voice dropped to a whisper. "What do I do if somebody else goes to sleep?"

Billy's sleeping image flashed through my mind. And I'd gone out to have fun instead of trying to find answers. I was never going to forgive myself. "We'll cross that bridge when we come to it, Robert. It'll be okay. I'll be right there. You did good, calling me. I'll be right there," I promised again, and hit the door at a run.

The Hollidays' home had a wonderful front yard that'd seen better days. Trees and bushes were mashed, and a section of the picket fence had been replaced but not yet re-painted. The front porch, similarly, was of fresh raw wood, though a can of stain sat on the corner of the railing, making a dark cylindrical spot against the lightness of the wood. Billy'd repainted the new boards above the front door where the frame had been torn apart and fixed, since the last time I'd been over. Even in the middle of the night and half repaired, it looked like the sort of place where a person would want to raise a herd of children. Billy and Melinda were doing just that, with four already and a fifth on the way.

There was a white Mercedes SUV parked behind Billy's car. I parked Petite behind Mel's minivan and didn't think anything of the SUV until I rang the doorbell, expecting Robert to answer. Instead, Brad Holliday, bearing the wild-eyed combination of alarm and anger people do when they're woken up at two-thirty in the morning, flung the door open and stared at me. Even straight out of bed, he wore the heavy ring that had helped annoy me at the hospital. It was on his right hand, wrapped around the edge of the door above his head, and I wondered if he wore a wedding ring on his left hand. I hadn't noticed earlier.

We stared at each other a few seconds, equally surprised, before I said, "I'm sorry, I didn't realize there was another adult here," and he started berating me for small-hours visits.

Robert appeared in the hall behind him and interrupted with "I called her, Uncle Brad," before ducking under Dr. Bradley's arm to take my hand and pull me into the house. Brad got out of the way, surprised into silence by his nephew's arrival on the scene. I gave Brad a fleeting, semi-apologetic smile, and hugged Robert.

"Told you I'd be here as fast as I could. How come you didn't get your uncle instead of me?"

Robert shrugged against my ribs. "You're the one who got the Thing out of the kitchen."

"Yeah." I ducked my head over Robert's, an arm around his shoulders as I pressed my mouth against his hair. I didn't want to call it a kiss. Kissing sounded all girlie and uncom-fortable, the wrong sort of thing to impose on an eleven-year-old boy. Comfort could be imparted by mouth presses, too. "Yeah, I guess I did."

"The thing in the kitchen?" From the tone of his voice, I couldn't tell which was worse for Brad: asking, or not knowing.

Robert shrugged under the weight of my arm, matter-of-factly. "There was a Thing in the kitchen a couple weeks ago. A big snake thing. Joanne got rid of it. That's what happened to the front of the house," he added, as if it cleared everything up.

Brad's mouth went thin and tight. "Robert, that was an effect of the earthquake. I'm sure your father explained that to you."

Robert and I exchanged glances and the kid sighed. "Yeah, Uncle Brad. I know." He didn't actually *say*, "Whut-ev-aaar," as people his age were prone to doing, but it sounded loud and clear in his voice. I swallowed hard to keep a smile from jumping into place.

"You think what put your Mom to sleep is the same kind of thing as the, uh, Thing?" I really needed to work on my Mystical Stuff vocabulary. I wondered if I could find a handbook. Robert shrugged against my ribs again and started leaning in a time-to-move way. I shuffled down the entry hall with him, hanging a right through the living room so we could go upstairs to the bedrooms.

"It's not the *same* kind of Thing," the boy said, "but it's the same *kind* of Thing." He cast me one quick look to see if I understood, concern that I wouldn't clear in his eyes. But since we seemed to be speaking exactly the same language, I was able to give him a reassuring smile and another quick hug.

"Yeah. I think you're right. I'd like to know how you know that, though."

"I dunno. It just feels the same. The air's kind of cold and wet-feeling. Kinda like it is when…" He looked back at his uncle, who couldn't get past us as we climbed the stairs together, and said, evasively, "When Dad does his thing."

"You can tell when he does that?" I asked, surprised. Robert gave me a look that suggested I wasn't too swift.

"Yeah. Can't you?"

"I've never tried," I admitted. *And a child shall lead them* popped into my head, the phrase a title of the painting that had led me to answers about the Wild Hunt back in January. I gave the top of Robert's head a crooked grin. "You'll have to teach me, if you can."

"Sure," Robert said, with all the nonchalant ease of a kid who hadn't stopped believing in six impossible things before breakfast. For a startled instant I thought of another little boy, not much older than the one at my side, and wondered whether he, too, would have held my lack of ability to sense what was apparently obvious in such casual disdain.

"Is this conversation supposed to be making any sense?" Brad snapped. I let go of Robert's shoulders to turn and look down on the doctor. Way down, since I was two steps above him and had several inches of height on him, anyway. Not that I was enjoying it. Honest.

And the strange thing was that was all it took. I'd been going to round on the guy, give him a lecture on things I was only beginning to believe in myself, and all of a sudden it simply didn't matter. Bradley Holliday had his own reasons for not believing in the esoteric, just like I'd had, and just like me, nothing anybody said was going to change his opinion. I knew enough about pissing into the wind not to start doing it, at least this once. Brad didn't look in the least bit qualmed, but he subsided, anyway, and the breath I drew in to scold him with slipped out as nothing more than a slow exhalation. I could feel Robert's round-eyed gaze of admiration as I turned away from his uncle and climbed the rest of the stairs.

Erik, the youngest, met us at the upstairs bathroom door, clutching his sister Jacquie's hand. The boy had the sour scent of an ill child, and Jacquie looked green around the gills. "He threw up. Twice. On me."

"He only threw up on you once," Robert corrected pedantically. I crouched to give Erik a sympathetic smile.

"Don't feel good, huh, lil' guy?" I ruffled his hair. It was sticky with sweat and he wobbled under the touch. The power resting behind my breastbone burbled, and I leaned forward to kiss his forehead, feeling very much as though I was running a diagnostic on a car. The wash of power that came back to me said there was nothing strange or worrisome wrong with him, just one of the innumerable bugs that children were routinely exposed to. It also told me, in essence, not to worry about it: other than Jacquie wreaking vengeance for being puked on, Erik was in no danger. I brushed my fingers over the scar on my cheek, remnant of the morning I'd become a shaman. That particular scar had refused to heal into nothingness, and it'd struck me at the time that not everything needed to be fixed. So it was with Erik; he'd get better on his own, and I didn't need to interfere. I stood up to smile brightly down at him. "Uncle Brad'll take care of you. You'll be just fine."

"I'm not—"

"You're the doctor, Doctor." I might've been enjoying myself a little too much, especially when Erik staggered forward to latch on to Brad's leg. Brad gave me a look that would peel paint, then bent to scoop the boy up, feeling his forehead. Robert caught my wrist and tugged me down the hall toward his mother's room. I watched him as he pulled me into the bedroom.

Goose bumps stood up on his arms as soon as he crossed the threshold. My skin felt warm under his grip, though not as warm as Erik had been. "Robert, did you feel cold when you visited your dad at the hospital?"

"It's always cold at hospitals."

An uneasy sense of profundity crept over me with his statement, and I resisted the urge to pull him into my lap as I sat down on the edge of Mel's bed. Like Billy, she appeared to be sleeping peacefully, but when I shook her, she wouldn't wake. "Always?" I asked, half to distract Robert from his mother's state, and half because I was curious. He curled a lip.

"Yeah. There's always bad stuff going on in hospitals."

"Bad stuff like this? Like the thing keeping your mom and dad asleep?"

He shrugged one shoulder, stiff. "No, but there's always people hangin' around. Dad sees 'em sometimes, but I can always feel them. They're cold."

My mouth, somewhat ill-advisedly, said, "That's creepy," but Robert only nodded, evidently in complete accordance with me. "How'd you learn to feel the cold?"

"I dunno. I guess I always could. It makes my skin itch. Like it's trying to crawl off." He gave me another uncertain look, hoping he was communicating. I puffed out my cheeks and glanced down at Mel. There was nothing in my car metaphor that allowed for skin itching like it was going to crawl off, unless rust flaking off a vehicle counted. I stuck my lower lip out, thoughtfully, then shrugged one shoulder at myself, much as Robert had done.

"I'm going to see if I can learn to feel that. Did the Thing in the kitchen feel cold, too?"

"Yeah." For a kid awake at three in the morning, lecturing an adult on paranormal activity, Robert sounded remarkably patient and composed. "It's how I knew something was wrong in the first place. My bedroom's right above the kitchen and I woke up all shivery."

I squinted at him. "Your dad didn't tell me it was there."

"He didn't know. We couldn't see it until right before you came over to take care of Mom. I just knew it was there."

When this was all over I was going to have a long talk with Billy about his family. "Can the other kids sense stuff like that, too?"

"Clara can. But it's different for her. You'd have to ask her," he said before I could put the question to him. "It's not that big a deal, Joanne. Mom and Dad are just kind of weird."

"Aren't all adults?" I asked automatically. Robert gave me a very faint smile.

"Yeah, but some are weirder than others. You're even weirder than Dad, but you don't know what you're doing."

I stared, then laughed to cover dismay. "What, it shows?"

"Duh. Everything about you's all patchy, like somebody dropped a mirror and stuck the pieces back together." He rolled his eyes, then looked at his mother. "So can you help her?"

I cranked my jaw back up. "We're going to have a talk when this is finished, you and me."

"Okay. But can you help her?"

I sighed and looked back down at Mel's snoozing form.

"Honestly, Robert, probably not. Not right away, at least. You're pretty much right. I don't know what I'm doing. But I'm learning, and I *am* going to figure out how to wake them up. Why don't you go back to bed? I'll get you up if I figure anything out, or if your uncle and I decide we need to take your mom to the hospital, okay?"

"Promise?"

"Yeah." I reached out to ruffle his hair, just like I'd done the three-year-old's. Robert looked put upon, but took it. "I promise. You're kind of the grown-up for your little brother and sisters right now, and you did a good job calling me, so I'm going to treat you like you're an adult. You've earned it."

"Do you mess up grown-ups' hair?"

I laughed, admitting, "Not usually. I'll try to remember not to do that again."

Robert climbed off the bed, looking like he'd won a small battle. "Okay. Thanks, Joanne."

"For what?"

"For telling me the truth about not being able to help Mom. Uncle Brad wouldn't have."

It was a strange world where admitting to my shortcomings was the right thing to do. I nodded and tilted my head toward his bedroom. "Back to bed now, Robert."

"Okay." He slipped out, leaving me to turn to Melinda Holliday's sickbed and see if there was anything I could do to waken her from a sleep of death.

CHAPTER ELEVEN

Trying to slip inside Melinda's mind was as difficult as getting through to Billy had been. Like him, she had solid mental shields, only a trickle of life force draining through them. Syrupy weight pinned her down, heavy with determination that bordered on malevolence. I didn't try the siphoning approach, or the equally unsuccessful needle. Instead I turned away from Mel and looked into thick shadow, wondering if I could find my way to its heart. Nothing like taking the fight to the source, after all.

It occurred to me, perhaps a moment too late, that such a decision could be terminally dangerous. But by then a pathway had melted open, like a dream obliging me by creating passage when I needed one, and I stepped onto the road offered.

I'd become accustomed to flitting through astral realms in the past six months, whether I wanted to admit to it or not. The world I belonged to in day-to-day life was the Middle World, caught between the Upper and Lower Worlds, places of mythology and mysticism. The names I had for them were Native American in origin, but they fit remarkably well over an ancient Irish structure of the universe as well. I suspected that if I ever entered the Celtic Upper and Lower Worlds, they wouldn't look like the ones I'd seen in my dealings with Native American gods and demons, but the structure seemed to hold true regardless.

There was also an astral realm I could tune into. That one could be tapped by turning on my second sight, without ever leaving the Middle World. It could also be entered wholesale: that was how I usually got to the Dead Zone, and it was how I'd found ancient Babylon and the ghostly, sad land of Tir na nOg. I wasn't quite sure how those places connected to Earth, or the Middle World or whatever I wanted to call it. Babylon had, ultimately, seemed to reside in the deepest parts of human consciousness, but Tir na nOg was somewhere else entirely, a world of fae creatures that were gods and immortals in my world. I thought someday I might understand how all those places linked together, but I wasn't knowledgeable enough yet.

What I walked through now was somewhere else yet again. I'd spent almost no time in the dreamlands, only using them as conduits in the first days of awakening to my shamanic powers, when I just hadn't known any better. They were a place where thought formed and melted around me, gray shapeless forms that looked like the stuff of nightmares. I could feel the weight of sleep pressing down on me as surely as it had caught Billy and Mel, trying to snare me as well. I didn't like it, in a more specific and visceral way than my general discomfort with traipsing through realms of Otherness. I knew there could be danger in any aspect of psychic exploration, but something about the dreamlands struck me as more actively alarming than the astonishing neons of the astral realm.

Maybe it was that the demons here grew straight up out of my own psyche. Dreams were personal, tailor-made to inspire exultation and fear alike, whereas the dangers in other aspects of the Other were their own creatures, able to prey on anyone who came too close. I guess the egalitarian approach made me more comfortable.

Someone walked beside me. In the fashion of dreams, it seemed like she'd been there all along, and when I tried to focus on her arrival it shimmered and faded away into ir-relevance. "It's okay," Barb said. "I won't be around for long." Morrison was on her other side, completely oblivious to my presence. They were holding hands and he was smiling at something she said. Something I couldn't hear, despite being right next to her.

See what I mean? I set my jaw and shoved my hands in my pockets. "This is a stupid dream. You two can just go away."

"I said we would," Barb repeated. My hands made them-selves into fists in my pockets. Wanting them to go away and wanting them to go away together were different. Stupid dream. The gray-on-black surroundings had changed while I wasn't looking, resolving into the precinct headquarters. Except the hallways didn't have this many windows in the headquarters, and the trim was a different color. I curled a lip and turned away from my walking companions, stomping down to the garage through a series of halls that weren't really there. The light over the last set of stairs was incandescent and not burned out, both of which were wrong. Even in the midst of the dream I wondered what it meant that the place I was happiest in the precinct building was well lit in my dreams, when it wasn't in real life.

"Joanie." My old boss, Nick Hamilton, nodded as I came around the corner, then waved me toward the coveralls the mechanics wore. "You're late. Get to work, would you?"

"I brought doughnuts." I put an oversize box of dough-nuts on the hood of one of the cars, a peace offering for being late to work. The Missing O, a local doughnut shop, had become a favorite hangout for the precinct cops, and we usually got discounts for buying three dozen or more dough-nuts at a time. Nick grinned at me, which he hadn't done since January, and popped the box open to dig out his favorite, a raspberry-filled vanilla-crème monstrosity that dripped all over the place. I took it as writ that I was forgiven and sauntered back to grab my coveralls, pausing for a round of mock fisticuffs with Nathan, one of the guys who *was* still talking to me. He was the SOB who'd handed over the Johnnie Walker at the picnic, in fact. I threw one extra punch that landed on his shoulder with a meaty *thwock* and he looked offended. "For my hangover," I said, and he laughed.

I swung down into one of the pits, coverall sleeves rolled up to my elbows, whistling jauntily to myself. "Joanie got laid," somebody said dryly, and I threw a rag in his general di-rection, calling, "At least one of us is getting some," back. Familiar faces and voices filled my peripheral vision and my ears. I hadn't had a chance to banter with the guys since Cernunnos rode through the garage six months earlier. Tears burned at the back of my throat for a moment and I inhaled harshly to push them away. The sharp scent of oil and gasoline thrummed through my brain, making me feel welcome and at home. Not sniffling took more than I wanted to admit.

A year ago this had been my life. I'd been a mechanic for the Seattle Police Department. I got up and went to work five mornings a week, got covered in grease, fiddled with computery bits and kept cars running. In my off time, I worked on Petite and hung out with the guys from the garage, or took out work in trade for some of my cop coworkers: I'd fix their cars and they'd feed me. It was a sweet setup.

But then the mother I'd never met called up to tell me she was dying, and invited me over to Ireland to watch it happen. What'd been a two-week...I hesitated to call it a vacation...had turned into a four-month leave of absence. Sheila MacNamarra had taken her own sweet time about dying, though I hadn't found out the reasons why until later. By the time I got back to Seattle, my position in the garage had been filled by someone else, although my Cherokee heritage and my gender made me too appealing, quota-wise, to fire. Morrison had a clever plan to get me out of his hair.

He made me a cop.

I mean, I had the credentials and everything. The department had sent me to the academy because of that whole heritage-and-gender thing, and I hadn't done too badly, but I'd hired on as a mechanic and nobody'd expected me to stop doing that and start arresting people. Neither, frankly, did Morrison. He figured I'd quit. I figured I'd rather poke myself in the eye than give him the satisfaction. It'd taken six months to get back where I belonged, back down in the garage. I yelled an answer to some half-heard question and crawled out of my pit, content with my place in the universe. That was all I really wanted.

The room changed around me, turning into the reception area upstairs. Dozens of cops moved around, doing their work, getting ready for the day, most of them little more than blurred faces in the background, though I picked a couple people out and waved greetings. Ray, who was built like a fireplug and who was usually the first to warn me when Morrison was on the warpath. Thin-faced Bruce, whose wife Elise made me tamales for fixing their car, looked up from the front desk and gave me a broad smile. "There you are. They're waiting for you." He looked me up and down, still beaming. "You look beautiful, Joanie."

I hadn't asked. That made me nervous. I looked down at myself to see I was no longer wearing jeans and a T-shirt, but an honest-to-God dress with a dropped waist and a fair amount of frothy cream lace. It could've been a wedding dress, though not one of the meringue ones that were so often advertised. It kind of suited me. Pretty but understated. I was also wearing fantastic shoes, with bits of gold glimmering through the straps. I said, "Who's waiting?" but it was too late: I'd gone around the corner to meet a man in a tuxedo.

Mark Bragg. He looked fantastic, goldy-brown hair brushed back, his tux navy-cut with long tails. I smiled automatically and looked past him; he wasn't the one I expected. After a few seconds, the one I did expect appeared. Morrison, also in a tuxedo, though his wasn't nearly as ornate as Mark's. Barbara Bragg appeared behind him, in a very simple, pretty yellow gown that made mine look all the more formal. I could see the butterfly fluttering on her shoulder.

A burp formed in my stomach and refused to go anywhere, just sat and collected nervousness until I thought I might sick up. I said "Um," very quietly, and the ridiculous music started. I started to sing, "Big fat and wide," beneath my breath, but Mark nudged me and shook his head. "No making fun of brides today, Joanne. Not today."

I nodded, but I didn't really hear him. Dad wasn't there. We weren't exactly close—I didn't remember the last time I'd called him, in fact—but it seemed like he should be the one walking me down the aisle. Walking with the man I was going to partner myself with was nicely symbolic and all, but I wanted that man to be waiting for me at the altar.

Barb was up there, in the maid of honor's place, holding a bouquet as bright as her butterfly tattoo. Morrison stood opposite her, and all I could think was he was standing in the wrong place.

I jolted awake with sweat beading on my forehead. Melinda still slept, cheeks flushed with color. The weight that pressed down on her seemed to fill the room, darkness trying to work its way into me, too.

I dragged in a breath through my nostrils and staggered to my feet, rubbing my eyes and then the scar on my cheek. "Arright." My voice was scratchy. "All right, Jo. You're awake. It's okay. Just a nightmare." Only I wasn't sure it had been. Overlooking that I thought weddings probably weren't supposed to be nightmare material, an awful lot of that dream had been just what I wanted. My old life back, my old friends back. It was a little early to be planning a wedding to Mark, but as a flight of fancy it didn't seem too awful. Except the part where color rushed to my cheeks when I thought about Morrison being the best man. I guessed it was nice my brain thought they'd be friends, but that didn't make any of it feel quite right.

I shivered and went to look out the window. The sky was graying with the coming dawn, suggesting my nap had lasted longer than it'd seemed. That was twice, first sleeping under Petite and now this. Sleep and me were clearly going to be a dangerous combination for the next few days, until I got whatever was going on figured out. I wondered if I could put in a petition for one of my adventures being done with plenty of extra snooze time, instead of operating on half-brained sleep deprivation, which had been the order of the day so far and appeared to be coming up on the roster yet again.

I put the wish aside and went back to Melinda's bedside, bracing my face in my fingers as I sat. The air still felt weighty, making me reluctant—or, more accurately, outright afraid—to try slipping into her mind again, or to try following the thing keeping her asleep back to its source. I'd woken up once. I didn't know if I'd do it again, not when I was sitting there by her side with dark pressure drawing me toward sleep.

I honestly didn't know which way to turn. I had nothing useful to work with, nothing I could go look up on the

Internet and find answers to. Gary, for all his sturdiness, didn't seem likely to come up with a solution for this one. The only person I could think to ask hadn't responded to me in almost three weeks, not since I'd encouraged him to shove off in the face of impending doom. Having a snit and staying away didn't seem like very spirit-guide-like behavior to me, but I'd never had a spirit guide before, so what did I know? "All right," I whispered out loud again. "One more try, Coyote. I don't know what else to do." At least going inside myself seemed less dangerous than questing outward in search of the right thing to do. My index finger started tapping against my cheek, rhythmic little thump-thumps that made a heartbeat pattern. I wasn't sure it would work, but it was quiet in the house and there was nothing .to distract me.

It might've been general tiredness that let me slide deep into my own psyche. Sleep deprivation was one of those tools shamans were supposed to use. Either way, it didn't seem to take very long, Melinda's bedroom fading around me in favor of a misty, moonlit garden.

There was no use standing around in there yelling for Coyote. I'd tried that several times in the last weeks, to no avail. But it struck me that when I'd come to my garden the very first time, Coyote had found me in an uber-Arizona desert and led me here. I thought if I could get back to that desert—which I vaguely envisioned as being a place accessible by anyone who knew how, rather like Babylon—I might just be able to get Coyote's attention again.

Of course, the key words there were *anyone who knew how.* Not for the first time I cursed my own amazing contrariness, and paced my garden, trying to determine how to get out of it.

You could try a door, the snide little voice in my head suggested. I swear, if I could have grabbed it and shaken it, I would have. I nearly clutched my own head to do just that before I got ahold of myself. Or didn't get ahold of myself, more accurately. "There isn't a door," I muttered, then ground my teeth together. I really hated that voice. I especially hated it because it was right a lot of the time.

I mean, technically, I was right. There wasn't a door in my garden. But it was *my* garden, and if I wanted a door, then there would be a door. It would be at the misty end, hidden by soft fog. I walked around the garden's edge, trailing my fingers over the rough stone wall and keeping my gaze forward, expecting the door to appear before my eyes or under my fingers.

Instead a robin twittered violently, the first animal I'd ever heard in my garden, and I tripped over my own feet as I jolted around looking for it. It peered down at me, one beady black eye and then the other, and chirruped again as if its little red-breasted life depended on it. Then it was gone, swallowed up by the fog. I rocked back on my heels, huffing a laugh as I looked at the ground. A robin; a garden. I knew a cue when my subconscious gave me one. I whispered, "Mary, Mary, quite contrary," and a glitter of silver in the damp earth caught my eye.

I tilted my head at it just like the robin had at me, taking a few seconds to convince myself to kneel and curl my fingers around the bit of metal. It was cool and heavy and felt solid in my palm, and for some reason holding it made an ache in my heart I could hardly breathe around. "Maybe it's been buried for ten years," I murmured to the robin, because that was what I was supposed to say, though I knew it was closer to thirteen years the thing had been buried and ignored.

"You've got it wrong," I said, still to the robin. "The key's supposed to be outside the garden, not in it." There was no answering chirp, and I pushed my way back to my feet feeling older than my twenty-seven years. "Close enough, eh?" I asked the silence, and stepped forward through the fog to brush a sheet of ivy away and reveal the door.

CHAPTER TWELVE

It opened upward, into the peak of a vast crater. I came through cautiously, feeling like I was caught in an Escher painting. My center of balance swerved dramatically and my stomach muscles constricted as I rotated onto the landscape, the world itself pulling me around until I was vertical by its standards. The door closed behind me, though by the time I looked down I was standing on it, the key still clutched in my hand. As I watched, the door faded into striated dirt, becoming a perfectly ordinary crater center.

Oddly enough, for the second time, I knew where I was.

It took rather a lot of huffing and puffing and even more sliding down the crater's steep sides before my stride remembered the ground-eating run I'd learned when Coyote had led me through the desert and to this place. I had to keep reminding myself it was a matter of will, of my own desire overriding the evident reality of the situation around me, that allowed me to move anywhere in the psychic realm. I suspected that subconsciously I'd expected the door to open in the crater, and if I'd been more focused, I could have just walked through into the desert.

Instead I went leaping and bounding over hill and dale, until the air went sandy and dry and the landscape below me turned beautiful orange-red. I skidded to a halt in the sand, tilting my head back at the sky, blue as robin eggs. Heat poured down from the white sun, too much for comfort, though I wasn't even sweating. There were no coyote tracks in the sand, no footprints left from my last visit here, although no wind blew to erase them. Then again, I wasn't sure this place existed except when people came to visit it, so the idea that it was remade new and whole each time someone encountered it seemed completely plausible.

I chose a patch of sand that looked as much like where I'd lay dying as anywhere else, and flopped onto my back. Grit seared through my shirt and jeans, bringing stinging prickles of heat rash to my skin, but I ignored it. The suntan I sported was thanks to a mystical desert heat considerably more antagonistic than this one, so I figured I could handle a little itching. I dropped my elbow over my eyes so the sun didn't make red spots through my eyelids, took a deep breath, and bellowed "Coyote!" into the desert air.

Only that wasn't what I did at all. It was the equivalent, maybe, but it felt completely different. It felt as if I was spread thin as hot butter over the sand, sending my consciousness over the whole surface of the desert. I could feel lumps and scrapes of earth beneath me, all over and everywhere. Curious lizards ran over my skin, hardly aware I was there. Water bubbled up through me in a few precious locations, and the dry earth considered whether I was something that could be drunk down for nourishment. It found the coil of power beneath my breastbone and tugged at it curiously, but I envisioned titanium shields protecting that power. Shot-blue sworls slipped into place, blocking the desert's hold, and it relinquished it without argument.

Somewhere in the back of my mind, very privately, I wished to holy living hell I had a nice sturdy-vehicle analogy to work with here, but my psyche and my power seemed to be getting along just fine without my metaphorical grasp on things. I didn't want to think any of it too loudly, in case my brain should notice I didn't really know what I was doing, and stop doing it. I had this idea I'd end up like so much hamburger all over the highway if the desert-wide awareness stopped suddenly.

Crap. Now I had the idea of a car wreck smeared across the desert in my mind. Well, I'd wanted a car analogy. That was what I got for wishing. Since I was stuck with the idea, anyway, I leaned on the horn, vibrating out a call to my spirit guide with all my will.

A tiny reverberation of recognition bounced back at me from what felt like somewhere around my left knee. I gathered the idea of the smashed-up car together in my mind, rebuilding the vehicle, purple paint shimmering bright in the harsh desert sun, in that place where I'd felt an answer.

The sensation that followed felt very much like watching Stan Laurel take a long slithering step across the movie screen. It began with inching a black-clad foot across the floor, then slowly whiplashing his whole tall thin body to its new destination. I expected to hear a *bloop!* sound effect, or at the very least a soft pop of air, as I reconverged on a completely different spot in the desert.

Usually I wasn't so much for telling one spot of desert from another, but this one had potential shade from rounded rocks piled up into wobbly pillars and hills, sculpted and buffeted by wind until they looked soft to the touch. The sun came down at enough of an angle to drop cooler shadows into hollows in the stone, a few of them big enough for a coyote to curl up in. Add a water source, and it would be a perfect hideaway in the landscape of the mind.

I should have been able to curl myself up in the idea of becoming a coyote, and fit into one of those little hollows all comfy and snug. That was one of the things about shamanism, shapeshifting on at least a psychic level. I'd read it could be done in the real world, too, but I wasn't exactly a believer on that particular topic yet. Thus far, my internal shapechanges had been either accidental or the result of having been eaten by a particularly huge and powerful spirit animal, the latter of which was not on my list of things to do again. I wanted to be able to coil up in one of the coyote-size shallows in the rock, but not enough to convince myself I was a coyote. Instead, with a sigh, I fit my Joanne-shaped-self into one of them, folding my arms against a higher curve of stone and resting my head on them. It wasn't all that comfortable, but as I settled in, I started to feel like I at least belonged there.

All I needed was a way to search the area. The heat made

me think of waves boiling off a car's hood on a hot summer day, the physical pressure of over-warm air something that could be used. I slid myself into the idea of that pressure, trying to feel the world from its perspective instead of mine. I wanted a hint of Coyote, something I could follow back to his consciousness. I wasn't sure what I'd do after that— probably read him the riot act for not talking to me for weeks on end—but I had to start with finding him.

Cooler air melted as easily as tissue paper under the encroaching heat of my search. The weight of my analogy rolled over the hills and hollows, exploring them until a thrill of recognition tingled through me. It was as if the stone where Coyote habitually lay tasted different, flavored with his tang and sarcasm and general irritating habit of never directly answering questions. I wondered suddenly if this rocky little oasis was his garden, but discarded the idea. It felt more like the place he entered this landscape from his garden, like mine was at the center of the crater.

I very much didn't want to know why he got an oasis and I got the scarred remnants of disaster striking. Rather than pursue that thought, I did the mental equivalent of *knock knock, I'm coming in,* and poured myself into the spot that had felt most like Coyote.

To my complete surprise, there was no resistance. Coyote'd lectured me up and down and left and right about my shields, so I expected to smack into his and be soundly rebuffed. I'd certainly slammed into Billy's hard enough to get a headache. But I slid through so easily that for a moment I thought I'd have screwed up and not gone where I'd wanted to at all. There was nothing of a garden around me, just amber-tinted blackness, and a sense of time draining away very slowly. I had no idea where I was, and was trying to cast an apology into the darkness and back away when Coyote walked out of the night.

He came in his brick-red man form, black hair loose and swinging to his hips. For all that I'd gone looking for him, finding him in the black simply astonished me, emotion rising up from within like its own kind of power. He put both hands on my face, thumbs against my cheekbones, looking down at me with such curious seriousness I thought he might kiss me. Spirit guides weren't supposed to go around kissing girls, were they?

It didn't matter, because he didn't do it. Instead he put his forehead against mine, a light touch that carried a staggering order: *get the* hell *out of here, Joanne.*

It wasn't rejection. It was desperation, a single panicked rally to try to keep me safe. I could feel Coyote's exhaustion behind it, as if he'd been struggling with the darkness for days. I couldn't tell if he'd been waiting for me, or if my arrival had forced him to split off from what he'd been doing so he could warn me.

Because he hadn't abandoned me after I'd thrust him out of the Dead Zone when I faced the ancient serpent there. He hadn't left me to struggle through the aftermath of my failures as a shaman alone. The knowledge washed into me with his touch, all the information he could share inside a moment. He hadn't been punishing me, these last two weeks.

He'd been a captive. There was something out there, an amorphous being awakened by enormous fluxes in the astral realm. Awakened, to put none too fine a point on it, by my clumsy use of power. It had slept for eons and had been waking for months, and when flickering life in the astral plain sped by it, it reacted, even half asleep. It trapped that life like a tiger in a tar pit, pulling it down into silent stillness until it roused itself fully and could decide what to do with it. My attempt to save Coyote from the serpent had thrust him right into this thing's arms, and now he slept in amber, neither dead nor alive.

Coyote gave me a push, the action gentle enough to go unnoticed by the thing that held him captive. I drifted out of the place that should have been the garden of his soul, and went bounced like a tumbleweed through the desert, all the way back to Melinda's bedside.

I spent a little while longer hovering at Mel's side, trying to get more sense of what was keeping her—and Billy, and Coyote—asleep. The only thing I came out pretty sure of was that whatever it was, it didn't have any idea Mel had a baby along for the ride. The only energy drain I could find was Melinda's, with no connection to her daughter. Moreover, there was a sense of sheer, raw power, a shield itself that protected the child's presence from the dangers of the outside world. I didn't think it was something she'd cooked up just for this occasion. I was willing to bet there were still remnants of that kind of shielding lingering around all of her children, Melinda's love made manifest. That was great for the kids, but not useful in the larger sense. I was feeling like a big fat loser when Dr. Brad tapped on the door and let himself in.

"She'll need to go to the hospital," I said, hoping to head

off any disgruntled lectures. "They won't be able to do anything for her except keep her fluids up and stuff, but I guess she needs to be there for that. It seems stupid," I added, mostly to Mel. "Hooking you up to an IV at the hospital will just cost more than hooking you up to one here would."

"There are other reasons for Melinda to be hospitalized," Brad said. I looked at the bump that was going to be the Hollidays' fifth child, and nodded.

"Yeah. I guess so." I could feel the baby's energy if I wanted to, all bright and vital and rosy pink. She was busy, that little person, busy growing and being made and buzzing with enthusiasm for the whole process. In another few months she'd be making her mother's life miserable with great wholloping kicks and punches as she turned somersaults in her confined growing space. My own stomach cramped with sympathy, and I rubbed it, wishing the flutter of power behind my breastbone would let me wipe stuff like that away. Apparently it considered them to be part of the hardships of living, because it showed no interest in responding. "I can stay with the kids if you want to take her over and get her admitted. I don't work until eleven."

A silence in which it became very clear Brad Holliday didn't trust me with his nieces and nephews followed. I finally looked at him, trying to keep my expression neutral.

Apparently it didn't work. His eyebrows drew down and his mouth tightened, which was enough to allow me an exasperated sigh. "Look, Brad. I'm Billy and Melinda's friend. Their kids know me. I get you don't like me, and I even get why. That's fine. But do you really want to wake four little kids up and herd them while you're trying to admit their second parent to the hospital? I'm here, and as far as I know, neither of them have any other family in the area. Who're you gonna call?"

There was one brief moment of camaraderie where Brad and I both all but swallowed our tongues, struggling against the obvious response. Brad passed a hand over his eyes and muttered, "That question is ruined for all time," under his breath, while I turned a nearly violent grin at my hands. Dr. Brad was human after all. "All right, fine," he said more loudly and very decisively, as if doing so could wipe away the moment of sympathy. "I should be back well before eleven."

"I think Robert's old enough to watch the little ones for a while, if there's a gap. I—crap." I turned my wrist up, looking at the watch I'd finally gotten fixed. Now that it worked again, I kind of missed it telling me the time in Moscow. "I guess I'll call Gary and get him to stop by my apartment for my stuff. That way I won't have to leave until a quarter till or so." I wouldn't be more than a few minutes late, unless traffic on Aurora was critically bad. Morrison would probably want to bust my ass for it, but that was nothing unusual.

I got out of Brad's way so he could bring Mel to the hospital, and stopped by Robert's room to tell him, as I'd promised, what was going on. He looked worried and sleepy, but when I whispered, "Shh, go back to sleep, kiddo," the coil of energy inside me sent a soothing warm splash of power over him that seemed to weight down his eyelids and help him fall asleep again. I actually thought that was kind of cool. It wasn't anything big or dramatic, but it was the first time I could remember being actively pleased with the gift I'd been given.

I'd been relieved in the past, and sometimes glad to have been of help, but this was a little warm bubble of genuine pleasure, and at something as simple as making sure a kid got some sleep. Maybe, just maybe, if I could learn enough to fix the crises that kept lurching into my life, it would all smooth out to little happy-making moments like this one.

That thought got me through the next several hours, in which Erik got up and vomited again and Clara discovered neither parent was at home anymore and cried until her face turned purple. Robert got Jacquie and himself breakfast while I cleaned up after Erik's Technicolor splatters, but Clara was too busy hyperventilating to eat. I liked kids in a sort of abstract way in general, and Billy's kids in particular, but by the time Gary showed up at ten-fifteen with my work gear, I was trembling with exhaustion. I had no idea how Mel got through a single day of this, much less three hundred-sixty-five of them, year after year.

Gary got Clara to stop crying by picking her up by the ankles and carrying her around like a sack of flour. Within ten minutes she was giggling and willing to eat breakfast, and I was collapsed on the living room couch staring at the old man in admiring disbelief. "I thought you didn't have any kids."

"Don't," he said. "Old army technique. Distract and redirect. Works, too, don't it?"

I said, "You're a god among men," which Gary rewarded me for with a toothy white grin.

"'Course I am. That kid called while I was at your place, to say he had a nice evenin' and to check up on you. You went out with him, Jo?"

"I—" I shot a guilty look at the kids that Robert, at least, read clearly. "Yeah," I mumbled. "Last night. I kind of crashed the evening by having a vision and passing out, though. And if I hadn't maybe I'd have been doing something useful and Mel wouldn't be in the hospital right now."

"Mebbe," Gary said. "Mebbe not. The last few weeks you've been steppin' up to the plate with your shamanism, and I'm proud of you, doll, don't get me wrong. But runnin' away from the rest of your life ain't gonna help matters any."

"Damn it, Gary." Great. I sounded like Morrison. "I'm sorry, but at what point did you turn into Mr. Bossy Telling Jo to Get Her Life Together, anyway? Who says you get to do that?"

"You." Gary sat down in Billy's easy chair and kicked it back, folding his arms behind his head and giving me a steely gray-eyed look. "Or didja forget the part where you said you had lots to learn from this old dog?"

I really hated it when people got all supercilious at me. Especially when they were right. I was searching for a biting rejoinder when I noticed there were four small people watching Gary and me as if we were the final pair at Wimbledon, bright interest writ large across their little faces. I said a word I absolutely should not have in front of Billy's kids, and they all brightened even further. I lifted my hands in defeat. "All right. Maybe you're right. I've got to get to work, Gary. Can you keep an eye on them until Brad gets back? He should be here any minute."

"Yeah. Told dispatch I was runnin' late today. Who's Brad? You got another guy on the line, Jo? Good for you. About time, I say." Gary looked pleased and I smacked myself on the forehead, then ran for the door, leaving poor Robert to explain who Brad was.

I made it to the precinct building in the nick of time, bewildered to find plenty of parking. The building itself needed expanding, and the parking lot was always full. I climbed out, looking around in confusion, and patted Petite's roof. "Stay brave, girl. Don't feel lonely. I'll be back for you." There were cars in the lot, including a news van a dozen spaces down from me, but it wasn't overflowing. That was even weirder than me having a date.

I turned away from Petite to find Morrison striding across the lot toward me, and hoped he hadn't heard me talking to my car. "Whatever you do," he said as soon as he was close enough to be heard without shouting, "do *not* talk to the press."

"What?"

Down the row, the van's sliding door rumbled open, and a pleasant, neutral expression slipped over Morrison's face. Only his eyes told me to get the hell out of there, and for once I was in complete agreement with my boss. I gave him a quick nod and managed about six steps toward the precinct building when a woman's curious, professional voice said, "Joanne Walker, right? We met in January at Blanchet High School in the aftermath of the murders."

I set the edges of my front teeth together in a grimace, then made it into a smile as I glanced over my shoulder. A lovely woman, her ethnic background clearly involving at least Asian and Caucasian, had climbed out of the van and was smiling at me. "Laura Corvallis, Channel Two News."

She offered a hand and I found myself casting what I hoped was a well-disguised helpless look at Morrison as I turned to shake her hand. "It's a pleasure to meet you again," she said. "I see you haven't been stricken by the Blue Flu. Do you have any comments on the illness that's bringing Seattle's police force to its knees?"

CHAPTER THIRTEEN

A muscle cramped in my neck as I tried not to look at Morrison. I had no idea what she was talking about, and worse, no idea if I should. My tongue felt like it'd swollen to choke my throat, which, all things considered, was probably good. It made it very difficult for me to say the wrong thing. I could practically feel Morrison telegraphing *keep quiet!* at me, and after a few seconds I got my tongue loose enough to croak, "I don't, Ms. Corvallis. No comment. Nice to see you again. If you'll excuse me, I've got to get to work." I tilted my head at the building, nodded at Morrison, said, "Captain," just like a good little police officer and made a break for it.

"Don't you think it's rather odd that a quarter of the North Precinct police force can't get out of bed this morning?" Corvallis called after me. "How do you suppose you've escaped the illness, Officer Walker?"

I nearly tripped over my own feet. A *quarter?* That explained the empty parking lot. I was afraid to look over my shoulder and see Morrison's expression, and I still had no idea how to respond to Corvallis. I repeated, "No comment," in a strangled voice and tried not to actually run for the building. Corvallis let me go, turning her shark's smile on Morrison instead. I ducked into the building hyperventilating and feeling sorry for my boss.

A quarter of the force? It didn't seem possible. The lot was empty, but that empty? It'd only been Billy, yesterday, and Mel this morning. Hollow laughter built inside me and faded away again. Funny how I assumed it was the same thing striking everyone, but Corvallis had said people couldn't get out of bed. I didn't know how else to construe that.

Morrison was going to want to talk to me. Morrison was probably going to want to kill me, but if I got into uniform before he came back into the building, maybe it'd remind him he shouldn't go around killing police officers. I barged off to the locker rooms, which were noticeably emptier than was normal a few minutes before shift change. I changed clothes and escaped the echoing chamber feeling like I was getting out of solitary. For a moment I just leaned on the wall outside the locker room, eyes closed and my cheeks puffed out. This was not going to be a good day.

What a firm grasp of the obvious I had. I huffed a breath and wrinkled my face, eyes still closed. Someone chuckled. "That's not such a good look for you."

My eyes popped open. Thor had just exited the men's locker room, the door swinging shut behind him. He looked, as usual, like a thunder god, all blond and broad-shouldered and chisel-jawed as he grinned at me. "Thor." I'd been going to try to call him by his real name. That was one of my new Joanne resolutions. "I mean, uh, Ed. Hi."

"Edward."

"What?" I needed a better comeback than that, for when I missed a beat. I felt like I was saying, "What?" a lot lately.

"Edward's better than Ed. Leftover childhood trauma."

It took me a couple of seconds, but I got it: "Mr. Ed, huh?"

He smiled, brief twist of one corner of his mouth. "Yeah. As far as nicknames go, 'Thor' doesn't seem that bad when you're used to being called after a horse."

"I guess it wouldn't." As if missing a night of sleep wasn't enough, I was now having a nearly normal conversation with the guy I'd been considering my arch nemesis ever since Morrison gave him my job. This was, once again, a whole different kind of weird than the weird I'd gotten used to. "Did you…want something?"

He cleared his throat. Actually cleared his throat. Put his hands in his pockets and pushed his mouth out in duck lips before asking, "You ever go out clubbing?"

"What," I asked in astonishment, "like cavemen?" No way the one night in the last however-many years I'd gone out a coworker had seen me. It just wasn't possible. Especially when it was a good-looking coworker. Especially when it was a good-looking coworker who didn't like me.

Edward laughed, an out-loud belly laugh that nearly knocked me off my feet from sheer surprise. He had a nice deep laugh, infectious enough to make me give him a confused smile in response. "No," he said a moment later, still chortling. "Dancing. I coulda sworn I saw you last night."

I was going to kill Phoebe. Or Mark. Or both of them. "Uh. I, um. Yeah. Was out last night. At Contour. Sort of a freak occurrence. Like, never happens. Probably never will again. Like, you know, a perfect storm or something. Not that I'm perfect. I dance like an accident victim." I bit my tongue to keep from babbling any more.

"Well, I thought you looked pretty good."

"So why didn't you ask me to dance?" I asked, suddenly full of inexplicable piss and vinegar. *Oh,* the snide little voice in my head said, *maybe because you've been nasty to him pretty much straight for the last seven months?*

"I figured you'd say no."

I stared. "Why would I do that?" *Oh,* the snide little voice repeated. I told it to shut up and go away.

Edward shrugged one shoulder and did the half smile again. It was a kind of nice smile. "Told you. It's like trying to follow Roth. We haven't exactly gotten along. Besides, you looked like you had a date." He hesitated, then crooked another half smile and said, "Promise you won't sue me for sexual harassment if I say this."

My eyebrows went up. "You're probably safe." To the best of my recollection, no one in my entire life had ever said anything to me that might set them up for a sexual harassment suit. I was almost hopeful.

"Well, you're usually…" He gestured at me: bulky blue uniform, clodhopper boots, broad-shouldered and without a discernible waist beneath the Kevlar. "I'd never seen you dressed up before. You were kind of intimidating."

"Intimidating?" I was beginning to think someone had replaced me with Folger's Crystals and I hadn't noticed. "You must be very confident to confess that to me."

He flashed me a genuine grin. "Yeah. Just not confident enough to ask a coworker to dance." He waited out my jaw-dropped, stunned silence for a few seconds, still grinning. "Maybe I'll catch you at a club sometime. Right now I better get to work."

He left me standing in the hallway, blinking in astonishment after him.

I lurked around the hall outside Morrison's office, mostly out of sight, until he came back from the Channel Two interview. He wasn't quite in dress uniform, but his clothes were crisper than usual, as if he'd known the interview was coming. But crisp or not, there were worried wrinkles around his eyes, and his gaze was concerned as it roved over the empty desks in the room outside his office. A frown pinched his eyebrows, and a wave of wry exasperation filtered through me. I was pretty sure he was looking for me. Even in the midst of a crisis I could annoy him with the mere question of my presence. Go, me. Morrison went into his office and I lurked for a couple more minutes, giving him some time to wind down after the interview before coming out of hiding to tap on his door.

He said, "There you are. Good job with Corvallis," as I came in. I actually looked over my shoulder to see if there was someone else behind me, which got a faint smile out of my captain. "I'm talking to you, Walker."

"So I see. It just seemed incredibly unlikely."

"Take what you can get," Morrison suggested, and gestured toward a chair. "Now tell me what the hell is going on with my police force." I sat, then sank into the chair as weariness swept over me. Morrison's mouth soured as I fought and lost to a yawn big enough to make my eyes water. "Did I interrupt your beauty sleep, Walker?"

"No." I squeaked it out on the last of the yawn. "Robert Holliday did. Mel's gone to sleep, too."

A subtle flinch went through him. "Melinda Holliday? She's not—" Morrison's expression darkened until his blue eyes were almost as gray as Gary's. "What's going on, Walker?"

"She's not a cop," I finished for him. "I don't know. I don't know, Morrison. Billy and Melinda kind of make sense. They're—" I struggled with the right way to say this. "Like me," I finally said, though it was incomplete. "I don't know why I'm still awake."

"Because they're not like you," Morrison said flatly. "Holliday's a believer, Walker, but he can't do what you do. You want to see the roster of people who are out today?" He shoved paperwork across his desk at me. I leaned forward to pick it up, not wanting to see it at all.

Almost everyone from the garage was on it. Nick, who hadn't smiled at me in months, except in the dream that morning. The guys I'd been drinking with on the Fourth; all the old friends I'd bantered with in my sleep. Bruce was there, and so was Ray. For a moment I thought I was onto something, but I let it go with a hoarse laugh. Morrison wasn't on the list, and he'd featured heavily in the dream. Damn. It'd been a good thought.

I slid further down in my chair and put one foot against

Morrison's desk and my elbow on the armrest so I could push my knuckles against my mouth and rub my thumb over the scar on my cheek. Somewhere during the fidgeting I got the impression Morrison was looking at me disapprovingly, but I couldn't stop. "All I know is whatever this is, I woke it up," I said through the barrier of my knuckles.

Morrison stood, then walked across the room to windows that overlooked the parking lot. He'd taken his jacket off before I'd come into the office, and sunlight softened the sharpness of his white shirt, making a faint shadow of his torso inside the fabric. The line of him was casual, hands in his pockets, but I could almost see tension rolling off his shoulders. Energy fluttered behind my breastbone and I pushed the heel of my hand against my stomach, then stopped fighting the push of power and let myself blink.

And I could *see,* with a capital *S.* Morrison's colors, dominant purples and blues, were stained with the tension I could now literally see. There was too much red in his purple, edging it toward burgundy, and the colors clouded over his shoulders in roiling dark swirls. Blues were tinged toward black, the color of anger mixed with fear. Not, emphatically not, fear for himself, but concern for his people, and anger at being helpless in the face of their illnesses. Compassion ran deep in him, royal-blue tempered to something more soothing, but gray ran through it, the frustration of being unable to act. Just beyond him, my second sight let the sky thrum with neon intensity, bright electric colors of life making Morrison seem unusually solid and grounded by distress.

I didn't really mean to get up and walk over to him, and I certainly had no idea what I was going to do when I got there. Morrison made it a moot question by turning to look at me when I was still a few steps away. A flicker of expression washed over his face, and he said, "Your eyes are gold again," before brushing past me and returning to his desk. I stood there alone, staring out the window at a world of garish colors.

Morrison said something else and I flinched, all the brilliance of my other sight disappearing in a flash. I closed my eyes, not particularly wanting to look at a dull-colored earth and more particularly not wanting to look at Morrison, though I turned my head toward the sound of his voice. "I'm sorry, sir. What did you say? I was…I wasn't listening."

"I said you sound pretty confident that this sleeping sickness is caused by an *it*." There was nothing at all about his phrasing that made it a question, but it was one. I nodded and my eyes came open whether I wanted them to or not. There was a Frank Lloyd Wright clock on one of the bookshelves in Morrison's office; I stared at its slim glass form and the seconds ticking away as I answered.

"You remember when the lights went out in January?"

"As if I could forget."

I ignored his tone and shrugged at the clock. "I really screwed up with that. I guess it was kind of like using a bulldozer to swat a fly. It sent…" My hand lifted and made a wave in the air, all of its own accord. "Ripples. All those snowstorms. The heat wave."

"You're telling me you can affect weather patterns, Walker?" Morrison sounded rightfully disbelieving. I squeezed the bridge of my nose, fingers cool against the corners of my eyes.

"You know, sir, if I could summon a little thundercloud above your head to prove myself, I'd do it, but I don't think I could even if it'd help anything. That's…" I struggled for a word, and the only one I could come up with was, "*magic.* Making something out of nothing. I can't do that. All I can do is manipulate what's there, move energy and shape it some, and if I do it badly, we get snowstorms and heat waves and thunderbirds, oh my. I don't know. Maybe I could make a ministorm above your head if I had the training. I don't." I dropped my hand and went back to staring at the clock, then at the calendars above it. Three of them, turned to the past, present and upcoming months. All three were covered in Morrison's handwriting, tiny but readable. I talked to the fine print, pretending my boss wasn't really in the room.

"Everything that happened a couple weeks ago, all that stuff with Colin Johannsen and Faye Kirkland. It got started because I should've started out years ago as a firecracker, and instead I showed up a decade too late as an atom bomb. It was like I threw up a big red arrow in the sky pointing to me and saying, 'Stupid newbie on the astral scene, please use and abuse to your heart's content.'" I had never once put all this into words, and I was pretty sure there were better people to be telling it to than Morrison. On the other hand, Gary and Coyote both basically understood the problem already, and right then I couldn't think of anybody else who might need to understand it more than my boss.

"I thought everything I'd screwed up had been fixed on the solstice, but I guess not. Whatever's putting people to sleep, I woke it up, and now it's hunting and I've still got that arrow blinking over my head." That sounded like I was completely concerned with myself, which was bitterly untrue.

I drew in a breath to try rephrasing, and Morrison interrupted with, "A decade ago."

It was very nearly the last thing I expected him to say. For all I didn't want to, I found myself looking at Morrison, who had an expression of cautious restraint pulled tight across his face. It was so careful it was clear he was asking a question, and that question told me just how detailed the research he'd done on me when I'd let slip my full original name. Captain Michael Morrison knew something about me I didn't want anybody to know, something I'd thought nobody outside of Qualla Boundary knew. My jaw and my stomach both tightened.

"Close enough."

"All right," he said after a long time. "I'm taking you off street beat, Walker. God knows I need you out there, but if my people are going down because of something only you can stop, then that's what your assignment is. Get. Go save the world, however you have to do it." He sat down at his desk, looking worn to the bone.

He hadn't said *because of something you did*, which was far more than I deserved. But because it was Morrison, I had to ask: "You believe me?"

"Don't ask questions you don't want answers to, Walker. Just get out of here and find a way to keep my people safe. Go."

I went.

CHAPTER FOURTEEN

I wish I could say I went boldly forth with a plan in mind, but what I really did was go to the locker room and change into my regular clothes. I wasn't going to be doing police work, and although the heat wave had broken, it was still in the eighties. Jeans and a T-shirt sounded a lot more pleasant for tromping around in than my uniform. I went out into the July morning with my head down and my eyes squinted against sunlight bouncing off the asphalt. Such diligent concentration on my feet led me over to Petite, and to a bright, semifamiliar voice saying, "Officer Walker. You don't look like you're on shift."

I felt distinctly deer-in-headlights as I looked up to see Laura Corvallis perched in the open sliding door of her news van, a *gotcha* smile pasted across her face. It took everything I had not to break into a panicked run back toward the precinct building. "Ms. Corvallis. I thought you'd be at the studio getting your tape ready."

"Oh, we don't air until six. I'm looking for some human interest sides of the Blue Flu story. Captain Morrison's got a real knack for looking handsome and not answering questions."

I let out a little breath of laughter. "Yeah." Crap. That was a bad confession to make. I didn't want to build any sort of camaraderie with a news reporter. I bit my tongue so I couldn't say anything else, unbit it and added, "That's his job," which I hoped would mitigate my agreement that my boss was handsome, and dug Petite's keys out of my pocket.

"So I thought you had to go to work," Corvallis said. "Don't tell me you've got the day off, with a quarter of the workforce out." Her voice was full of polite curiosity, but I glanced up through my eyebrows as I unlocked Petite's door, and saw the dark glitter of a hungry hunter in her gaze.

"Ms. Corvallis, that sounds like a good idea. I won't tell you anything." I smiled, winked and got into Petite before she had time for a rebuttal. Cranking the engine made a satisfying lot of noise that drowned out any chance of me hearing her follow-up, and I pulled out of the parking lot feeling like I'd gotten a reprieve. Morrison had given me rope to hang myself with. I wasn't eager to use it explaining why I'd ended up on the evening news babbling about Laura Corvallis's poorly named Blue Flu.

About three blocks farther on I realized the news van was following me.

* * *

I pulled into a drive-thru, mostly to waste a few minutes and see if the van was actually following me. I emerged from the other side with a burger I didn't really want and a bag of fries that would kick off a month-long craving for more if I gave into their evil seductive ways. The Channel Two van was waiting in the parking lot, so I pulled up alongside it and rolled down my window. "Want a burger?"

Corvallis was in the passenger seat, grinning at me. "No, thanks."

"Hey! Yeah, if you're giving it up!" The cameraman-cum-driver leaned across her, looking eager. I handed the food over, figuring the best way to a man's heart was through his stomach, and I might need a friend on the news team if Corvallis was going to insist on following me.

I was trying not to think too hard about a reporter following me. I barely had any idea what I was going to do even without a monkey wrench in the works, and the only thing I could think of that would make it worse was broadcasting my bizarre talents on local TV. In the best-case scenario, nobody would believe her. In the worst, they would, and I'd be like Christ in the temple.

Which was not to say I was Christ-like in any way. Gah. I put on the nicest smile I could, trying to rid myself of the thought. "Are you following me, Ms. Corvallis?"

"As a matter of fact, I am."

Outright honesty had not been the response I was expecting. I blinked up at the woman. "Why?"

"It strikes me you've been involved in some interesting events the past few months." She smiled at me. I didn't like it, and did my best blank expression. It usually worked to irritate and distract Morrison.

It didn't work on Laurie Corvallis. "An officer—not a detective, just an officer—at the Blanchet High murder scene. Immediately after that you were on the list of approved visitors for Henrietta Potter. Mrs. Potter died quite violently, didn't she?"

A bolt of cold loss shot right through the flutter of power behind my breastbone, making bile rise up in my stomach. For an instant I was desperately grateful I hadn't eaten the food I'd bought, or I'd be revisiting Erik's early-morning sickness right there in my car. The smell of vomit lingered in leather forever, too. I shuddered the feeling away, knowing Corvallis was watching my reaction with professional interest. I'd barely known Henrietta Potter, but I'd liked her enormously. Her sudden, violent death had shocked me to the core. "Yeah," I managed. "She did."

"Then your name came up during the police investigation of Faye Kirkland's death," Corvallis went on conversationally. I inhaled through my nose, long slow breath.

"That was weeks ago. Why are you following me now?"

"Well, the third time's the charm, Officer Walker. I see you going into the precinct building, saying you're on your way to work on a day when a quarter of the North Precinct police force has been admitted to the hospital, and half an hour later you're walking out, still in civilian clothes and getting in your—" she broke off to consider Petite briefly, then gave me a quick grin "—shiny Mustang." The smile faded into something more predatory. "And I start putting all these little strange things together, and I start to think maybe I have a story here."

Nausea kept burning in my belly, churning up until it felt as if it was encouraging my heartbeat to rattle too fast. My fingertips were cold and my cheeks were hot, physical reactions to what I thought was best referred to as blind, screaming panic. I wanted Laurie Corvallis to go away, far away, from my weird little life, and to never come near me again.

Saying that, of course, would pretty much guarantee she'd be on my back like black on night. I gave her a rueful little smile that I hoped hid the ninety-mile-an-hour pulse in my throat, and managed to keep my voice steady as I said, "Ms. Corvallis, if you really want to investigate me, I can't stop you, but you're going to be disappointed. I'm not a very interesting person. As for being at work, I have some personal things to take care of today. I just needed to stop by the station to talk to a couple of people." I wasn't a very good liar, and hoped that was close enough to the truth to hide it.

Interest glittered in the reporter's eyes. "And you weren't pressed into service, given the situation?"

I tipped my chin down and looked up at her through my eyebrows. "A lot of people are out on sick leave, Ms. Corvallis, but we usually do get paid for sick leave. The department doesn't have a lot of money for overtime. Sorry to disappoint you."

Corvallis pursed her lips, looking as though she was in fact disappointed. "You're lying to me, Officer Walker. You said you had to get to work, when we spoke in the parking lot."

I stared at her. First, how she remembered exactly what

I said was beyond me. Second, "Do people typically say, 'Please excuse me, but I've got to run inside and talk to a couple of people before I leave and go about my day' to you when they're heading into their work building, Ms. Corvallis?" Sure, I was lying now, but now I had a moral high horse that made it easier.

"People often find being very specific in what they say to a news reporter is a good idea."

"I'll keep that in mind," I said in genuine, pointed incredulity. "Now, if you'll excuse me, Ms. Corvallis, I've got some personal business to take care of." I clipped the words off and she smiled at me.

"I hope you're telling me the truth, Officer Walker. I'll find out if you're not."

"I'm sure you will." I bared my teeth at her, which was as close as I could get to a smile, waved goodbye at the driver, who lifted the half-eaten burger in salutation, and backed out of the parking lot to drive home with shaking hands.

Wednesday, July 6, 2:20 p.m.

By the time I got there I at least had a plan. I had no illusions that it was a good plan, but at least it was a plan, and that was better than sitting around with fast-food coffee going sour in my stomach, worrying about Billy and Mel and a whole lot of other friends. I turned my computer on and prayed the gods of the Internet would have some answers for me.

They didn't. Mystical sleeping sicknesses and the Net turned out to have little in common, although I did learn more than I ever wanted to know about African trypanosomiasis. The only references that covered both sleeping sick-nesses and mysticism were stories about African evil spirits who'd turned into the mosquitoes that carried the disease. It was a long shot, especially since there just weren't that many mosquitoes in downtown Seattle parks. On the other hand, these evil spirits were evidently sensitive to topaz, so if I got really desperate I could always start collecting topaz and hand it out to people.

Actually, that didn't sound like a bad idea, which in and of itself made me wince. I hoped I wasn't going to turn into one of those New Agers with the frizzy hair and the gypsy skirts. I punched in a search on topaz's inherent qualities and came up with an Indian—the subcontinent, not the Native Americans—belief that it helped bring good dreams and peaceful sleep. Between that and the evil spirits, handing out chunks of it sounded like an actively *good* idea. I couldn't believe I'd fallen so far, and at the same time I was incredibly relieved to come across something that might help.

I took a deep breath, accepted my doom and Googled "magic sleep," which turned out to be just the ticket for a Dungeons & Dragons cleric in search of spell statistics. I put my forehead down on the keyboard, depressing keys until they started a long painful beep.

The sound was enough to send me shoving away from my desk purposefully, gripped with the determination to do something, even if it was stupid. I drove Petite down to East Asian Imports, the incense-filled shop I'd met Faye Kirkland at only three weeks earlier, and bought every piece of topaz they had. Half an hour later, my pockets full of rocks, I marched into the precinct building, a woman on a mission.

Morrison was the first stop on my mission, and he wasn't there. That took the wind out of my ambition and I stood there staring at his desk for a while, relief warring with disappointment. He was the hardest person to talk to, so I wanted to get it over with. On the other hand, more sympathetic ears might make it easier to work my way up to him. I went back to Missing Persons, a flawed piece of stone clutched in my hand.

I didn't like the Missing Persons office. It always seemed cold, even in July, and the door stuck, making a draft that riffled all tidy rows of photographs and vital statistics that lined the walls. I thought it sounded like the lost whispering for help, and found it overwhelmingly depressing. Homicide was bad, with all its raw violence floating at the surface, but Missing Persons was worse. It had the tang of hope sullied by desolation, the knowledge that every day a case wasn't closed meant it was that much less likely there would ever be a happy ending. Murder was concrete; it made an end to things. Hope could hang on like a bitch.

"You always get that look when you come in here." Jen Gonzales, the woman I was in search of, came out from one of the inner offices, offering her hand to shake. I put mine in it automatically, her fingers startlingly warm in the perceived chill of the office.

"Hi, Jen. What look?"

"Makes your eyes sad, and no offense, Joanie, but a lot of the time you don't have the happiest eyes, anyway." Jen had a faint Spanish accent and always shook hands when people came into her office. It'd finally struck me that doing so might give her a better sense of the people she was meeting, and their emotional state, than anything else could. The one time I'd asked she'd brushed it off.

But she'd been one of the people who had known how to focus her energy and offer it up like she'd been trained in it when I'd faced down Cernunnos in the precinct's garage. I rubbed my thumb over the topaz, watching it more than her. "This sleeping thing," I said after a minute. "It's not a virus or anything. It's…" I gritted my teeth and scowled at Jen's knees, working myself up to what I needed to say. "You've got the same kind of talent Billy does, the ability to focus your energy."

I dared a glance through my eyebrows to find Jen ghosting a smile at me. My shoulders relaxed marginally and I sighed. "Yeah. This thing hit Billy first, and then Mel before it started spreading like wildfire. I don't know what this morning's explosion's about, but I think it might be a good idea for people who've linked up with me to keep their heads down, if they're still awake." I presented the piece of topaz, my hand palm-up. "The only thing I've been able to find so far that might help is topaz. It's supposed to be protection against non-viral sleeping sicknesses."

That was playing fast and loose with the truth on a lot of levels, but Jen probably didn't need to know about the evil African spirits, and it was a lot easier to say "non-viral" than "mystical." Even as I said it I felt like I was trying to cheat my way out of admitting what was going on. I wondered if it'd ever be easy for me to admit, "Yeah, it's magical in origin," and didn't know if it'd be better or worse if it was easy. I lifted my hand a little, offering Jen the topaz.

"I don't know if it'll help, but you might want to hang on to this."

Jen picked the stone up without touching my skin, lifting it to examine its clarity. There wasn't much; smoke and scars filled the golden stone, which was the only reason I'd been able to afford a box of the stuff. As far as semiprecious jewels went, topaz wasn't expensive, but gem-quality rocks would've put me back more credit than I had. Just watching her fold it into her pocket made me feel a little better. The stones had only been in my possession a few minutes, but I really *wanted* them to offer some protection, and maybe that in itself would do some good. So, I thought, would the bearer believing in its power.

The bearer. God. All the people I'd mocked for getting weird with language when they got into otherworldly stuff deserved an apology. It really did do something to the brain, because now I was doing it.

"Let me know if I can help at all," Jen said. Her hand was still in her pocket, making a bump in her pants where her fingers were curled around the stone. I ducked my head in a nod and backed toward the door, then stopped in it to look at her.

"Look, Jen, if this thing starts sniffing around you, don't throw anything at it, okay? It siphons off life force. Just make yourself as quiet as you can."

Jen gave me a quick smile. "You're getting good at this, Joanie. That sounded like you knew what you were talking about." She lifted her chin, ushering me out. "Get going. You're letting the draft in."

* * *

Almost nobody was as cool with my little weird gifts of topaz as Jen had been. I found myself saying things like, "I thought this might make a cool good-luck stone for you," to almost everybody who'd helped me back in January. I don't think most of them wanted to know why I was handing out good-luck stones. People preferred to forget the bizarre things I'd done. On the other hand, with a noticeable number of coworkers out of the office, nobody said no. They just didn't quite look at me when I handed over the stones. I couldn't exactly blame them, but I was starting to have an inkling of what it would feel like when I was actually good at being a shaman, and the rest of the world refused to see what was going on around them.

I plodded down to the garage, not really wanting to enter what I'd once considered my haven in the station. I'd seen the roster. I knew how many people from the shop were out sick. I came around the corner at the base of the stairs watching my feet, and nearly crashed into Thor. For once I darted to the left and he held still, so it didn't turn into a dance of trying to circumvent each other. I even managed a faint smile, then blurted, "Hey, Thor, uh, I mean, dammit, Ed. Edward!" to his shoulders as he started up the stairs.

He turned and looked back at me with a curious expression. "You weren't in my dream," I said, more to myself than to him, and his eyes went even more curious. "Guess you wouldn't have been," I mumbled. "I mean, it was my job." I was making sense to me, anyway. "Never mind." I followed him up the stairs a couple of steps and offered a piece of topaz.

"Hang on to this, would you? It's kind of a..." To my surprise, I found I didn't want to prevaricate. "A protective charm."

His golden eyebrows rose. "You serious?"

"Yeah." I managed another little smile. "I don't know how good it is, but there's some kind of weird stuff going on, and it might be a good idea to have it."

He shifted his shoulders uncomfortably. "You and weird go together like beer and pizza, you know that?"

My smile faltered, not that it was very good to begin with. "You noticed, huh?"

"Yeah. Kinda hard to miss, really. The guys down here—" He broke off with the look of someone realizing he was about to betray ranks. I turned my face away, mouth twisting.

"Yeah. I know. Good old Joanie used to be awesome. The Girl Mechanic, kind of like the garage mascot, until she got screwy in the head. Trust me, I know what they say, and I know how half of them don't like talking to me anymore, and—" It was my turn to break off and take a deep breath. "It doesn't matter. Anyway, you want this or not?" I hefted the little stone, looking back at my big blond nemesis. I'd just decided he was going to say no and was thinking about putting it in his locker when he reached out and plucked it from my hand.

"What the hell. Anybody who can drink as much whiskey as you did the other day and look as good a night later is okay in my book." He lifted the piece of topaz with a quick smile and stuck it in his pocket as he turned away and went upstairs.

Not that Morrison had any reason to avoid me, but a fruitless search of the station didn't turn him up, and I left feeling vaguely out of sorts. I was supposed to avoid him, not the other way around. It was the whole pulling-rank thing. I'd ended up leaving one of the pieces of topaz on his desk with a note that said, "Put this in your pocket" and no signature. I couldn't decide if my name on it would have made him more or less likely to do as I asked.

Okay, ordered. No wonder I didn't date much. I had the social skills of a laboratory gorilla.

My next stop was the Ravenna area east of the university. Scraping up my nerve to get out of the car at the ranch-style house I pulled up at was harder than I wanted to admit to. Giving Morrison a topaz talisman face-to-face would've been easier than knocking on the door. The house emanated sorrow, old grief mixed with fresh. It didn't take any particular skill to pick that up. I'd been there barely ten days earlier for the gathering after a funeral.

The young man who opened the door had lost weight since I'd seen him last, his sandy hair grown a little too long and flopping into his eyes. He wasn't surprised to see me, but he wasn't happy, either. He leaned heavily on the doorknob, making it clear he was a barrier between me and entering the house. "Joanne."

"Garth." I offered a little smile, then pulled my lower lip into my mouth. "How're you doing?"

His gaze skittered away from me, the shoulder his weight wasn't on twitching upward in a shrug that was supposed to be dismissive. "Okay. Dunno if Dad said thanks for coming to the funeral, so..." Another twitched shrug. "Thanks."

"He did." My voice was hardly a whisper, the smile I tried for weak and unhappy. "It was the least I could do."

Garth's gaze flickered back to me, and I saw him swallow the words: *yeah. It was.* His brother had died because of mistakes I'd made, and I deserved the rejoinder. That he didn't make it was a lot more than I'd earned. "So what do you want?"

"I don't know if you're still part of the coven," I began. Garth cut me off with a slice of his hand and a harsh sound.

"Yeah, you know, what with everything that went down, between Colin and Faye, the coven kind of decided to take a step back. I'm out of it. That kind of shit doesn't do anybody any good." Bile filled his words, the bitterness of a true believer who'd seen his god's feet of clay. While I would have shared his sentiment not very long ago, it left me with a hollow feeling where I was accustomed to my power being settled.

"I'm sorry to hear that." My throat had gone all scratchy and my eyes stung with disappointment that struck me as inexplicable, even if it wasn't really. "You had some real power. Look, I just came by to offer you this." I took one of the topaz stones from my pocket and held it out. "It's kind of a good-luck charm. I thought maybe..."

"No. Thanks." The second word was perfunctory, thrust at me like a weapon. "I don't want anything else to do with magic or spells or any of that crap." Garth moved out of the door as he spoke, retreating and rejecting. "Maybe I'll see you around."

I let the topaz fall from my fingers into the lawn as I walked away, a host of regrets at my back.

CHAPTER FIFTEEN

Returning home felt anti-climactic. Garth'd rejected me, I hadn't found Morrison and I still didn't have any actual answers. I climbed the stairs slowly—for once it might've been faster to take the building's ancient elevator—and bumbled the key into my door's lock. Turning the knob proved it'd been open and that I'd just locked it, which didn't strike me as too unusual. I'd been known to forget to lock the door before. But when I reopened it and entered my living room, I found Gary snoozing on my couch. He had his hands folded over his belly and his ankles crossed on the arm, so his knees were locked. My own knees ached in sympathy, but my mouth said, "I *know* I didn't give you a key, Gary!"

He cracked one gray eye open. "That ain't stopped me yet, darlin'. Welcome home."

"I thought you had to work. Are the kids okay?"

"I thought you had to," Gary said in a perfectly reasonable rejoinder, kicking his feet off the couch arm. "Called Keith and told him I wasn't comin' in today after all. Kids are fine. What've I missed? Start with passin' out." He sat up and clapped his hands together, making an unexpectedly loud pop.

I dropped into the other end of the couch and pulled my knees up until I could put my chin on them. "Did I tell you I fell asleep on the concrete outside yesterday?"

"Jo," Gary said in astonishment. I couldn't tell if there was reprimand in it, too, and had to look up to find Gary's bushy eyebrows drawn in concern. "What's goin' on, doll?"

My hands fluttered, making a useless circle in front of my shins, which were in the way of my stomach. "I don't know, Gary." I recounted the larger part of the past twenty-four hours as best I could, a feeling of unease settling inside me. It was centered in that coil of power I carried, the same pressure that'd driven me to find a woman I'd seen from an airplane seven months earlier. I took a breath, trying to dispel it, then moved my legs to press my hands against my stomach. It wasn't as bad as it'd been then, but that didn't surprise me. I'd had a whole lifetime of unused magic to tune into then, and now I was at least sort of used to it. "I'd think it was this sleeping sickness, except—"

"'Cept you woke up," Gary said. "You been dreamin'?"

"About all kinds of things." I didn't want to go into dreams of marrying Mark Bragg while Morrison looked on. "Yesterday it was about a coyote. Not a real one. Like a—I guess I dreamed about a spirit quest. But it wasn't mine. I mean, it wasn't the one I did with…Judy." I said the name slowly, a prickle of shame stinging my cheeks. "It was like a real one," I added more quietly. "Like the one I did for you."

"Makes sense, don't it? You got Coyote as your spirit guide. Mebbe he's just tryin' to show you the way."

"Yeah, but this isn't—have you eaten?" I wasn't trying to change the subject, though Gary gave me another bushy-eyebrowed look. "All I've eaten was cereal this morning. I'm starving."

"Got any Pop-Tarts?" He followed me into the kitchen and snitched one of the doughnuts he'd brought by the previous morning. "I could use a snack," he allowed. "Ate lunch before I came over. Now, finish what you were sayin', Jo."

I sat down at the table with a glass of water and watched Gary putter around the kitchen while he ate his doughnut. "My Coyote, Little Coyote, doesn't look like the spirit coyote I saw or like your tortoise or any of the other animals who came when I asked for help for you. They were all luminescent and drawn out of fine lines, like they didn't exactly have bodies to them. Like constellations. Little Coyote's solid. I've never seen him get all starry like that. So he's not the same."

"How 'bout Big Coyote?" One of the things I loved about Gary was that he went along with my terrible naming scheme. Even so, referencing Big Coyote made me shiver and take my hands away from the glass of cold water.

"Big Coyote was like the thunderbird, Gary. *Solid*'s too weak a word for him." The scent of burned sand filled my nostrils, memory so vivid I felt a wash of heat come over me like it was renewing my tan. "Big Coyote and the thunderbird and the serpent, for that matter, are all solid like the earth is solid or like space is empty. You couldn't move him even if you had the lever and a place to stand, unless he wanted you to. Little Coyote's just not like that. And the spirits aren't, either."

"You're startin' to sound pretty sure of yourself, lady."

"I know," I muttered at my water glass. "I just wish I knew if I was right."

"Arright." Gary came to lean on the table, making knuckles against its hard surface without appearing to suffer any discomfort. "So you're dreamin' about spirits quests like one you've never done, is that it?"

"Pretty much." I drank my water and put the glass down again as Gary cocked his head at me.

"Maybe it's a hint, darlin'. Why doncha do one?"

I opened my mouth and closed it again and looked intently at my empty glass. "Because last time I did, I was hoodwinked by the bad guys?"

"You think I'm one of the bad guys, Jo?"

Every vestige of good cheer drained out of me like somebody'd opened a valve, complete misery rising to take its place. My throat went tight and my eyes stung with tears, color heating my cheeks even as my stomach twisted and my hands turned icy. "If you are I'm throwing the towel in now, because I just couldn't handle that."

"Aw, hey, Joanie." Gary took my wrist, pulling me to my feet and into a bear hug that left me snuffling in his shoulder. "I was teasin', sweetheart. I ain't one of the bad guys. Just an old dog with a pretty girl to look after."

I snuffled again, leaking tears. "'m not little."

He chuckled against my head. "Didn't say you were, darlin'."

"Oh." I sniffled again and extracted myself to find a tissue. "I guess you didn't." Gary turned to watch me.

"You all right, Joanie?"

"Yeah." I scraped up a smile and offered it to him. "You never call me Joanie."

The old man waggled his head dismissively. "Tough broad like you don't usually need to be called by a little girl's name. You sure you're okay?"

"Yeah. Just don't turn out to be one of the bad guys, okay?" I gave him another weak smile, then put my cold hands over my too-hot face. It felt good, so I stood there until my hands warmed up again. "You think maybe there are some real spirit animals out there for me?" I asked into my palms.

"Only one way to find out." Gary came up to me as he spoke, slinging his arm around my shoulders to give me another brief hug. "You found one for me, didn't you? If an old tortoise could spare some time for me, there's gotta be somethin' out there for a powerhouse like you. I'll get the drum."

"Thanks, Gary." I dropped my hands to watch him exit the kitchen, then slumped against the counter, trying to remember if my little emotional breakdowns were usually followed by getting my act together. Maybe I needed to start keeping a journal: *Wednesday: burst into tears on Gary, then saved Seattle. A good day.* The idea made me smile and I pushed off the counter to get ready for a spirit quest.

I had an almost complete lack of things that struck me as appropriate for preparing for a spirit quest. I had no over-heated hut like the dream had featured, I had no drum circle, I had no guide and I had pretty much no idea what I should be doing, except for the examples of the dream and the success of the quest I'd done for Gary. With any luck, that would be enough. I forewent the towel I usually tucked against the front door, as the draft from under it felt nice in July, and plunked down in the middle of my living room floor.

There was no electric shock when Gary picked up my drum, and the beat he picked out didn't send shards of light through my soul and out into the world. Overall, I thought that was probably a good thing, even if it did make my heart skip a thud with missing Morrison's rhythm.

Wow. There wasn't anything wrong with the thought, exactly, but it brought me to all sorts of places I just wasn't prepared to go. I fought down a blush, totally without success, and hoped Gary didn't see it. It took a while to get my heart rate back to normal after that, and visions of Morrison kept popping up in my head. I hadn't gone out with him. It didn't seem right for him to hang around my brain, clouding things up.

Wow, again. I'd had a real, honest-to-gosh date. I couldn't remember the last time I'd gone on a date. It'd been before my mother died, which meant at least a year ago. My social life was an absolute disaster. I was going to have to call Phoebe and see if she wanted to go out again, although maybe not to the club Thor had seen us at.

Then again, maybe. I felt a grin creep over my face and tried to push it away. I was sitting in the middle of my living room listening to a drum. It was not supposed to be the time to reflect on my personal life. This was the bit where it was all deep and dark and serious and mystical, so I could get inside my own head, or outside of it, and maybe meet a few spirit animals out there in the black.

That was, of course, the problem with trying to think of nothing. All sorts of somethings kept crowding around in my mind, vying for attention. Morrison, Mark, Thor…for a moment I paused to admire all the men suddenly in my life, then shook my head. Morrison was certainly not a man in my life. I mean, he was, what with being a man and in my life, but he wasn't a Man in My Life. And a compliment from Thor probably didn't make him a Man in My Life, either. I was getting a big head.

Mark, on the other hand. Mark was nice to think about. He was quirky and charming and absolutely no doubt too good to be true, and made a warm little bubbly place in my tummy that I liked. I let out a tired, content sigh and thought about Mark until his image dissolved and let me drift thoughtlessly in the dark behind my eyelashes.

Warmth and comfort and safety gradually surrounded me, all caught up in the sound of the drumbeat. My heart had staggered into the drum's pattern, or maybe the other way around. Both felt languid and unworried, a part of me but not to be terribly concerned with. Distant sparkles glittered and faded in the dark, almost familiar now. I sat myself down, folding my legs yoga-style, and resolved in a laid-back kind of way to be patient. Judy'd said it was easier to do spirit quests for others than for yourself, and while I had good reason not to trust most of what she'd told me, that part actually resounded with some of what I'd read.

I'd asked for help for Gary—and for Colin, though that was something I didn't want to think about in the middle of my own spirit quest—but doing so now seemed presumptuous somehow. My spirit animals, if they wanted to come to me, might take their own sweet time about it. I just had to be patient.

One of the distant shimmers took on a harder glimmer, making a seared sharp edge of brightness in the darkness.

It brought with it color, desert-blue sky meeting red stretches of earth, coalescing at a horizon that seemed a thousand miles away. A road, straight and narrow and plumed with dust, cut toward that horizon, and the hard line of light glinted again. I walked forward, raising a hand against the shadowless skies, and squinted at puffs of dirt ambling up from the far-off vehicle.

I could hear people behind me, voices rising and falling with as much enthusiasm as could be generated in the heat. Someone was keeping an eye on me, not worried, but because I was a kid, and so someone had to watch out for me. I felt a hand on my shoulder as an adult stopped to watch the car with me, then a double-pat as he left me on my own.

Time folded, the car pulling up in a cloud of dust. It was an enormous old boat of an Oldsmobile, built in the seventies, four-doored and powered by a massive V8 engine. A fleeting thought, *this is not your father's Oldsmobile,* scampered through my mind, but as the driver's-side door pushed open and a young man got out, an unsettling jolt made my stomach cold.

It *was* my father's Oldsmobile. The car I'd grown up in was out there in the desert, my dad climbing out to hail one of the adults behind me. I shook myself, realizing that for the second time, I was having a dream in which I was somebody else. I hadn't known it this time, though, until I saw Dad. I knew him, but whomever I was dreaming as didn't.

He was tall, taller than I thought of him as being. That was the kid's perspective; I remembered Dad from my adult height, only an inch or two shorter than his. He gave me an impersonal nod before he passed me, offering to shake someone's hand. I turned to watch him a few seconds, unused to strangers.

His height was compounded by a ranginess that I shared, both of us lacking my mother's elegance. He wore his hair long and smooth beneath a bandanna, just as he had all through my childhood. I'd loved it when I was little, though not enough to try to grow my own out. Long hair on men was in at that time, and it suited my father's angular Cherokee features. The rest of his clothing was conventional, nothing native about it, but his hair and cheekbones set him apart. He couldn't have been older than I was now, if that.

I turned away from him when another car door slammed. A little girl, maybe five years old, came around the vehicle's enormous hood from the passenger side, her palm flat against the hot gold-painted surface. Blunt-cut black bangs were nearly in green eyes, the sides of her bobbed hair hitting a baby-round face just at chin length. She stopped in front of the Oldsmobile's left headlight and stared at me, defiant to the point of excluding curiosity. My stomach did another lurch and flip, though the reaction seemed in both cases to be my own; the dreamer wasn't surprised or confused at all. How I could separate myself from the dreamer, I didn't know, and for a moment teetered on the precipice of a mental death spiral about the philosophy of dreamers and dreams.

The kid saved me from it by thrusting her chin out and saying, "Hello. I'm Joanne."

A thunderclap sounded, ripping the sky asunder. Starlight fell down from the blue, making a blazing path that ran from me and under the little girl's feet, then farther and farther into a blazing future I couldn't see. A coyote appeared before me, standing between little Joanne and myself, his every strand of fur so sharp and vivid it might have been etched in pure copper. He brought with him air too hot to breathe, the weight of it pressing down and making the sky turn white with expectation. I swallowed against the dryness in my throat, wondering how I kept my feet as he paced forward to stalk around the dreamer me. I watched him as best I could without moving more than my head, and when he'd made a full circle, he stopped and let out a single bark that broke the world in half.

A second path shot up out of the darkness that made up the earth's insides. It ran at right angles from the first one, burning through the sand into a different future. I could see farther down that path: the little Joanne wasn't in the way, and I got sparks of information: family, community respect, long life, satisfaction. I felt joy down that road, and a lot of years of laughter. Looking back at the other, all I could see was the little girl, so vivid and clear that nothing beyond her was visible.

Coyote sat down between the two paths, arranged his paws mathematically, and waited.

A warning of imminent danger splashed over me, darkness suddenly cutting through the brilliant sky and the brighter paths that lay before me. I flung a hand up, knowing which road I intended to travel, but before a step could be taken, a raven made of thin glowing white lines and avian grace fell down out of the sky and dug its claws into little Joanne's shoulders.

CHAPTER SIXTEEN

Agony knotted my shoulder muscles, just as if the raven's talons had buried themselves in *my* flesh and not in young Joanne's. I felt like I was being dragged skyward, the raven's wings whispering against desert air that thinned and turned bluer as we rose into it. The world hollowed around me until it had cylindrical walls, just like the vision I'd had in the dance club. There was nowhere to go but up or down, and the raven kept climbing higher. I set my teeth together and tried not to either squirm or scream, afraid the former would get me dropped and figuring the latter to be pretty much pointless.

I didn't know if a bird could actually wheeze from breathlessness, but by the time we broke out of the cylinder into a blue world, I had the impression that was exactly what the raven was doing. Well, I hadn't asked it to haul my hundred-and-sixty-pound self through the sky.

As if in response, it dropped me and I tumbled down to the earth, bumping and whacking myself on mountains along the way. Clouds wafted above me when I finally came to a rest, lying on my back and staring up.

I'd called it a blue world, when we broke into it. Normally that would mean I'd been looking skyward, except I hadn't been. I had no need to watch a raven's butt as it hauled me around. I'd been looking down, and the mountains and the dirt and the plant life had all been different shades of cerulean.

The sky, it turned out, was also blue, though not a typical Middle World blue. It was a hard flat blue, dark enough in hue to be pushing dusk, except the sun burned down, blazing so white the edges of its corona were—I regretted the descriptor, but it was true: sky blue. I turned my head, looking for a horizon, expecting it to be like the Lower World's horizon, like my last vision's horizon: too close.

I found no horizon. There was instead a lithe, long cat staring at me. For a few critical seconds I forgot how to breathe, my heart clogging my throat and cutting off air. Another cat padded up, standing above me with the blue-eyed curiosity of a wild animal. Another and another appeared, all of them watching me as if to see if I was about to become dinner. Their stomachs were pale, almost white, and their faces and the tips of twitching tails were dark.

Dark blue, actually. So was the rest of the fur on their bodies, paler blue instead of tawny like I expected it to be. Mountain lions didn't come in blue, as far as I knew. Not cobalt and powder-blue, anyway, as if somebody'd carved them out of this strange sky and made them into cats with clouds for underbellies.

The first one, delicately, put a large paw onto my chest and pressed. I hadn't been breathing, anyway, but the weight brought that home, and I gasped. He shifted forward, liquid movement that took his bulk from long hind legs and leaned it into me. This was not a spirit animal. I didn't know what it was, but I felt pretty confident of that. It was something entirely Other, belonging to a world that wasn't my own. Spots danced in my vision, blocking out his wide eyes.

Thin voices cried out from the mountains around me. I turned my head the other way with effort, to find other humans pinned to the ground in the same manner I was. Innumerable Prussian-colored cats leaned into uncountable people, squashing the life from them, and like me, they all seemed too frightened to fight back. I twisted my head forward again and wrapped my hands around the cougar's paw, pushing back enough to drag in a lungful of air.

As if my inhalation called them down, sparrows flocked from the sky by the thousands, sparks of darting sapphire against the stillness of the dusky sky and blue-smoke mountains. For a moment I thought they would attack the cats, but instead they swept down to the captive humans, pecking and plucking at tender flesh and tasty eyes. The sky blotted into darkness from their numbers and from mortal screams.

Then the sky broke apart, fragile as an eggshell, and black poured in.

I flung my hands up, half warding off sparrows and half as if I'd catch the sky. Power came without bidding, spilling from my hands as I pushed toward the pieces of sky as they fell. I tried to shore up the world, and it almost worked. For a few seconds destruction came to a halt, and the people around me cried out in gladness.

Then a huge whacking straw burst up through the heart of the world and shattered the remaining sky into a billion pieces. Sparrows and cats alike chittered and yowled with fear, springing away from the men they held captive and feasted upon. All around me, people scrambled to their feet and ran for the tube that pierced the sky, while I lay there heaving with a useless attempt to save the world.

Blue mountain broke apart beneath me and I fell a hundred miles, all the way back into my apartment. I was just about to hit my body at terminal velocity when I felt myself jerk, as if wings had spread, and popped back into myself just a little more gently than I'd expected. My shoulders ached. I pressed on one, trying to work the pain away, and encountered slight resistance and the fluttered offense of a man-handled bird. I even thought I heard an undignified squack of dismay, and looked up to find Gary gaping at me without the slightest apology.

"You got—it's gone now—you had a—you had wings, Jo."

"What, like an angel?" I slid my hand down my shoulder, half expecting to encounter angel wings.

He pushed his mouth out in exasperation. "Around your head, you crazy dame."

Right where the raven had snagged me. I could feel its presence on my shoulder, claws dug in for purchase. It had no weight, just a peculiar *thereness* I couldn't otherwise identify. "Gary, can you feel that tortoise?"

Gary drew himself up, mock dignity almost hiding the

amused twinkle in his gray eyes. "Lady, I ain't sure that's the kinda question a nice girl asks an old man."

"Gary!" I couldn't get enough exasperation into my voice. It came out sounding like laughter. Gary let the twinkle overtake dignity and gave me a wicked smirk.

"I guess I kinda can," he allowed, "if I think about it. I got kind of a sense of havin' somebody watchin' my back, like maybe I got that big ol' shell keepin' me safe. Why?"

I rolled my shoulder, seeing if I could dislodge the faint sense of having a bird clinging to it. I couldn't. In fact, it hung on harder, so I stopped that nonsense. Well, I tried, anyway. I found myself still shifting around a bit, getting used to the idea of having somebody—or something— watching over me. "I think it worked."

"That's good, ain't it?"

"Yeah, but it wasn't like your spirit quest. Or the one I dreamed about. I had another..." I hesitated, frowning. "Dream, I guess. I didn't think I was asleep."

"You didn't fall over," Gary supplied helpfully. "What'd you dream?"

I shook my head and got to my feet, stretching out some of the stiffness of sitting still. "I dreamed about meeting my dad and me out in a desert someplace. I don't know where. And I saw Big Coyote in the dream. He was giving me a choice of some kind, but then the raven grabbed me—the little me—and then—"

"Raven?" Gary turned my drum toward me so I could see the raven sheltering the rattlesnake and the wolf under its wings. I stared at the rich dye job and pressed my lips together, nodding. "Think somebody knew somethin' you didn't?"

"I don't know, Gary." I couldn't even decide if I hoped the answer was yes or no. I'd had that drum since I was fifteen. The idea that somebody'd seen the potential for what I might become that long ago, without me ever knowing anything about it, made me both sad and nervous. "I don't know," I said again. "That didn't exactly go like I thought it was going to."

"Nothin' ever does," Gary said, far too cheerfully. "That's how life is, Jo. You gotta run with the punches."

I smiled. "You're mixing your metaphors, old man."

Gary sniffed. "Mix a few words up and she starts callin' me old. How you like that?" he asked of no one in particular, before shaking off his snit and adding, "So you got yourself a little spiritual protection goin' on. That gonna be any use?"

"Honestly?" I dropped into the couch. "I have no idea."

"Oh, good." Gary put my drum aside, folding his hands behind his head. "I always like it when you got a nice solid game plan."

I grinned despite myself and leaned against his rib cage, feeling like a big cat demanding attention. Reminded, I straightened before I got comfortable. "The world ended again. I forgot. The raven distracted me."

"That s'posed to make sense?"

I gritted my teeth impatiently and tried once more, explaining the second part of the dream I'd had. "It was kind of like the vision at the dance club. The world—some world—came to an end and I couldn't stop it."

"Some world?"

"It wasn't this one. It was like the Lower World, except

not. I mean…" I screwed up my face. "Everything was blue. *Everything*. The first one was all kind of primary colors. So it was like the second one was more real, more like this, than the first, kind of. If that makes sense." I was pretty sure it didn't.

Gary harrumphed. "If they're gettin' realer, I guess that kinda gives us an idea of what we're up against, don't it?"

I leaned against his side again. "You always sound so cheerful about things like that. 'Hey, Gary, I saw the world ending.' 'Great!' I don't know why you stick around in the face of that, but I'm glad you do."

Gary put his arm over my shoulders and wrapped it over my collarbone to squeeze me, dropping a kiss on the top of my head. "How many times I gotta tell you, you're the most interesting thing—"

"That's happened to you since Annie died, I know." I smiled. "I just think you must be crazy, the way you run with all this and just kind of let it come without freaking out."

"Darlin', you get to be my age, and you start figurin' there's two ways to take the world. One's like it ain't never gonna change and you're not gonna, either. The other's ta keep right on believing in six impossible things before breakfast. Guess I'd just rather do that."

"Is that what Annie would've done, too?" I closed my eyes, inhaling the old man's mellow scent. "I wish I'd met her."

"Me, too. She woulda liked you, Jo. You woulda liked her."

"I'd like anybody who could stay married to you for forty-eight years."

"Harrumph." Gary gave me another squeeze to let me know he didn't mean it. "Always thought she was the practical one," he said after a moment. I turned my cheek toward his chest, eyes still closed as I listened. "She was a nurse, didja know?"

"I think you told me," I said with a nod. I felt Gary nod, too, pride coming into his voice.

"She said it was in case I never came back from the war, so she'd have somethin' to do. I always thought it was so she could work with the little ones without bringin' 'em home to remind me of what she couldn't give me. Damn fool woman never did understand." Sorrow mixed with pride by the end of his words and I squirmed around to put my arm over his chest and hug him.

"How come you didn't adopt? I think you would've made a fantastic dad." Gary had mentioned once, in passing, that Annie couldn't have children. He didn't know I'd seen more than that in a moment of revelation, seen the illness that had nearly claimed his wife's life and had taken her ability to bear children instead. It was one of those things there was no less-than-awkward way to confess: *sorry, Gary, but I accidentally spied on your history a couple days after we met.*

Gary chuckled. "Annie was the breadwinner then. Me, I was wanderin' around playin' the trumpet at jazz clubs and drinkin' too much. Guess we never thought we fit the right mold to adopt."

I sat up, an incredulous smile blooming over my face. "Trumpet? You? Were you any good?"

"I was all right," Gary said with such deprecation I suspected he'd been a lot better than all right. "Brought in enough spare cash to take Annie on some nice vacations."

"You still play?"

Gary made a noise that sounded suspiciously like *pshaw*. I poked him in the ribs, grinning. "You do, don't you? How come I don't know this? What other secrets are you keeping?"

Gary gave me a white-toothed grin and shrugged his big shoulders, looking thirty years younger than the Hemingway wrinkles and white hair told me he was. "A fella's gotta keep some secrets, Jo, or you'll stop comin' around."

"I'm not the one who goes breaking into your house," I pointed out. "You're doing the coming around." Gary looked not at all repentant, and I climbed off the couch, smiling as I looked for my cell phone. "Come on down to the car with me. I left the topaz and my phone there." There was absolutely no good reason I couldn't use the phone in the house, but Gary ambled down to Petite with me, anyway, and I dug a particularly nice piece of topaz out of the bag and handed it to him. He held it up to the light, and I dialed Morrison's number into my phone. I hadn't figured out how to program numbers into the phone's auto-dial—or, more accurately, I hadn't figured out how to make the stupid keypad give me the right letters so I could spell people's names when it offered to store numbers for me—and so I still had to actually dial phone numbers. For someone who owned a Linux box at home instead of a Microsoft or Mac PC, that was an embarrassing failure in the technical department. I liked to imagine that memorizing numbers was a good mental exercise that would stand me well while all of my contemporaries' brains turned to mush from lack of use.

"Walker." Morrison spoke through gritted teeth before I

even heard the connection go through. How I could tell his teeth were gritted, I wasn't sure, unless I was just making the relatively safe assumption that if he was talking to me, his teeth were gritted. "Tell me you've got a better solution to my police force calling in sick than leaving pieces of rocks on people's desks."

"Technically," I said, "if they're sleeping, they can't be the ones calling in."

I don't know why I did things like that. Morrison erupted in a nearly incoherent bellow of frustration while I leaned on Petite's hood and watched Gary admire his stone. "Captain," I interrupted when he sounded like he was winding down a little, "get that piece of topaz. It's the only thing I've got that might be protecting people from this. I really mean it, Morrison. Put the topaz in your pocket."

"How in hell is a rock going to do any good?"

"It's symbolic, Morrison, if nothing else. Haven't you ever gone to church?" I hung up before he could answer, although I was suddenly curious as to the answer. My own church-learnings were sketchy at best. Once in a while, and only when we were in the South, Dad would feel the urge to stop by a Baptist temple and absorb some gospel music and the high-rolling passion of belief, but that was as much as I'd ever had in the way of formal church attendance. Still, the power of faith wasn't something you had to go to church to pick up. I just hoped Morrison would put the stupid rock in his pocket. That conversation had not gone as planned. I don't know what had made me think Morrison might start listening to reason. Or listening to me, which wasn't really the same thing at all. I spun the phone in the palm of my hand, trying to decide what to do with it. "Was it only this morning Mel went to sleep?"

"'Fraid so, sweetheart." Gary lowered his stone, then slid it into his pocket. "Maybe you oughta sleep, Jo."

I shook my head. "I think that's a bad idea. I'm already getting stuck in dreams and being blindsided by visions. I don't want to give this thing any more opportunity to snag me than I have to."

"And how many is that?"

I looked up. Gary's white hair was bright with sun, almost glowing, and his eyes were concerned. I smiled despite myself. "Enough to figure out what it is and get everybody free from it. I'm being careful, Gary. As careful as I can be, anyway. If this thing can grab Coyote, it's a lot stronger than I am." As if the admission was a weakness, I yawned until my nose stung, and felt my expression go wry. "Maybe I'll get a caffeine IV and drop by the hospital. If they've got Billy and Mel in the same room I might be able to get more off both of them than just the one. Hang on to that rock, will you, Gary? Please?"

"'Course I will." His eyes sparkled in the sunlight. "I don't want you givin' me the look you gave Morrison a minute ago. Coulda peeled paint, and he ain't even here."

"That's my goal in life," I muttered. "Peel Morrison's paint." Something sounded unbelievably wrong with that and I felt my ears heat up. Gary cleared his throat too loudly and looked somewhere else, trying not to grin. I slumped somewhat melodramatically, feeling put-upon, then straightened. "Anyway," I said, also too loudly, "I'm going to the hospital."

Gary came around to Petite's passenger side and bopped his hand against her door handle. "Arright, let's go."

"This became a we?" I crawled in and popped the lock on Gary's door open. He swung down into the seat like it was natural, a marked difference from Morrison, and shrugged.

"I took the day off, doll. Might as well be in on the good stuff. Besides, you kept me out of it last time."

Like clockwork, guilt swept through me, bubbling around the core of power in my stomach. I reached over without thinking, putting my fingers on Gary's chest, and magic spilled out.

CHAPTER SEVENTEEN

Magic was okay. Magic was what I expected. What I didn't expect was the depth it crashed to, wholesale ignoring my intent to work a little good mojo into Gary's heart and call it done. A jungle rushed up around me, shaking into place with such force I staggered while leaves and branches settled into place with rustling whispers. Water splashed around my ankles, cold and fresh and urgent. I stepped with it, letting its current guide me. Within a few steps it deepened and pulled me off my feet, buffeting me and carrying me to wherever it wanted me to go. I laughed, breathless with surprise, and twisted in the water, looking to see how far back it went.

Following me came a flood of inky-black wings, so rich in their darkness that I could see hints of purples and blues within them. Blackness tainted what it touched, sucking life away. Horror seized me as surely as the stream had and I snatched for shore, trying to stop my plummet before I fell any deeper and brought death to everything that surrounded me.

A big hand reached down and snagged my arm, hauling me out of the water and onto a branch dangling over the river. I yelped and clung to it, dripping and astonished. Below me, darkness bubbled and boiled in place, apparently unable to go farther than I was, regardless of things like physics. I could see it roiling against clean water as if they were two wholly different substances, never meant to mix. From above, it was easier to see into the depths of the black, and to imagine eyes of indigo and violet, fluttering like urgent wings against the air. The rapid, soundless beats carried pressure with them, as if someone had made a corset of the earth's core and squeezed the breath from my lungs with its weight.

"That what I think it is?"

I twisted my head up to look at Gary, who'd righted himself on a branch above me and was drying his hands on his khaki pants. There was a pink flush to his arms, telling evidence of the burst of strength that had hauled me from the river. His army-issue shirt was a little different this time, *Muldoon* still printed in yellow block letters on a black nametag over his left breast. Below it, though, there was now a medal, so discreet it faded when I tried looking at it directly, and only reappeared when I caught it from the corner of my eye. His eyebrows had gotten a little farther away from him than they'd been the first time I'd been in the privacy of his own garden, as if he'd learned to see himself as slightly older than he had then, only a few weeks ago. I guessed a heart attack would do that to a guy. His hairline was flushed, too, from hanging upside down to catch me in the river, but his hair was dark and the wrinkles I knew so well had only just started settling into his face.

"Annie was so lucky," I blurted, and my old/young friend gave me a sly grin that made me laugh and blush at the same time.

"You're avoidin' the question, Jo." He nodded beyond me at the river and the flittering, dangerous surface that tried to rise from it. I shuddered as I glanced at its alien blend, then lay on my stomach and reached down.

Weight swam up my arm, black and heavy, as if it was trying to drag me into the water. Flutters of magic danced through that weight, a feeling like eyelash kisses on my skin. I yawned, and the lethargic murkiness came to life, no longer content to be slow and drowsy. It rose up, not like water at all, but like a wave of enclosing wings that worked to buffet me into them. Oil-slicked patterns formed in the darkness, delicate purple eyes and blue threads between them, familiar without quite being recognizable. Softness swept in around me, diminutive feathers tickling and bearing a promise of sleep making everything all right.

"C'mon, doll."

I looked up, eyes glittering from holding back another yawn, to find Gary offering his hand and a smile. The lush trees were gone, and he looked younger than I'd ever seen him, in his twenties. His eyebrows were groomed and his smile was as strong and white as it was when he was in his seventies. His uniform was crisp and new, not yet worn comfortably like it was in his self-image a decade hence. A dance floor lay behind him, uniformed men dancing with women in full-skirted dresses. They looked absurdly young and beautiful to my eye, semiformal atmosphere tinged with hope and desire and the rush of falling in love as quickly as possible. Gary tilted his head, an eyebrow rising in a rather endearing look of puppy-dog anticipation. "Don't break a soldier's heart, lady."

I laughed, unduly charmed, and put my hand in his, discovering I wore wrist-length white gloves. A startled glance down at myself told me I was wearing one of those period dresses, too, in a forest-green that I suspected complemented my skin very well. The dress had a prim collared throat opened just far enough to be not that prim after all, and a nipped waist that fitted over my hips and flattened out into pleats. I had no idea I had so much hourglass to my shape, and wondered briefly just how sturdy my underwear had to be to keep me curved that way. My hair brushed forward against my chin, fat black undercurls, and I touched my forehead to discover bangs, just as well coiffed as the rest of my hair. A mirror on the far wall gave me the startling impression the outfit made me look taller, not something I normally needed, and then I was dancing with Gary and no longer worried about my clothes or hair, or even the fact that I couldn't dance.

Because I could. Whether it was Gary's lead or magic shoes or the music lending me its gift, I followed him on the dance floor without thinking or worrying about it, and instead laughed and nestled close when the music slowed, unable to remember being so happy. At breaks between songs, other boys cut in and asked to dance, and Gary let me go graciously, unconcerned, and that was as much a reason to come back to him as anything else. There were young men who scowled when their girls danced with someone else, sulking around the edges of the dance floor, but Gary put a hand in his pocket and got a glass of punch and watched, eyes full of confidence and pleasure.

"I thought boys didn't like to see their girls dancing with other men," I said when I came back to him after one dance, and he let go a belly laugh that all but knocked me off my feet.

"Darlin', if they've got that much to worry about, I guess I wouldn't like it, either, in their shoes." He winked, then cast an exaggerated look toward the dance hall clock and lowered his head to say, "Your mama staying up waitin' for you to come home at the stroke of midnight?"

I lifted my chin in a mixture of pride and offense. "I'm nineteen years old, Gary Muldoon, and in college. I can go home when I want."

He gave me a grin that melted all the offense out of my expression, then caught my hand. A moment later we were in sweet-scented woods, Gary offering me his coat as I shivered. I slipped into it, feeling silly for leaving my own coat behind, though a tiny part of me knew I'd done it on purpose so I could huddle in the warmth left from his body. "I'm lost in here," I protested in amusement, which was more true than I expected. Gary had height and breadth on me even as an septuagenarian. His younger self was wonderfully broad-shouldered.

"That's whatcha get for leavin' your coat inside," Gary teased. "C'mon, this way." He nodded ahead of us, taking my hand to lead me over a root-ridden forest pathway, an incline leading us to a bluff that looked over a night-black ocean. "They're sendin' me to Korea," he said abruptly.

My heart caught, little white pulse of pain. "When?" Gary watched me out of the corner of his eye, as if afraid of my reaction. I'd let go of his hand, and mine were knotted together in the sleeves of his army jacket, worry tasting like copper at the back of my throat.

"I leave Saturday. You gonna wait for me, sweetheart?"

"Wait for you," I said quietly. "What do you think I've been doing the past four months, Gary?"

Relief swept the big man's expression and he turned all the way to me, hope bright in his eyes. "It ain't much, but I wanted to…" He slid a hand into his front pocket and came out with a small black box. My heart caught again, a lurch so profound I wasn't sure it would start again, and Gary gave me a funny crooked grin as I lifted my gaze to his. "It ain't much," he repeated, "but maybe it's enough. I'll getcha somethin' better before we—well, *will* you? *Will* you marry me, Annie?" He opened the box and a soft golden glow sprang up from the ring within. I laughed, and touched the stone with a fingertip—

—and flinched awake in a surge of alarm that pushed sleep away. I could feel it consciously now, a pressing blackness trying to enter me more forcefully than it had Billy or Melinda. There, it had the sense of having all the time it needed. With me, it felt disturbed, as if my power drew it out of its usual languor and encouraged it to action. I jerked back from the river, shaking darkness from my skin, and put my hands against my mouth. I didn't want to look at Gary. I was afraid I'd start crying, which would be impossible to explain.

"Jo?" Concern colored Gary's voice and I bit my knuckles, eyes wide as I stared into the unblended water. "It's what you think it is," I whispered. "It wants to put you to sleep. Or me. I don't know. It followed me in here. I'm sorry, Gary. I didn't mean to do this. I just wanted to put a tingle on your heart to help it heal some more."

"Jo," he said again, the word more solid. "Darlin', something's stoppin' it. What?"

"The…" I closed my eyes, the yellow chip of stone set into silver metal against a black box playing behind my eyelids. "The topaz," I whispered. "I think it's the topaz. It woke me up."

"Woke you up?"

"I think it's trying to give me things I want. Dreams. Dreams I want. Like they're real." My voice was tight, and I wasn't sure I was really talking to Gary. The last dream swam around in my mind, its focus on Mark and the mechanic's job I'd been so happy with. I wondered, sharply, if the only reason it'd lost its hold on me was Morrison's intrusion into the scene. I wondered, too, if Gary had been able to afford a diamond fifty years ago when he proposed to his wife, if I'd be content to stay in that dream of happiness they'd shared for five decades.

I shook my head, trying to push the questions away, and climbed down the tree so I could crouch at the river's edge without touching the water. "Come here." My voice kept playing in that same scratchy whisper, too tight and small to really be heard. "Take the topaz out and take my hand."

I reached for his without looking, waiting until he'd dropped from the tree and done as I asked.

His raw strength rumbled through me, the big V8 engine I always thought of around him. I didn't so much gather it up as focus it through the topaz, like I was letting the darkness know that this man, at least, wasn't an easy target. The stone held in our hands thrummed with its own kind of defiance, like it knew what I was doing. I couldn't sense any natural antipathy for the gem on the part of the darkness, but the rest it offered was far from peaceful, and the topaz seemed to have an opinion about that. I added my own whisper to the barrier against sleep the gem presented, a shoring up of its will, then said to Gary, "Push it out. It's your mind. Your garden. You're the one with the power to reject it. I'll be right behind you."

War fell down on us, clods of earth spraying from the sky as we crawled forward, doing more than just holding the line against the enemy. We were encroaching on Korean territory, the black scent of powder in the air and screams of anger and fear tearing through smoke and gunshots. I dragged in a breath that somehow sounded too loud in the noise and Gary reached back to silence me, a warning hand lifted. I bit the heel of my hand, tasting mud, and waited.

The surge forward came before I knew it, a final call across the lines that was a promise of victory or death. Enemy fire lashed out in rays of colored heat, more seen in my mind's eye than in reality. Only the aftermath, puffs of dirt rising where bullets hit, men falling in their path, were truly visible. But for every encroachment I saw another of my brothers in arms stand fast, stagger forward and reclaim a span of land. My vision blurred, confusing me: those warriors had faces of their own, but when I looked too closely they became my face, contorted with determination that bordered on rage. Even *my face* was a confusing concept; I saw myself, *Gary,* reflected all around, doing battle against an unseen adversary.

Once routed by even a single step, our attackers fell back, slowly at first and then faster, slipping through cracks and hollows as if they'd never been there at all. As quickly as a syringe might draw blood. And then we met a wall, as if the forty-ninth parallel had been given physical, real presence, and then the enemy lay beyond that wall and I stood at the edge of Gary's garden, fingers against it, panting from an effort I could hardly conceive of. I thought I saw feathery eyes glowing, dark in the shape of the wall.

Then sparks of gold and blue darted through it, the colors of topaz half daring anyone to test them. I dropped my hand with a wheezed laugh and turned to Gary.

He was battle-torn and bleeding, gray eyes gone darker than I'd ever seen them. Youth had fled him, for all that he was no older than he'd been at the USO dance. That boy was gone, though, leaving behind a man who'd learned mortality belonged to everyone. All my laughter fell away and I stepped forward, reaching up to take his face in both hands. "Come on back to me now, Gary. It's gone. Whatever it is, it's gone."

He flinched when I touched him, staring down at me as if I were a stranger to him. Then a shudder ran over him and he folded one of his hands around one of mine, taking it from his face. "Jo." The name seemed to bring him back to himself a little, and he drew a sharp breath, eyes clearing. "Jesus, I ain't had dreams like that in forty years."

I pulled a smile. "I probably would've gone for more of a pickup truck with a snowplow metaphor, myself, but whatever works, right? I didn't know you'd fought," I said with a little less humor. "I mean, I didn't know it was like that."

"It's not somethin' I care to dwell on, doll." He'd folded my hand over his heart and smiled at me. "I figure I'm all shored up now, Jo. Do your trick and get us out of here, you crazy dame. You've got a lotta work to do back there."

"Right." I slid my hand out of his and turned to the strong wall we'd come to, putting my fingertips against it again. I knew the topaz, steady as stone with its intrinsic gift of quiet sleep had done its work there, but there was something else—

—yes. As much a part of those defenses as anything I'd done, maybe more, rested the complacency of the tortoise spirit that helped protect Gary. I wasn't at all sure it could keep him awake, but along with his deliberate, forceful rejection of the thing that had followed me into his soul, and the piece of protective stone in his pocket, there was something of a trinity working in his favor now. He'd been struck down twice because of me, once by Cernunnos and once by Faye. I was not going to let it happen again.

I said, "Okay," and opened my eyes again in the real world. My hand fell away from Gary's chest and he took a deep, startled breath, then looked at me, gray eyes opened wide. I said, "I don't know," before he could speak, and rubbed the heel of my hand against my breastbone. Scattered thoughts danced through my mind, barely letting me catch hold of them. "Unless it's following me. I might've gotten its attention, poking around at Billy and Mel." I was speaking more to Petite's dashboard than anything else, and Gary kept quiet, letting me talk. "I'm trying to think. I've been falling in and out of trances all over the place the past couple days." I tried for a smile. "See how I said that, like it was totally normal?"

He gave me a quick grin and I leaned forward to put my hands and forehead against the steering wheel. "But that was the first time since Billy went to sleep that I've tried healing anybody. I ran a diagnostic on Erik—"

Gary laughed. I found I couldn't blame him, and returned a sheepish smile. "Well, I did. But I didn't try healing him, and that was before the dream at Mel's bedside, anyway. I think...crap, Gary." I sat up again. "I think if I try healing anybody I might lead this thing right into them. Come *on,*" I said to the roof, and the sky beyond that, and to any gods who might be listening beyond *that,* "I finally agree to play ball and now I don't get to? What kind of joke is that?"

"Cosmic irony," Gary offered in a dry voice. I eyed him, then exhaled and nodded, tapping my fingertip against the steering wheel.

"Change of plans." My voice sounded hoarse again. "I've got to learn more about this thing, Gary. Even if it sucks me up, I've got to try. Maybe just one thing will go right today."

My cell phone rang.

CHAPTER EIGHTEEN

I shrieked and dropped the damned thing in the foot well, nearly stomping it for good measure, and decided to let it ring. After the fourth ring Gary gave me a look I preferred not to interpret and reached for it, answering with a gruff "H'lo?" A moment later he handed it over, looking sanguine. "It's for you."

I muttered, "I'm going to kill you," and took the phone.

"I'd hate for you to think I was following you," a woman's voice said, "but if your personal business is necking with older men in your Mustang, do you really think that's more important than being at work?"

It took a few seconds for the voice to click. Then I dropped against the headrest and groaned. "Ms. Corvallis."

"Officer Walker," she said far too cheerfully. "He's not really my type, but whatever floats your boat. Sugar daddy?"

"What do you *want,* Ms. Corvallis?" I didn't want to call her Laura, for fear of creating some kind of bond between us.

"I want to know what you're doing, Officer Walker, since it doesn't seem to be protecting Seattle's citizens. I'm almost certain that's your job description."

"I'm..." I had no answer for her. Gary, who knew whom he'd handed over to me, raised a finger in suggestion. I put my thumb over the mouthpiece and lifted my eyebrows at him.

"Why doncha just tell her?"

"Tell her." I more mouthed the words than spoke them, afraid she'd somehow overhear. "That some kind of mystical, contagious virus is making people sleep and I'm trying to find its source?"

"You could leave out the mystical part," he suggested. I gave him a dirty look that gradually faded into a moue of surprised agreement. Maybe it would get her off my back. I took my thumb off the mouthpiece.

"Actually, you might be able to help me."

"Really." I couldn't tell if she sounded amused or delighted. "Do tell, Officer Walker."

I pressed the heel of one hand against Petite's steering wheel. "I'm trying to find the source of this sleeping sickness. You're a news reporter. You've probably got easy access to files, right? If you could look up every case of unexplained sleeping sickness since the seventh of January..."

"That's the day after the lights went out," Corvallis said. The woman didn't miss a beat. I wished she had. "What's the relationship?"

I really didn't want to say, "Me." I glowered at Gary. This was his fault, somehow. He didn't seem to be bothered by my glowering. "If you can find that out, Ms. Corvallis, you'll be on to something." I was putting a lot of faith in me being such an unlikely link she'd never figure it out. "One more thing."

"What?" She sounded like a cat pouncing.

"The origin point's probably not going to be anything handy like a CDC containment-facility breach. It'll just be people going to sleep for no reason and not waking up."

"How do you know this?"

I sighed and pushed Petite's door open, climbing out and closing it with a thump before answering.

"Magic."

Wednesday, July 6, 4:50 p.m.

Gary followed me back upstairs once I got Corvallis off the phone, and I paused to stare longingly at the day-old doughnuts on the counter before going to take my contacts out for the first time in days. The problem with not sleeping—one of them, anyway—was I got used to the idea that I could see, so I tended to forget to give my eyes a break. Gary, the heartless monster, was eating doughnuts when I came back out wearing my glasses. "What're we doin' now, doll?"

I stared hungrily at his doughnut. "I have to go inside again. You shouldn't be eating that."

"You're the one who can't be grounded, Jo."

"I know, but it's not nice to torture me." Gary waved the doughnut at me, filling my nose with its scent and my gaze with his gleefully malicious grin. "Are you *trying* to torture me?"

"Somebody's gotta."

I shook my head and sat down in the middle of my living

room floor, spine straight and hands on my knees. Gary blinked and scurried for my drum, but before he started drumming I was halfway to my garden, flashing through what had once been a difficult journey. Once the drumbeat kicked in I fell completely into myself, deeper and faster than I was accustomed to. Good cheer bubbled up through me, infiltrating my power and making my skin tingle even as I left my body behind. I was maybe starting to get the hang of this shamanism thing.

I already had the key in my pocket when I stepped into the garden, and took too little time to glance around at the green growing things springing up all around. The misty southern end of the garden seemed to be farther away this time, though a handful of steps folded space and I found myself standing in cool drifting fog in front of the door I'd willed into being. I stepped through it, still trying not to think too hard about what I was doing, for fear it would bungle my plans.

The one person I'd been able to speak with through the wall of sleep had been Coyote. I had no doubt that what I was facing was as dangerous to me as he thought it was, but unless I could find out more, I'd be going into battle unarmed, and no matter how you cut it, that couldn't be good. Passing through the crater and desert to Coyote's entrance place was easier this time, too, as if I'd made tracks in my mind with the first journey, and, like a river, power took the path of least resistance.

The good humor turned into a brief body-shaking chuckle. Working through me was probably the path of most resistance any kind of magic could have taken. Coyote'd once told me—

and it had been independently verified by a clairvoyant dead girl—that my soul was a new one, cooked up by world-creating archetypes who wanted an unburdened conduit to help heal the world with. I almost felt sorry for Grandfather Sky. I could not possibly be what he'd had in mind.

Too bad for him I was what he'd ended up with. I found Coyote's entrance spot and curled up in it, much more comfortably this time, though I maintained my own form. I didn't want to broadcast my presence as loudly as I had before, cautious for once about announcing myself to whatever held Coyote trapped in amber darkness. I needed an image that wouldn't draw attention, which purple Mustangs speeding through the desert definitely would.

Tumbleweeds popped to mind. They were completely out of my natural vehicle-based analogy, but they certainly fit into deserts, and could bounce along to wherever the wind drove them. I wasn't sure how to direct a tumbleweed, but on the other hand, dreams were as random as wind gusts, too, so I wrapped semiwistful thoughts of Coyote in spiky tumbleweed images and let them scour their way across the desert floor. Wisting was easier than I liked to admit to, not just because I badly felt in need of some guidance. Coyote in his man form was wonderfully easy on the eyes, and that might've had a bit of effect on his wistability.

Of course, that put me in mind of Mark, which brought a dumb smile to my face until I remembered his sister and Morrison.

Concentrate on the job at hand, Joanne.

My tumbleweeds took the self-directed reprimand and

spun into the air with it, sending me soaring on vast howling winds through blinding sand. Dizziness swept me, the vertigo of a falling dream, and darkness closed in all around, the blue desert sky funneled away. Stars took its place, hard and bright in the cold night. The scent of baked sand, its heat now lost but distantly remembered by my nostrils, lingered at the back of my throat. I floated a few inches above myself, lying on ground too hard to be comfortable and too smooth to be uncomfortable. I lifted a hand to point at the stars above, and could see myself twice, spirit and physical body both making the motion, like the shadow of a bad photocopy.

I traced a shape in the stars and heard an older voice say, "What do you see?" A man's voice, one I didn't know at all, and yet did. I couldn't get my head to turn so I could look toward the speaker.

"A raven." I dropped my hand. "I see ravens everywhere."

"As guides," my grandfather said hazarding a guess, but I could tell from his voice he said it only to give me something to continue from. I shook my head against the sand, staring up at the corvidae in the sky.

"As a path." I sounded pretentious even to myself and tried again. "As a warning. A choice. It's scarier than a guide. It would be something else if it was a guide. It wouldn't be a trickster." Now I sounded confident, though I faltered again as my grandfather asked, "What would it be?"

"I don't know. But not a raven. I see shadows of other animals around it, but the raven is the important one to me."

"Your spirit animal," my grandfather offered, but I shook my head again.

"Someone else's. Mine hasn't come yet."

Surprise, wholly my own, coursed through me. This dream was out of sequence, before the sweat lodge or the day I'd seen myself and my father's car out in the desert. Whoever dreams I was sharing, he hadn't yet experienced some of the things I'd dreamt, our disjointed realities not yet converged. I crunched up, hoping to pull my spirit into a sit so I could twist and look down at myself and see whose body I inhabited.

Instead I snapped free and flew up to the stars on raven wings.

They say stars appear to be different colors because of interference in the atmosphere. Maybe it was my near-sightedness, but I'd never thought stars twinkled yellow and blue and the various other colors people assigned to them. I always thought they pretty much looked white, up there in the night sky. I supposed it was a limited existence, but I'd gotten used to it.

So the stars taking a clear bend toward amber struck me as noticeably odd. They left tracks in my vision, streaks of warm gold as I passed through them, and instead of the night getting darker it turned warmer and thicker, until I felt like I was struggling through honey. In time I stopped moving, wings straining to beat against the weight that held them, and the stars began to take shape.

They coalesced into a slow golden form, shining as brightly as Big Coyote's every hair did, though without the pinprick edge that made him seem more than real. Shoulders, hips, a mane of long hair; they were familiar to me, though I was used to seeing them in Little Coyote's normal colors, brick-red and black, not starlight and sable. Triumph should have welled in my breast, except my plan in finding Little Coyote had not included getting stuck in amber-laden stars. He was much, much larger than life, as if I was seeing him from a raven's point of view, and the expression he turned on me was sad and worried. I drew breath to tell him it was all right, when I realized how very all right it wasn't.

Night's blackness had butterfly eyes in it. All the hints and shapes of colors I'd seen in my dreams and visions, when I'd tried searching pulling Billy and then Mel out of sleep, when I'd drawn this demon toward Gary, finally resolved into something recognizable. I'd known the form without recognizing it; butterflies weren't something that I thought of as malicious, and the familiarity of form had simply slipped by me.

Little Coyote's hair, strung out through the sky like a spiderweb, was caught by indigo and violet spots, watching us. If I took my gaze away from the darkness and concentrated on Coyote, I could see the ripple of life that went through the watching eyes, like endless wings fluttering in a breeze I couldn't feel. Under different circumstances, the living night might have been overwhelmingly beautiful, traces of green and blue so dark they could hardly be seen washing through the empty spaces of sky. Instead, the feeling of being examined sent a stab of fear directly through the center of my power, beneath my breastbone. It hurt in an almost familiar way, like the cold of a silver blade being slammed through my chest.

For a painful, unfunny moment, laughter bubbled up

through that familiarity. Karmically speaking, it was probably less like having a sword shoved through me than a butterfly collector's pin. I focused hard on Coyote, afraid if I let that idea get too far out of hand I'd see a giant needle piercing me through. To my relief, I didn't see any such thing in Coyote's starry self, just an outline of sorrow and regret written in the stars. He'd told me to stay out of the ether. Just then it struck me that he might've had a good reason for doing that. I could feel amber hardening around me, sticking me in place, and behind my breastbone, the slow build of panicked power. My only thought was to release it like a grenade, a concussive explosion that might shatter the golden warmth that held us, but there were a number of problems with that plan.

First, I didn't know if my power could even be used that way. I remembered, as if through someone else's mind, an already-dead shaman telling me there was more than one path to be had, and that some shamans chose the warrior's path. The implication had been that that was the road I was expected to travel, and I could make an argument for it with my experiences thus far. Whether that meant I could go commando on a sleepy butterfly monster's ass was not a question I'd thought to cover in Shamanism 101.

Second, and somewhat more important, I had a sinking feeling that if I went the blow shit up route, Coyote and I would get blown up, too. That was the problem with grenades. They weren't picky about who they exploded. Coyote and I both knew how to shield ourselves, but me going kerblewy struck me as the psychic equivalent of friendly fire. It didn't really matter how friendly the fire was if it went off on your side of the barricade. I'd needed answers, but coming to Coyote to find them might very well have killed both of us, and now I didn't know how to get out of it.

We stared at each other across what felt like an impossible distance, the space between stars, and Coyote inclined his head, slow movement in the amber.

It looked horribly like a goodbye.

CHAPTER NINETEEN

I came awake with my heart sick in my throat and my ears ringing. My vision had streaks of golden stars in it, the aftermath of a rupture of power that looked like something I would do accidentally, not something my irritable guide would do deliberately. The butterfly darkness had swept over him so quickly it'd seemed to devour him, one moment his lanky form and starlit eyes saying goodbye and the next all the sarcasm and smart-mouthing drowned in blackness. My eyes burned and my chest hurt, like I was waiting for tears.

"Jo?" Gary crouched in front of me, a big mass of man that I could only see as an abstract shape, my gaze still focused on things that had happened in other worlds. "Jo," he said again, more urgently, then took a big breath and blew it in my face as if I were a baby screaming the last air from her lungs.

It worked just as effectively, too, making me drag in a

sharp, startled breath and blink, which went a long way toward relieving the pain in both my lungs and eyes. It did nothing for the sickness in my heart, though, and the second breath I took exited again as a shuddered, "Oh, God."

"What happened, Jo?" Gary's bushy eyebrows were drawn in concern and he had both hands on my shoulders, grip tight enough to hold me up. I diverted my gaze to him, still staring almost sightlessly, then leaned forward to wrap my arms around him and knot my hands in his shirt. I was afraid I might collapse if I let go. "Joanie? What the hell's goin' on, sweetheart?"

"I think Coyote just committed suicide to keep me safe." My belly knotted as I spoke and I lurched to my feet, scrambling for the bathroom. A minute later I wasn't sure if I was grateful to Gary or not, as it was largely his fault I had nothing in my stomach to heave up. I tried, anyway, stomach twisting and clenching as tears fell from my eyes. Gary followed me into the bathroom and crouched beside me again, waiting until I fell back against the bathtub before speaking.

"What happened, Jo?"

I wiped my hand over my mouth, shaking my head as tears rolled down my cheeks, my eyes still wide and aching. "I think it ate him. The bad thing. He let go this huge burst of power, and he was so tired before, Gary." I stared at the old man without quite seeing him, my whole body shaking with chills.

"He's a spirit guide, Jo. You think somebody like that can even get killed?" It was a genuine question, one I had no answer to. All I could do was shake my head.

"It felt like me, Gary. It felt like me fucking something up. I don't know what it's supposed to feel like when a spirit uses his power, but this felt like me telling the city to hit me with its best shot. It was everything. And the butterfly thing just…ate him. It jumped on him and just let me go." My stomach roiled again, but there'd been nothing for it to evict the first time. "I think he's dead. And it's my fault."

"Joanie…"

I had to be a mess if Gary kept calling me Joanie. I shook my head, still staring through him as I whispered, "I'm not taking blame where it doesn't belong, Gary. He didn't want me out there and I ignored him. That thing had me trapped and he chose to let it eat him instead of letting it take me."

"Chose to, Jo," Gary said quietly. "You keep tellin' me that's what shamanism's all about. Makin' choices."

I finally focused on him again, feeling bleakness carving itself into my face. "That doesn't make it any less my fault." There were so many recriminations to heap on my own head I could've stayed there for the rest of my life, paralyzed and shriveled by guilt and misery. I reached out to fumble the toilet lever down, washing away the spatters of bile I'd choked up, then used the bowl and the tub to push myself upward.

"Where're you goin'?"

"I don't know." I sounded like someone'd flattened me with a rolling pin and stabbed holes in what remained, to make sure I'd never rise properly again. "I've got to get somewhere I can think. I'll call you, Gary. I'll call in a while. I'm sorry."

I stumbled out of the apartment and down to my car. A

minute later she pulled out into five o'clock traffic, me feeling like she was steering herself.

Pretty much the last place I expected her to go was Thunderbird Falls.

I had to park along the road near Matthews Beach Park, as the parking lot itself was still a hopscotch of fallen land and broken pavement. There were boards up over the deeper and wider crevasses, and the yellow danger tape spread everywhere was torn and cut away, left to rustle in the evening breeze. I made my way through the mess left of the lot, watching my feet instead of the passersby. There were more of them than I expected, given the area had been cordoned off two weeks ago and was still supposed to be unused. No one in the neighborhood seemed to be taking that seriously, voices raised in good nature and kids running about, leaping over the cuts in the earth as if they didn't exist. Evidence of the earthquake that had torn Lake Washington's western side was everywhere, and people were just going about their lives without concern despite that. It was as if the magic that had been thrust into Seattle's atmosphere a few weeks earlier had sluffed off, putting everything back to normal. If someone had not just died for me, I might have taken comfort in feeling I wasn't making irrevocable changes to strangers' lives.

Instead, I felt like something worse than panic had taken hold inside me. It felt cold and resolute, the feeling of despair tangled with destiny. Coyote'd died for me. Colin and Faye had died because of me. I would be God damned if I was going to lose anybody else on my watch. I wished my newfound resolution felt good, but it only felt like some-body'd sealed over my emotions with lead piping and was waiting for my body to realize my soul was dead. Spiderweb cracks slid through my vision, a windshield shattered. My soul hadn't notified my body of its pathetic, miserable state for half my life. I'd been used to feeling cut off. I'd have thought feeling that way again would be comforting.

There were more voices down at the falls than I expected, doing something that sounded suspiciously like chanting. Sunlight caught a glitter on something gold and metallic through the trees, and I slowed down. It wasn't like I'd intended to come here. It'd been my car's idea. I was going to have to rename her Kitt.

For some reason my feet kept moving me forward while I peered ahead of myself, uncomfortably certain of what I'd see once I got clear of the boardwalks and wooden steps that made hash of what had once been treed waterfront. I could hear the stream made by the falls, and wondered briefly what people were calling it. Probably not *Jo's Hand's Stream*. I kept catching mere glimpses of people ahead of me, as if the sunlight was helping them deliberately evade my sight. They winked in and out of my vision as if they didn't quite belong in this world, and by the time I got to the bottom of the board-walk, I wasn't sure they did.

Not that they were Otherworldly. They were perfectly human, all of them, even the guy wearing white robes and a beard down to his belly button. He was behind a set of skin drums broad enough to be heard halfway across Seattle, but rumbled them so quietly I didn't realize I'd been hearing them until I saw him playing. I came to a stop, still standing on the boardwalk, and looked over what I automatically and uncharitably categorized as an enormous group of long-haired hippie freaks.

There were several dozen of them, women in long skirts with long hair, men in bell-bottom jeans and tie-dyed shirts. There were also a fair number of incredibly normal-looking people mixed in with them, but even the ones wearing slacks and button-down shirts looked too damned cheerful to fit into my idea of natural behavior. They were mingling, laughing, chatting, waving their hands passionately as they disagreed without venom. They stood together in groups or pairs, no one alone at a single glance, though a second look showed me individuals sitting or standing in meditation, apparently consumed with personal joy that required no sharing.

Even without the sight triggered I could practically see their auras, glowing with good-naturedness and excitement. The air tingled with it, as if people were doing—

I brushed my hand over my eyes, knowing when I lowered it, I would see in two worlds. *As if people were doing magic, Joanne.* I finished the thought forcibly, and dropped my hand.

Right at the foot of the falls, there was a group weaving power together, a delicate construction that took form before my eyes. I could see where it was going, and it was going to be beautiful: an arch that would rise over the edge of the fallen lake, fifteen or twenty feet into the air, made of starlight and sunlight. Glimmers of a thunderbird were already in place at its apex, like a sign of welcome to anyone with eyes to see it.

And it was clear nearly everyone here had those eyes.

Power, far more than the eleven coven members had shared, was palpable here. It strengthened auras and built on itself, like static charges from winter-dry wool. The earth itself announced its presence, torn and battered as it was: magic had been done here, and had left its mark. These pleasant, joyful people had been drawn here by power I'd laid down. By mistakes I'd made. And they were glad of it, the whole area having the sense of a giant coming-out party. They weren't pretending or hoping or hiding, for the most part. They were there to share themselves, their experience, their lives that they'd tried to live quietly, for fear people like me would stare and call them crazy.

These were my people.

I sat down on the boardwalk and put my face in my hands, less to hide the activity from my gaze than to wrap my mind around that appalling idea. These were my people. The men and women who'd gathered here, at the site of my battle with an ancient, deadly serpent, were the ones who would believe in me and in what I could do without fail and without hesitation. They would accept me as one of their own, and very probably revere me if they figured out I was the one who'd shared skin with the thunderbird. The idea was horrifying.

"Joanne?"

I knew the woman's voice and wasn't entirely surprised to hear it here. It still took a few moments to lift my head and look up to find Marcia Williams standing before me. She was in her fifties, the lines of wisdom around her mouth now more deeply etched with sorrow. She'd held the position of the Crone in the coven I'd been a part of for a few days. Her power, genuine and pale in its colors, washed around her as she offered a sad smile and took a seat beside me on the boardwalk. "I wondered if you'd come here," she said. "I wondered if it would draw you back."

"How is everyone?"

"Thomas is here. The others—" Marcia spread her hands in a shrug. "They may never come back," she admitted. "I've thought about staying away myself."

"But you're here." It was a question, and Marcia heard it as one, spreading her hands again.

"My life has been dedicated to the Goddess, Joanne. We made…terrible mistakes, but I believe She can and will and does, forgive us. I can't walk away from my faith out of fear, not now. Maybe especially not now." She was silent a moment, then said, "You're also here."

"You noticed that, huh? Look at them." I nodded at the gathered magic-users, knowing I was avoiding Marcia's own implied question. "I don't know what to make of them. A lot of power and arrogance, used blindly, made the falls and a mess of the land here, and they've found it and they're just so damned happy. I don't know what to make of it."

Marcia cupped her hands together, wrapping her fingers in the opposite palms to make a kind of yin-yang. "Nature prefers balance, Joanne. If our arrogance created this place, then maybe it's meant to be used as a place of healing and joy. It becomes the balance."

"Our." I looked up at her, absurdly grateful for that.

"We're rarely alone, Joanne. Even in our worst moments,

we're rarely alone." She touched my shoulder, gave me a sad smile and walked away to join the throng of people.

Leaving me alone.

I didn't know how much time had passed when I got up again. The sun still colored the horizon, but sunset came late in Seattle in July. My second sight stayed on, astounding neons and shimmering enthusiasm of growing things helped me breathe a little easier. One of the things I didn't like to admit was how much I loved the crazy, vivid world I saw through the second sight. It made me feel as though I'd been wearing blinders all my life, and when I lost control of the sight and the blinders came back on, it was like I'd lost something important. I was grateful for its cooperation right now, even if I hadn't really intended to call it up. Driving with it on turned out to be a lot easier than driving with my vision inversed.

It was after eight by the time I got to the precinct building. The parking lot was worryingly empty, and the garage, when I skulked down in hopes of finding comfort there, was worse. I'd never seen it so quiet, its usual din replaced by the noise of fluorescent lights buzzing overhead. They were loud enough to give me a headache, and I wondered how I'd never noticed them before. I sat down on the bottom step leading into the garage and stared at the echoing room. Even its sense of purpose seemed faded without any of the mechanics there. I'd felt the garage's force before, an animation of color that wasn't exactly sentient, but knew it existed and why. Seeing it drained so badly made me feel even more alienated from myself than I already did.

"Depressing, isn't it?"

I turned my head, only unsurprised because I didn't seem to be able to feel any particular emotion. Thor came down the steps and sat down beside me, his shoulder brushing mine. "It's not quite as bad upstairs. Not good, but not this empty. I'm the only one left down here."

"You're the only one who wasn't in my dream." My voice was dull. "What're you still doing here?"

"You said that earlier, about the dream. What're you talking about?" He shrugged a little. "I don't know. There were a lot of cars to work on today, even with so many people out. I guess I just wanted to try to keep up. Stupid, huh?"

"No. It's something to do. So you don't feel so helpless." I knew exactly what that felt like, but I hadn't yet pulled the rabbit out of my hat. I was still useless. "Thank you." The words came out abruptly and I shifted my shoulders, feeling my shirt brush against Thor's again, cotton grabbing. "For helping me in March when my eardrums exploded. I never said thank you."

"You're welcome. I think you paid me back." He leaned back to slide a hand into his pocket—he was wearing jeans and a T-shirt instead of the mechanic's uniform the department issued—and came out with the piece of topaz. I glanced at it, glowing warm in his hand, then at him, getting an eyeful of aura that brought a faint smile to my lips.

"You really are a thunder god." He was all stormy grays and deep blues, shot by streaks of bright silver, like lightning. Some of the turmoil that darkened his colors was from the absence of our coworkers. *His* coworkers, I had to remind myself. I didn't belong down in the garage anymore. I didn't have enough in me to find the thought as miserable as I once would've, and tried focusing on Thor's colors again to take my mind off that and everything else. I imagined there'd normally be less stress discoloring the colors, but even so, they suited the nickname I'd given him to a wonderful degree.

"Do I want to know what that means?"

I shook my head and looked back at the garage. "Probably not." I felt, more than saw, his frown, and was completely taken aback when he reached out and turned my face toward him again. His eyebrows were drawn down with curiosity.

"What color are your eyes?"

"Green. Hazel. Why?"

"Hazel," he repeated after a moment. "Yeah, I guess."

I sighed and moved my face out of his touch, closing my eyes. "They look gold right now, don't they."

"Yeah. I guess I can see the green in them from here—" I felt the warmth of his hand as he reached for my chin again, and looked back at him in bewilderment. People didn't go around touching me that casually, unless it was to sock me on the shoulder in a one-of-the-guys routine. He'd sat up and his face was closer to mine than I was used to a man's being. Nerves cramped my stomach, the closeness seeming uncomfortably intimate, but I didn't know how to get away without being obvious to the point of rudeness. "—but if I were more than ten inches away I'd think your eyes were gold. Kinda cool. I've only met a couple of people with gold eyes before." He sat back again, releasing me from the tête-a-tête without seeming to notice it himself.

"I don't think I've met anybody with gold eyes." Except

Coyote. Misery swept up unexpectedly and seized me by the throat, shattering the cold that had settled on me for a little while. I stood up fast enough to be rude after all, reaching for the railing. "I'm sorry. I've got to get going, go do some things." Action, moving forward purposefully, was the only thing I thought would get me through the next few days without wanting to die myself. If it could keep emotion at bay long enough, I could find a way to deal with Coyote's death and the butterfly thing that had killed him. I could break down after that, or better yet, just build up that wall of cold until I didn't feel the need to cry anymore.

"Yeah, I guess you probably do." Thor didn't sound offended as he squinted up at me, and twisted to watch me walk stiffly up the stairs. "Hey, Joanne."

I looked back, taken off guard. He'd never called me by name before, and I'd half expected him to have a nickname for me as obnoxious as the *Thor* I'd saddled him with.

"I said maybe we'd see each other at a club sometime...."

I felt my back muscles tighten, like I was waiting to take a hit. "Yeah. Don't worry about it. I don't go out much."

"Yeah, you said that, so I thought maybe I'd better make it a specific sometime. I've got tickets for an Alan Claussen gig at the end of the month. You want to go?" Silver shot through his aura, looking like hope.

I thought of Coyote's last gambit, the burst of sheer orange and blue power that had broken me free, and wondered if I had any right to go ahead and go on with my life when everything I'd done with it so far had been to fuck up in one dramatic fashion or another. I opened my mouth to say no, and Thor saw it, disappointment dimming the silver streaks to gray.

You gotta balance things out, Jo. The way you go ain't healthy. Gary's words came back to me and I tightened my fingers around the railing. Punishing myself wasn't going to bring Coyote back. Trying to maintain the damaged hermitdom I'd imposed on myself was a hundred percent counter to what he'd wanted me to do. It shouldn't take people dying to get me to pay attention, but if it did, I was goddamned well going to listen.

"Yeah," I heard myself say, very quietly. "I'd like that. Thanks."

Surprise lit his face like a sunbeam and Thor waved me off, smiling broadly. "Awesome. We'll talk about it later. Go save the world."

CHAPTER TWENTY

That wasn't the first time a good-looking man had given me a *go save the world* send-off. It wasn't even the first time today. I could feel my usual sarcastic litany running through the back of my mind, things like, *that can't be a good sign,* and *it's clear the world is in a lot more trouble than words can summarize if it needs somebody like me to be its savior.* I usually enjoyed wallowing in that kind of woe-is-me patter.

Right now I was so disgusted with myself I wondered how I'd ever gotten any relief from it. That I couldn't stop it from nattering on made a bad taste in my mouth, bitter and sharp enough that I felt like I was holding back vomit. I could even feel it in the way I held my face, as if what I really needed to do was get to a bathroom and spit out a mouthful of nastiness. I was still holding my mouth that way when I walked into Morrison's office.

He was in the midst of shrugging a jacket on, and for the

first time in history he said, "What's wrong?" instead of berating me or looking frustrated that I was still around. I ignored him and got a cup of water from his cooler and washed the dredges of coffee out of my mouth, then sat without answering. Morrison stared at me, then slid the jacket off again and came around his desk, leaning on it as he folded his arms and looked at me. Concern flashed through his aura, dark patches in colors already blackened by stress.

Part of me admired how fast I'd adapted to seeing auras. Half an hour of it and it hardly seemed worth mentioning anymore. The rest of me just sat there and gave the button above Morrison's belt a thousand-mile stare, like it might turn out to be hiding the secrets of the universe. It was more likely hiding Morrison's belly button. For a few seconds I was actually grateful for my mind's idiotic tangents while I tried to remember where standard-cut men's waistlines hit the waist in relation to a standard-man's belly button, and decided that yes, probably the first button above the belt was about right.

The jeans Mark wore rode considerably lower than that.

I crumpled the water cup and put my hand over my eyes, beads of water making like tears down my cheeks. "How many more?"

Morrison was so quiet I thought he hadn't understood my question. I'd just about convinced myself to look at him when he said, just as abruptly, "By the end of the day it'd piled up to a quarter of the force. Some of their families, too."

"Like Melinda." Not that Mel was really a good example, as she and I had been mystically involved. Which sounded like the sort of thing a person might call a 1-900 number for. Great. I didn't know how I was going to break it to Billy that I'd been having an illicit psychic affair with his wife while he slept, but I'd give just about anything for the chance.

"Like Melinda," Morrison agreed, blissfully unaware of my unfortunate internal monologue. I had a brief moment of envying him. At least he could get away from me. I didn't like me very much right now, and I was stuck with me twenty-four/seven. "You all right, Walker?"

"Fine." I dropped my hand, fingers still curled loosely around the cup, and looked at the jacket he'd left on his chair. "You're here late. I'm keeping you. You have plans." I wasn't sure if that last was a question or not. Morrison took it as one, nodding.

"Dinner."

"Sorry. I'll get out of your hair." I got up and Morrison stepped into my path. I was wearing sneakers, so he had the very slightest height advantage, less than half an inch. Nobody else would've noticed it, but we both did. I wanted to take a step backward to make it less obvious, but there was a chair behind my knees. Morrison knew perfectly well he was in my personal space and didn't have the slightest intention of moving out of it, so I just waited, looking that all-important fraction of an inch up at him.

"Talk to me, Walker. You look like your best friend just died."

"No." An image flashed through my line of vision, a petite pretty girl with hair like buckwheat, thick and straight and long. For some reason I could see her aura, too, though I certainly hadn't been able to thirteen years ago. It was tight against her skin, bubbling with wrath, just as her expression was full of rage. She'd been the only person who'd ever called me *best friend,* until I'd gone and slept with a boy she'd said she didn't like. "Just a friend." Butterfly-winged blackness swept Sara Buchanan's memory away as easily as it'd swallowed Coyote, and for an instant I wanted to thank the nightmare thing for taking away that image.

Morrison wouldn't step out of the way, his mouth tight with concern. "Who?"

"Coyote. My…it doesn't matter, Morrison. He's dead because I screwed up again. He got caught in whatever's making people sleep, and if he can be dead, other people are going to be, too, so I just need to get out of here and do my job. I just came by to see how bad it was today."

"Walker," Morrison said again, this time as if the name was insufficient. I debated telling him my first name was Joanne and he could try it out for size, but I had the very real feeling that would lead right back around to a discussion of *Siobhán Walkingstick,* and I didn't want to talk about her. "Coyote is your spirit guide, isn't he?" It was barely a question, and I wanted to know how he knew that and what it cost to ask, but not enough to pursue it. I closed my eyes and turned my head to the side.

"Yeah. Or he was. Now he's dead."

"I wouldn't think a spirit guide was something you could kill." Morrison was treading on very thin ice, the words strained, and the only reason he was doing it was for me. I looked at him and wondered what he'd do if I curled myself against his chest and held on. I didn't even think I had it in me to cry. I just wanted to be somewhere safe for a little while, and Captain Michael Morrison's arms seemed like the safest place in the world right then.

"Walker," he said, one more time, and sighed.

I was actually changing my weight to damn the torpedoes and step closer to him when his office door opened and Barbara Bragg walked in.

Had there not been a chair immediately behind me I probably would have leapt back like a guilty puppy to put distance between myself and my boss. As it was, I had to clench my stomach muscles to keep from simply falling into the chair.

Morrison, who neither shared my guilty conscience nor, very likely, any half-formed fantasies about sweeping me protectively into his arms, glanced toward the door and smiled. "Barbara. I'd like you to meet Officer Joanne Walker. Walker, this is Barbara Bragg." He stepped away from me easily, making space for Barbara and me to shake hands.

She came forward, giving me a smile sunny enough to make Kewpie dolls look dour. She wore another sundress, different from last night's, but just as becoming to her. It had capped sleeves, and I found myself staring at her left shoulder, where the butterfly tattoo was hidden. She and Mark both had one, all vibrant dark colors like the ones that haunted the nightmares. My heart started pounding too hard, heat burning my jaw and working its way toward my cheeks.

"We met again at Contour last night. How are you doing, Joanne?" Barbara's eyebrows drew down, concern making fine lines on her forehead. "We were all pretty worried about you." She put her hand out, and I took it automatically, braced for a wash of darkness.

She clasped my hand in both of hers as if she genuinely was concerned, and also possibly a close friend, but there was no dangerous hint of power in her touch. I pulled my gaze from her shoulder to our hands, then up to her eyes, tongue-tied with confusion and trying to figure out how to extract myself from her grasp without being rude.

"Contour?" There was slightly too much incredulity in Morrison's voice. I felt like I should be insulted, except, frankly, I thought it was as unlikely as he did. "What happened?"

Whether he was asking what had happened at Contour to worry Barbara, or what unlikely event had transpired to get me to a dance club, I never got a chance to answer. Barb turned back to him with a teasing smile. "It's a club, Michael. Stop looking so dour. I *will* get you to come out dancing with me, so you might as well accept it now."

Morrison looked as though he couldn't conceive of that idea any more than the idea of me going out dancing. I was with him on that, but Barb continued on merrily, stepping back to Morrison's side.

"Joanne had—" she cast a quick glance at me, as if she was verifying the accuracy of what she was about to say, but barreled on without any actual input from me "—a little fainting spell. Probably dehydration," she said, attention back to me now. I felt slightly dizzy, like sunshine was sweeping back and forth from me to Morrison, pouring radiant enthusiasm at us in turn without particular regard as to whether we were prepared for it. "You did drink most of a fifth of Johnnie Walker Monday night," she pointed out. "If you didn't hydrate yourself properly after that, going out dancing last night would do you right in."

Even her aura was as cheerful as her chatter, spinning through every other color of the rainbow as I watched. There was nothing sleepy about her at all, no languid dark power to taint her smile or her touch. The butterfly on her shoulder was probably nothing more than an impulsive joy in pretty things, although I had no idea why Mark would have an identical one. That was actively bizarre. Barb smiled at me, and I had the sudden awful feeling that I would probably like this woman if she weren't hanging on Morrison's arm.

Or maybe if Morrison wasn't smiling down at her with a delight I couldn't remember ever seeing on his face before. Then again, usually when I was around, there was a specific reason for him not to be delighted. Today was no different. My stomach hurt. I looked away as Barbara squeezed Morrison's arm, then stepped back. "You're already late leaving work," she said a bit sternly, and I had the even more horrible feeling that she might be *good* for my boss, if she wasn't going to let him get away with working too many hours even after two days' acquaintance. I swallowed and tried to imagine away the burning at the back of my eyes. I was being ridiculous. Over-emotional. "But if I'm inter-rupting a meeting I'll give you a few more minutes, okay? Dinner reservations are for eight-thirty, though, so we leave in five minutes."

"Not at all." Morrison went around his desk to get his jacket. "Officer Walker and I were just finishing up."

Barbara turned her half rainbow of good cheer on me again, interest lighting her eyes. "Oh, well then. Are you on shift, Joanne? No, you must not be," she added, taking in my tank top and jeans. "Why don't you come along with us? I'll call Mark and he can meet us at the restaurant. We can all get to know one another."

Morrison shot me a look of abject horror over Barbara's

head. For once I was in complete accordance with him. I made a stiff jerking motion, encompassing her sundress and Morrison's suit, though the latter was tired from a day of heat, and said, "Oh, I, I—" I hadn't managed to say a word since she'd come into the office, and my first vocal foray didn't exactly cover me with glory. "I'm not dressed for it." Morrison's dismay faded, then leapt into relief again as Barbara sniffed.

"Nonsense. I'll tell Mark to dress down a bit and it'll be fine. Everybody talks about the relaxed dress code up here in the Pacific Northwest, anyway. I'll call the restaurant and change the reservations to four." She swept out the door, opening her purse to retrieve her cell phone as she went.

Morrison and I stood there staring at one another. I wanted to say something funny, not that I could remember easily amusing my boss. It seemed, though, like there ought to be something I could say. All that came out was, "Sorry."

Morrison flinched. "Barb's persuasive." He followed her out, leaving me to trail behind.

"Persuasive." Mark echoed the word at the end of the story with a laugh. "Barb's a bulldozer." He elbowed her, earning a mimed throw of the olive from her drink in return. We'd ended up with the pairs who knew each other best sitting next to each other: me and Morrison on one side of the table, Mark across from me and Barb across from my boss. Presumably that allowed us to focus on the person most important to us. I could smell Morrison's cologne when he moved.

"Barb the bulldozer," Mark repeated happily. His colors were an astounding complementary mix to Barb's, all the opposite colors of the rainbow. When they laughed together, their auras jumped up and spun into a breathtaking light display. "That's my big sister. Well, I'm glad, Joanne."

I twitched, focus torn away from their entwining auras. "What? Oh. Yeah." I retrieved a smile and pasted it on. "Big sister?" That was probably the wrong thing to say when a guy said he was glad to go out on a date with you, but the people who were having fun at this table were not Officer Joanne Walker and Captain Michael Morrison. Barb and Mark Bragg hadn't seemed to notice.

"Seventeen minutes older," Barb said triumphantly. "That makes me the boss of him."

"And she never lets me forget it," Mark said, full of mock despair. Morrison and I caught each other giving the other guarded looks, establishing that this was news to both of us.

"Twins?" I asked more than a little inanely. That was me, super-cop. They both laughed, sending their auras whirling together again in a rainbow of colors. Twins certainly explained that, anyway. It also explained the identical tattoos. I slid down in my chair, less happy than I thought I might be at clearing the Braggs of any likely connection with the sleeping sickness. At least if Barb was evil I'd have a legitimate reason not to like her. Instead, the more she talked, the more I felt like a jerk for hating her straight off.

"Identical," Mark said, pulling his face straight. Morrison chuckled, a quiet sound, and I managed another smile, nodding.

"I can tell. All night I've been trying to figure out which one of you I was supposed to be playing footsies with." I had no idea where that'd come from, but it got laughter from Mark and Barb. Morrison shot me a startled look. Mark leaned forward, lowering his voice conspiratorially.

"What, can't you tell with, you know." A subtle eyebrow waggle suggested I was supposed to pick up on what *you know* was, but he wasn't sure everybody else at the table was in on my shamanic practices. I sighed and flipped my fingers out, indicating a go-ahead. Morrison already knew. One more person thinking I was a weirdo wasn't going to change the balance of my life. Barb leaned in curiously, and Mark put his elbows on the table to announce, with obvious relish, "Joanne's a shaman."

Her eyebrows shot up. Morrison exhaled quietly, a sigh that probably nobody but me heard. I didn't look at him. "Really," Barb said, then straightened up as the waiter came by with glasses of water and our menus. As soon as he was gone she folded her menu into her lap and leaned forward, all interested eyes and enthusiasm. "What's that about, really? I mean, magic, right? You do magic?" Her voice was full of lightness. I couldn't tell if it was laughter or teasing or humoring me, though I assumed all of it had a fair degree of mockery in it. Still, I was going to have to find a way to deal with this one way or another. No time like the present to start. Poor Morrison. I sighed, a half-conscious echo of his expression.

"It's about healing. Magic." My smile felt half-assed. "I'm really not all that comfortable with it. Normal people don't do magic."

"Oh, I don't know," Barb said in evident seriousness. "I think it kind of depends on how you look at magic. When Mark and I were driving up here we went by Wild Horse Monument, out in eastern Washington. Have you been there?"

To my utter surprise, a little something loosened in my

chest for the first time since I'd woken up from Coyote's sacrifice. It hurt, like cracking a scab you didn't know was there, both a relief and painful at once. From that break came a smile that bordered on tears. "Actually, yeah. I drove by it when I came to Washington, too. It's amazing." I'd glanced out my window to see horses on a cliff top, and pulled Petite over so I could scale the hill and stand in the midst of an iron herd, larger than life as they charged recklessly toward the edge of the cliff. The leading stallion had a wild abandon to him, as if in recognizing death he embraced it. I'd stood up there among them for hours, watching shadows bring them to life as the sun moved through the sky.

"Tell me that isn't magic," Barb said triumphantly. I laughed, a rough sound that went along with the tightness in my chest, and shook my head.

"I can't."

Barb sat back, smug. "See? I think it's all over, if you want to see it. So healing. Does that mean you can help the people who are going to sleep?"

"I'm trying." I found myself looking at Morrison.

"The topaz works as a charm against the sleeping sickness," I heard myself add. Morrison's expression went indecipherable.

"Good," he said after a moment. "I gave that piece to Barb."

CHAPTER TWENTY—ONE

I'd thought the wall of cold that had come down over me was going to be a permanent fixture. It turned out to have nothing on sheer, irrational jealousy. The muscles in my neck creaked audibly as I turned my head to stare at Barbara, who showed no signs of understanding the mortal danger she was in. I was much bigger and stronger than she was. I could probably claw her eyes out before Morrison could stop me.

She smiled brilliantly and tilted over, scooping her purse up from the floor so she could dig through it and moments later display the piece of topaz I'd given Morrison. It wasn't a remarkable piece of topaz, except that it was supposed to be his and he was most definitely not supposed to have given it to her. "I love topaz," Barbara was saying happily. "It's my favorite stone. Our birthstone," she said to Mark, as if he didn't know, and he grinned and nodded. "I really didn't expect Michael to give it to me, but I noticed it on his desk this afternoon when I dropped by to ask if he'd like to go out to dinner. So it's magical? How does it work?"

I heard everything she said through heavy static, my ears and cheekbones so hot I thought they must be glowing. Even my vision was fuzzy, white noise buzzing around the edges of it as I stared furiously at the stone in Barbara's palm. I wanted to snatch it up and throw it at her or at Morrison or through a window. In fact, I jolted like I might do that, a violent spasm that knocked my knuckles against the table. The spike of pain sent me shooting to my feet, full of clumsiness and blind anger. My chair fell over behind me with a noisy clatter, a pool of silence rippling out around us in the restaurant.

Normally that would only last an instant before the usual sounds of dining reasserted themselves. Not so with me as a focal point, misbehaving in public. My stomach muscles trembled from being held so tight. The whole restaurant seemed to inhale expectantly, waiting to see what happened. Mark pushed his chair back, concerned, and Morrison came half out of his seat, angry perplexity at my display written across his face. I still felt heat in my cheeks, but my hands were icy and I felt like the color had drained from my face, leaving me with an expression of childish injury. Morrison reached for my elbow and I jerked away hard enough to pull myself a step back.

That step proved my betrayal, undoing whatever it was that bound me in place. I whipped around and bolted for the door, smashing my thigh into the corner of someone's table as I ran. A hard knot of pain formed in the muscle as silverware jangled and glasses crashed over. Morrison shouted, "Walker!" and I threw a raspy apology at the diners, breaking for the door again. In all the horrible silence of everybody watching drama unfold, I heard Morrison mutter an apology at Barbara and come after me. I slammed my shoulder on the door frame on the way out, half clumsiness and half punishing myself for something I barely understood.

I got to Petite before Morrison caught up with me, shaking hands fumbling the keys repeatedly. My heart hammered so badly it hurt, taking up all the room in my chest so I couldn't get any air, and the only clear thought I could form was that I didn't want to scratch Petite's paint job with my shaking hands and key.

Morrison put his hand on my shoulder. Confusion, anger, concern all flared in the touch, tainting the purples and blues of his aura. I felt it all the way through me, the same bright agonizing definition of things around me that I'd experienced when he'd picked up my drum and played it.

Under the circumstances, it was an unforgivable intimacy.

I turned around and threw a punch, catching him in the chest with a meaty *thwock*. My keys, folded into my fist, cut into my fingers, and that, like the knot in my thigh and crashing into the door, was better than the hurt that squeezed my chest until I couldn't breathe. Morrison staggered back, more from surprise than the power of the blow, and I dropped my keys to grab his shirt in both fists.

"Do you just not get it, Morrison? Are you just totally failing to comprehend that I'm trying to protect you? Do you think sheer blind arrogance and ignoring what's going on is going to get you through it unscathed?" I let him go with a shove, taking the step with him so I could stay right in his face. "Let me tell you that I've learned the hard way that *it doesn't work.* I know you don't want to believe it. *I* don't want to believe it, but goddamn it, Morrison, you've got to be smarter than I am, and even I'm finally listening."

My grip on the second sight slid off somewhere in my outrage, so the only way I could tell Morrison was building up a head of steam was the way his face darkened into a dangerous shade of red, instead of watching his aura do the same. I jerked my hand at his throat as if I'd cut his words off before he spoke, and it seemed to work. He inhaled, but didn't yell.

Maybe that was because I wasn't giving him a chance to get a word in edgewise. I'd backed him up another several steps, until he hit a row of hedges. Once he did, he didn't lean away from me or move forward, just stood his ground while I shouted. "This sickness is killing people, Morrison! It killed Coyote!" I slapped my palm against his chest, not quite the outright punch I'd thrown before, but enough to cause a sharp crack of sound and a sting in my hand. "You think you're special? I promise you, you're not! That goddamned piece of stone is supposed to keep you safe while I try to figure out how to fix all the crap I've fucked up. I need you to have that rock, Morrison, because how am I supposed to do my job if I'm worrying about you? Sure, great, you gave the fucking thing to a beautiful woman, guess that makes you a real hero, doesn't it? Just like you're supposed to be, the handsome cop saving the girl. Good for goddamned you, Morrison, but what the hell am I supposed to do if something happens to you? I'm trying to *protect* you, Morrison, because I don't know what—"

I finally broke off, my anger going cold and lonely as the rest of that sentence finished itself in my head. Morrison was florid, his jaw set and eyes blazing with fury. At least a couple dozen people from the restaurant had come out to watch me berate my boss, including Mark and Barbara. Barb had her hands over her mouth, eyes wide with distress, and Mark stood with his gaze cast down, as if he couldn't watch or look away, either. A bunch of others looked delighted, the thrill-seeking sons of bitches. Some of them were clearly embarrassed for the people causing the commotion, and a little of that started to sink through my stomach-churning emotion.

"Are you done?" Morrison asked, so softly I was surprised I could even hear it, for all I was only standing three inches away. I turned my head to the side and pressed my lips together, embarrassment and anger welling up in equal parts. After a couple of seconds I nodded and Morrison took one abrupt step forward that sent me back a couple of steps.

"I'm going to cut you some slack, Walker, because a friend of yours just died." The quiet rage in my boss's voice was about a thousand times worse than the shouting I'd gotten used to. "But if you *ever*. So much as *think*. About throwing another punch my way, I will have you up on assault charges so fast your head will spin, and I am goddamned good and certain that your bag of tricks doesn't hold a get-out-of-jail-free card. Do I make myself perfectly clear, Officer Walker?"

Blood curdled in my face, so thick and painful I wanted to cry just from the weight of the blush. I nodded twice, stiff motions, then forced, "Yes, sir," through still-compressed lips.

Morrison didn't say anything else. He just turned away from me and went back to Barbara and Mark. I heard him making apologies to them, to the restaurant staff, to everyone, while I stood there like an unstrung marionette, my heart beating so hard in my throat I thought I would be sick. Mark broke away from the others and approached me. I shook my head before he got close enough to speak, and then did it again, lifting my palm to ward him away. It was a nice gesture on his part. I could almost feel sympathy and unhappiness coming off him. I just didn't want to even try explaining myself just then. After a few seconds I saw his shoulders slump, and he turned away, joining the breaking crowd in returning to the restaurant.

Only when I was more or less alone in the parking lot did I wet cracked lips and whisper, "Because I don't know what I'd do without you," to the empty pavement.

My skin had gone numb, sometime between my breaking off and Morrison dressing me down. My head was hollow and my ears were ringing, eyes too dry and mouth sticky. I knew myself well enough to feel like I ought to have some witty rejoinders, a way to blow off what I'd just admitted to myself with a sarcastic comment or two. Instead I stood there staring at the pavement. I had the idea that finding a sword to fall on was probably the appropriate thing to do. It was what I'd do if I were the heroine of a Chinese film, having just confessed to the unreachable hero that I was in lo—

My own self-censorship wouldn't even let me finish that thought. I supposed the only small thing preventing me from having to throw myself on a sword was the fact I hadn't actually made an idiot of myself in front of Morrison.

Boy. Some things sure were relative. I hadn't made an idiot of myself over that particular topic in front of Morrison, to be somewhat more accurate. Besides, seppuku was for people with moral resolve, not windshield-shattered police mechanics whose mystical backgrounds were catching up to them. I wondered how long I might've gone on, able to deny to myself what was obvious, if Coyote hadn't interfered with what would have been an otherwise very dramatic death seven months earlier.

There was a flaw in that thought process, but I didn't want anybody pointing it out to me, not even me.

It wasn't as if I hadn't known what was going on behind Melinda or Gary's sideways smiles when my tongue got tangled up over Morrison, but hunching up and looking away had worked as a denial method. Besides, there were half a million good reasons to not think about it, starting with the screamingly obvious one: he was my *boss*.

He also didn't like me very much, didn't like my gifts at all and knew nothing about cars. In no way was it a match made in heaven, or even by a canny matchmaker planning to rake in her profit for arranging an unlikely marriage. Kate and Petruchio, comparatively, were a sure thing.

I could almost feel thoughts whirling around in my head, like I was deliberately trying to keep them on the surface, nice and superficial. It seemed like a very me thing to do, which in and of itself made me uncomfortable. I didn't particularly like being aware of my emotional status. I especially didn't like being aware and suspecting it was equivalent to the maturity level of your average turnip.

"Siobhán."

No one but Morrison knew to call me that name, and he had already left. The voice wasn't his, anyway, and it repeated "Siobhán" after a few moments' delay.

I tried to put my hand over my throat but couldn't. The voice wasn't mine, either, but I thought it was me talking. I turned around in the parking lot, looking to see who was there, and discovered I wasn't in the parking lot at all.

Stars, distant and meaningless, surrounded me in a place between worlds and dreams. They went on just less than forever, to a horizon so distant it made me feel insignificant. I stood among the blackness and the stars, comfortable with it: I'd traveled there an uncountable number of times already, though this was the first time I'd made the journey on my own. It was dangerous in the way any new territory was dangerous. An unwise show of power could attract things that were never meant to find fragile humans, but a judicious asking could as easily call up protectors for that same delicate psyche. My own protector danced around me even now, lithe and furry and looking for a chance to cause trouble.

Not trouble, I chastised myself, or thought I did. It could as well have been Coyote, shaking his golden head at me. He never caused trouble, only learning opportunities. Who did the learning was beside the point, and the fact that he never seemed to learn himself even more so.

"Welcome, Siobhán," I said one more time, and finally someone else appeared in the Dead Zone. A girl I knew, all elbows and knees, her black hair cropped short in defiance of the big bangs and perms that were stylish when she was that age. She was more than half asleep, a frown etched between her eyebrows, and she glowered at me suspiciously.

I offered out a brick-red hand and smiled. "This is where it begins. Brightness of body, brightness of soul."

A doorway opened up in my mind.

CHAPTER TWENTY-TWO

I fell through myself and memory and dreams until I was no longer capable of telling up from down or me from him. In every room of memory a brick-red boy waited, golden eyes bright and cheerful while I argued with him. I was thirteen and gawky and even I knew shamans didn't just *happen.* You had to do a spirit quest and be guided and be prepared to focus yourself on the good of the community. I barely knew what a community was, much less had any interest in making it healthy. I felt distant and sullen even contemplating it. I was new to North Carolina at that age, still the outsider, and the part of me that wanted desperately to fit in was overridden by the part that just didn't know how. I never had figured it out.

"That's why I'm here," Coyote said over and over again,

showing patience far beyond his apparent years. I could see him through my own eyes, a brick-red young man of about eighteen with hair past his shoulders, long and gleaming blue-black in the darkness. The part of my mind able to think about it thought that made sense. A prepubescent girl was more likely to respond positively to an eighteen-year-old knockout than a thirty-something...well. Knockout. Coyote in any form was beautiful, bequeathed with the striking features that seemed par for the course when it came to otherworldly beings. But watching him now had a peculiar echo to it, as if what I saw was somehow being filtered through more than one set of eyes. It didn't exactly diminish him, but it gave him a slightly more human cast. The red brick of his skin was warmer, sun-kissed instead of masonry, and his golden eyes were touched with brown. Looking too hard made me dizzy.

"You're unusual," Coyote said. My thirteen-year-old self snorted with the same lack of delicacy the woman twice her age had at her disposal.

"Siobhán," he said, and I watched me hunch my shoulders up and shift, as if I was dragging a blanket over them.

"Stop calling me that. My name's Joanne."

A wave of sorrow caught me off guard, not my own emotion at all, but Coyote's. Unexpectedly, it brought clarification. I wasn't visiting memory on my own. These were Coyote's memories, not mine, and the double vision was brought on by both of us remembering the same thing from different vantages. I had the impulse to gather up the younger me into my arms and hug her. Rather, *Coyote* had the impulse. *My* reluctance might have been what stopped him. I wondered if the me now could affect the him then. I wouldn't put it past me.

I shook my head without moving his at all, unable to keep my selves straight. "Hang on." That was actually me, breathing the words while I looked for the coil of power inside me. It felt awkward, tangled up in Coyote's dreams, especially as his power wasn't centered the way mine was.

Separating myself felt like making taffy candy, pulling and stretching and bringing it back together. Coyote's power was recognizable to me, in the same way the Eiffel Tower was: I'd never seen it before, but all the representations and reproductions looked like the real thing. I'd dealt with enough magic from other people to recognize what I was facing.

His magic was all rusty oranges and hard blues, desert colors that had a faint taste of grit to them. Everything that was mine was silver and shot-silk blue. His were a part of him, as natural as breathing, and mine were still bunched together at the center of me, tendrils feeling their way into me as if they weren't certain they were welcome. A touch of green sprouted in my silver, envy at how easy it was for Coyote, then disappeared again as I folded taffy one more time and found myself untangled from my spirit guide.

For one truly alarming instant I didn't belong anywhere. I had no attachment to my own body, not even the pulse of silver cord I'd seen when my mother and I had come together to fight the Blade. I hung in the Dead Zone, numbed by a coldness that went beyond anything I'd ever felt before. Even Amhuluk's presence hadn't held the bone-draining chill that was death in such a profound manner.

Panic clenched my heart and I dove forward, taking up residence behind the eyes of my thirteen-year-old self.

She didn't notice a thing. I wondered once more if it'd been like this all along and I just hadn't known I was visiting back then, or if this was only memory, and nothing I did could affect what was to play out. Not that I had the foggiest idea what was going to play out. My subconscious seemed to remember this conversation, but I certainly didn't.

"Joanne." I could hear the sadness in Coyote's voice as clearly as I'd felt it rise in him. My mother had sounded much that way the first time I'd corrected her as to my name. Right after that I'd done something that turned her from being a light-hearted woman with a ready smile into someone with the strength to will herself to death on a specific date. I very much didn't want a repeat of that scenario.

The younger me didn't hear anything beyond the brick-red boy in her dreams using the name she wanted him to. It was enough to satisfy her, at least for the moment. "What do you mean, I'm unusual?" The question was cautious, guarded, like somebody'd said Tom Cruise was on the phone for her. She wanted to believe it, but couldn't fathom it being true. She had half-formed ideas that I remembered, wanting to be told she was *really* the lost daughter of some insanely wealthy family who would dote on their missing child, not the half-breed daughter of a reclusive father who didn't know what to do with her. Probably every kid in the universe had that kind of fantasy, whether they'd been abandoned at three months old or not.

The adult me didn't expect anything at all. I remembered

this dream. It'd come the night my period started, and I'd woken up after Coyote'd said *brightness of body, brightness of soul.* He'd shown up in my dreams a few times after that, never more than an instant or two. I usually woke up as soon as he appeared, to the best of my recollection. I wasn't sure why I wasn't already awake, instead of lingering in the Dead Zone. Coyote put his hand out again, inviting.

"Let me show you, Joanne."

I got up, rubbing my eyes like a much smaller kid, and put my hand in Coyote's, feeling grubby and gangly next to him. He dropped a wink and said, "Down the rabbit hole!"

The Dead Zone opened up a funnel and zipped me down a swirling tube at about a thousand miles an hour. Wind ripped through my hair and the tube took a rise and dip, making me squeal and laugh and reach for support that wasn't there. The adult me thought there ought to be friction burns on my thighs—I was wearing shorts and a T-shirt, my usual sleeping apparel as a kid—and the younger me thought she'd never been on such a totally excellent roller coaster. Light suddenly enveloped us and Joanne shrieked gleefully as we exploded out of the tunnel over a body of water. We were in the air just long enough for me to catch a glimpse of greenery, and then we hit the pond with a tremendous splash and a whole lot of giggling. Joanne came to the surface laughing and wiping her eyes, merrier than I could ever remember being, and stood there looking around, thigh-deep in water.

A lush, misty garden spread out in front of me, cobblestone paths wending through it into a foggy distance. Enormous trees grew up, branches braiding together to make arches over the pathways. A scent of cherries filled warm air, blossoms drifting down like soft rain, and thunder filled my ears. There were lily pads and floating cherry blooms on the water's surface, and Joanne trailed her fingers through the water, scooping one of the flowers up. She actually tucked it behind her ear, a feminine gesture I couldn't imagine doing, and turned to look behind her while she waded out of the pool.

I knew what I'd see: a waterfall filling the pool from the garden's northern end. I thought maybe it'd been the water-slide we'd come in on. But the falls I was accustomed to tended to be a trickle, or a thin sheet of water over granite facing, hardly enough to play in.

Joanne's waterfall ran higher than I could see, blue sky and pounding mist obscuring its top. For all its enthusiastic fury and the white water it made when it hit the pond, the pool itself was remarkably still, so clear I could see the depths it plunged to near the waterfall's foot.

Joanne backed up until a bench hit her in the knees and she sat, arms braced as she smiled at rainbows brought into relief by sunlight playing over the falls. "What is this place?"

"Your soul, for lack of a better word," Coyote said. He was sitting beside me on the bench, apparently unconcerned with having temporarily disappeared, and he wore the coyote form I was most familiar with. Joanne did a double take that even I found funny, and Coyote himself snapped air in a doglike laugh.

"I'm not a dog," he said, nearly before the thought was

finished, and *I* laughed while Joanne wriggled sheepishly. Some things, it seemed, hadn't changed.

"Sorry." She sounded like she meant it, which was more than I'd ever done. "Does everybody have a garden like this one?"

"Everyone has a garden," Coyote said with a bony-shouldered shrug. "Nobody's exactly alike. It's the source of who you are, Joanne. The heart of your power."

Joanne curled a lip, the expression familiar to me. I'd tried hard to train myself out of it once I'd grown up, for a couple of reasons. One was that sneering only looked good on James Dean. The other was that I'd eventually figured out nobody wanted to be friends with somebody who perpetually looked like she'd bite your head off if you spoke to her. But that was years ahead of the girl I was right now, and she sneered with the best of them. "I don't have any power. I don't even have a boyfriend."

Oh, God. Reliving being thirteen was going to be a lesson in humiliation I could do without. I tried closing my eyes and putting my hands over my ears, but it was amazingly ineffective against things that were happening in my own head. Coyote cocked his ears, as if doing so would explain the logic behind the younger me's statement, then rolled out his tongue and let it go. "Close your eyes, and tell me what you feel."

Joanne eyed him, then shrugged and did so, straightening her spine as she did. I didn't remember having such good posture at her age. Then again, being tall had kept me out of some fistfights, so there were reasons to stand up straight.

Being tall and standing up so straight had come across as

arrogant, the snide voice in my head reminded me, and had gotten me into a lot more fights than it'd gotten me out of. I told the voice to shut up and go away, even if it was right. Especially because it was right. I'd learned, too, to never let them know they'd beaten you, and standing up straight went a long way toward that. I'd stood up so straight every goddamned day of my pregnancy that my back hurt again just thinking about it. Pride had kept me stiff-spined for eight months. I guessed maybe it'd been doing that for a lot longer than I cared to think about.

"I feel like I'm going to puke," the younger me announced in the midst of all that introspection. She rubbed her hand over her stomach and opened her eyes again, nose wrinkled. "Like somebody hit me in the stomach with a golf club."

Coyote's mouth opened and his tongue lolled out, as if he'd been about to say something and Joanne's comment had caught him off guard. "Golf club?"

"Yeah," she said, oblivious to his surprise, while I remembered the club sinking into my diaphragm like it was meant to be there, hooking under the breastbone with a solid *whump*. It'd been an accident, the kid who hit me considerably younger than I was, but the club's backswing had still taken the breath out of me for what seemed like hours on end. Even now, more than fifteen years later, the memory made a sick little pit beneath my breastbone, and I realized Joanne was right. The power, when it wanted to be noticed, did feel a lot like that had. It wasn't something that could be ignored. "It feels kind of connected to something," she added. Coyote shook off his curiosity about the golf club and looked pleased.

"Connected to what?"

"I dunno." Joanne turned around in a circle, still rubbing her tummy. "Maybe to this whole place. Maybe to you." She let go a sudden burp, clapped a hand over her mouth and looked back at Coyote with wide eyes. "Feels better now," she said through her fingers. "Maybe it's just gas."

Humor creased Coyote's long face and he lifted his chin, ears pricking up. "Close your eyes and try again. Imagine reaching out with that feeling so you can touch everything with it."

"You want me to puke all over everything?" Joanne asked dubiously, but closed her eyes. I couldn't see when she closed her eyes, and twitched impatiently, trying not to order myself to open my eyes again. I could feel the power inside her—us—respond when she reached for it, flowing cool and silver-blue out from her center. There was nothing sluggish or reluctant, as there'd been in the worst moments of my denying it, nor did it feel in any way gleeful or glad to be used. It just *was,* as much a part of my younger self as breathing or messing around with cars was. For an instant I envied her, and wished there was a way to get her not to make the mistakes I'd made.

Joanne didn't even have to open her eyes. The world began to come into focus through closed eyelids, the gorgeous, powerful neon colors I'd become so fond of spilling into her vision through the power of magic. I'd never tried looking at my garden with the second sight, and wouldn't have thought an imaginary place representing my soul would have all the colors of life inside it, vibrating with excitement and potential.

The waterfall was made of crystal, crashing down with a liquid music that raised hairs on my arms. The pool it splashed into rippled into prisms, colors riding tiny waves to the pool's edge, where they crawled up over the banks and spilled into grass and trees with all the joie de vivre imaginable. I could see Coyote in both his forms at once, the lanky good-natured animal shape seeming to settle inside the young man's torso. His own power, his aura, was less tempered through Joanne's eyes than through his own, burnt sienna and bright cobalt-blue, but it was infused with joy and patience.

"Open your eyes," he murmured, and Joanne did, very slowly, until the spirit world and the normal world amalgamated and became one in her vision, neither seeming complete without the other. I felt raw delight rise up in her, so overwhelming her throat tightened and tears swam in her eyes as she split a smile broad enough to hurt her cheeks.

"It's magic!"

"It's your birthright," Coyote said. "I've got a lot to teach you."

Joanne turned that blinding smile, an expression I couldn't remember ever having, on the coyote, then reached out to hug him so hard I could feel bony ribs and shoulders digging into my cheek and arm. There was greed and hope and excitement in her voice as she said, with more enthusiasm than I'd ever shown, "I want to learn."

CHAPTER TWENTY-THREE

The sun had set when I became aware of it again. I didn't know why no one had disturbed me, the scene-causing woman standing mindlessly still in the middle of the restaurant's sidewalk, but then, I didn't know why nobody'd awakened me when I was sleeping beneath Petite a couple of days earlier, either. I had the sensation of being veiled, as if I were sleep-walking, or maybe as if everyone around me was. I'd have thought Morrison would see through the veil, and the idea made my stomach clench. Me being cosmically attuned to him in some way hardly meant the reverse was true.

I remembered, now. I remembered Coyote dreams so clearly I could barely fathom why I'd forgotten them for so long. I remembered his patience in teaching me how to draw my powers out, how to heal, starting with the most superficial of wounds and working toward the most profound. I remembered that even as a kid I'd had a hard time with the idea of simply seeing something as whole and it being that way. I had never quite achieved that to Coyote's satisfaction, and I remembered that back then, I'd used the same tire-patching and car-fixing analogies to rebuild bone and sinew as I did now.

I remembered the tricks I'd shown him: the way I'd learned to bend light around me so I was invisible, the idea taken from some comic book I'd read. I remembered a night when it'd been pouring rain in my garden and I'd changed the rain to flowers, daisies and sunflowers and dandelions spilling out of the sky, and I'd realized then that I could do that in the waking world, too. I remembered touching on a river so deep and fast I'd almost drowned in it before Coyote put his teeth into my belt and tugged me back. I remembered learning to create things from my will alone, and I remembered that the basic rule of magic was the same one a coven had taught me a couple of weeks earlier: *do what thou wilt, and it harm none.* Neither the coven nor I had done so well with that, but it was still the immutable rule.

What I did not remember was walking through school every day, cocky and proud of my knowledge and power. I didn't remember using it to make myself popular or stronger or better, to push myself into the place I'd always wanted to be: belonging. I turned my palm up, creating a silver-shot ball of blue energy there. It swam around my fingers, darting and dancing like it had life of its own, and I wished it was sheer moral superiority that had kept me from making a place for myself in Qualla Boundary. That was what my fictional Chinese heroine would've done, kept her gifts quiet and worked silently in the background to the betterment of the people around her.

I was nowhere near that good a person. I hadn't eked out a position for myself using my power because in the waking world, I didn't even know about it. I could just about see it now, a thin line across my psyche that Coyote had drawn, keeping my awareness of burgeoning power apart from the often bitter, sullen teenager I was in day-to-day life. On one side of that line lay the memories of dreams, and on the other was what I'd been meant to remember until I'd grown beyond the emotional maturity of a turnip. On *that* side, I remembered Coyote visiting a handful of times, always waking me up immediately, until the day he'd stopped visiting at all.

I thought I should be bubbling over with resentment at my spirit guide, for all the trouble he'd put me through by walling up my power until I was grown-up enough to use it. It was arrogant, high-handed and officious, assuming I wouldn't have been able to handle the responsibilities he was offering me.

It was unquestionably the right move.

I walked back to Petite, my body stiff from standing motionless on concrete, and crawled into my car. I wanted to stay there, small and hidden, and sleep until I understood everything that had ever happened to me. Dreaming would help sort it all out. That was what dreams were for.

Only lately, they seemed heavy and dangerous, too, and I didn't think this was a good time to risk letting my subconscious do all the work. I put my hands on the steering wheel and let intellect unfold creases of memory I was too drained to deny.

The advantage of being a new soul, Coyote'd told me not that long ago, was I didn't have the burdens of past lives to weigh me down. The disadvantage was I didn't have the experiences, either. I had thirteen short years of existence behind me when we first met, and in all that time I'd never really belonged anywhere. Maybe someone with a little more history would have felt the weight of smart choices and understood that shamanic gifts weren't for personal gain. I'd known that on an intellectual level at thirteen, but I wouldn't have given a rat's ass, and Coyote knew it.

The bitch of the thing was there wasn't much choice about whether I'd have those powers or not. I'd been built that way by a Maker I wasn't quite convinced existed, but Grandfather Sky and Mother Earth didn't care if I believed in them or not. They believed in me. That was all that mattered. So Coyote'd been stuck teaching a kid who'd use her powers in all the wrong ways if she'd known she had them. In his position, I'd have kept me in the dark, too.

I'd like to think I'd have grown into learning the truth. In retrospect it was clear other people did—the drum that lay at home on my dresser was proof of that. It'd been a gift when I turned fifteen. Maybe it'd been a sign that the elders saw that I was finally coming into myself.

But then I met Lucas, and everything went to hell.

I leaned forward, putting my forehead on Petite's steering wheel, my eyes closed. I didn't let myself think of him by name, not since he'd hightailed it back to his mother's people in Canada when I told him I was pregnant. The First Boy.

That was how I thought of him. It was safer that way, as if he was a symbol more than a person. School had just started and he was new, newer than even me, visiting his father and cousins in North Carolina. Even now, almost thirteen years later, when he came to mind I still thought he was beautiful, with broad cheekbones and a white smile. I'd hoped going to bed with him would make him like me, or make me fit in better. It hadn't worked, though it'd lost me the only best friend I'd ever had.

I wasn't dumb enough to pretend not to know what a missed period meant, under the circumstances. Lucas had left at Christmastime, maybe as he'd always intended. It certainly gave him a legitimate excuse to be far away from Qualla Boundary before it became obvious I was pregnant. It didn't really matter: I hadn't told anybody but him and my friend Sara, and still haven't. The father's name is left unknown on the birth certificate, and that was probably as much the reason for Morrison's concern as my lousy phrasing yesterday morning. Part of me wanted to get out of the car and go find Morrison and tell him right then that it hadn't been rape, just a stupid mistake, but I knew I'd never do that. I hadn't even told my father I was pregnant, just let it become obvious as time went on. He never asked.

Other people did, but I'd learned that stiff-spined solitude by then, and didn't answer. The only two people I'd ever admitted my pregnancy to out loud were Lucas and Sara, and I'd lost them both. I didn't know how to break that silence anymore, even if I wanted to.

I'd thought Coyote'd stopped visiting my dreams around then. Sitting there in Petite, the steering wheel making a dent in my forehead, it was finally clear he hadn't stopped visiting. I'd stopped answering. He'd taught me shields back then, just like he'd had to teach me all over again, and that was a lesson I'd learned by God well. I'd kept them up so well for more than twelve years it'd taken almost dying in order to bring them down again. By then I was so set against the whole idea of a mystical world I don't think he stood a chance. Getting back inside my head, or helping me to, in order to access the dreamworld training he'd given me more than a decade earlier would have required at least a smidgen of willingness on my part. I'd been about as willing to listen as a man might be eager to walk to the gallows. And, frankly, if I'd been my spirit guide at that point, I'd have been tempted to throw in the towel and let me figure it out by my own damned self. Coyote was a better person, so to speak, than I was.

Some of it had made it through, anyway. Healing came naturally to me, even as I fought it. I'd pulled out gimmicks that felt instinctive, and now could remember they'd been learned and figured out. I was torn between relief and disappointment. Being able to do what I did on instinct really seemed like it meant I was supposed to be doing those things. There was nothing like a little predestination to make a girl feel like she's got a place in the world. On the other hand, having studied with Coyote, in however esoteric a fashion, made sense in a way that I was much happier with. Being able to do something because I'd studied it fit much more nicely into my rational world than the uncomfortable idea I'd become part of a massive sportswear campaign and could Just Do It.

I spread my fingers and thunked the heel of my hands against Petite's steering wheel. Part of my mind was demanding, *so why didn't he tell me? Why didn't he at least try?* Blaming Coyote for my shortcomings was much easier than taking responsibility for them myself. The truth was, I just couldn't imagine me listening six months ago. I couldn't fathom a better way to get me to dig my heels in and refuse any of what was happening to me than saying, "Hey, you liked it when you were fifteen." I was nothing if not contrary. Even the slightest hint that we'd been there, done that, would've slammed me back into my shell. I wasn't sure even the gods could've pulled me out of that one, and they'd been running rampant around Seattle at the time. Better to treat me like the sulky, snotty rank beginner I'd grown up into than try to pick up where we'd left off.

I wished I could tell Coyote I was sorry, and that I remembered now, and even that I understood.

Instead I whispered a promise to him that I'd do my best, and let Petite take me to Northwest Hospital.

Wednesday, July 6, 10:29 p.m.

It was well after visiting hours when I got to the hospital. Odds were good that I could slip in under the *forgiveness is easier to get than permission* axiom, which had worked for me in the past. On the other hand, seven months earlier, I'd wrapped light around myself until it bounced away and pretended I wasn't there. People who'd been looking straight at me frowned in confusion, then slowly walked away. I hadn't known then how I'd done it. I remembered now, and part of me wanted to see if I could replicate it.

Part of me also thought, a bit grimly, that it would be a good way to find out if the sleep demon was triggering to any external magic I did, or just attempts at healing. I wasn't strictly sure the light trick was external, but it was far more external than visiting my garden and the realms accessible from there to find Coyote.

My heart spasmed again and I got out of the car, hoping that moving and taking deliberate deep breaths would help me get through the impulse to burst into tears.

My reflection, highlighted by a streetlamp in a night-dark window, caught my eye before I got to the main entrance. Light bounced around me, warping and weaving in smooth glass, like I'd been stretched out of shape. I stopped, watching my distorted self. Disappearing had come from far within me back in January, anger and desperation pushing me to use my power for something other than healing. Choosing to use it in a different way.

Choice. My reflection's lips parted with the word, though I didn't say it out loud. I felt out of focus, staring at a corner of glass, listening to a running patter that went on in the back of my mind: *c'mon, baby, you can do it. This is what the magic's there for, right? Shamanism's about choosing different paths, so you just have to choose to embrace it, Joanne. Choose to use it. You know you can do it.* I knew the cajoling rhythm: it was what I used with Petite when I needed just a little more out of her. I honestly couldn't remember ever using it on myself to encourage a little more out of the gifts I'd been granted, much less encouraging the power itself. I'd paid for that, too, and so had others. Without really thinking about it, I walked forward to put my fingertips against my reflection's, looking at myself without seeing.

For two weeks I'd been running helter-skelter, looking for answers and quick fixes and a crash course in using the powers that had grown up inside me. I'd drummed and gone in and out of my body until it was halfway natural, and I'd faced up to being stuck with magical talent. All of a sudden I wasn't sure that facing up was the same as accepting.

An evil spirit had told me that I might very well have to struggle every single day to accept what I was and what I could do. I'd let myself forget about that, because, hey, evil spirits. Standing there staring through my reflection in the dark, I wondered if the message had been right, even if the bearer had used it to confound me. I could not imagine there'd come a day when I was happy or comfortable being a shaman. The idea that my natural skepticism would eventually give up the fight seemed ludicrous.

It also seemed inevitable. How long could I keep not quite believing in my own gifts? How long was I going to wince when somebody like Mark wanted to know about them? I wasn't even letting him judge for himself whether I was nuts or not. I was doing the job for him, putting it out there so he couldn't reject me first.

That was uncomfortably like another one of those introspective thoughts I never enjoyed having. I finally focused on my reflection, my eyes dark in the overhead lights. Like it or not, this was who and what I was. I said, "Shit," under my breath, very quietly, and the black-haired woman in the window looked about as unhappy as I felt.

Conviction, a grim dark feeling of knowing I could pull this off, was right there, waiting for me to sink into it again. I'd done it before, more than once, pulling belief around me like a cloak to be shed when the crisis had passed. I didn't exactly feel guilty about dropping it when the moment was gone, but I was getting tired of it. I just didn't know how to stop. I closed my eyes, prickles of weariness stinging the inside of my nose like a warning of tears. The power behind my sternum waited, so calm and patient it felt like mockery. For the first time I could remember I just stood there, paying attention to what it felt like. It was cool and still, mostly centered in my diaphragm, but if I concentrated I felt it welling up higher, running through my veins like blood, as if it was a part of me. If I called up the second sight and looked at my skin, I thought I'd be able to see it, silver and blue and flowing inside me. It wasn't conscious, but I could be subsumed by it, giving myself over to its strange and scary potential.

The idea terrified me. I wanted to be in control, rational and intelligent and logical, not at the mercy of a healing magic sufficiently greater than myself that I couldn't even recognize what to do with it half the time.

I also wanted to go in and visit Billy. I opened my eyes again and whispered, "Okay. I'm trying this your way," to my reflection. "You can do it. It's who you are. You taught Coyote, remember? Just let yourself…go."

Feather-soft warmth enveloped me. For an instant I thought I saw a white ghost of wings in the reflection, making a shelter that fell around my shoulders. Inside that hollow place of safety, I felt as though I slid inside myself, a cool drink of water sliding down my insides. It brought the Sight with it, the world visible in two realities for a few seconds, one ordinary and night-dark, the other neon brilliant and vibrating with life. Then the second one settled out, leaving me with whispers of encouragement reverberating through my mind and echoing in the power centered within me. I did my best to formulate a *please* without making the word, afraid something as mundane as language would screw my attempts up for good, and magic responded.

It burgeoned out of me, pushing out in bubbles and bursts of pleasure at being used, and slithered over my skin like a coat of thick paint. It started with my chest and ran downward, distorting even my own vision so that light bent and I seemed to be looking through myself. It ran over my fingertips and touched the glass, then splashed back up my arm to my throat and face. The last thing I saw was my eyes, oddly gold in the darkness, and then my reflection wasn't there at all.

Absolute sheer panic erupted in my stomach, cramping it and making cold sweat stand out all over my body as I stared at where I ought to be reflected. I clenched my teeth and breathed in and out like a Lamaze mother, half convinced that if I couldn't see my reflection, I wasn't there. I wondered if vampires felt that way, then had to remind myself severely that there was no such thing.

God on high, how I hoped there was no such thing.

The thought seemed to be a source of amusement to the

power hiding me from myself. I ground my teeth and willed myself to take a few steps backward, seeing if the magic would hold. To my complete fascination, moving made me visible, but only just: if I didn't know where to look, I wouldn't see me. I'd seen news stories about technology that did what I seemed to be doing, projecting images of what was around me over where I was. The tech I'd read about only worked from one direction, but as I peered over my own shoulder, it appeared that magic was a more effective invisibility cloak than technology. A very tiny pop of glee burst through me. There was no actual crisis and I'd talked myself into doing something pretty dramatic with my power. I actually whispered "Thank you" to myself, and headed for the hospital doors.

It was then that it occurred to me to wonder if the hospital's sliding glass doors were triggered by weight or motion. The question kept me paralyzed for several long seconds as I stared at the doors a few yards ahead. Then someone exited and I made a mad dash inside, never knowing which it might've been.

A noseful of sharp sweet hospital smell made me sneeze so explosively I staggered to the lobby chairs, leaning on one while tears ran down my face and I sneezed again. More people than I'd hoped were about at that hour. Every single one of them stared around in confusion at the sneezes evidently coming out of nowhere. I got myself under control and snuffled my way to the elevators, still wiping at my eyes and nose. I couldn't remember Harry Potter ever having this sort of problem while he was running around in his invisibility cloak. I was going to have to speak to the management.

The elevators and halls upstairs were bustling with exhausted-looking doctors and nurses and the buzz of worried confusion. More and more people were being admitted with the sleeping sickness, and nobody'd woken up yet. I flinched my way around gurneys and frustrated medical personnel, whispering promises to make it better as I slipped into Billy's room and sank against the door, eyes closed for a few seconds as I muttered another internal thanks to my gifts and let the bubble of invisibility slide off me. Then I shoved away from the door and took two steps before jolting to a halt in complete dismay.

Bradley Holliday was conked out in a chair by Billy's bed.

CHAPTER TWENTY-FOUR

My first thought was, *shit, what if he wakes up?* And my second was, *shit, what if he* doesn't? I stood where I was, foot half off the ground with indecision, then swore noiselessly and crept forward. A tile creaked beneath me and Brad snorted and stirred, far more reaction than Billy gave. Despite my not wanting to be caught, my shoulders dropped in relief: far better to have Doc Holliday wake up than go into a permanent sleep like his brother and sister-in-law had. I put my foot down and exhaled carefully, looking around the room.

Mel was in the bed closer to the door, now that I was noticing things. She, like Billy, looked well, except for the unbroken sleep. Brad Holliday looked uncomfortable as hell. I thought about waking him up to save him the crick in his neck, but he probably wouldn't appreciate it. Besides, I didn't want to explain how I'd gotten in there.

Which led me to the good news. Nothing had come out of the dark to attack me through my use of power.

The bad news was I could feel the feathery heaviness of sleep in the room, as if it gathered there and waited for something. Even'd get you odds it was waiting for me.

And I didn't know what to do about it.

I tiptoed to the middle of the room, seeing if I could touch both Billy and Melinda at once. I couldn't, and edged back to Mel's bed to see if it could be moved a few inches without noise or pulling any important-looking tubes loose. I didn't want to try moving Billy. For one thing, he had almost a hundred pounds on me, and for another, it was his bed Brad was next to.

Mel's bed was actually surprisingly easy to move. I lifted the foot and swung it over eight or ten inches, then snuck forward to move the head as far as I dared. Air stirred around me, thick and slow, and seemed to stick to my skin as I moved. Like tar. I thought of Coyote, and thought, *like amber.* It took another minute of maneuvering to get the beds close enough together, and then I stood there between them, panting quietly and trying to order my thoughts.

As best I could tell, Billy and Mel had been the first two to go to sleep. I'd spent more time psychically linked with Billy than anybody, and I figured the events of a few weeks past had bound Melinda and me together in some fashion as well. If there was a place to start ending this plague of sleep, it was probably with them.

But I was on my own. Coyote was gone and my forays into other realms were stung left and right with darkness and encroaching sleep. There was a real possibility I wouldn't be able to snap out of it if I went to do battle with this thing.

I also didn't see that I had much choice in the matter. I wasn't going to let my friends die. I wasn't going to let Coyote have died for nothing.

Besides. A ghost of humor passed through me. At least if I got myself caught by this thing I wouldn't have to face the embarrassment of seeing Morrison again. That made the prospect of getting stuck in dreamworlds almost appealing. The extra chair in the room was on the far side of Billy's bed. I didn't want to move it and risk waking Brad up, so I took a deep breath and knelt down between the two beds, reaching out to touch the sleepers, making myself a conduit. It wasn't very comfortable. I thought it'd take a while to get myself into a trance state.

Instead, the weight in the room crashed down on me like a waterfall.

The world around me was golden, the color of a warm summer day, but with no sun to light it. The earth itself gave off brightness, mountains glowing with cheer and good purpose. A river cut through the land, gold as the sky and ground, and reached to the horizons. They were farther away than I expected, a certain curvature to the earth, unlike the flatness of the burning world or the near mountains of the blue world. It wasn't the Middle World, certainly not with the warm glow of the land and no sun in the sky, but this place was the closest yet to my own time and place that I'd seen.

Around me, in the distance and close by, I half heard and half knew that men and women and beasts and plants, all the creatures and things of the world, spoke the same language, communicating easily with one another. It reminded me of Babylon, though the land I'd entered was as different physically as it could be from that city of twisting spires and hanging gardens. That had been a metropolis, and this world was an agrarian desert. For an instant I grasped how they might still be the same thing, but my understanding was lost as red streaks appeared in the sky, pocked and marked like comets.

People fell ill and struggled to survive, their distress worsening with every heartbeat. Accusations rose up, turning a land of joy and peace into something far more like the world I knew. Blame fell down gender lines, anger and fear thrown all around me. The women said it was the men bringing illness, and the men said it was the women. They separated themselves from one another, making the streaks in the sky and the pain of loss even more difficult to bear. A protest formed in my throat and caught there uselessly; watching the world collapse around me was like watching a time-elapsed video of a train station. It moved too quickly and too violently for me to affect. I stood outside it, gasping for air as the world fell down.

And then something slipped through the midst of the world's breakdown, moving at the same slow, normal rate of speed I did. My eyes, accustomed to the lurching hurry of the dying world, took a few seconds to pick out details that were as much physical as known within the depths of my mind. It wasn't a human creeping through the world's end, not on four legs, not furry and sly and furtive.

Coyote.

My heart leapt and lost hope in almost the same instant,

leaving me with an ache bordering on whimpers. This coyote's fur was acid-etched, each thread of it gold and copper and bronze, strong with power. Not a spirit, not a guide, but an archetype, the trickster who helped make and unmake the world. I wondered if every trickster was Coyote, and Coyote every trickster, one eternal concept that took form however the people thought to see it. That left me with the bemusing idea that Coyote and Brer Rabbit were exactly the same thing underneath, and for an instant I saw through to the truth of that. *Saw,* not just saw, the very concept that lay beneath Coyote's recognizable form.

A fractal pattern exploded in my vision. Chaos bled in bright beautiful spikes, sometimes doing damage where it struck, other times ricocheting into mutation, creating new life. It wasn't caring or uncaring or anything but *there,* senseless in the way that most of the universe often seemed to be.

Curiosity hung over it like a cloud, not an inherent part of its random magic, but so heavily imposed by limited human understanding that it seemed to wear that impulse like a cloak. I kept my eyes wide, afraid to blink for fear I'd lose sight of that thread, and while I watched the cloak shifted. Rabbits and spiders, gods I could name, like Loki, and an astonishing series of creatures and beings I couldn't, interspersed with a handful of icons so familiar they made me laugh despite the oddness—Charlie Chaplin and Daffy Duck—shimmered through that cloak, and then it settled down again into a coyote shape, leaving my eyes burning.

I had thought Cernunnos with his Wild Hunt had been a thing of chaos. I stared, still unblinking, at Coyote darting through the people of the yellow world, and understood with great surprise that Cernunnos had been an agent of order, if there was such a thing. He belonged to rules and a pattern of life and death, only able to lead the Hunt in certain times, in adherence to specific ritual. He had made his play to be a creature of chaos, trying to break free of the place written for him in the laws of creation, and I'd put him back in his box.

I wondered where the hell that put me, in that pattern of life and death, order and chaos. Did I straddle some kind of neutral line? That seemed pretty much unspeakably arrogant. I made a face at myself and pushed the thought away. With any luck there would be plenty of time later for navel-gazing and deciding my place in the universe. For the moment I scurried after Big Coyote, just as grateful, all things told, that my sight had settled out and I didn't have to look at his discordant soul.

Behind me, the men went to live on one side of the river and the women on the other, never to be together again. The crimson slashes faded from the sky, and Coyote explored the world in front of me, nosing high and low. He dipped his nose in the river and pulled something out, and even I knew enough about Coyote and chaos to think *uh-oh*.

Storms rose up all around, dark colors coming from each direction. Rain fell and water began to rise. I turned back to the village separated by the river, finding men and women together again and climbing frantically up an endlessly tall hollow reed that stretched to the sky. I waited for all the men and all the women, all the animals and insects and the winds and the people of every sort to climb as high as they could, and then climbed up myself, looking for a new world to live in.

But the water kept rising, and the reed didn't reach high

enough. Spider-people wove webs for us to climb, and the insects made their way to the hard shell of sky and began to gnaw and chew and break their way through, until finally there was a hole big enough to scramble through. All the creatures of the world made their way through and gathered around the hole, watching to see what happened.

And the water kept rising, threatening to flood this world, too, just as it had done with the old one. Every world had an end, and I realized I was once more throwing power out, this time like I was the little Dutch boy. The hole in the world wouldn't plug up, and from the corner of my eye I saw Coyote slinking away, his head hung low from the weight of carrying something. I shouted "Coyote!" and he stopped, shoulders hunching high.

I strode to him, men and women and beasts and bugs making way for me, and stood above him. "What are you carrying, Coyote?"

He wouldn't meet my eye. Instead he lowered his head farther, gently putting a bundle on the ground. A black-haired baby looked up at me, his dark hair streaming very long.

For one wretched moment visions collided with memory and dreams, and the child lying wide-eyed and serious, bundled there on the ground, was my own. For that moment all the sorrow of a child lost was my own, and the breath I took caught in my chest until it brought tears to my eyes.

I had never planned to keep them, not at fifteen. Not having been myself dumped on a father who didn't want me by a mother I'd grown up assuming didn't like me. I had wanted them to grow up in a home where they were wanted and loved and could be raised by adults able to care for children. I wasn't ready. The only way I could see to love them was to let others be their parents. I'd known from the start they wouldn't stay with me.

But the girl, Ayita, *first to dance* in Cherokee, had left long before I thought she would. She was born second, the only moments of her brief life that she spent apart from her brother Aidan those few while he blinked at the outside world and waited for her arrival. They nestled together in life just as they'd done in the womb, tiny bodies huddled in an incubator as I watched Ayita fade away. Aidan's eyes seemed clearer after she died, as if the two had only had enough life force for one, and she, smaller and weaker, had given Aidan the strength he needed to survive their early birth. It was his gaze I saw reflected in the serious little person before me, though I'd only seen him for a matter of hours before he went to live with his family.

I had not known much joy in my life after that. The image of a silver key, buried thirteen years, flashed through my mind. Buried since I realized I was pregnant, keeping me apart from the heritage the makers of the world planned for me. I had not been any unhappier in the half a lifetime since then than I had ever been before it, but I had not been happier, either. It was a hitching point, the center of my spider-webbed soul, and the only thing I'd given myself over to fully in the intervening years was lavishing attention on my Mustang. I swallowed hard and cleared my throat to give myself voice.

"Bring him back, Coyote. Send him back to the world we came from, so the water will not rise and try to find him."

Coyote sighed, a very human sound, and picked up the baby in his teeth, carrying him back to the hole between worlds. He set the child down in the rising water, and a sigh of joy rose up from the world below. Water receded, and all the men and women and creatures that had survived another world smiled and began to explore their new home.

All but Coyote, who sat with his back to me, looking into the hole. "Who do you think you are?" I rasped. "Playing games that bring the world to an end. Who do you think you are?"

He looked over his shoulder at me, and his face was my own.

I recoiled so violently it reflected in the physical world, pulling me loose from the bridge I'd made between Billy and Melinda. I came awake falling to the side, and grabbed for the first thing I could to regain my balance.

Unfortunately, it was Brad Holliday's leg. He yelled and jolted to his feet. I yelled and fell over, still flailing at bedsides and chairs. It was a good thing there weren't any IV racks near me. I sprang to my feet in a flurry of embarrassment and dismay, not sure if I was more upset by waking Brad or by what I'd seen. I was looking for a way to explain myself when he demanded, "How'd you get in here," and my mouth replied, "Magic," flippantly, without consulting my brain.

Anger contorted his features sharply enough that I lifted a hand in apology, though my mouth went on without any evident concern for what it was getting me into. "What's the story, Doc?" I asked with genuine curiosity. "I know Billy's side of it. Is it just that it's incredibly frustrating to have a little brother everybody thinks is nuts? Don't get me wrong." I let go a huff of air that I thought passed for humorless laughter. "I'm really on your side of things by nature. I don't blame you for not liking the superstitious stuff. I don't, either. But Billy's so into it. What's your story?"

"That's none of your business, Officer Walker."

That much was certainly true. I squinted, hoping to take a look at his aura, but even that tiny shift toward using my power seemed to alert the sleeping thing in the room. I felt it gather, ready to pounce, and let go my grasp on the Sight before it even came into focus. Brad Holliday and I might not get along, but I didn't want to be responsible for putting him into a coma. I was a little surprised he wasn't already, after hanging out in this sleep-laden room for hours. "You're right. I'm sorry."

Brad turned away, folding his arms across his chest as he looked down at his brother. His ring caught blue light from one of the monitors, turning it green, and I found myself staring at the jewel in its weighty setting. I still hadn't noticed if he wore a wedding ring. "Class ring?" I heard myself say.

He glanced at me, frowning, then at his hand, and scowled even more deeply. "From medical school, yes."

A thin band popped around my heart, releasing a thin wash of satisfaction. African evil spirits seemed ever-more unlikely, but my enemy did seem reluctant to mess with topaz. I didn't know how, or by whom, the stone had first been recognized as conducive to easy sleep and pleasant dreams, but I thanked them for it. It wasn't a lot, but it was something, and I was grateful for a reprieve, small as it might be.

Right on cue, my cell phone rang.

CHAPTER TWENTY-FIVE

I was really beginning to detest that thing. Strike that: I detested cell phones on general principles. I was starting to have a deep personal and abiding hatred for mine in specific. Visions of taking a sledgehammer to it drifted pleasantly through my mind as I took it out of my pocket and said, "Please tell me nobody's dead."

"Can't help you there," Laurie Corvallis said. "Sorry."

I reached for the railing on Mel's bed, using it to support myself. "What do you mean?"

"Tell me something first. How'd you know to start on the seventh of January?"

"You wouldn't believe me if I told you. What do you mean, you can't help me there?"

"Try me," Corvallis said. "You'd be surprised what I

believe." She left it alone, though, a note of cockiness coming into her voice. "There was a whole burst of sleeping sicknesses around the tenth of January, down in the southwest. Half of the Navajo Nation dropped off the planet for a couple days—"

"Half?" I demanded, genuinely alarmed. "Isn't that about a hundred thousand people, Laurie?"

Silence was followed by an impatient sigh. "All right. Maybe one percent. There's no drama in that, Officer Walker. Regardless, literally hundreds of people dropped off, then woke up two days later and quietly started making preparations for the end days. There've been some news stories about it, but they've gotten about the same amount of attention than your average Christian sect predicting the end of the world does."

"I've heard of a couple of those," I objected. I could almost hear Corvallis shrug.

"There were thirty-seven separate dates that various sects believed the world would end in the year 2000. How many of those did you hear about?"

"Does the Y2K bug count?"

"No. You see my point." She went on without worrying about whether I did or not. I did, anyway. "That was it. No more of the Dine went to sleep, and un—"

"Dine?"

"The Navajo, Officer Walker," Corvallis said, impatient all over again. "It's their name for themselves. It means—"

"The People," I guessed. The Cherokee's original name for themselves meant more or less the same. A lot of Native

American tribe names did. I felt vaguely guilty for not knowing the Navajo called themselves something else.

"Would you like to tell this story?" Corvallis asked. I was smart enough to keep my mouth shut, and after a moment she said, "Until a few weeks ago, nobody else did, either."

I tightened my grip on Melinda's bed frame. "How many?"

"Ten or twelve. Nothing like what's going on here."

"Do they have anything in common?" I pushed my glasses up to rub my eyes.

"Yeah. This is the weird bit. The new group who've gone to sleep worked in the University of Phoenix physics department. Grad students, professors, you name it. The CDC is still down there trying to figure out what did it, but it looks like it was something called Project Rainbow. I haven't gotten past the classification yet, which probably means it's a weapon of some kind under development for the military. You were right, Walker. You gave me a story. I really didn't expect it. Maybe somebody's been running tests on their weapon or, hell," she said, sounding suddenly enthusiastic, "maybe it's a terrorist attack. My God, that'd be a story."

I sat down on the edge of Melinda's bed and stared at the floor. "Physics?" I thought shamanism was outside my realm of expertise. I didn't have any idea what to do with a bunch of physicists. "Has anybody died? Are they still asleep?"

Corvallis hesitated, which I hadn't known she could do. "Nobody's died, but nobody's woken up, either. No, that's not true." I could almost hear her shrug, and then sly pleasure came into her voice. "Two people did wake up from the university plague. The weird thing is that they apparently have Navajo blood themselves. If I worked for a tabloid I'd be all over that link. Magic Indian blood saves—"

I pushed my hand against my stomach, feeling power flutter there like, as my younger self had said, a burp. "Ms. Corvallis. Who were they?"

I didn't even need to hear her say it. She did, anyway, of course, triumph in her voice as I mouthed the same words she announced: "Mark and Barbara Bragg."

I would've laughed, if I'd had it in me. I didn't, so I only got off the phone with my vision blurred and my stomach roiling. I didn't know what the link between a physics project and the sleeping sickness was, or what either of them had to do with Mark, who was an English major—

—Mark, who had *told* me he was an English major. I hadn't had any reason to disbelieve him, except he was too good to be true. But then, so was Thor, who was good-looking and genuinely into cars and who apparently thought I cleaned up well enough to ask me on a date. So was Gary, whose steadiness and good heart had gotten me through the past seven months with something like my head on straight. So was Morrison, who might be short-tempered and grumpy with me, but whose inherent qualities were inarguably golden. I hadn't exactly done an extensive background search on Mark, but I honestly thought that this time I'd approached the new arrival in my life with enough skepticism to give myself some credit.

And I'd been wrong despite my caution. That was bad enough. What was worse was that, however Mark was tangled up in the sleeping sickness, at least I was semiprepared for it. I'd had enough brain cells to wonder if the person who'd been dropped into my life was too good to be true, even if I'd settled into an incorrect complacency.

Morrison didn't have anything like that kind of warning. I had to tell him, and I didn't want to have that conversation while standing in front of Bradley Holliday. I waited until I was safe in Petite, who offered me some kind of psychological comfort, before dialing my boss's cell phone.

He didn't answer, which was so incredibly unlike him I immediately began to worry. Then I remembered it was well after midnight, which might just have something to do with it. I was about to redial the number when my phone rang, startling the bejeezus out of me.

"It's a quarter after one in the morning, Walker," Morrison growled in my ear. "This had better be very good."

"This sleeping sickness. First it was Billy and Mel, but when I went in to try to help Mel, I had this dream. Everybody in the dream was asleep by the time I got to work yesterday, Morrison." I thought it was yesterday. I was pretty sure it was the wee hours of Thursday morning now. I hadn't truly slept since Tuesday afternoon. My grasp on when things had happened was starting to slip. So was my coherency. I struggled for a point: "Everybody but you, Barb, and Mark."

"You called me up at one in the morning to tell me you're dreaming about me, Walker?" Morrison sounded utterly disbelieving. I didn't blame him.

"No. I mean, yes, but no. They're tied into this sleeping sickness somehow, boss. I don't understand how yet, but I just talked to Laurie Corvallis, and the point is, you've got to stay away from Barb."

Morrison said, "For Christ's sake, Walker," and hung up the phone. I stared at it, then called back. Maybe he had the same Pavlovian response to ringing phones that I did, because he answered even though he had to know it was me.

"She's there, isn't she?" The very idea made my eyes hot. "Morrison, listen to me. That topaz is working. If you don't have it, there's nothing protecting you, and if she's there you're in danger. You've got to get out of there."

I heard him pull a deep breath. His voice was very steady a moment later when he said, "Walker, you sound ridiculous. Yes. Barbara's here, though that's none of your business. You need to go home and go to bed. You're obviously overwrought."

"I'm over—I'm…Morrison! You told me to solve this thing! I'm telling you, she's got something to do with it! She and Mark were—"

"Walker, listen to yourself. You sound like—" My boss was at a loss for words there for an instant, then finished as if he couldn't believe what he was saying. "You sound like you're jealous, Walker."

I slammed the heel of my hand into Petite's horn and shouted, "Of course I'm jealous, you idiot!" over its blare. "Could we get past that and get you out of the house, please?" I pounded on the horn, short bursts of noise that emphasized my words. Then I remembered I was sitting outside a hospital, and stopped hitting the horn.

The silence that followed was profound. Not just the silence in the car, but Morrison's quietness on the other end of the line. He finally said, very gently, "Go home and get some rest, Walker. We'll talk about this tomorrow." He hung up, and I wrapped my hand around my cell phone and smashed my fist into the opposite palm until I stopped wanting to cry.

It took long enough to let me decide that if Morrison wasn't going to listen to my irrational, embarrassing self over the phone, I was just going to have to go to his house and talk to him in person. Because that would go over so well. It might help if I started with an apology, though that wasn't going to help my general feeling of humiliation any. I was pretty sure that karmically speaking, though, the universe would approve of it as a first step.

The problem was I didn't know where he lived. Or even if he was at home, for that matter. He could've been with Barb, for all I knew. The whole idea made my stomach hurt, a fishhook tug that felt like I was being pulled where I didn't want to go. While my mind ran in circles trying to figure out how to figure out where he lived, my hand opened up and dialed the front desk at the precinct building. The guy who answered wasn't Bruce, which it wouldn't have been, anyway, because he didn't work a night shift, but my heart missed a beat and hung there miserably in my chest while I asked to be, and was, transferred to the missing persons department.

Intellectually I didn't expect anybody to be there at going-on two in the morning. My intellect, though, was still working on how to find Morrison's house while some other part of my mind, working on automatic, actually tried doing something about it. My stomach hurt even more, a bubbling mess of sickness that roiled and twisted beneath my breastbone. I made a fist and thumped it against my diaphragm, trying to work some of the discomfort out, and narrowly avoided burping in the ear of the woman who picked up the phone, her Spanish accent tired.

"Jen? What're you doing there?"

"Joanie? What are you doing calling?" Tired didn't cover it. She sounded exhausted. I thought I probably sounded the same. "I'm popping NoDoz and drinking Jolt," she answered. "I fall asleep if I'm at home, so I thought I'd hang out here and try to get some late-night work done."

My face crumpled. "Are a lot of people doing that?"

"All over the place. Everybody's trying to stay awake. What are you calling MP for, Joanie? Is everything okay?"

Talking about staying awake made me yawn. I tried to keep it tight so it wouldn't set Jen to yawning, too. "I have kind of a weird question."

"Is it weirder than asking me to find a modern-day kid from a reference painting of mythological figures?"

I lifted my eyes to look blankly through Petite's windshield. "When you put it that way, no." For a moment my vision fused with the Sight and I could see spiderweb cracks all through Petite's window, streetlight glinting on the damaged lines. "I need Morrison's home address."

The silence that followed was long and profound enough I found myself shifting uncomfortably in Petite's bucket seat. "What," I finally said, "is that weirder than the painting?"

"The jury's still out," Jen said after another long several seconds. "Why don't you just call him?" She sounded, I thought, suspiciously like a teenager waiting to get the dirt on a topic she'd been polite enough not to ask about until now. I began to wonder if I was the last one who'd picked up on my own emotional conflict regarding Morrison. I hoped not. I hoped, at least, that *Morrison* was still a step behind me.

That seemed painfully unlikely, especially at this juncture.

"Can you just get me his address, Jen?" I had to at least try to draw a line in the sand. I had no illusions about how long it'd stay drawn if Jen insisted, but I wasn't going to go down without a fight.

Jen said, "Huh," and then, "Just a second," leaving me to eye my reflection and the phone in the rearview mirror. It couldn't be that easy, could it?

"All right, here it is. You have something to write with?"

Apparently it could be. I scrambled for a pencil, writing down the address and repeating it back to her. "Thanks, Jen. Look, the topaz seems to be working. You can probably sleep safely if you're hanging on to it. It looks like it's keeping Billy's brother from going under, anyway."

She said, "Huh," again, then, "Ok, if I get desperate. Thanks," and hung up on me. I glanced over my shoulder as I keyed Petite on, and pulled out onto the street wondering what I was going to do if Morrison wasn't home.

I didn't have to worry about it. Morrison's Avalon was parked next to a quarter-ton Dodge Ram in the driveway of a two-story cream-colored house with trim that looked black in the nighttime city lights. Curtains lined the insides of windows. I didn't have curtains on my windows, only the blinds the apartment had come with when I'd rented it in college. At a glance, Morrison was Suzy Homemaker, compared to me. Of course, the Four Horsemen of the

Apocalypse were probably Suzy Homemaker, compared to me. I bet Morrison cooked his own meals, too. He certainly mowed the lawn, right up to the edge of a picket fence that matched the trim. I'd never thought of Morrison as a picket-fence kind of guy. Young spruce trees bordered the fence, with hedges growing up between them. They looked like they probably reduced the noise off the street, which might help a cop sleep better at night.

Unless, of course, he had employees calling him up in the middle of the night to rant and rave and profess jealousy to him. This minute examination of his front lawn was not getting me any closer to dealing with my embarrassing behavior or the woman in Morrison's bed. The Ram had to be hers. I couldn't imagine Morrison owning a recreational vehicle.

I gritted my teeth and left Petite, following a stone footpath up to Morrison's front door. Yellow rosebushes lined the front of the house, and a wheelbarrow sat up against the bushes on the porch's far side. A blue tarp was tucked neatly around the barrow's burden, a plastic-wrapped set of shears weighing it down for good measure.

I knocked on the door, staring at my feet, and nobody answered. I could think of a lot of reasons why someone might not answer the door at two in the morning, and none of them were reasons that suggested pushing the doorbell was a good idea. I did it, anyway. For a moment I thought it was broken, then heard it bong twice with increasing volume, and decided it probably rang three times, working its way up to being heard instead of starting out shrill and scaring the hell out of the people inside. It seemed like a good doorbell for a cop.

Nobody answered the doorbell, either. My tummy did a quick dive and swoop to the left, bringing illness intense enough to break a cold sweat on my forehead, and I finally clued in to the familiarity of the sensation. A similar sickness had prompted me to get off an airplane and go running across Seattle in search of a woman trying to outrace a pack of dogs, seven months earlier. The younger me had referred to it as being hit in the stomach with a golf club. I had more than justifiable nerves going on here.

The power inside me lit up like the Fourth of July once I finally recognized it. Gary was right. I really did need to figure out how to balance my life somehow. My focus was so limited I could either have power running or I could have emotional awareness turned on. I was almost certain that those two things ought to be intimately tied up in each other, instead of being divisive as the Grand Canyon.

That was about all the recrimination I had time for. The Sight fell over me again, doubling my vision for a few seconds, then settling out in a manner that was starting to feel familiar, if not quite natural. The walls of Morrison's house thinned, support structures glowing strong and purposeful, and objects within became clear in their own neon bright colors. If I wanted to become a thief, this second sight thing could be very useful for casing out a joint ahead of time.

As if in disapproval, my vision wavered and flickered, darkening. I lifted a hand in silent apology to the power and it steadied again. I could practically hear a disapproving sniff, and despite everything found myself smiling. I wasn't sure if it was me sniffing or if the magic I carried actually had a personality of its own, but either way I thought it was funny. Only I would end up with opinionated magic. Maybe that was the price of ignoring it for over a decade. It'd struck out on its own, forged new territory in the heart and soul of the Other realm, and came back with a smart-ass little voice that pointed out the obvious to me and didn't like it when I thought about being naughty with my power.

I was doing it again. Procrastinating. I'd been staring through Morrison's front door at the discreetly ornate wooden frame of a picture, not letting the Sight take me farther into the house. I had no words for how much I didn't want to get an eyeful of Morrison and Barbara Bragg in bed together. On the other hand, I noticed I was physically leaning backward, my heels dug into the porch, and that my stomach was cramping from wanting to move forward. I hadn't felt anything like this much impatience when I'd astrally snuck through Suzanne Quinley's parents' home. Somehow it suggested my power knew something I didn't, and the more time I wasted the worse it was going to be.

Not that I could think of anything worse than getting to watch Morrison making love to his cute redheaded evil girl-friend. I ground my teeth together and let loose the dogs of war, separating from my body entirely so I could follow the urgent power that had brought me to Morrison's home.

CHAPTER TWENTY-SIX

Last time I'd done this I'd walked through the whole house as if I was there physically. This time there was no transition. I snapped to Morrison's side without heed to intervening walls or worry about the house's layout.

He lay sprawled on his back in the kitchen, for which I was perversely grateful. Kitchens were common areas, a room to invite people into. The bedroom, where I feared I'd end up, would've been unbearably intimate. Invading Morrison's privacy was one thing. Invading his bedroom was something else.

He hadn't, I remembered with a flush of bewilderment, had the slightest compunction about walking into my bedroom a couple days earlier. I suddenly had no idea how to react to that.

Lucky for me, it wasn't a good time to be thinking about

it. Barbara crouched at Morrison's side, her hand over his heart. Her colors, half the rainbow in hue, were so vivid it hurt to look at her. Even in my astral form, when she moved it left blurs of crimson and sapphron and azure smeared across my retinas like acid etching into my eyes, sheer radiant power.

It was also incomplete, as if someone had thoughtlessly cut away her left hand, unaware that doing so maimed the whole. There were gaps of darkness as razor-sharp as the colors, spots of black that didn't complete the whole. I hadn't seen those slashes earlier, neither when she'd come into Morrison's office nor when she was with Mark. I hoped that was because she was actively pursuing magic now, thereby exposing her flaws, and not because I was blind and stupid. I had a sense of patterns in the darkness, but looking that hard made my head ache, and there were other things to focus on.

Like the fact that it appeared she was trying to make up for her lost colors by feeding on Morrison's. The solid purples and blues were already depleted, far worse than Billy's or Mel's. Morrison didn't know how to build shields to protect himself. I hoped, abruptly and painfully, that I'd get the chance to teach him. Knowing he'd never do it was beside the point.

I extended a hand, all washed with silver-blue, and put it below Barbara's, over Morrison's heart, actually within his chest. Cold infused the back of my hand, then feathers as edged as scalpels lacerated the skin. It hurt like tiny paper cuts, more academic in the moment they happened than they would be in a few more seconds. My own shields pushed back against the injuries, healing sparks flying upward like a muffler dragging against asphalt. It tingled and itched, then flared bright in the instant that Barbara drew back in surprise.

That was all I needed. The timing was flawless, like the pit mechanics at a race. Seven-second tire change, though nothing like that much time passed in between Barb's falter and my sliding shields into place, protecting my boss the only way I knew how. Silver power washed into him, building protective walls around a psychic garden I didn't dare invade, but which I knew the peripheries of well enough to risk defining. I built points of contact, his complete lack of knowledge about cars tied with the practical safety of the Toyota in the driveway; practical safety bound with compassion that had brought *him* to tell a mother her daughter had died, when it could easily have been someone else's job. And that tied to another daughter, six years old, treated with due respect and seriousness, which came around to the frown Morrison had bestowed on me when he ordered me not to belittle myself.

Endless details I hadn't realized I'd known, from the Frank Lloyd Wright clock on his desk to his father's seaman's coat, from our identical heights making it hard for either of us to back down to the guts it took for him to point my magically talented self at problems mundane policework couldn't explain, helped me to build a shield around my captain that cut off the life force that Barbara drained from him. Everything, his rare smiles and his steadfast belief in right and wrong, his stiff-necked acceptance of my talents and his exhaustive concern for his police force, hammered through me in waves of recognition.

No wonder I loved the man.

I closed my eyes against a blush that burned my cheeks, even in astral form. I could see it with my eyes closed, the physical action having no effect at all on my projected vision: red infusing the cool silver-blue that was my usual aura. I suspected there was strength somewhere in embarrassment, but if there was, I didn't know how to use it for myself. I thought it might help maintain the shield I'd built, though, as it was intimately bound to Morrison himself.

I lifted my eyes and met Barbara's gaze square on, totally unsurprised that she could see me. Her mouth pinched, eyes tightening, and her shoulders went back. Not with shock, but preparation. Even knowing that for some reason she was only at half strength, watching the changes in her body language sent the primitive lizard part of my brain running screaming into the dark recesses of my mind. I didn't know what exactly Morrison's new lover was, but I was very sure I didn't want her to hit me.

A very small blossom of rage opened up inside me and I realized that more to the point, I didn't want her to hit *him*. I felt my lip curl as I leaned forward, literally bracing myself against whatever onslaught she had prepared.

Time went desperately weird.

It went still all around me, worse than the slowed-down clarity of a fight. It *froze,* as if I'd be able to see raindrops hanging in the air. Barbara's breathing stopped, though there was no flatness in her eyes that bespoke death. I couldn't tell if I did the same, because I wasn't sure I even breathed when I left my body.

I hadn't been particularly aware of my body for the last several seconds, though I knew in a clinical sense it was out there standing on Morrison's front porch. Having now spared it a thought, I could almost feel the memories of the past few moments pouring through it, as if it was catching up on details of a movie it hadn't been paying attention to. Everything rewound, a blur of silence and images, until I'd reamalgamated with myself and all my memories and awareness were in one place, back there on the porch.

I snapped forward again.

This time it hurt, a concussive smash into—

—the future. The present. For a bewildering instant I wasn't sure where or when I was anymore. Morrison's kitchen floor was hard under my knees, my body having joined its spirit, apparently without bothering to travel the distance separating the two. My ears rang with a disrupted song of power, jangling noise fading away even as I noticed it. I felt like there were eddies swirling off my skin, as if I'd become a sticking point in a river and that river had briefly bent to my will.

I still saw with the Sight, but ordinary vision lay beneath it, picking up details that hadn't been important to my projected self. The lingering scent of meat and tomatoes was in the air, reminding me I hadn't eaten for hours. The dishes hadn't been done, a frying pan sitting on the stove. I wondered if they'd come back to Morrison's for dinner after my little display at the restaurant. Streetlamps colored the walls through big windows, no lights on inside.

My outstretched hand now rested on Morrison's chest, no longer just beneath the surface of his skin. Barbara's hand, warm and sweaty, lay on top of mine. My own skin shimmered with the silver-sheened rainbow slick of power, but not translucently. And Barbara was breathing again, time loosing its hold on her. Fury glinted in her eyes as she recognized that time had hiccupped, and she drew breath to spit something at me.

I twisted my right hand up to grab her wrist, and brought my left fist around in a roundhouse blow that caught her squarely in the teeth.

With all due modesty, I really think she'd have gone flying if I hadn't had a grip on her wrist. As it was, the weight of her body pulled me forward as she recoiled. If I hadn't had thirty pounds on her, I'd have flopped ignominiously across Morrison's chest. Some rescue that would've been.

Although as far as rescues went, this one pretty much sucked, because Morrison wasn't waking up. I tensed my stomach muscles and surged to my feet, hauling a dazed Barbara with me. I let go of her wrist and knotted both hands in her shirt before she got her feet under her, and discovered I could actually pick her up far enough that her feet dangled just above Morrison's chest. There was a certain amount of genuine glee involved in whirling around and slamming her up against a wall so I could yell, "What the hell are you?" into her face. I felt like an action hero.

She got enough focus back to stare at me, which I thought was a good sign. Then she smashed her head forward into the bridge of my nose, which wasn't nearly as good a sign. I dropped her, yowling with pain, and she slithered down the wall. Women, especially cute petite women, weren't supposed to head-butt people. Girls like me, who stood almost six feet tall, could head-butt in a fight. That was okay. Little women were supposed to shriek and flail and use their fingernails, not their foreheads.

I bet Phoebe would kick my ass just for thinking that. In something like my defense, instead of kneeing me in the crotch, which is what I would've done if I'd been her, Barbara dropped to hands and knees and scrambled around my legs while I swore as violently as I could. It didn't help my nose any, but it made me feel better enough to turn around and deliver a swift kick to Barbara's ribs. She lifted up a gratifying few inches and went over on her back to land on Morrison's shins with an *oomf!* I wanted to take a minute and fix my nose so tears would stop blinding me, but Barb rolled off Morrison and staggered to her feet, reaching toward the counter for support.

Wrong-o, Joanne, I heard myself think, far too brightly. Barb's actions telegraphed through tear-blurred vision just an instant before she completed them. The counter wasn't her goal. The frying pan on the stove was. She slung it at me, marinara sauce splattering everywhere. I flung up my arms with another yell, crossing them in front of my face.

The impact bounced off my arms hard enough to leave a bone bruise. I shouted again, half in anticipation of burns than the immediate pain of the pan crashing into my arms. It took a good three seconds to realize there wasn't any accompanying singeing of my arms or thick boiling liquid dripping down me. I squinted one eye open to discover a sheen of blue-tinged power dancing over my skin, my mental shields made manifest in reality. Only very belatedly did I realize the sauce wasn't hot, anyway, but had it been, I'd managed to protect myself.

It was the second time that had happened, but this time a sudden crash took place between my ears. I remembered one very long tiring night where Coyote coaxed those shields out, exhausting my brain with the idea of sheltering my whole body in shielding when I thought it was hard enough to protect my mind.

I also remembered falling asleep in English class the next day, with one ear half listening to a discussion on *Hamlet*. The teacher, suspecting me of sleeping, had called on me and I'd sat upright blurting, "Polonius!" without the foggiest conscious idea of what was being discussed. The teacher's irate expression and a sense of smugness on my part still lingered, so I knew I'd been right.

I muttered, "Thou canst not then be false to any man," as I lowered my arms, shielding still washing over my body protectively. I was starting to think the old windbag might've been on to something, which would have gratified my English teacher to no end.

To my complete astonishment, the same cool blue protection danced over Morrison, who was almost as liberally spattered with sauce as I was. Once I'd seen it, I could feel the stretch in my mind that said I was maintaining the mental shielding. The connection went deeper than I'd thought, and I had the sudden uncomfortable sensation that I might not be able to undo it.

It didn't matter, at least not for the moment. Without the shields I could provide, Morrison's life force would be drained away in very little time, so undoing the thing was out of the question. I wondered, briefly, if other people were as vulnerable as the captain was, and thought it unlikely. For one thing, people I knew would be dying in droves, if it were so. For another, I was pretty certain I'd been right in what I'd told Morrison: it was those I had the deepest emotional connections with who were in the most danger. I guessed it was lucky for Seattle in general that I didn't have many close friends, or deep hatreds. I'd done what I could with more casual acquaintances with the topaz pieces, and would have to hope they'd work.

Topaz.

I could *kill* Morrison for giving away that topaz.

My attention came back up to Barbara, who stood by the stove looking very human and confused, so much so that my heart went out to her. I knew that look. I felt like I'd spent an awful lot of time with it on my face. I was actually putting my hand out to her, like I might offer some kind of comfort, when whatever uncertainty had surfaced was swallowed whole again, and Barb sprang across Morrison's body at me, her hands clawed.

That was more what I expected from a chick. I braced myself, but not enough, and her weight drove me over backward into Morrison's kitchen table. I heard wood splinter and the smooth surface lurched downward beneath us while Barbara skimmed her lips against her teeth and hissed from the back of her throat. I grabbed her wrists and rolled, crashing off the table into the chairs. More wood splintered, and I wondered how I was going to explain the remains of the kitchen when Morrison woke up.

If Morrison woke up.

For a few seconds I couldn't see anything except red, and I wasn't sure if that was the Sight or just my normal vision full of fury. Barb got a hand loose and jabbed her fingers into my eyes. I screamed, as much with anger as pain, and grabbed her wrist again to bite into the webbing between her thumb and forefinger. She shrieked and jerked away, sending us off the chairs and onto the floor, the light dimming. I spat out a mouthful of coppery blood, gagging on the flavor. My vision cleared again, tears streaming, and I snatched her hand out of the air as she drove it toward my eyes again. Her wrists were tiny, and once I had both of them I knotted the fingers of one hand around them, imprisoning her and leaving me with a hand to punch her with.

Triumphant, I reared back on my heels to get my weight behind a hit, and clobbered my head on the table. Stars sparkled in my line of sight and I realized a little too late the reason the lights had dimmed was we'd rolled under the table. Barb pulled her legs up and kicked me in the stomach with both feet, sending me back far enough to smack my head on the table again. I did my best mindless beast roar and flung myself on her, no longer trying to get a hit in. I would just smother her with my superior body weight. And whack her in the eye a few times with my elbow, if I could. For a few seconds we were biting and rolling and scratching and screeching, the indignity of fighting like girls ridiculously clear in my mind. I couldn't remember getting in such a noisy fight before.

The table crashed over sideways as we rolled into its legs with enough force to knock it down. The smash made us both freeze for an instant, as if we expected a parent to come storming downstairs to find out what was going on.

I recovered first, probably because I had no siblings to

wrestle with, and therefore less expectation of getting in trouble for wrecking the house. The table no longer hindering me, I grabbed a fistful of Barb's shirt and hauled her to her feet so I could hit her. This time I let go when the punch landed and she staggered back into the window.

Which shattered, and she went head over heels through it with a shriek.

I stood there a couple seconds, completely unprepared for that. My first thought, I admit, was, *hah!* but it was followed by the somewhat more alarming, *Christ, she could be dead.* Glass was still shimmering and trembling as I took the couple steps to the window and put my hands on the sill gingerly, looking out.

Barb popped to her feet and hit me in the face with a pair of plastic-wrapped pruning shears.

CHAPTER TWENTY-SEVEN

It had been a while since being hit on the head had knocked me into the realm of Other. Overall, I liked it better when I was sliding in and out of psychic realms on my own cognizance, though I had to say there was something for waking up in my garden without my head hurting. It was a big fat psychological fib, because I knew perfectly well that out there in the real world I was going to need a nose job. Fortunately, my self-perception didn't include a mashed-in face, and in my garden, imagination trumped reality.

"Joanne." The thin, weary voice seemed to come from all around me and nowhere at the same time. It made my heart lurch, one part panic at my garden being invaded and two parts hope: I knew that voice. "Jo," it repeated, and I whispered, "Coyote?"

I could almost sense him. His presence was more a wish than a fact, as if he'd been mixed up with oxygen and smeared liberally through the atmosphere: I couldn't see it, but I knew it was there. My heart pounded so hard it made my stomach hurt, and for some reason there was a film over my eyes, blurring my vision. "Coyote?" My hands had gotten all cold and shaky and my cheeks burned hot, until I felt like I might fall apart from conflicting temperatures in such a small space. "Coyote, are you okay? Where are you?"

A breath of a chuckle came through the air, but that was all. No more words, nothing reassuring, no explanation as to how I might go about stopping Barb from sucking my friends' life forces. "Coyote, I need you." I sounded young and so tremulous I'd moved beyond pathetic into outright fear.

He didn't say anything else. The garden seemed to shift and sigh, like it was waiting for something, and I put my face in my hands with a hoarse laugh. "Imagination trumps reality. Please, oh, God, please help me get this right."

I reached for my power, still whispering pleas into my fingers. It spilled upward, delicate as a filigree net, pouring through me until I could see my garden the way the younger me had, some fifteen years ago. Life infused it, though not as thoroughly as it had then. Here, it simmered below the surface, instead of bursting free and full of laughter. My waterfall, always off to my right, was as I remembered it, sheeting down a wall of granite, rather than thundering so hard and fast it made mist, but at least it held the promise of more. Everything felt that way, as if it waited to come to a boil again. I was absurdly grateful it thought it still could.

I dropped my hands from my face and reached out, casting my net of power as if I would be able to draw Coyote in. It shimmered blue, ocean-colored, and rode the air like feathers on the water. I had no car analogy to suit this, but nets had worked for me in the past, and the one I wove now was so fine it might catch raindrops and cradle them between its threads. I clung to the idea of my spirit guide, trying to gather him in so he could become cohesive and whole again, instead of just a voice in the ether.

A pulse ran through the net, silver power that rippled and overwhelmed the blue that was predominant. It caught me in the belly and pulled me forward with unexpected strength. Panic seized me and I resisted, for which trouble I earned a snort I knew all too well, and a distinct sensation of dismissal.

I couldn't tell if it was surprise or dismay that caught me out, but it didn't matter. I faltered for just an instant, a hiccup of concentration lost. Silver swept my net, wrapped around me, and hauled me through space and time like so much flotsam.

Joanne was tall at—more than thirteen, now. I'd had one disastrous flirtation with perms as a teenager, the summer after my freshman year. The ends of her short hair were still curled, so she'd been fifteen for a few months, and if I remembered my own haircuts correctly, that meant in another six or eight weeks she'd be pregnant. My stomach cramped up and I knotted my hands into fists, staring down at the younger me. I was less than two inches taller than she was, and by the end of her sophomore year she'd be able to look me in the eye. Right now, height was the only thing I had on her at all.

I could see the cohesion of her power, riding under her

skin and sparking through her aura. The net I'd woven was gone, replaced by a silver cord that thrummed back and forth between us, twisting and writhing in the air like it had life of its own. I wanted to bat at it and make it lie down. Joanne ignored it, looking over me like I made a bad taste in her mouth.

"Jeez," she said, "you don't know anything at all. What the hell happened to you?"

"Wow." I startled out of staring at the cord and stared at Joanne instead. "You really were a little shit, weren't you? Anybody ever tell you that you catch more flies with honey?" Wow. I wasn't going to like me at all. From either side of this conversation. Joanne's eyes narrowed and her sneer settled into place. I wanted to reach across and smack it off her. "I need to talk to Coyote."

Joanne tossed her head, which would've been more effective if her hair was long enough to swish. "Too bad."

My hands were still fisted at my sides. I took a moment to explain to them that I did not approve of giving my younger self a knuckle sandwich, no matter how much she deserved it, and deliberately unknotted them and put them in my pockets so they couldn't act on their own.

"Seriously," she said. "What happened to you? You're a total mess."

I actually *felt* her reach into my head and draw out my own private image, the shattered windshield that reflected the state of my soul. It superimposed itself across the whole of my garden, which was *Joanne's* version of the garden, verdant and lush and full of life until my cracks and seams sucked some of the health from it.

"I mean, look at that," she said, somewhere between admiring and horrified. "You've got a bullet hole right through the middle of you. What happened?" A note of urgency threaded through her voice with the third repetition of the question, and to my surprise I felt sorry for her.

"It doesn't matter, Jo. Just—"

Her hackles went up. "Don't call me that."

A muscle cramped in my shoulderblade and I reached around with my left hand to massage it, startled. "Sorry. I forgot." Dad called me Jo, like he wanted a boy if he wanted a kid at all, and I'd hated it. Sometime in the past six or seven months I'd gotten used to Gary using the nickname, and it'd worked its way into being a name I used for myself. The younger me stared.

"You forgot? I *hate* being called Jo."

"I know. You get over it."

Outraged disbelief settled on Joanne's features. She wasn't unattractive, I thought rather clinically, although the sneer and the chip on her shoulder made her much less pretty than she could be. I wondered how much of that I still carried with me, and glanced around the shadow-stained garden. Probably more than I wanted to admit to. "I would *never* get over it," Joanne announced with furious dignity. I shrugged.

"I know. That's why I'm not going to tell you what happens."

Her lip curled again, this time with incomprehension. It was good, I thought, that I could at least consistently and properly read my own expressions. "Look, if I try to warn you, you'll say, 'That'll never happen to me,' and go charging along on your predestined path, and if I don't, you will, anyway, so there's no point in telling you what happens. It happened. It's done."

A narrow breach appeared in the tightness of her face, a place where fear could enter. "But I don't want to end up like that." She waved a hand, encompassing my shattered soul. I managed a faint smile.

"I don't want you to, either. Sorry, Joanie."

"You're not either sorry. You don't care at all."

"Wouldn't it be a lot easier of that was true. Look, Joanne, I don't really have time to hang out and argue with you. I really do need to talk to Coyote."

"No."

I abruptly recognized the tone, as if I could hear the rest of her words echoing in my mind: *he's my friend. You don't get to take him away from me.*

I thought, *oh, crap,* and let the lead weight that suddenly filled my stomach pull me to my knees. I felt my hands cover my face, a fingertip bumping over the thin scar on my cheek, and all I could think was, *crap, no, crap, shit, no, don't do this.* I could feel Joanne's distress rolling off her in waves as I put my hands forward in the earth of the garden and brought my forehead down to it, clutching grass and fighting against misery. I could see, could *see* the path opening up in front of me, in front of Joanne, and I didn't see a way to get off it.

"Please." Hotness dripped from my eyes, staining the grass with sizzling spots, salt burning away the green. "Please don't do this." Even as I spoke I reached for my power, the ball of energy that seemed to lie behind my breastbone, separate but part of me.

And Joanne's answered, pure amalgamated strength that was as much a part of her as her eyes or fingers. The river

Coyote'd pulled me from swept around me, time shifting and flexing as I borrowed what was mine thirteen years earlier. I didn't drain my younger self, no more than she could drain me, but I did take her control, whispering, "I'm sorry, I'm sorry, I'm so sorry, Joanie, I'm so sorry," as I did so.

"No!" Rage and pain and fear split her voice in a shriek, and she jumped at me. I reared back onto my heels and caught her in a hug, my arms over hers. In the garden that we shared, neither of us had the psychic advantage, but I was an adult woman, physically powerful from years of working on cars, and I held her easily as she twisted and sobbed against my chest.

"I'm not taking him," I whispered, knowing it was completely useless. "I'm not even taking your ability to talk to him, Jo. I just need to be able to do it myself in my time, and I need your power. Your skill. Your training. I am so sorry, Joanie. Don't let it ruin you. Coyote's not gone. You're not alone, sweetheart. You're not alone."

"What do you know about it!" Her voice was a hoarse scream, making my own throat ache. "You're a grown-up, you don't understand! You don't know anything!"

"I was there, Jo. I do know. I lived it. I do know. You don't have to let it drive your choices. You're going to be okay, Joanie. You really are." I sounded so soft and confident that even I believed me for a moment.

But I did know. I had been there. I knew that the fifteen-year-old girl I held wouldn't remember her dreams about Coyote, or my visitation, when she woke up. She'd only remember that she felt more outcast and abandoned than ever, because she thought I'd taken her one friend away.

And that loneliness would drive her choices, just as if I'd deliberately wiped away every other path she might have taken. The beautiful skin drum lying on her dresser would go unused. The power she had such control over would be shut away, left to fester, its only release the creation of impenetrable shields and a stubbornness so profound it might well have been born of magic. She would take desperate actions to try to fit in during her sophomore year of high school, and she would pay for what I had done here for the next thirteen years. Just as I'd made my mother a woman who could will herself to death, I'd made myself into the ragingly lonely, angry young woman I was in high school, and the ill-adjusted, reluctant shaman I'd grown up to be. It was a closed circle, endless, flawless.

I lied, "You'll be okay," into Joanne's hair, and let her go.

Time pulled me back to where I belonged.

The net I'd cast out shone with a power I'd never seen before, not without help from my friends. It felt as if I'd been breathing without one lung for half a year and simply hadn't realized it. I still had a sense of centering, the healing magic resting behind my breastbone, but it wasn't any more separate from me than my heart was. I didn't need to blink or concentrate to bring auras into focus, the young Joanne's training fully accessible to me. I should have been glad.

Instead, every heartbeat felt heavy, regret weighing it down. There had to have been a better way, and the closed loop of time and paradox told me even if there was, it was too late for me, too late for Joanne. We'd traveled the path we needed to in order to arrive here and now, and without starting completely anew, I saw no way around it. I hoped

Grandfather Sky was happy with what he'd wrought, and wondered if I'd ever be what the Makers of the world had intended for me to be.

I drew my net in with the skill of an ancient mariner, fistful after fistful of shimmering blue and silver light, waiting to see what I'd caught. Weight burdened it as I pulled it in closer, thin air coalescing into familiar shape. When I'd gathered all the particles spread through the atmosphere together, they became Coyote, translucent and tired in the mist of my waterfall. We looked at each other awhile, both silent and weary, his eyes gold and mine green, for all I couldn't see them. Magic in the outside world might make them gold, but my idea of myself had hazel eyes, and I would not relinquish that to the power.

When I finally spoke, it wasn't what I expected to say. "When are you?" came out, as if it made perfect sense.

"I'm not sure." He lifted a hand to examine it, turning his fingers this way and that. I could just see his face through his fingers, and from his glance, he could just see me through them, too. Disconcertingly, the coyote form mixed with the man, bones and paws and heads twisted to work together until I couldn't quite tell which was which. Joanne had seen him this way, and I wondered if I always would now, or if he'd be able to hold to one form in my eyes when he was at full strength. "I don't remember this," he said, "but it doesn't mean I'm now." He lowered his hand, turning his golden focus on me. "So now you know."

"You didn't warn me." I couldn't bring heat or accusation to the words, much as I wanted to. "Couldn't you have done something to change how it happened?"

"I tried. I tried, Joanne. I did try."

Dreams filled my mind, seeing myself from the outside as a raven fell down from the sky to sweep me up. Then Big Coyote, settling himself between two paths, the raven down one and a comprehensible future down another. The sweat lodge, and my grandfather, a man that Joanne didn't know, but Coyote did. The path I'd taken in dreams, following the raven in hopes of somehow guiding the black-haired little girl who had stared at me from beside her father's Oldsmobile, twenty years earlier. I stared through the dream images at Coyote's thin form and shook my head, eyes wide with incomprehension. "What are you?"

He smiled, tired and sad. "A shaman. A guide. Your guide."

"But—" I shook myself, trying to clear my mind. "But…you're…" Certainty filled me, washing away an abstract concept: the grandfather who'd guided me in Coyote's dreams was not the Maker Grandfather Sky, but Coyote's own grandfather, a kind wise man of flesh and blood.

"Human?" His smile came again, brief and brighter this time. "You never asked, Jo."

"I asked if you were a spirit guide!"

His smile crinkled a third time. "I am."

"But—but—you're—!" I wasn't doing well with clearing my mind, much less getting a coherent thought out. "But I thought you were magic! Not real!"

He lifted one eyebrow. "After all this, you still think there's a difference between *real* and *magic?*"

"*Coyote!*" Frustration burst through my voice and he laughed, gentle sound beneath the rumble of waterfalls.

"I wondered for a long time why you never asked my name. You always called me Coyote. Even when you were a girl. I finally realized you thought I was something else. A power animal. No wonder you kept thinking I was a dog."

"Coyotes aren't dogs," I said, so automatically I surprised myself. Coyote's eyes widened and he threw his head back in another laugh.

"After all this time, you've finally learned that. There may be hope for you yet, Siobhán Walkingstick."

"Why didn't you ever *tell* me?" My voice rose and broke like a kid's. "You *tricked* me!"

Coyote flashed into his animal form, lolling a cheerful tongue at me. "I *am* a coyote."

Spluttering outrage stopped my throat while he cocked his head, tail wagging in admonishment. "There isn't a lot of time, Jo. You're coming into your own now. I don't know what's going on around you, so tell me. What do you need me for?"

All the burgeoning betrayal fled, leaving me on my knees in the garden clutching at grass again. "The usual," I heard myself say in a small voice. "Save the prince, fight the dragon, be home in time for dinner. I'm all alone, Coyote. You…" I didn't want to tell this Coyote, whenever he was from, that in my time he was dead. His golden burst of power, whatever he'd done to stave off the butterfly darkness and free me, suddenly made more sense. It hadn't been a spirit creature at all, and it felt like me because he was like me. Human. Only human. I didn't see how he could have survived. "You can't answer me," I said to the grass. It was longer than I remembered, halfway up my forearms as I knotted my fingers in it. "I set something loose, something that was sleeping and is awake now, and it's got you. It's getting everybody. I don't know how to stop it." I laughed, thin little sound, and shook my head. "And I haven't slept in days, except for these magically induced comas that I dream and dream during. I'm tired. I'm tired and I don't know what to do."

"Trust yourself." The words were so bald they made me look up, even as I swayed in the grass. "You're not alone, Joanne. You have a teacher. Trust yourself." His voice thinned as he spoke, as did the rest of him. I could feel my net fraying, not because I lacked power, but more as if it felt it had done its job, and the time to hold him was over. "You'll be all right."

It was the same promise I'd made to a much younger version of myself. I'd lied. I watched Coyote as he got up, shook himself, and turned to trot away, wondering if he was lying, too.

"Coyote."

He turned back, furry spots where his eyebrows would be raised in curiosity, one paw lifted in a pretty pose.

"What's your *name?*"

A man stood before me, looking back over his shoulder, hip-length black hair swinging free over brick-red bare shoulders. His eyebrows were still lifted, his foot paused in preparation for a step. I could see the coyote form nestled inside him, wholly a part of him. He dropped a wink, then disappeared into the mist, leaving a word lingering in the air: "Cyrano."

CHAPTER TWENTY—EIGHT

I had actually forgotten about the pruning shears to the face, while traipsing around with Coyote and ruining my younger self's life. Memory came back to me with blinding vengeance as Coyote's name rang the round two bell and dropped me into my own body. So little time had passed I was still in the midst of falling over. I twisted in midair, wrenching my back but managing to get my hands under me so I neither smashed into the table nor bashed my head against anything else. That had to count for something. What, I didn't know, but I was sure it was something. Still, I hit the floor hard enough to jar my whole body, all the nerve endings of which seemed to be centered in my face. Whimpering and rolling over wasn't very manly, but it was about all I had in my repertoire right then.

Barbara didn't appear to be climbing back in the window to whack at me with the shears, so I took a moment to lie there and focus on my nose. Not literally. My eyes were too full of tears to see it even if I could've gotten them to cross, which hurt too badly to try after the first time. I put my fingers over my nose, gingerly, then tried really hard to think of something else while I yanked it straight.

Turns out you can't really think of anything else when you're doing that. I wasn't surprised, but I was very disappointed. The good news was, once I was done straightening the mashed cartilage, it only took a moment's visualization for cool blue healing power to suction-cup the dent and pop it back into place. I knew there was a chance I'd bring the darkness back down on my head by healing myself, but I just flat-out couldn't imagine trying to chase bad guys around with my face throbbing so hard I could barely see straight.

Pain faded so quickly it left me with a headache that felt blissful and frothy in comparison. I braced, waiting for the weight of butterfly darkness to come back, but instead I heard the sound of an engine cranking. I crunched up and climbed to my feet, leaning out Morrison's shattered kitchen window to catch Barbara backing out of the driveway as if a banshee was after her. She hadn't thought to stop and slash my tires, which I would've done in her position, and which was good for her health. I'd have had to found a way to fly through the air, land on her hood and pull her through the windshield a few times in vengeance. I could feel power settling into my bones, comfortable as if it'd always been there, but I didn't think a newfound confidence also covered superheroic leaps across wide empty spaces.

It'd be cool if it did, though.

Rather than try, or even go tearing out to Petite to give chase, I turned back to my boss. He lay in the shambles of his kitchen without the slightest awareness of what had transpired around him. I figured if I didn't get the mess cleaned up before he woke up, he'd automatically assume it was my fault. The idea made my heart cramp. I took a deep breath to push pain away, then crouched to get Morrison into a fireman's carry and take him to the hospital. Barbara could wait.

I knew Northwest was swamped, but I brought Morrison there, anyway. Even before dawn, the admitting nurse's hair was sticking to her temples, tiny pin curls taking shape in the dampness of perspiration. She gave me a look bordering on despair and got Morrison into a wheelchair while I filled out paperwork that asked awkward questions about the captain's weight and general health. I was sure he had a wallet in his pocket that would hold a driver's license and insurance card, but it took me fifteen minutes to talk myself into looking.

His driver's license picture was one of the best I'd ever seen. I wondered if police captains got to stand around making the DMV take pictures until one came out well enough to satisfy their vanity, or if Morrison was just photogenic enough to overcome the general awfulness of identification photos. Since I was being nosy, anyway, I looked for a passport to compare pictures with, but he wasn't that thorough about carrying ID.

The sun was peeking over the horizon by the time I got the paperwork filled out, as much because I kept nodding off and jerking awake as not knowing the answers. I hauled myself to my feet and went back to the admissions desk, where the frazzled nurse gave it a perfunctory glance. "What's the J stand for?"

"I have no idea. He goes by Michael." It was Morrison's first initial. J. Michael Morrison. I'd always assumed Michael was his first name.

Sort of like he'd always assumed Joanne was mine. I crinkled my face at the desk and waited until the nurse signed him in and gave him a room number.

Billy's room number.

My stomach knotted up again and I reached for the nurse's hand, astonished at how warm it was. My fingers felt like they were turning blue. "I know the people who were in that room. William and Melinda Holliday. Are they... okay?"

The nurse put her hand over mine momentarily, a gentler gesture than I'd have expected, given that I'd seized her, then extracted her wrist to check the computer. "They're fine. We're just finding it necessary to sta—" She cut herself off with a look of dismay.

Relief brought laughter to my lips. "Stack 'em and rack 'em?"

"I would *never* say such a thing," she admonished me, then smiled briefly and shrugged. "As you say."

I nodded, almost reached out to grab her hand again and stopped myself by folding both my hands together on the counter hard enough to turn my knuckles white. "Thank you. Thank you so much. Would it help if I brought Morrison up to the room? I want to see Billy, anyway."

"You really shouldn't. Visiting hours don't start until eleven." Then she looked around and exhaled. "Just tell the nurse's station I couldn't find an orderly and you offered to help. It's a madhouse around here, anyway. They'll be too busy to fire me." She pulled out another smile, this one wry, and handed me Morrison's chart before turning into the noise to help another incoming patient.

Somebody at the nurse's station upstairs took Morrison away from me, and I went down the hall to Billy's room, where a harried-looking orderly was changing sheets and cleaning up as fast as his legs would let him. A third bed had been inserted into the room, making it claustrophobic but worthwhile. Mel's bed had been pushed up against Billy's. Robert Holliday was there, and I wondered if he'd stayed the night in the hospital, too, and had simply been elsewhere when I visited, or if he'd found a way in himself. I didn't know if strict visiting hours counted for immediate family, but they didn't seem to apply to Brad Holliday, who, it appeared, had never left.

The two of them were hunched over the beds like weary gargoyles, one on each side. I tapped on the door frame and they both looked up, Robert brightening and Brad glowering. I said, "Hey," before Brad had time to say anything mean, and came into the room pushing my hair back with both hands. "How're they doing?"

"No change." Brad held his mouth in a thin line of disapproval, as if he was trying to drive me out through force of will alone.

"I guess that's a good thing, under the circumstances. At least they're not getting worse." I stepped up to Robert to give him a one-armed hug, then brushed my fingers over Melinda's temple. Silver-blue sparks leapt from my fingertips into her hair, sparkling down her body like a quick vehicle diagnostic, and came back to tell me she was fine and the baby was very very bored with Mom just lying there on her back. I heard Robert draw a sharp breath and looked down at him. His pupils ate the irises, black swallowing light brown.

He blurted, "You're warm," then sucked his lower lip in, not sure I'd understand. I put my arm around his shoulders again.

"That's good. Hospitals are cold." The kid sagged against my side and I hugged him harder. "How're your sisters and brother? Who's watching them?"

"My wife came up from Spokane." Brad's tone told me I could leave any time now. I lifted my gaze from Melinda and studied him a moment, then tilted my head.

"Can I talk to you out in the hall for a minute, Brad?"

Robert stiffened under my arm and I gave him another hug, wishing I could reassure him that I wasn't leaving him out of grown-up talks. I left the door open so he could eavesdrop when I followed Brad out of the room.

Leaving the meager sanctuary of the room dropped us back into the chaos and sound of the hospital hallways. Orders blared over the PA system. Hospital personnel called out to one another as they coordinated their workday. Frightened, worried families hovered in doorways and in waiting rooms, whether visiting hours were open or not. I said, "I don't know how you do this every day," without thinking. "Just standing here exhausts me."

Brad's face relaxed from its pinch, surprise taking over for a few seconds. His "You get used to it" sounded almost friendly, though he looked like he didn't know why he'd responded politely.

"I don't know if I would. Look, Doc, I'm sorry." Apologizing was not high on my list of favorite things to do, and I listened to myself with nearly as much surprise as Brad's expression showed. "We got off on an incredibly bad start, and that's my fault. I was completely out of line and I'm sorry. I was…" I raked my hand through my hair again and sighed. I needed a shower. "I was trying to protect people, and trying to show off, and I was a total jerk. I'm not going to ask you to forgive me, but Robert's not stupid, and his parents are in there asleep and nobody knows if they're going to wake up. He doesn't need you and me bristling at each other."

"So you want me to bury the hatchet." Brad spoke so suddenly I hiccupped, caught out of an apology that was only starting to build up steam.

"Yeah. Please. You want to go *mano a mano* with me when Billy and Mel are awake again, okay, fine, name the time and place." Last time I'd challenged somebody to *mano a mano* it had been a god. Brad Holliday was a real come-down, comparatively. "We're not really on opposite sides, you and me," I added more quietly. "Just traveling from different directions."

"I don't want to know." Brad's voice went thin and stressy. I lifted my hands in another apology.

"Sorry. Peace?"

He jerked his chin in a downward nod and walked back into Billy's room. Robert watched him, then watched me, his clear gaze telling me he knew perfectly well I'd let him listen in on the conversation. His hand crept into mine for a squeeze when I came back to his side, an eleven-year-old's way of saying thank you without drawing notice to himself. "They're bringing Captain Morrison in here," I said as if that had been the topic all along. Robert held on to my hand harder, dismay radiating off him.

"Captain Morrison's sick, too? He can't be. I thought you'd keep him okay." Robert's voice rose in alarm. "Gary's okay, isn't he?"

"Gary's fine." Robert relaxed a little under my arm, then gave me the same sideways look he'd gotten when he'd first met Gary. Even he thought I was dating the old man. "How come Gary's okay and Captain Morrison isn't?" he asked, somewhere between suspicious and testing. I groaned and closed my eyes.

It did nothing to make the world go away. My second sight just slid into place, letting me see everything in vibrant neon glows and swirls of color. Robert's aura spiked orange, pulses of curiosity. "Gary's okay and Morrison isn't because Gary listens to me." I opened my eyes and looked down at Robert. "*Not* because Gary's my boyfriend."

Robert said, "Hnh," through his nose, and assumed an expression of innocence as he looked away.

I could feel Brad's gaze turn curious and nearly groaned again. After all, Gary had been the one to ride to the rescue Wednesday morning when Melinda'd gotten sick. It all made sense, from an outside point of view. I muttered, "He's not," aware that the lady was protesting too much.

I was rescued from further attempts at extracting myself from a relationship with the old cabbie by a tired orderly wheeling my sleeping captain into the room. Brad got up from the far side of Billy's bed, said, "I'm a doctor," and gave the orderly a hand in getting Morrison into bed. After one look to see who'd entered the room, I kept my focus wholly on Melinda and Billy. For some reason I really didn't want to watch people manhandling my boss into a hospital bed. I was going to take that piece of topaz and hammer it into Morrison's skull when this was all over.

It took a while for them to get Morrison settled. Robert, rather too loudly, asked Uncle Brad to take him down to the café for breakfast, and I wondered if the kid was just teasing me about Gary for form's sake. Either way, they left me alone and I found myself by Morrison's bed, sitting on my hands so I wouldn't take his in both of mine.

The poor man looked like he needed the sleep, honestly. I didn't know if a coma was proper rest or not, but the inability to worry wiped some of the lines from his face, making him look younger than his thirty-eight years. If I let my eyes unfocus just a little, I could see the shielding I'd put in place, sparking blue along the silver threads in his hair and swimming over the surface of him. I could feel it, too, if I wanted to, and I was trying hard not to. I didn't think Morrison would appreciate the intimate invasion, and the last thing I wanted was full-body memory flashes when I went to work and faced my boss every day.

After a while I noticed my face was in my hands and there was salty wetness leaking through my fingers. For someone who didn't think of herself as the crying sort, I'd sure done a lot of it recently. More in the last six or seven months than I could remember in years. I had a fair idea that said nothing good about my ongoing emotional status.

Eventually I stood up and put my fingertips on Morrison's shoulder, as polite a farewell as I could manage, and said, "Sorry about your kitchen," before I went out to finish what I'd started with Barbara Bragg.

CHAPTER TWENTY-NINE

That was one of those easier-said-than-done plans. I didn't know where to look for Barb, or what to do when I found her. Finishing kicking her ass was definitely on the roster, but that was sort of nebulous, in a specific way.

I shuddered. My brain was starting to show the lack of sleep. I stopped at a drive-by coffee shop and got a quad shot of espresso and had them pour a generous splash of amaretto flavoring in to make it drinkable. I was tired enough to find myself balancing the coffee and my cell phone, making a phone call while I was driving.

That had to be one of the stupider things I'd done lately. Except the scene at the restaurant, which I hoped took the cake for at least the next couple years. But if I was ever going to mar Petite's bumper with a sticker, it would probably be one of those *hang up and drive* ones. Watching people drive juggling coffee and cell phones made me the bad kind of crazy. Doing it myself and compounding it with no sleep was the sort of behavior that made me want to take my keys away for a week as punishment. I promised myself I'd do that later.

By the time I'd muttered and scowled and scolded myself I'd also dialed my home phone, which got snatched up so fast I thought Gary must've been sleeping on it. "Jo?"

"I'm okay. Are you?"

"Worried sick," he said grumpily. "Where you been, Jo? What's goin' on?"

"Thank you," I said instead of answering. "For staying there. For looking out for me. Thank you, Gary. I'm really sorry. I kind of lost it last night." I flicked my turn signal and almost poured coffee in my lap. "Did Mark call?"

"He finally stopped callin' around one," Gary growled. "I been chewin' my fingers to the bone tryin' ta decide if I should call you or not, Jo. What the hell happened?"

I laughed, hoarse sound. "I don't even know where to begin, Gary. The really short version is I completely embarrassed myself and my boss, saw the end of the world has my face on it and learned Mark and Barbara are involved in it somehow. Did he leave a number?"

"Same one as before." Gary rattled it off like he had it memorized, and I wondered why he did and I didn't.

"Thanks. Gary, I...look, I don't know when or how this is going to go down. I'll try to call you, okay? Are you going to be—where are you going to be?"

"I'll be here," the old man promised. "If I need ta go out I'll give you a call. You okay with that?" Worry colored his voice again and I wished I could give him a hug. Stupid phones.

"It's fine. Thank you," I said again. "I've…I…" I didn't know what to say. I hung up, drank as much coffee as I could at a stoplight and called Mark's number despite the fact it was barely six in the morning.

He sounded less awake than Gary did, though like the cabbie, his opening volley was "Joanne?" instead of a more typical hello.

I said, "Yeah" and "Is Barb there?" in almost the same breath. There was silence before Mark exhaled.

"She came over at two in the morning, Joanne, saying you'd showed up at Captain Morrison's place acting like a jealous girlfriend. Is there something I should know about there?"

"How about I come over and explain myself?" I found myself holding my coffee cup very carefully. I wanted to squeeze a fist around it, but it was a paper to-go cup, and I already couldn't remember the last time I'd changed clothes. Pouring hot coffee over myself didn't sound like a good idea.

Mark sighed. "All right. I'm staying at one of those short-term rental places right next to Microsoft, on Northeast Fortieth. Oakwood, I think. You know where that is?"

"I'll be there in twenty minutes." I hung up and concentrated on driving. Without traffic, it took less time to get there than I'd expected. I drove through the complex to the unit number he'd given me and threw my coffee cup away on my way up. He opened the door before I even knocked.

Concern colored his expression and his aura, blotches of worry that flashed through the opposite colors of the rainbow. Where Barb had red and yellow, Mark was orange and green, fading into indigo, all of it sunshine-bright. It was easier to see, without the two of them together, and I could now see the same razors of blackness between those brilliant shades. I didn't know if I just hadn't been looking closely enough before, or if believing they were the bad guys helped me see it. Either way, without thinking, I reached out and put my fingers into the murky splices, pulling them apart.

Butterflies swarmed out of the opening I'd made, midnight-blue and violet, darkness upon dark. They took the air around me away, settling onto my skin with grazing light brushes from their wings, and they fed on the silvery sheen of my own power. Spots swam through my vision like butterfly eyes, feathered with tiny piercing needles. I struck back, forming a fine-woven net with ease that surprised me, and swept it through the crevasse that butterflies pounded from.

They caught in the net and drained it dry, gobbling up the power there and becoming ever more solid, more real, themselves. They swooped together, making a fluttering, always-moving body in the darkness, like a photograph mosaic made up of hundreds of other tiny photos. My head hurt, looking at it, and it only got worse as the form shifted and changed, never quite satisfied with its shape.

The butterflies on my skin kept nibbling away, tickling sensation bordering on pain. Power fluttered beneath my breastbone like a warning, and I strengthened the shields I'd built, both physical and mental.

Light shot off my skin, braiding into a thin cord that flashed away into the distance. Hundreds of butterflies followed the brightness, and for an instant I left my body, racing ahead to see where in hell they were going. It was my cord, my power; I could travel it instantaneously, just as quickly as I'd snapped out of myself and into Morrison's house.

Morrison. I was there by his hospital bed a breath ahead of the butterflies, staring down at him in horror. The shields I'd left for him were vulnerable to my own power use, making a clear line for my enemy to follow.

I shut down every aspect of magic I could think of, slamming back into my body so hard I swooned. It was old-fashioned and fakey of me, but I didn't think collapsing against the wall yet managing to keep my feet quite qualified as a faint. It was unquestionably a swoon. No self-respecting woman from an era beyond 1910 should find herself in a swoon. I was offended on my own behalf. I leaned there in my swoon, completely bereft of any of the power I'd gotten used to. No mental shields protecting my core self, no physical ones to keep butterfly feet off my skin. No auras blazing, not even a hint of impatient power bubbling behind my sternum. For the first time since the beginning of the year, I felt completely, wholly, absolutely and totally normal.

It was awful.

I'd gotten used to the nudging insistence of power within me, to a sparkle at the edges of things that told me how much more to see there was than what I saw through ordinary eyes. I'd gotten used to a vague sense of people, even when I was deliberately ignoring my power. I'd gotten used to a very slightly heightened awareness that I didn't even *know* I'd gotten used to until I cut it off and made myself invisible to the butterfly demon residing in the dark places of Mark's aura.

Mark—to whom it must have looked as if he'd opened the door, I'd reached for him and then tumbled sideways in a faint—caught me and pulled me into his arms with the strength and confidence of a fairy-tale hero. He drew me into his room, closed the door and looked down at me in confusion that had no place on a fairy tale hero. "Joanne?"

"I thought you were an English major." Even my voice sounded wrong, all thin and raspy. I couldn't tell if it *was,* or if magic had done something to my hearing, too, and now it was gone.

Bewilderment swept Mark's handsome features, darkening his eyes. "I am. Was. What?"

I pushed away, trusting him less than my feet, which weren't any too steady. It was a nice little apartment, with a hall off to the left that presumably led to the bedrooms. The furniture in the living room we were in looked comfortable. I put my hand on the back of the couch, hoping it would steady me. Mostly its squishiness made me want to curl up and whimper until I fell asleep. I rotated myself a few degrees so I could watch Mark.

"What's an English major doing working in a physics department? What's Project Rainbow? Why are you here, Mark? Who are you?" My voice was changing again, high and thready. Maybe it wasn't my ears at all.

Mark moved around to look at me worriedly as I swayed. "How do you even know about Project Rainbow? It's a—I worked for the physics department because physicists need people to translate what they're writing into plain English so they can get grant money, Joanne. Barb got me the job. She's been the department's receptionist since college." He spread his hands, expression twisted with confusion. "Project Rainbow's a quantum physics project my lab's been working on, this thing about dimensions and other worlds lying alongside ours. They've been trying to open a—well, the plain English translation is a wormhole. A passage into other worlds. They did their first test just a couple weeks ago. The project's named for the song, you know? *The Rainbow Connection.* Joanne, what's wrong?"

"A couple of weeks." Just at the same time Coyote had gone missing, I bet. "Wormholes. Jesus Christ. Congratulations. I think it worked. You punched through to another reality and finished what I started." I laughed, high-pitched painful sound. "Oh, that makes sense, in a completely screwed up way. No wonder you got hit. They're all sleeping down there in Arizona, Mark. How come you and Barb woke up?"

His gaze went fuzzy with uncertainty. "What are you talking about?"

"Your mom must've been right." I wasn't talking to him anymore. "You must have Navajo blood in you somewhere, if the rez got hit and everybody woke up, and then your department did, but you're awake, too. So it's another demon." My voice dropped, all my thoughts and attention turned inward. "Okay. That gives me something to work with. Some kind of Dine demon." That was kind of fun to say, plus I was proud of myself for remembering the Navajo word for themselves. "*You're* some kind of Dine demon."

"Joanne." Mark came toward me cautiously, holding his hands wide. "Are you okay? You're not making any sense."

"Get away from me!" I clutched the back of the couch, trying to keep my balance. I'd think after a whole lifetime of not having any power, cutting myself off from it after six months wouldn't totally disrupt my system. I knew I could turn it back on, access it again, but with Mark in the room and Morrison so exposed, I didn't dare.

Mark stopped dead, hands still spread. "I don't know what's wrong, Joanne."

"Your aura! It's all screwed up and it fits with Barb's perfectly! And there are butterflies in the dark spaces!" I sounded like a lunatic. Mark took a slow step backward. I didn't know if he was trying to calm me down or trying to get away from the crazy lady.

"Barb and I are twins, Jo. Fraternal twins. We told you that." He offered a lopsided smile that was endearing even when I was in the midst of half-panicked uncertainty. "I guess it'd make sense our auras would fit together. What do you mean, it's screwed up? Butterflies? Dark spaces?" His smile went a little more fragile. "I'm glad you want to talk about your shamanism thing, but I don't have the frame of reference for your use of the language. And I hate to change the subject, but I really think I need to know what's going on with you and Captain Morrison."

"You're such an English major," I whispered. I wanted to like this guy. I *did* like this guy. It just figured he'd turn out to be some kind of monster in larger scheme of things. Then my head shifted of its own accord, small motion that made the muscles in my neck creak. "Nothing's going on. He's my boss. Is Barb here?"

Mark held up his hands, careful appeasing gesture. "Maybe we can talk about Barb in a while, Jo. I want to talk about us right now."

"Us? There isn't an us. Usses are for people who—who—" I was not doing so well with the words. "Who aren't us. She's here, isn't she? What are you guys doing here, anyway, Mark? Why'd you come to Seattle?"

He hesitated. "Barb wanted to, and I'd never been."

"You always do what she wants?"

A tiny smile played over his mouth. "Yeah, pretty much. Bossy big sister, you know? Seventeen whole minutes older than me. She's got the adventuresome streak, I guess. She's kind of the tough one."

"The female of the species is more deadly than the male? Great." I got to fight with the mean sibling. On the other hand, at least she didn't have Mark's reach. "When'd you two get here?"

Mark's eyes went fuzzy, eyebrows drawn down over them. After a couple seconds he frowned more deeply and looked away, shaking his head. "A few days ago. Maybe on the Fourth."

And Billy'd gone to sleep that night. "Mark." I said his name carefully. "How'd your sister get herself invited to the North Precinct Fourth of July party if she's never been to Seattle before?"

"Well, she..." His forehead wrinkled until I thought it must hurt. "I don't know. She makes friends fast. She's cute."

"Yeah," I said. "She is. And I bet she does." As easily as Mark had made friends with me, in fact. I was starting to get a list in my head, gifts that my opponent seemed to have in his repertoire. Charm. Good looks. I remembered the dreams I'd had, and shivered. The ability to offer a girl things she wanted through the sleeping world. A vampiric tendency to drain life from people, an affinity for butterflies and a dislike of topaz. It seemed like a bizarre combination of talents for a demon of any sort, but the razors in the blackness of Mark's aura and my sleeping friends made me more inclined to believe it than not.

Very, very cautiously I reached for the power lying quietly inside me. It stirred and sparked like an engine rolling over, not quite sure it wanted to start. Since I wasn't quite sure I wanted it to, either, I didn't object to its reluctance. But those sparks set something off inside of me, a very thin trickle of magic that spilled through my veins like a promise. It felt like Petite idling at a stoplight, with me grinning at the guy in the souped-up Civic next to me 'cause I knew I could dust him at the drop of a hat.

Not that I, a good, law-abiding citizen and one of Seattle's finest, would ever, *ever* think of street racing, or a ten-second quarter mile. Especially not down that long stretch of Aurora that got relatively little traffic late at night, with kids listening in on police scanners while a lot of money got put on the line. Because, after all, Petite was a very recognizable vehicle, and Morrison would *kill* me.

If he could catch me, anyway.

Which was sort of the same principle I wanted to try on Mark. I didn't know if Barb would've noticed me, psychically speaking, if I hadn't gone in on the astral level first. Once I did, there was no going back, but Mark's butterfly-ridden rainbows didn't seem to be actively considering me a threat, despite my initial foray. If the power he and Barbara shared really was split up, she might be carrying the aggressive side— red and yellow in her colors even suggested that. Mark's power might be more passive, so if I didn't attack it directly, it might ignore me. He might not even realize it was there.

That might mean I hadn't fallen for a bad guy, which would be nice. I wasn't counting on it.

The trickle of power running through me finally made it to my eyes, sliding the Sight on. Mark's aura still flexed and bent with uncertainty, but the black slashes between colors didn't strike out at me, or suddenly fill with butterfly eyes. I rubbed the heel of my hand against my breastbone, then exhaled deeply. "Okay. You're coming back to my place."

"No," Barb said from behind me, "he really isn't."

CHAPTER THIRTY

She would've been a lot better off if she hadn't said anything. I ducked, which was not at all my usual response to people speaking unexpectedly behind me, but it proved to be a good choice. A lamp sailed over my head and smashed into the wall. Mark, who had to have seen her sneaking up on me, lamp in hand, yelled with surprise, anyway. I spun around, still crouched, and charged full-bore into Barbara's rib cage.

I only had about two steps to build up momentum, but it was enough. I got my shoulder in her gut and she whooshed out air, unable to dig in and stop my headlong rush. That was okay. The bathroom door frame stopped it a handful of steps later. Barbara croaked like a dying frog as her spine impacted the frame and my shoulder drove farther into her belly.

It was incredibly satisfying.

Less satisfying was the way she heaved in a breath of air and used the energy to bring her knee up into my left boob.

Insomuch as people aim in fistfights, she was probably aiming for my diaphragm, but crushing my breast was at least as effective. I went, "Glork," and staggered back, still doubled over, clutching an arm over my chest. Barbara kicked me in the jaw with her bare toes, then howled and fell back herself, hopping on her other foot. Despite having head-butted me earlier, she pretty much fought like a girl, which was to say, without any experience at it. Anybody who's gotten in a couple of real fights learns to hit soft parts with hard parts. Kicking me in the face was a good idea, but she should've done a side kick and made the impact point my nose with her heel.

I actually thought all of that during the course of a couple ragged breaths, by which time the radiating pain in my breast had lessened enough to let me move again. Barb was still hopping up and down and shrieking when I dragged in one more breath and let it pull me to my full height, so I was looking down six inches at her. I wanted to have a really good view of slamming her into the floor. She stopped jumping around when I reached for her, eyes widening as she twigged to the fact that the fight wasn't over yet.

A pair of strong arms wrapped around me, pinning my own arms to my sides. Mark, through gritted teeth right next to my ear, said, "I—" and the rest of it was lost to me bracing myself against him and lifting both feet to kick Barb in the gut.

She flew back and crashed into the wall. Mark staggered under a hundred and sixty pounds of unexpected weight in his arms. I got my feet under me again and slammed my head back, Mark's lovely nose crunching quite horribly against my skull. He shrieked like a girl and let me go, and for a moment there I stood there, a panting, breathless, triumphant king of the hill. I hadn't gotten into a fight with ordinary, unarmed people since I was a teenager. It was nice to know I hadn't lost my touch, and that brawling was still in my repertoire. "Now that I have your attention."

Like Barb, I should've kept my mouth shut. She got enough breath back to produce a howl of outrage and flung herself on me, hands clawed all over again. Her weight was enough to drive me back into Mark, and all three of us went down in a clawing, scratching, shouting pile of arms and legs. I caught an elbow to the ear and my head started ringing. I grabbed a shoulder and pounded on it, which just felt good. It was better than not knowing what to do, and it was much better than remembering that Coyote'd died to keep me safe. White fury rose up in me and I smashed down all the harder.

The shoulder moved and gave me room for purchase on a shirt—Barbara's, slippery soft sleeping satin—and I dug my hands in, lifting her away bodily. She kicked and squealed and I grunted, dropping her heavily to the side. A couple of seconds later I ended up on top of the dogpile, straddling Mark's chest with his arms pinned by my knees and shins. He gave me an unexpected rakish grin that really didn't go with a bleeding, swollen nose, and said, "Dis has probmis."

I was so taken aback I actually laughed out loud. Barbara lunged and I drew a fist back and said, "Eht!" in warning, not threatening her at all, but Mark. He might make me laugh, but that wasn't enough at this particular moment in time to save him from getting the tar beat out of him. Barb lurched to a halt and a thrill of triumph went through me. She was protective of her baby brother. "Here we are, then," I breathed. "I need some answers. Who are you? What are you? Why are you doing this? What in God's name have I done to you?"

Barb all but hissed at me. I rolled my eyes, settling my weight on Mark's chest. "I can sit here all day, you red-headed bitch." I didn't know if it was true. I thought I might fall asleep if I had to sit there for more than a couple minutes. But Barb didn't know that, and it sounded good.

"Leave him alone," she muttered, "and I'll tell you."

"Tell me and I'll leave him alone."

She gave me a baleful look and snaked a hand out, cautiously, toward Mark. It didn't look like an attack, so I let her.

That, too, was a mistake.

I did not think of rainbows as something that had sound. Nonetheless, rainbow thunder rolled over me as she touched her brother's shoulder. Their auras melded and fit together, dark spaces between them filling up with missing color. Color and noise slammed into me and I grabbed my head, aware I was yelling fruitlessly at the thunder rumbling in my mind. I didn't want to respond, not even to protect myself, for fear of sending up that beacon that pointed straight to Morrison again, and so all I could do was yell.

The end of the world unfolded before my eyes. Fire, like the first one I'd seen, only this time the spirit of flame came in mushroom clouds and burning wastelands. A very human destruction, incinerating cities and poisoning the air. One people survived, carried by a yellow-haired god up through a tall hollow reed that broke through the sky and into another world. Only they were ready; only they lived.

Time rewound, a blur of images faster than thought could process. Coyote slunk away from the hole in the earth where the water baby floated away to the floods that were its mother. Coyote, wearing my face. I watched him go, turned to the People and warned them, the words tasting like ritual in my mouth.

"This world, too, might someday be destroyed by fire, flood or cyclone, and then I will come again. You must live the right way, or this will happen. The signs that you must watch for are the rainbow around the sun, or when the sacred yellow rabbit bush, *Giss-dil-yessi*, does not grow, and most of all the rainbow that lasts all day. This means something dreadful will happen, and I will come then."

The People all nodded and took note of my words and wisdom, telling them to each other so they would not be forgotten, and I slipped away into the darkness of sleep. Only one being stopped me, and that was Coyote, standing in my path. He wore his own face now, and I said to him again, "Watch for the rainbow that lasts all day. Then I will come."

Time skidded forward an unending number of years, and slammed to a halt.

I looked down at myself from somebody else's point of view. I was lying outside a diner, a silver sword stuck through my lungs. Then I sat in a coffee shop across from Morrison, my eyes gold as I looked through my own skin. Then outside Suzanne Quinley's house, asking the city to hit me with its best shot. Then the Seattle Center deserted at an hour it should have been busy, all but me and Gary and the Host of the Wild Hunt in a battle between gods and sons.

Through all of it, *all* of it, silver rainbows of power bled off me like diamonds washed by sunlight. My aura, now mostly settled down to silver-blue, had glowed like rainbows for days, an endless, beautiful threat to the world. I remembered staring into my own skin, watching spirit unbound by flesh, rainbows of power held in by what seemed to be surface tension.

I heard myself whisper, "Oh. Oh, shit," somewhere in the waking world, and then a little louder, "I'm not—"

Barbara clobbered me over the head.

As far as being hit on the head went, it wasn't nearly as bad as pruning shears to the face. Stars shot through my vision and I sort of collapsed forward, muffling Mark. He grunted and I tried to get enough focus back to push myself off him. I heard Barb scramble to her feet and run for the door. By the time I sat up, it'd slammed shut. I put a hand on the back of my head and winced. "I'm not whatever this thing thinks I am. I'm not the end of the world." I was practically certain. I hoped.

Mark didn't appear to care much. After a couple seconds I realized that was probably because I'd fallen on his face when Barbara hit me, and I'd just bashed his nose in a minute earlier. "Oh, God, I'm sorry. Hang on a second."

For the second time in as many minutes, I did something really stupid. In my defense, I hadn't known that letting Barb touch Mark would throw me into a vision, but I did know that trying to heal somebody when all that dark power was waiting to pounce was a bad idea.

Unfortunately, I'd already gone down the rabbit hole toward Mark's garden when I remembered that.

Just as it had with Gary, overwhelming blackness rose up and followed me, so fast and sure of itself this time I had no way to stop it. I wasn't carrying topaz, and Mark didn't have the slightest familiarity with my intrusions to help me fight back with. His aura split apart, all the rainbows colors widening, and butterflies rose from the darkness between color to cloud out the sun.

I thought, quite clearly, *this is going to get very confusing,* and then it did.

In so far as there was good news, it was in my adversary being no better at planning than I was. My attempt at healing Mark had lit a path for it to follow, and it'd done so without hesitation or compunction. I had the sense that each time I built this sort of link to another person, it gave my enemy strength to draw from, a new route for it to take. I had a sudden awful concern for Ashley Hampton, but worry disappeared again under trying to untangle what my opponent had wrought.

Because it had just driven its own host into deep slumber. I felt Mark's breathing change, both from inside where I was caught, and from outside where I was sitting on him. Butterflies whirled around me in obvious agitation, their rapid-beating wings making rainbows that danced in the corners of my vision. For the first time I got a feeling for Mark's own aura, and realized I hadn't even known I wasn't seeing it. His was rusty-brown, so flattened that most of the red had been pulled from it. I thought it ought to be warm and friendly with life, but the butterfly colors had ridden it so long it was like he'd lost the ability to recognize himself at all. Standing inside the darkened garden that represented his soul, I felt energy draining out of it, sapped through uncountable needle-fine points. The trees and grasses and bushes in his garden were hole-ridden, as if it'd been attacked by voracious insects that neither knew nor cared that their feasting would ultimately destroy their food source and themselves.

Cold shocked through me, making hairs stand up all over my body. *Destroy their food source.* I doubted that doing so would be the end of whatever demon was carrying, but *Mark* was dying.

Standing there in the midst of a butterfly storm, my hands clenched and cold anger built up inside me. Not on my watch. I actually spoke the words out loud, then tilted my head up and shouted them into the sky: "Not on my watch, do you hear me, Goddamn it? Not again! Nobody else! *Not on my watch!*"

As if I'd thrown a challenge into my opponent's teeth, half the colors of the rainbow bled down from above, butterflies by their thousands coming to feed off the sheer raw anger I flung out. I felt safe in drawing them to me: as long as Mark slept I thought they couldn't escape the confines of his garden, which left the link to Morrison untouchable. That I wasn't sure how *I* could escape was a matter to be dealt with later.

Rust under paint. In a way, that's what this thing was, rust encroaching on the metal beneath a vehicle's painted surface. It could be sanded out, replacement sheets soldered in and polished up, and with a professional job, the car'd be good as new. Mark's soul needed replenishing and some TLC, but first the damage had to be excised.

I met the onslaught of butterflies with a belt sander.

There was something particularly awful about that image if I let myself think about it too hard. Working with the idea of damaged paint was easier, since it didn't involve delicate beautiful bugs being turned into so much ichor and smeared all over the place. Those that had already landed on my skin dissolved into fine mist, like paint drifting in the air, and I tried not to breathe too deeply at first.

Then I thought better the connection be in me than in Mark, and inhaled sharply, sparks of an otherworldly power crashing into me. Every breath I took replenished me enough to keep pouring power out, and the dark swarm of hungry butterflies kept coming to it, rather literally like moth to flame. The more I took in, the more distinctly I felt *recognition*, as if I was allowing whatever had ridden Mark to see me, and it knew me for the world-ending herald it had seen within Coyote. A certain delight began to feed through the loop as it drew closer, and I had the unfortunate feeling that my clever plan to rescue Mark from the clutches of sleep might not have been so clever after all. If it got inside me, I might go to sleep, too, and then we were all screwed.

I would just have to hold my ground and drag it out into the real world somehow. It had so much strength, so much weight to it, that I thought I might be able to. I'd brought an immortal child across worlds once, and a demon after that. There was no reason I couldn't pull it off a third time.

Except those other two had been willing to go, and I

wasn't sure this thing was. I pushed the thought aside with an audible sniff, as if contempt for the details would make them go away.

By that time my whole body was buzzing from running a belt sander over my own skin. My own power was its usual burnished silver-blue, now gleaming over the rainbows of magic I'd obliterated with my psychic belt sander. The colors gleamed as if in defiance or mockery of the prophecy that had gotten me here, and the endless attack of fluttering creatures began to slow. I felt full up of power, like butterfly wings might lift me up from within and carry me away.

Beyond me, the pinprick holes that damaged Mark's garden were healing, green returning to grayed-out leaves, blue fading back into a pale sky. With the butterflies focused on me, he had a chance. That was all I asked for. Triumphant, I turned my focus back on myself, looking for a way to seal the multi-winged dark power inside me long enough to wake up again.

Barbara, wreathed in red and yellow and violet flame, stepped into the garden of Mark's soul just as I was about to sever the link, and pulled all the magic I'd stolen from my adversary to herself.

CHAPTER THIRTY-ONE

I gasped, wrenching my eyes open, and to my surprise they did open, leaving me awake and breathless and still sitting on Mark's chest. His nose was no longer mashed in, and Barbara was nowhere to be seen. I got up, the change in pressure reminding me I'd just been hit on the head, and dialed 911 on my way out the door. An ambulance would have to pick up my snoozing paramour. I had to find Barb.

Which would be a lot easier if she would stop running away from me. I gave the emergency services people the address Mark was staying at and climbed into Petite, gnawing on my cell phone. Not that I could blame her for running away: except for the pruning shears thing, I was pretty much on top of things physically. She wasn't exactly the sort of person who could beat the tar out of me. Keeping the fight from me was the smartest thing she could do.

I straightened up so fast I hit my head on Petite's roof and said, "Shit!" both because it hurt and because wisdom had fallen down on me like a load of bricks. I pulled out of the parking lot and dialed Gary, telling myself I was grounded from driving for another week.

He wasn't home. At least, he wasn't at my home. I whacked the phone against the steering wheel a few times, like it was its fault, and tried calling him at his house. No answer there, either. He'd said he'd be there.

I whispered, "Shit," one more time, this time with worry. The topaz should be protecting him. He couldn't have gone to sleep. Then again, I didn't think Mark would've been a potential victim, either, so what the hell did I know?

There were absolutely no cops on the roads. I hoped it was just because I was getting lucky this morning, not because the wave of sleeping sickness had gone beyond the North Precinct and was starting to overtake Seattle. Given the general lack of vehicles at seven in the morning on a Thursday, though, I thought I was probably pipe dreaming. I got home and pounded up the stairs, afraid of what I'd see.

What I saw was an empty apartment with a box of two-day-old doughnuts on the kitchen table. I said something unladylike and ate the last two doughnuts, too hungry to care if they were stale. I couldn't remember if I'd had lunch the day before. Or breakfast. I knew I hadn't had dinner. The second half of the last doughnut stuffed in my cheek, I called Gary's house again, still getting no answer. He didn't have voice mail or an answering machine, on the logic that if it was important, they'd call back. He was right, but that didn't do me any good when I wanted to rant worriedly at him.

Which was probably exactly how he'd felt when I'd run off last night and hadn't called until this morning. Properly chastised, I went and sat at my computer, desperate for a little research on butterflies and nightmares.

Half a minute later I was scrubbing my eyeballs with my fingertips after clicking through to a pair of DVDs that came up with those words in the title. Never once in my life did I suspect butterfly nightmares might be just the ticket for determining just how much of a prude I really was. I tried a second search, using the ill-advised combination of "butterfly dream," and really should have expected the innumerable Chuang Tsu hits. At least they weren't brain-scrubbing. It took another couple minutes to find anything something useful.

Butterflies, it turned out, were across-the-board erotic little things. Mythologically and legendarily, they were associated with all sorts of sexiness. Mark and Barb fit that bill very nicely. Of course, butterflies were also associated with insanity, which didn't make me particularly happy, as well as rebirth and, in fact, sleep. None of it, though, suggested that butterfly demons flapped around the psychic ether putting people to sleep and draining their life forces. I sucked on my teeth and tried another search, adding in the end of the world and some of the elements of my vision-dreams. My hands grew cold as I began to get hits.

By the time my door banged open half an hour later, I had an unfortunately clear idea of what I was facing. Gary came in red-faced and huffing, and looked startled to see me there. I got up and went to hug him hard, not caring where he'd gone as long as he'd come back safely. He grunted with surprise and returned the hug. "You okay, doll?"

"I've been better." I spoke into his shoulder, muffled. "I was worried when you didn't answer the phone. You're okay?"

"'Course I am. What's wrong, Jo?"

I breathed a little laugh and held on tighter. "I think I really blew it this time, Gary. I woke up a god."

Gary extracted himself from my hug and leaned back, looking at me. "You've gone up against gods before."

"Yeah. Except the last one just wanted free of his constraints." I managed a smile and stepped away. "This one thinks I heralded the end of the world, and he doesn't like it. Is that interesting enough for you?"

To my never-ending surprise, Gary cracked a grin. "Just about. What are you, crazy, lady?"

"You tell me. I mean, you've got to admit, as the pinnacle of half a year's screwups, bringing the world to an end is hard to beat. I start with the Wild Hunt, I move on to unleashing earthquakes and demons on suburban Seattle, and I wrap it up with signaling a god that it's time to end the world. I think I've got the escalation about right."

"Yeah," Gary said, "but what're you gonna do for an encore?"

Laughter caught me out. "I hope to God," and for a moment there I wasn't sure if I should be pluralizing that, or if I had a specific deity in mind, "that when we get through this I'll have laid all the ashes of my spectacular opening act to rest, and that anything else I get to deal with isn't quite as cosmic in nature."

A thread of cold warning slithered down my spine, bringing with it a vivid image: a cave in the lit-up astral realm, a place of real beauty and unending life. That cave was blocked off, its depths cut away from me by my mother's will, but beyond it lay something that thought of me as a tasty morsel. It knew I was out here, and every time I tripped through that part of the Other worlds, it taunted and teased me. I'd resisted it once, and been forbidden that path by Sheila MacNamarra's power, but moonlit blue darkness waited for me. I didn't think it would prove to be a puff of dust to be blown away, not when it was so well buried, so deep in the astral planes.

As if thinking of it—him; I had a sense of maleness about the thing, and if I was right in my summation of connections, the banshee I defeated had called it Master—as if thinking of him brought me to his attention, a soft wave of rich, malign amusement danced over my skin, raising goose bumps. I shuddered off thoughts of that particular monster in the dark. I had others to deal with.

"The visions I've been having. The waking visions?" Gary nodded, reassuring me that I'd told him about them. I couldn't keep my thoughts straight anymore. I was so tired I wanted to cry on general principles. "I thought I was supposed to be fighting those dreams. I mean, the world kept coming to an end. It flooded, it burned, it…kept ending. And there I was trying to fling everything I had against that, to stop the destruction of the world. And I couldn't. They were Navajo history, Gary." I looked at him in unhappy exhaustion. "I finally had enough pieces to do research."

"So what're we up against, Jo?" That was something else I loved about the old man. He meant it when he said *we*. Even if I was the world's biggest screwup, Gary was on my side.

"A god," I said again. "Begochidi. He led the Navajo from one world to the next. And now he's come back to do it again. I think I just told him it was time. I think a bunch of physicists working on wormhole theory accidentally set him loose. Like I did with the Lower World demons. I think they made the walls of the worlds thin enough to pass through, and Begochidi was just waiting to step through." I caught Gary's expression and shook my head. "The point is he's here now, to deal with the threat and lead his people to the next world. To deal with me."

I let out a hoarse laugh and looked away, like I could see through the walls of the apartment. Actually, I could, but I didn't want to right now, so they were solid and normal. "Begochidi's not just a minor character in Navajo legend. He's the Maker of the world, both male and female. Mark and Barbara," I heard myself add wearily. Gary made a sound of dismay and I couldn't bring myself to look at him or explain that particular misfortune any further. "Twins, male and female, to carry his spirit toward the blight that endangered his people. Only I think I freed Mark from his hold, so now it's just Barb out there someplace and I've got to fight her."

I was used to running behind, trying desperately to catch up. It turned out being ahead of the curve sucked just as much as not knowing what I was getting myself into. Maybe more. There was a certain blind hope associated with playing catch-up. Having a clear idea of what I was up against made me feel pretty damn grim.

"You sure 'bout this, Jo?"

I nodded. I didn't have the impression that shamans went through quite such dramatic trials by fire under usual circumstances, but nothing about my life had been much in the way of normal for a long time now. Longer than I'd thought, really, looking back to my Coyote dreams. Longer than that, even, if I'd really been mixed up by the Makers of the world. Not Begochidi. He wasn't one of the ones responsible for me, or he'd recognize me. But even the Navajo had more than one creation myth, and from what I'd read, Begochidi didn't feature as powerfully in all of them. The Makers, it seemed, weren't necessarily in on the Making together. I'd have to give them a scolding about that, if I ever got the chance.

"Arright, Jo. So what do we do now?"

I shook my head, taking a deep breath. "You don't do anything. *I'm* going to sleep."

Thursday, July 7, 7:37 a.m.

Nothing in my dreams of Coyote or in any other experience in my life had taught me how to say "I'm going to sleep" as a declaration of war. Consequently, it sounded nothing like one, which disappointed me. I wanted it to be dramatic and world-shaking, but it just sounded like exhausted relief. I wanted to sleep so badly I could taste it. Gary's bushy eyebrows went up.

"You're goin' to sleep? Are you nuts? You just said this guy's power is comin' from everybody who's asleep!"

"I know. Dreams are his domain, Gary. If I don't meet him on his own ground I'm not going to be able to fight him at all. Barb keeps running away from me." That made me laugh, huff of sound. "At least that's something."

Gary took another breath in protest, then exhaled and slumped his broad shoulders. "You sure," he said again, but it wasn't a question this time. "Arright. Lissen to me, Jo. You stay right there." He got up from the couch and went into my bedroom while I wondered where exactly he thought I would go. I didn't think dreamland was a place to be entered physically.

He came out of my bedroom with a sword. "Under the bed's a lousy place to keep a sword, Jo."

I blinked, getting up to meet him. "It's a perfectly good place to keep a sword. It's not like I use it a lot." He offered to me, so I took it, surprised as always at its heft. The weight hadn't meant anything to me when I'd first seen it in Cernunnos's hand, silver metal gleaming beneath prosaic fluorescent lights, but it'd meant a lot later on when the damned thing got shoved through my lung. I'd struck back with iron-based steel, and Cernunnos had fled without his silver blade. It was only considerably after the fact that I brought it to a dealer to have it appraised and found out it really *was* silver. In retrospect, it made sense, as the Celtic god couldn't touch anything made of iron.

The dealer had almost literally drooled over the blade. Its swept-silver handle protected the hand easily, the rapier blade impossibly sharp, holding its edge flawlessly despite the metal it was forged of. And that was something else: the forging was unlike anything he'd ever seen. Almost as if it had been cast, like a sculpture. He'd offered me such a ridiculous sum of money for it I hadn't believed him, and I'd gone home to read up on the Internet about Celtic magic and silver. I'd learned about somebody named Nuada, whose hand, lost in battle, was re-made in silver by a god. I'd tapped a finger on the blade cautiously and wondered.

A week later the dealer called me up and offered twice what he'd offered in the first place. He was still calling occasionally. There had to be a price I couldn't resist, but so far keeping Cernunnos's sword beneath my bed was more appealing than cold hard cash. Of course, if the car insurance company didn't pay up soon, I might start reconsidering my stance."

"So you don't go in unarmed," Gary said to me as I took the sword. My eyebrows rose and I glanced up at him, half smiling, not sure how seriously to take him. He wasn't smiling at all, eyes serious beneath untamed eyebrows. The lines in his face were deeper, as if the weight of the moment made him seem closer to his seventy-three years. My smile fell away and I just watched him, rapier balanced across my palms as I waited for whatever he had in mind next.

He didn't disappoint. He pulled a copper cuff bracelet, one that usually sat on my dresser next to the drum, from his pocket. It'd been tarnished and green until recently, when I'd had cause to buy metal cleaner and scrub a silver necklace clean of my own blood. I'd done the bracelet then, too, tracing my fingertip over etched knotwork that might have been Celtic around its borders, and the cut away shapes of Cherokee spirit animals between the borders.

"Gary." My voice came out small and tight as he turned the bracelet sideways and slid it over my wrist.

"'S from your dad, right?"

I nodded, unable to trust words, and he tapped the metal

against my skin. It was already warm from the minute in his pocket. "Left wrist," he said. "Protects your heart."

My heart tightened as he spoke, throat closing even more. "Gary," I said again, scratchy whisper, as if it would stop him, but he wasn't done. He dipped into his pocket again and came out with what I knew he would, a silver choker necklace I hadn't worn in months. Hollow tubes of metal rattled gently against its chain, the curved stretches broken apart by triskelions, the Celtic three-way knot that represented the Holy Trinity in modern days, and a much older trio of goddesses from a time before Christianity. The center pendant hung from the chain itself, just far enough to rest in the hollow of my throat: a Celtic cross, a circle quartered by two bars. My mother had given me the necklace as she lay dying, the only thing she'd ever given me besides life. Gary fastened the necklace around my throat with unbelievable delicacy, his big old hands far more certain than mine ever were when I put on jewelry. Something happened as the clasp shut, a soft sparkle of warmth that danced over my skin as powerfully as Gary's words did.

"To guard your soul," he said. My heart contracted again, tears blurring my vision, though I managed a painful little smile as I looked down at the sword and the bracelet. The necklace made an uncomfortable pressure against my throat, something I'd never given myself time to get used to. Then I looked up again, smile shaky.

"What about you?" I was trying to tease him, but emotion rode me far too hard. I felt girded for battle, as if I'd been entrusted with a kingdom's honor and my loved ones had helped me don my armor. "Don't I get anything from you?

Mother's got my soul covered and Dad's got my heart, but without you, jeez, Gary, I wouldn't be here at all. You took the damned sword out of me when I was dying so I could heal myself. And all I get is a lousy little ritual?" I was afraid to blink, for fear tears that burned my eyes would scald my cheeks. My smile was so tremulous I thought it might shake those tears loose, anyway.

A complex expression darkened Gary's eyes, more facets of sentiment there than I could easily recognize. Pride and love and laughter, mixed up with wry chagrin and just a touch of smugness, and other things that flickered so quickly I couldn't read them. He slid a hand into his other front pocket and came out with a small, nondescript black velvet box, the kind that makes a girl's heart slam into her throat when a man pulls it out. My heart did exactly that, cutting off my breath, and I blinked despite all my efforts not to, sending tears rushing down my cheeks. Gary chuckled, barely a sound, and opened the box toward me.

A heart-shaped purple medal, bordered in gold, lay below its ribbon against smooth black velvet, the metal bright by comparison. He only gave me an instant to see what it was before he took it from its case more brusquely than he'd done with the jewelry, and with gruff quick movements pinned it to my shirt. "Never meant that much to me," he muttered. "Just a way of sayin' I made it back when a lot of other good fellas didn't. But since I did, maybe it'll shield you, too, sweetheart."

A chime rang out as he dropped his hands, the medal fastened safely to my shirt. I didn't think he could hear it, but it sounded sweet and loud in my ears, pure tone like silver bells. I felt a click behind my breastbone, profound latching that welded those four items together within me. They whispered recognition to one another: *rapier for the hand, to wield in battle. Copper for the wrist, to shield the heart. Silver for the throat, to shield the soul. Bronze for the breast, to shield the body.* Four cardinal points burning a bright circle in my mind, heat flaring through each of the items Gary had bestowed on me. With that flare came the Sight, showing me how they shone with purpose and power. When I lifted my eyes to Gary, he blazed with the same resolve, in that moment an icon of all the best things that drove humanity onward.

"My girl," he added, but less roughly, because I'd dropped the rapier and stepped forward into his arms to let tears run freely down my cheeks. He bowed his head over mine, hand in my hair, and murmured nonsense at me while I held on to him with everything I had. When I finally snuffled and edged back a little, he gave me a soft smile that had nothing to do with the wolfish, toothy grin he liked to disconcert people with, and everything to do with family bonds that couldn't be broken. "Normally a man don't like to make a pretty girl cry, but I think maybe this time it means an old dog did somethin' right."

I smiled idiotically through the remnants of tears, nodding. "You know you did. You were what, just carrying this around waiting for the right moment?" My voice was still all hoarse and tight, but I didn't care. Gary beamed down at me.

"That's good, then. Nah. S'where I went, home to get it. Been thinkin' about that sword and everything you got for a while now." He shrugged, big lumbering motion of dismissal. "Thought maybe I could bring somethin' to the fold, if you asked for it, s'all. And you did."

"I don't know what I'd do without you, Gary." The words, whispered, were as true as anything I'd ever said. "Thank you."

"Anything for my girl." His smile reminded me of the younger Gary I'd met in his garden, full of warmth and gentle strength coupled with a linebacker's ability to clear a path. "I know you're goin' to sleep instead of into a trance, but maybe I'll drum you under anyway, arright?"

I nodded again, crouching to pick up the blade I'd dropped. I curled one hand around the pommel and the other around the blade very carefully, and made my way to the couch. The drum was already there, and Gary came around the other end of the sofa to pick it up. I tilted over, nestling my head on a pillow as I pulled the sword up to my chest like it was a teddy bear.

I heard about three beats of the drum before I fell asleep.

CHAPTER THIRTY—TWO

Back in January it'd seemed like every time I went to sleep, that little death drew me into the realm of Other. Letting it find me now, deliberately, seemed awkward after slipping in and out of the astral realms so much. The world of dreams, though, was not quite the same one I skimmed through when I left my body, and very much not the crisp, clear-aired Upper World or the red-skied Lower World I'd made my way to a few times. They all shared a commonality, but in the same way France and Germany shared a border: it could be crossed, but I didn't want to expect that the same rules would apply on both sides of the border. And I'd spent very little time in dreamworld, using it mostly as a transitory point. Now that I wanted to stay, I found myself with almost no idea how to travel or bring forth the things that I sought. Trusting my subconscious, which was usually how dreams were traversed, seemed both time-consuming and potentially dangerous.

I held on to all of those thoughts for what felt like whole minutes, maybe even longer. It was far more likely they'd formed and dissolved between the third and fourth drumbeats, in that pseudo-waking moment between dreams and the living world. Some brief, eternal time later the darkness of sleep began to take shape. A blaring voice, only half intelligible, echoed against forming hallways, the overhead lights both flickering and too bright. People rushed by me, knocking into me without setting themselves or me off balance, as if I wasn't there. Gurneys and wheelchairs were pushed against the walls, which faded out suddenly, leaving me standing amid rows and endless rows of hospital beds.

The people in the beds thrashed in their sleep, all of them opening their mouths to let out soundless screams. As if the silence carried their life, like a cat stealing a baby's breath, they weakened as they cried out.

Harried, faceless medical workers kept crashing by me until I realized I was shouting, too, my hands trembling as I stretched them out toward the agitated sleepers. My protests went unheard, caught in my mind: *I can help! Just let me help!* No one saw me, no one heard me, no one believed me. Nor should they have: for all my wordless calls, I *couldn't* help, not from amid this chaos. The noiseless shrieks from the sleepers pounded at the small bones of my ears, making me nervous and twitchy, like I waited for attack.

Bradley Holliday appeared in the middle of the hall in front of me, holding a patient chart on a clipboard and a distasteful expression on his mouth. "You don't belong here.

Leave now." He looked and spoke directly to me, so unexpectedly I nearly glanced around to see who was behind me. "I'm talking to you," he snapped. "Joanne Walker, police officer. This is a hospital. You don't belong here."

It was like his words were an eraser, sweeping at me with wide strokes that wiped me away. I leaned forward against the urge to disappear, shaking my head. "But I can help."

"How?" he demanded, encompassing a thousand hospital beds in one wave of his clipboard. "What do you think you can do that all these doctors can't?"

Uncertainty washed through me, since I hadn't been that much use so far. "I—"

"You see?" He put on a very good sneer, the sort my younger self would have tried to emulate, and flapped a hand at me. "You don't belong. Leave now."

"But I've done okay," I whispered. "I got Mel to not drain herself fighting this thing. Begochidi. I kept Gary awake. I got Begochidi off Mark's back." Even as I made the argument it felt hollow to me. Too many people had fallen asleep, their strength drained to bring a god back to waking. I hadn't done enough to keep Morrison awake.

The flickering white light closed down to a pinpoint and left me in darkness for just long enough to realize it was happening, then came up again inside a hospital room whose four walls were as solid as reality. Morrison lay resting on the bed there, vague figures holding shape in the background. Billy and Melinda, sharing a room with the captain. But they weren't what had called me to this space of the dreamworld.

A shield, glittering blue and silver, spun over Morrison's

skin. When I reached out to touch his shoulder, that shield danced up my fingers, becoming one again with its originator. "I can't fight, boss," I heard myself say. "Not with you in here like this. I've got you all mixed up with me. Even Begochidi's nice side went after you when I opened up." I sat down on the edge of his bed, folding his hand in both of mine. What the hell. It was a dream, right? With him so still and asleep, I didn't expect his fingers to be warm, but mine felt icy, wrapped around his. "I wish you'd kept the topaz. I wish you hadn't given it to Barbara." That seemed the greater insult, all things considered. Not just because I defined her as some kind of rival in my little world, but because I was half afraid gifting her with it would ruin any protection all of it offered. It didn't seem to work that way, but the fear was there regardless.

The fact that boys weren't supposed to go around giving girls gifts other girls had given them was, if not beside the point, at least a heartache I didn't want to dwell on. Morrison hadn't considered the topaz a gift, anyway. More like a burden.

Darkness fluttered through the room, a whisper of silence like feathers on the air. I closed my eyes, lowering my head toward my hands tangled with Morrison's. Guess I shouldn't have said Begochidi's name out loud, though now that I thought about it, that was pretty obvious. Nothing like sending up a beacon to the bad guys saying *here I am, come and get me*.

I could feel, though, the protective amulets I carried. I could feel the connection of three points to protect my body and spirit, and the fourth, the weapon at my hip. I didn't need to look to see it there, though I hadn't noticed its weight here in the Land of Nod. I was armored, ready for battle. My weakness lay in Morrison, sleeping beneath the shield of my making.

The funny thing was, I thought maybe my strength lay there, too. "C'mon, Cap. You've got to wake up. I need you to be safe so I can do what it takes to stop this sickness." I poured a little more into the shielding, looking for the weak point that allowed Begochidi to keep my boss asleep, trying not to invade his psyche while I did it. Power sparked against my skin, running under it like silver-shot blood, until I found the one narrow fissure I hadn't closed off.

The Dead Zone lay on one side of that fissure, black starry eternity less a threat than a fact. I could clip the thread Begochidi held into Morrison's heart, but it would change sleep into death.

On the other side lay me. My power. My magic and my healing skill. Life, which struck me as not a little ironic. And suddenly it was very clear what I needed to do, and I felt foolish for not having seen it before.

All I needed to do, as it were, was change drivers. It was one of those film stunts nobody ever needs to do in real life, clambering awkwardly from the passenger seat into the driver's seat without ever letting the vehicle lose power. Usually it meant dodging bullets and firing guns at the same time, and if you were lucky, you got to jump a sixty-foot gap in the bridge ten seconds after you made the switch.

That, right down to the bridge jump, struck me as an

alarmingly good analogy for the situation. I gave myself a heartbeat to wonder if Petite could make that kind of jump, then put my faith in her solid steel soul and let my dreaming consciousness slide under Morrison's skin.

I had never tried to be aware of a body without being aware of the person residing within it before. Snooping was bad enough. Snooping on Morrison was beyond the pale. I thought maybe I could slither along the surface and cut into that drainage point without going deeper.

I should have known better. It was his life force—his soul—that was at risk here, and that sort of brought me to his garden whether I wanted it to or not. It wasn't like trying to work with Billy, who had shields as solid as the day was long. The only reason Morrison wasn't already hung out to dry was my shielding, and I could get through my own creation easily enough.

His inner world was nothing like I would have imagined.

I'd have guessed his garden might be like mine, clean lines and short-cropped grass, with everything in its place. Hedges trimmed, pathways paved, all ordered and restrained.

The place I stepped into was breathtakingly tumultuous.

I stood on a craggy ledge above evergreen wilderness, wind strong enough to push me off balance. The sky above whipped with clouds that did little to dim the brightness of the day, a hard white sun blazing heat down on me. The horizons were faint with blue mountains, snowcapped peaks catching the sun and setting it free again. The air buffeting me scented of the outdoors, earth and rain and green things.

A whitewater river crashed far below me, enough that its rush only came up on blasts of wind instead of being a constant. It bent into the woods, glimpses of it visible in low points where valleys spread with low-brush meadows instead of trees. Irritable squirrels chittered at me, a bird of prey circling overhead as I gaped. It wasn't the lush jungle that Gary carried in him and it was further from my own small, ordered garden than I could have dreamed. It was a place of confidence and raw beauty and stark challenges.

And there was a darkness in it, behind me where bare, broken stone became pristine forest again. The sleeping god drew strength through that point of darkness, and that was where I had to go and cut him off. I took a deep breath of the clean air, feeling regret prick at my eyes, and turned away from the vista to face the woods.

Morrison was waiting there, behind me. He leaned against a spruce tree, its rough grey bark between his shoulder-blades, with one foot kicked out and crossed over the other, hands in his pockets. Even in his own mind, he wore a button-down shirt, solid slate blue and soft-looking, like brushed flannel. He wore jeans, not slacks, and boots sturdy enough for hiking or working. I looked at my feet, wondering which of us would have the height advantage. He would: I wore tennies.

I looked up again to catch an indecipherable half smile on his mouth. His hair was as silvered in his self-perception as it was in reality. Either there was no vanity about graying, or he knew the look was attractive on him. He didn't say anything, so I said the first thing that came to mind: "What's the *J* stand for?"

Morrison actually laughed, glancing away as he let go a burst of chuckle, then pushed off the tree and walked up to me. He had the height advantage by at least an inch. I restrained the impulse to stand on my toes, or change my shoes. "James," he said, completely to my surprise. I didn't think he'd tell me.

"J—Jay—mmm—your parents named you Jim Morrison?"

Real amusement curled my boss's mouth. He shrugged, easy casual movement I couldn't remember seeing him use before, and said, "There's a reason I go by Michael. Nobody in their right minds in 1968 would call a boy with the last name of Morrison 'Jim.' I was named for my grandfather. So was Holliday," he added, and it took me a moment to parse that he meant Billy'd been named after his own grandfather, not Morrison's.

I said, "Oh," reflexively, because that explained his unfortunate name. I'd never known.

"How'd you know about the *J*?" Morrison was alarmingly relaxed. Never, in four years of acquaintance, had he been so pleasant with me. Then again, I was quite literally and completely on his territory.

"I—you went to sleep." My hand fluttered up to my forehead as I squinched my eyes apologetically. "I had to look at your driver's license to fill out your insurance paperwork at the hospital. Sorry." I meant it. Morrison pushed his lips out, then shrugged one shoulder again, just as easily as before. Apparently I was forgiven. If I'd known it was that easy, I'd have…I didn't know what. *Snuck inside his head earlier* didn't seem likely.

"I'm sleeping," Morrison said, as if he'd just caught up with that. I pressed my lips together and nodded. His eyebrows rose fractionally. "So what is this? A dream?"

"Are you in the habit of dreaming about me?" My mouth bypassed my brain once more. I considered giving myself an emergency tonguectomy. Morrison's eyebrows went back down, eyes turning stormy blue, and he didn't answer, which was probably all to the good. "You're not dreaming." I cast my gaze at his workboot-clad feet and muttered the words at them. "I had to shield you, and now the only way I can get you loose of the shield is to take the thing that's keeping you asleep and hook it up to me instead of you. And I have to do that from inside. I'm sorry. I've been trying not to snoop."

"Hook it up to you," Morrison repeated. That was the part I hadn't wanted him to catch. I twisted my lip in discomfort and nodded. He said, "Absolutely not."

"Morrison—"

"Walker!" Ah. That was the boss I knew. "This isn't a negotiation."

"No, sir," I said with a sigh, "it isn't. If I don't do this, when I go to fight this thing it's going to follow this link right into you and suck you dry. I would rather die. But if you'd like to not be pigheaded about this, for once I don't actually think I'm *going* to die, so it'd be nice to just get this done and then I'll be out of your head. I promise."

"Why me?" And there was another part I'd hoped he wouldn't pick up on. "Why not Holliday?"

"Because Billy can shield himself, and he wasn't the one dating half the monster."

I saw all the obvious questions and all their answers dart

through Morrison's eyes. What he said, after a measured few seconds, was, "Who's dating the other half?"

Laughter caught me off guard and I said, "God, I love—" before my tongue fell down my throat and tried to strangle me. I choked, coughed and wheezed "—the way your mind works. Sir," as I wiped tears from my eyes. "I am. Of course I am. Because what fun would it be if I was just having a normal social life."

"What was that at the restaurant, Walker?" That was as abrupt a transition as I tended to make. My hands went cold and I skittered a glance toward Morrison. The wind around us still blew wildly, and the light had grown gradually dimmer.

I closed my eyes against the first spatters of raindrops. "Does it really matter, sir?"

"It might," he said in such a peculiar voice I opened my eyes again. But he'd let it go, or moved on, stepping away from me to look out over the evergreen valley. I half turned, watching him. Lightning split the sky in the distance, and moments later a puff of smoke rose up from the trees. "Barb woke up when you called," he said eventually. "She said I should be flattered that my officers worried about me that much. She said—" and now he looked back at me, though I wished he wouldn't "—she said she'd have thought you were jealous, if you weren't dating her brother. I told her she was being ridiculous."

My chin came up a little, like I'd taken a hit. That, then, was what I should have said when he'd accused me of the same thing. Pounding on Petite's horn and confessing to the green-eyed monster hadn't been the right move. As if that was a surprise. For some reason I said, "Why'd you tell her that?"

"Because it's what anyone would expect me to say."

We weren't high enough in the mountains for the air to suddenly be so thin. I clenched my fists and tried to breathe, not knowing what to say, or how to say it. After a little while Morrison looked out at the valley again. The skies went darker, and rain began to come down harder. "The next thing I remember is this conversation."

"You're—" Damnit. I could feel it, a thread that didn't lie flat in the weaving of his story. It'd bumped up and tangled when I'd found myself unable to speak. I curled my hands into fists and stared at the granite beneath my feet, frustration washing off me in waves. I felt them, and if I'd wanted to slide the second sight on, I had no doubt I'd see them, too, bright silver-blue splashes of power coming off me like a beacon in the dark. "What do I say, Morrison? How am I supposed to get out of this conversation alive? You're my boss. What do you want me to tell you?"

"The truth," Morrison said. "I wonder if you've got so much as a passing acquaintance with the truth, Siobhán."

My heart twisted hard, drawing a rough small sound from my throat. My knees seemed to have stopped working, because I was abruptly on them, kneeling on hard rock and reaching for stone to grind my hands against. I still couldn't breathe easily, or maybe it'd gotten worse. "Not fair, Morrison. Not fair at all."

He looked down at me. "Isn't it?"

I could feel more than the wondering, in the air of the wild valley. For a moment, as he asked that, something thin and hard pulled taut, a fishline that made a vulnerable space inside him. A space that the goddamned topaz was supposed to protect. Only he'd given it away, and I only saw one way to seal it up again.

"What kind of truth do you want?" I said, more to the view than to Morrison. "My name is Siobhán Grania Mac-Namarra Walkingstick. I—" I swallowed the next words, then clenched my stomach muscles, forcing myself to speak. "I got pregnant when I was fifteen—" I cast a quick look at my boss, almost an apology. "Out of stupidity, not violence." That much, at least, I could give him, for the concern he'd shown more than once in the last couple of days. Every breath was an agonizing challenge to my too-tight throat.

"I had twins, a boy and a girl. Ayita, the girl, died right away. Aidan's growing up somewhere in Cherokee County. I don't date because I'm scared of repeating my mistakes." New thunder rumbled, this time the sound of blood in my ears, and I raised my voice over it. "Which probably leads directly to—" I couldn't do it. Couldn't say *falling for* or *loving,* and I didn't want to use a phrase as stupid as *crushing on* or its ilk. The weaker word I defaulted to was hard enough: "Caring. For someone totally unobtainable." It took a long time to make myself clarify that further, to push the words out: "For you."

"I'm dating Mark because he was the nearest cliff for me to jump off, after she turned up looking all cute and perky and…cute." There was another cliff right in front of me that I could jump off. The idea held appeal. "It is ridiculous, and I'm sorry, and I'm also not particularly proud of my behavior. So if that's enough truth, if it'd be all right, I'd like to just go get this monster off your back now so you can wake up and I can do my job."

"I think you already have." Morrison's voice was light and hollow, unlike I'd ever heard it before. I looked up, then looked back toward the woods.

Black threads, flowing and alive with butterfly darkness, swam from me into the woods, and far beyond that. They danced beyond Morrison's personal area and back into the battleground of dreams that I intended to fight in. I stared at the link without comprehension, unsure when I'd slipped myself between Morrison and Begochidi.

Oh, said the sarcastic voice, *probably when you played ball and admitted, with your usual lack of grace, the truth*. I didn't know who was more surprised by my answers, Morrison or the sleeping god, but either way, I'd made somebody do a double take, and when the power reattached, it did so to the magical powerhouse instead of the police captain. I said, "Good," in a harsh small voice, and flapped a hand at Morrison. "Go. Wake up. Get out of here, boss. You wake up and my dream of you will end and then I can go fight this thing." There was no real reason it should work that way, except I wasn't traversing the dreamworld as an ordinary sleeper. I could move in and out of my shamanic trances here, and generally when I wanted to wake up from one of those, I did. The rule should hold.

Except it didn't. Morrison took a breath as if he were waking up, but it caught and held like the blankets were too heavy in the morning. Perplexity danced across his expression and I got the idea that Morrison never had mornings when the blankets weighed too much. "I can't," he said in some astonishment. "I never have trouble waking up."

"You probably never sleep hard enough to," I muttered. "Come on, Morrison. Wakey wakey."

"I'm trying," he said irritably. "I feel like something's keeping my eyes closed."

"Begochidi. Damnit!" The first word was under my breath, the second a shout at the skies. "He's not yours, you redheaded bitch! You want a taste of something that'll get you through the day, try *me!*" Power flared with my outburst, silver burning away the black threads that tied me to the dreamworld. Heat sizzled with a nasty dark smell, and Morrison himself flinched. I couldn't fight from here, inside his garden. It would destroy his mind or his soul or something equally important. I swore again, taking two long strides over to my boss. "This always works in fairy tales."

I slid my fingers into Morrison's hair and brought his mouth down to mine for a kiss.

CHAPTER THIRTY-THREE

It turned out an inch in shoe height wasn't enough for either of us to have to give ground in order to share a kiss. It turned out all the times I'd thought he was close enough to kiss hadn't been quite right, either. There was a hell of a difference between what I thought of as close enough to kiss and actually closing that last half inch or so. Frustration and anger and needing to get the job done and innumerable other emotions spilled away in the compass of Morrison's arms, leaving me light-headed and warm and absurdly, blazingly happy. Silver-blue peaked and swooped all around me, a dance of joy that lit the insides of my eyelids.

The best part was Morrison kissed me back. There wasn't even a moment of complete startlement where he drew away before giving in to it. For a few brief, glorious seconds it was just the two of us, surprise flaring through Morrison's rich colors until our blues tangled together for an instant. Desire and pleasure zinged through me so brightly I blushed. I wondered if astral sex was better than real sex, or just different, and if a girl could manage both at once. Then reality, such as it was, intruded, and I pushed Morrison away. He blinked down at me twice, and the second time, the Rocky Mountain wilderness disappeared from all around me and left me falling through a place between dreams.

There was a sensation of gray cloudiness in the midst of formless nothing, instantaneous and immediate. For a moment I thought I might get away with sneaking through the dreamworld and taking Begochidi unawares, if only I could find my bearings.

My bearings found me first. I tumbled to an upright stop, still breathless and dizzy, though I could no longer tell if that was from falling or kissing. Either way, I had about enough time to look around before a maw of butterflies cropped up out of the dark and swallowed me.

Typically, this was the point at which I would either panic, shriek and try to run, or dig my heels in and hang on to where I was with everything I had. Getting sucked into a vortex of butterflies—or anything else; getting sucked up by vortexes in general just couldn't be good—was not the best game plan a girl could come up with. Ideally, I'd take a lance and a white charger and gallop my way through the dream realms to throw down a gauntlet at a god's feet and challenge him to single combat.

But I didn't have a gauntlet, much less a lance or a white charger, and I hadn't ridden a horse since I was fifteen, anyway. I had to trust to my silver sword and my array of shields, and I had to find Begochidi one way or another. Letting him scoop me up and bring me to the battlefields seemed as practical an arrival as any.

Butterflies melted all around me, dark dangerous colors bleeding into ordinary walls in a room with no floor. I fell at an alarming rate, jerking upward into wakefulness with a lurch of my heart that made me feel sick. Gary dropped my drum and caught my arm, concern in his eyes. "Jo? Jeez, there you are. You been sleepin' for a week, Joanie."

I stared around me at the familiar walls of my apartment, then sank back into my couch with a groan. My left wrist ached like hell, pounding and burning as if a rope had been twisted around it and pulled. I wrapped my fingers around it, encountering smooth heat that I rubbed without looking. The ache went up my arm to throb in my heart. Taking a deep breath lessened the pain enough for me to focus on what Gary'd said.

"A week?" My voice sounded dry, as if I hadn't drunk anything for…well. Days. "What's happening? What's going on? I've been having…" I stopped rubbing my wrist and went for my eyes instead, turning over to bury my face in the couch back. The throb came back, less intent as I mumbled, "Awful dreams." Except the one about kissing Morrison. I felt a tiny grin develop. "Mostly awful." I rolled back over to stare at Gary, whose bushy eyebrows were drawn down. "I dreamed Morrison had a girlfriend. A cute little redhead. I hated her."

Gary's eyebrows went down further, until his eyes disappeared beneath the gray beetles of them. "Mike?" His voice rose, worry still evident in it. My own eyebrows went down far enough to give me a headache. I didn't know any Mikes. The closest I'd come was what's his face in my dream. Hey, I'd had a boyfriend in my dream, too. I guess it was fair for Morrison to have a girlfriend, if I got to have a boyfriend. I squinted my eyes shut, trying to remember my guy's name. Matt. Something like that. Good-looking, sandy-haired. Maybe I needed to conk out for a week more often. His image was already fading, nebulous as a dream.

"She's awake," Gary said, presumably to somebody else, since I knew I was awake. "She's been dreamin' you got a bit on the side. Got anything you want to confess?"

I heard an inhalation behind the couch, then a rough laugh that had more to do with relief than amusement. "Thank God. All this living a lie was getting too much."

Gary chuckled while I frowned. I knew the second voice. It was incongruous in my living room, but I knew it, and I knew the scent of the man who sat down on the couch and pulled me into a bear hug. For a few long moments I just knotted my fists in the back of Morrison's shirt and held on, inhaling Old Spice cologne and wondering why I was trembling. My wrist still ached, all the more now that I was using my hands. "It's all right now," he murmured above my head. "Tell you what, I promise to dump the girlfriend now that you're awake again. You had me worried, Joanie. You had us all worried."

"I'm okay," I croaked. "Thirsty. What're you doing here, boss?" Morrison didn't call me Joanie. Neither did Gary, for that matter. They had to have been worried.

"'Boss.'" Morrison sat back with a chuckle, looking down at me. "You haven't called me that in a while."

"Nah, I guess it's been 'Cap' lately."

Morrison's eyebrows drew down and he frowned toward Gary. "She's still not quite awake, Mike. Give her a few minutes." Gary got to his feet, jerking his chin toward the kitchen. "I'll get her some water."

"Thanks." Morrison nodded at the big old cabbie, who went around the couch while I tried working my brain around the idea of anybody, much less Gary, calling Morrison "Mike." They called each other by their formal titles, Mr. Muldoon and Captain Morrison, when they had cause to call each other anything at all. It was one of those weird male rivalry things I neither understood nor wanted to understand.

"Mike?" I said, which was intended to convey all that unspoken commentary. Instead, Morrison looked down at me curiously.

"Yeah?"

"No, I mean...why's Gary calling you Mike?"

A shadow passed over Morrison's expression, to be replaced a few seconds later by something of a wry grin. "We got some things settled out while you were asleep. Being worried about you trumped our differences. Guess I've always been a little jealous of him."

"Jealous? Of *Gary?* Morrison, how often do I have to tell you, he's—"

"Morrison?" Another funny thing happened to Morrison's expression, hurt tempered with an attempt at humor washing through tightness around his eyes. "Boss, Morrison, what is this? I thought we were past that, Joanie. That was the idea behind you leaving the department and setting up your own shop, wasn't it? I know it hasn't been that long, but—"

"Shop?" A sort of thrilled hope leapt in my chest, reversing the ache in my heart back down toward my wrist. "You mean I've got my own shop?"

"Joanie, it's been open for a month. You've been working eighteen-hour days. She's still really muzzy, Muldoon," Morrison called. "Maybe we should call the doctor again. It's all right, Joanie. I guess anybody'd be disoriented after sleeping for a week."

The ache in my wrist took up as a sense of wrongness at the base of my brain, dissoluted by my preference to leave things just the way there were. Unfortunately, my mouth wouldn't let it go. "Joanie. You're calling me Joanie. What's that about?"

Morrison's smile went crooked and concerned, voice lowering. "I thought we agreed neither of us wanted to go by *Jim* or *Siobhán* in public. Muldoon'll get the doctor here, all right? You haven't woken up all the way yet. Just give yourself a few minutes." He ducked his head to bump his nose against mine, so intimate it'd have been unforgivable if it wasn't also so incredibly bizarre, and then he kissed me.

Pain flared through my left wrist, cold hot enough to burn. I thought *aw, crap* far too clearly, and put my forehead against Morrison's chest with a sigh. If I'd been asleep for a week, why wasn't I in a hospital bed? Why was Gary sitting on my floor with my drum, like he had been when I went to sleep? What was Morrison doing there at all, much less calling me by nicknames and intimating we were in a relationship, or that I had my own mechanic's shop? It was perfect. It was the kind of life I didn't even let myself dream about.

"Nice try, Begochidi," I said into my boss's shirt. "But no cigar. I'm not awake yet."

I gave Morrison a gentle push, trying not to see surprise

and injury in his eyes in the moment before he dissolved in an upward rush of butterfly wings. The heat in my arm finally subsided and I rubbed it again, then looked down. My copper bracelet gleamed with firelight, making me wince in embarrassment. "Sorry," I whispered to it. "I didn't pick up the hint. That Joanne, she's a nice girl, but not too bright."

To my unending relief, the bracelet didn't respond. I curled my arms around my ribs and looked up into the realm of dreams, watching trails of color left behind by the flock of butterflies. Flock? Herd? What was a multitude of butterflies called? It probably didn't matter, but I was suddenly curious. There had to be a good word for it. I'd have to look it up when I woke up again. If I woke up again.

I actually lifted both hands to my head in an attempt to stop my brain from derailing itself. If shamans were meant to have disciplined minds, I was doomed from the start. The unfortunate fallout of that was it might mean the world was doomed from the start, too, and that just wouldn't do. I needed to learn to stop distracting myself from the task at hand and face the music when it played, or something with similarly mixed metaphors.

I was doing it again.

"This is a dream," I said out loud, on the off chance it might help me focus. "And I'm aware of that, so it's a lucid dream, which means I can control what happens. Okay? Okay. I'd like a ladder, please. I need to follow the butterflies." Soaring up into the darkness after them sounded like a much more fun, dramatic pursuit, but my experience with flying dreams was that either I couldn't go as fast as I wanted, or just as I was getting the hang of it, I remembered I couldn't really fly and went plunging to the earth. Typically falling in dreams wasn't fatal, but given that I was here by deliberate action and choice, I didn't exactly want to take the risk. "A ladder," I repeated firmly, and dug my fingers into the ether.

Darkness protruded and gleamed, iron runs like a submarine ladder stretching up to the faint streaks of color left behind by retreating butterflies. I gave myself a mental pat on the back and began climbing, keeping my gaze up. I thought I'd actually won that round with Begochidi, recognizing his dream of my life for what it was. Maybe he was regrouping. Maybe I could get to him before he'd come up with a new game plan.

Maybe a fantastic indigo and violet wall of feather-light touches could slam down from nowhere and knock me about a thousand feet to the ground. I slammed against a black shapeless floor, unable to breathe with the weight of butterflies on me. They fluttered about my face, tiny razor touches keeping me from screaming for fear of inhaling them. I batted at them, trying to get free, and those I brushed away ghosted back to amalgamate and create a shape in the darkness. Tall, well-built, sandy-haired, smiling pleasantly. I wanted to cry. "Joanne," Mark said cheerfully. "There you are."

"Here I am." He didn't look like a god. He just looked like himself, a decent, rather charming young man who cooked as well as he lounged naked in bed. I could fight Barbara. I didn't *like* Barbara. I didn't want to beat Mark up. "You're not the one I expected. I was kind of hoping for your other half."

"I was kinda hoping you'd be my other half." His nose wrinkled and he looked sheepish. "Okay, that was incredibly corny. But it's true, too. I mean, I like you, Joanne. You're a little scary with this shamanism thing you've got going on, but you really seem to care a lot about what's going on around you, and I guess it's better to be a little weird and scary with caring than not. I'd kind of like to stick it out and see if we could make it work."

I found myself knotting and unknotting my hands like it would lead me to some kind of salvation. Morrison's sleeping form kept splashing through my vision, as if I needed the reminder. "I meant your twin sister, Mark, not your soul mate." I barely knew Mark Bragg. Pretty much everything I'd shared with him had been the machination of a god searching for the danger to his people. It wasn't a normal relationship. It wasn't even a *real* relationship. So why in hell did shooting him down make my heart ache?

Maybe because I hadn't had anything like a real relationship in longer than I could remember.

Maybe because at the bottom of it, he was an ordinary man who'd gotten caught up in the mess of a life I'd led. I didn't like my magic reaching out and touching people outside my immediate sphere. Mark was god-ridden, and that, plain and simple, was my fault. I might have done better by him.

There were so many people I might have done better by.

The thought made my throat tighten, a cold knot settling in its hollow. Faye Kirkland's fanatical expression as she died blurred into Colin Johannsen's pale face, all forming in my mind's eye. Colin no longer wore the weary good cheer I'd seen in him in the few days I'd known him. He was drawn up thin and tall, much thinner than the boy I'd known had been, with the weight of cancer treatments bloating his body, and his eyes were accusing. Hard eyes, the expression of a young man used, and used badly. Cassandra Tucker, the only way I'd ever known her: blue and cold with death. I couldn't breathe, cold at my throat burning with despair, but the faces wouldn't stop.

Three young women, dead at a banshee's hands, strewn about a baseball field and hidden beneath unseasonable snow. I had memorized their names, too: Rachel and Nikki and Lisa, who had died because I'd distracted my mother from the all-important task of banishing their murderer. And before them a handful of schoolchildren and their teacher and the Quinleys and Marie D'Ambra and shamans whose life's blood began a legacy of death that tied to me. All of them were people who might have lived, had their paths not crossed mine.

And before that, a strong and determined woman who willed herself to death because I had turned away from the road I was supposed to travel, and before that, a baby girl whose dying breath seemed to give her brother the strength to live.

I could not breathe. Despair brought me to my knees in a jerky fall, pressure at my throat so intense I struggled to lift a hand to claw at it. Dark spots washed through my vision, indigo and violet, like eyes watching my death without remorse or pity. I had not expected this. Had not, for once, thought I was going to die. But the legacy that lay behind me spread so easily before me, so obviously. I could name the faces, count the numbers, now, of those who had died for my mistakes. Now. Soon I wouldn't be able to, not with the plague sweeping out across Seattle and in time over the world. The end of the world, heralded by my too-late arrival on the psychic stage, by my clumsy use of power that whispered *apocalypse* to slumbering gods. So many deaths, with me as the focal point.

My fingers snagged in metal, cold and hard and smooth under my hand, and I remembered, incongruously, Suzanne Quinley and Melinda Holliday and Ashley Hampton, all alive and healthy because their paths had crossed with mine. I knotted my fingers around the necklace, feeling the cross press into my palm, and lifted my gaze to stare across butterfly-swarming darkness at Mark Bragg.

"The shamans weren't my fault," I heard myself whisper, voice scratchy, as if the cold pressure from my mother's necklace had scraped my vocal box into disuse. "I probably could've done better, but I did my best. And I saved Suzanne Quinley." I felt a weak, miserable smile tweak my mouth. "That's got to count for something. I saved Gary."

A flash of warmth spilled through me at that, make me break out with a hoarse laugh. "I even saved myself. At least, I'm working on it." I could feel so much of the angry, resentful child I'd been still knotted up inside me, her world taken away from her in the moment I'd reached back through time to borrow the training she'd worked so hard to master. A shattershot image of a spider-webbed windshield flashed through my vision and I laughed again, another coarse sound. "I'm out of balance right now," I admitted. "More people dead because of me than alive. But I'm working on it. And I'm not the one pulling life force from others to stay awake. That's what you're doing, isn't it, Begochidi?"

I knotted my fingers around the necklace, hanging on to it to keep my thoughts in order, and advanced a step toward the god's avatar who stood before me. "You woke up without meaning to and took strength from the first people you could reach. The Dine. Your people. But you're supposed to save them, not put them all to sleep forever, so you had to let them wake them up again, didn't you? They woke up and started getting ready for the end of the world, while you looked for the strength to wake all the way up yourself. The poor bastards at the university."

I reached out, searching for Mark's memories and dreams in the darkness. "Is that what happened?" I whispered. I could sense excitement in their dreams—daydreams, night dreams; it didn't matter. Both could be found in this place. I should know. I'd been offered the stuff of daydreams repeatedly in the last few days. I clung to their anticipation, spinning out misty recollection from the recesses of Mark's mind, so foggy it seemed he didn't actively recall the day.

They invited everybody in the department down to the lab to watch the first test of their machine. I'd seen photographs of a machine other physicists had build that could teleport a photon from one place to another. I'd retained a critical disappointment that it hadn't looked like the beam-me-up sort, and felt similarly about the wormhole-maker. It looked more like a 1980s movie laser than a machine that could tear space and time asunder, and when they turned it on, there was little more than a pulse that rippled the air, and then silence.

Terrible silence, as everyone in the lab fell, soundless, to the floor. Everyone, including Mark and Barbara Bragg. The memory/dream faded into unconsciousness, Mark no longer able to provide information about what had happened, and me with no idea how to draw memory out of a god of sleep.

Mark stood very still, a sign I took as hopeful. I'd fought

a god and won once. I didn't want to put money on pulling
it off a second time. "Is that what you had to do all the other
times, Begochidi? The world's ended a lot of times before.
Did you have to reach out beyond the People for your
strength? It shouldn't be this hard, should it? If it's really
supposed to be the end of the world, shouldn't you have
just woken right up and gone to save your people? You
shouldn't have to fight so hard, should you?"

I inhaled, tasting my own sorrow in the dreamland. "All
my friends," I said quietly. "If you think taking their lives
will weaken me, you're wrong. If that's why you're choosing
them to take life force from, let me tell you, it's not going to
work. Not any more than me threatening your people with
annihilation would keep you from fighting. You're putting
me in a position where I've got nothing to lose, Begochidi."

Mark turned his face away, almost submissive action, and
for one bright moment I had hope. There didn't have to be
an end-all, be-all battle. We could work it out with words.

And then something happened in his eyes, something deep
and profound that turned them to agate blue, like Barbara's.
The color of a hard desert sky. My jaw set and I let the Sight
film over my own vision, looking to See what I suspected.

I hated being wrong, but there were days I hated being
right even more.

Mark's aura was no longer split. The full spectrum of rainbow colors bled out so sharply it hurt to look at, throbbing and pulsing with power. There were no empty razors of blackness between the brilliant shades, nothing suggesting a weakness. Then again, it wasn't really Mark. It wasn't even Barbara, and I had no idea what had happened to her, if Begochidi had consolidated his energy to the dreamlands. The image of her collapsed somewhere wasn't entirely unappealing, though I knew that was petty and nasty and should be scrubbed from my brain. I'd scrub it later.

Assuming there was a later.

Two attacks. One emotional, trying to trap me in a dream, the other intellectual, trying to weigh me down with implacable logic. The lingering burn in my throat felt tied to the dissipated ache in my wrist, the talismans Gary had girded me with reminding me of what they protected. My heart. My head, which was, for all intents and purposes, where I thought of my soul as residing. That left one obvious method of attack.

I snatched Cernunnos's sword from my hip and flung up my free hand as if I bore a shield, just as Mark gathered his hands in to his chest, then released them in a burst of winged color. Butterflies swarmed over me, parting with such force as they hit my shield and sword that I felt the reverberations up my arm and through my body.

They were a distraction, nothing more. In the instant they cleared I saw that Mark had disappeared, dreamtime swallowing him as if he'd never been. Swallowing him as effectively as he'd absorbed Coyote. My heart lurched, painful missed beat, and I tightened my hand around the rapier's hilt. It would not do to keep thinking of him as Mark. This was Begochidi I faced, a god wrapped in a sandy-haired man's form. I lowered my blade and my shield arm, casting out with hyper-natural senses to see if I could locate Begochidi in the darkness.

A rainbow of color hammered down on me, grasping the narrow threads I put out and draining their silver-blue dry. I reeled back, and lifted my sword again. Begochidi's assault faded away again, as if he couldn't attack directly unless I provided him with a power line to feed on, or find me by. I hoped so. I thought that meant he wasn't drawing any more from the people in Seattle who slept beneath his spell.

A net had done nicely to catch the god of the Hunt. It seemed more than a little ironic that it wouldn't work on a butterfly god. On the other hand, standing here sending out dribbles of power until he sucked all the life force out of me wasn't exactly the best plan I'd ever come up with. I took a moment to wonder if there was some kind of handbook on how best to fight powerful otherworldly beings, or if I was going to be stuck making the best of it every time I faced one. I was pretty sure I'd be stuck. That seemed excruciatingly unfair.

On the other hand, maybe it meant the powerful otherworldly beings didn't have any idea how to fight me, either. The thought cheered me, and I found myself doing like I'd seen in the movies, banging my sword against my shield to call my enemy out. It was only then that I noticed I was in fact *carrying* a shield, that the purple heart Gary had pinned to my breast had become a small round shield, quartered by a cross, clutched in my left hand. I had no idea how to fight with a sword and shield. I was going to have to go back to fencing lessons, and see if Phoebe could teach me.

Right after I took some names and kicked some godly butt.

I smashed my sword and shield together again, letting out a yell. "Hey! C'mon! You're going to have to do this the hard way, Begochidi! I'm not going to stand here and spoon-feed you power. You want me, come and get me!" I liked shouting things like that. It made me feel all studly and stuff.

Unfortunately, it also got the god's attention. He hadn't been hanging around in the dark waiting for me to lure him out with power, after all. He'd been off stage for a costume change, and nobody'd told me whether I got to have one or not.

On the positive side, he no longer looked like Mark. All the sandiness was gone from his hair, leaving it bright and golden as sunlight, so shadows seemed to slip away from it unnoticed. His eyes were cornflower blue, so mild as to be intense, and his features were strong and regular and handsome, like Aztec paintings had been modeled after him. He was bare-chested and wore a cloak of emerald and violet and sapphire, butterfly patterns woven into the vivid colors so beautifully that when he moved it looked like the cloak flowed with life. He wore leggings with a loincloth over them, and his feet were bare. He carried a massive feathered spear in his left hand. The entire ensemble looked as if it were meant to impress and intimidate.

It worked.

I looked down at myself. Jeans. A button-down shirt with three-quarters length sleeves. Tennies. Impressive I was not. On the other hand, I felt my singular lack of impressiveness gave me license to skip the posturing that he appeared to be going through—he'd stopped and stood there impassively to let me admire his glory—so when I looked up again, it was with a lunge that brought my rapier point a hair from his belly. I actually saw the inhalation that kept me from drawing blood, and an instant later when I met his eyes there was a mixture of outrage and astonishment in his expression. Come to think of it, Cernunnos had looked a lot like that when I'd fought him, too. Gods were apparently not accustomed to mere mortals taking the fight to them.

I stopped having any time to continue my entertaining internal commentary right about then, and started trying to keep myself alive.

Begochidi, unlike the last god I'd fought, didn't have any inclination toward seducing me, or persuading me in any manner. Or, I thought, given the dreams and visions I'd had, he'd tried and failed, so killing me was just fine, no holds barred. He slapped the spear up so the length of it followed his arm, and swept it around with massive grace. I skittered backward, holding my own breath to keep from being sliced in half. My shirt ripped silently under the spear's point, giving me an idea of just how sharp the metal head was, and just how much I didn't want it to touch me. Surprise flashed across Begochidi's handsome features, as if he'd expected me to hold still and be skewered.

I lunged forward again, six months of fencing classes overriding my brain. It was just as well: muscle memory observed how he'd exposed himself without my mind consciously registering it. I brought my shield up to ward off his spear as he drew it back to strike again, a forward attack instead of a sweeping one. He'd taken the haft in both hands now, as if I'd moved up a notch from *easy kill* to *respectable opponent*. I parried, tangling our swords together, surprised to find that move actually worked in battle. Then I swung the shield around and clobbered him in his pretty face.

He howled with outrage, which would have been satisfying if a heavy wash of black-and-crimson butterflies had not erupted from his mouth, beating at the air so heavily I suddenly couldn't breathe. Panic swept in and I staggered, releasing his spear as I gagged on soft feathered wings and honey-sweet thickness all around me. It felt hideously like a dream, being too far underwater and unable to claw my way to the surface for air. I'd lost sight of Begochidi entirely, scraping and flailing at butterflies instead. I wanted to run, but my feet were thick and slow and I couldn't get my legs to move fast enough. I knew there was something horrible behind me, something that would tear me to shreds if it caught me, but I was stuck, and there was nobody there to save me.

White terror closed my throat. I sent out an instinctive thread of power, searching for the help I'd had all the other times I'd faced something awful. The coven had helped me; the thunderbird had. Billy'd nearly given his life to keep me on my feet with the banshee, and my coworkers had banded together, even not knowing what was going on, to help me capture a god with a net woven from our energy. Coyote'd been there to guide me, however cryptically, and Gary's solid presence had anchored me when I felt most adrift. The whole of Seattle had given me what I needed when I first tuned into the shamanic world.

It was all gone now. There was me in the dark, drowning in butterflies, and nothing else. The only thing responding to the signal for help I'd reached out with was the god I had to defeat, and the butterflies around me grew heavier and stronger as I kept that desperate plea open.

"Idiot," I heard my own voice say, bitterly. Butterflies erupted in a shower of brightly colored confetti, and I discovered I was on my knees, choking until tears came to my eyes. I looked up to find myself, fifteen and angry, staring down at the me who couldn't breathe.

"Idiot," she said again. "You took all that power from me, and you still don't get it. What'd they tell you, Joanne?" A cord of power thrummed between us, not giving or taking, just linking. Shadows reformed around its brightness like it was food, delicate wings moving in the dark. Joanne-the-younger batted at them, silver-blue light surging, and for an instant they retreated, leaving us alone in a ball of light. "That the only way to win was to fight?"

"Yeah." My voice scraped. That was the path the dead shamans had set me on: the warrior's path. I'd tried talking to Begochidi already. I didn't know what else to do. My younger self sneered.

"Coyote told *me* that the whole idea was to get somebody to change his perceptions, even just for a second. So you can get inside. So you can heal."

"He's a *god!*" I yelled. "How the hell am I supposed to heal a *god*? I can't even tell what's wrong with him!"

She stared down at me disdainfully. "Who says it's him you're supposed to heal?"

A golf club to the stomach couldn't have been more effective. The air went out of my lungs and I stared back at her wordlessly. "You're supposed to be your own hero, Joanne. How can you be anybody else's if you're not?"

"When'd you get so smart?" I whispered.

"Somebody's gotta be," she retorted. "You're doing a crappy job of it. Get up and figure out a way to live. I don't want to die this way."

I could think of a number of ways I'd like her to die. Throttling her was top on the list. I swear I didn't remember being that much of a shit at her age. "You don't like me very much, do you?"

"Why should I?" she asked. "You don't." Then she was gone, all the demons and darkness she'd been holding back swarming in on me again to take the air away. Great. I was having oxygen-deprivation-induced illusions of my own temperamental teenage self. Just how I wanted to go out, scolded by a bratty me.

Well, she didn't want me to go out this way any more than I did. At least we had something in common. I climbed to my feet as I spoke, pushing at the darkness with my mind. It felt rather like wrapping myself in bent light, only now I was using that light to send sleeping night into retreat. I held my sword and shield like I was used to them, competent with them. Like I was ready to face the darkness and do battle.

My younger self had told me not to fight. Of all the people in the world, my fifteen year old punk-ass attitude-ridden self...

...had told me not to fight.

I lowered my sword, swaying in the ball of light I'd made in the heart of darkness, trying, for the first time I could remember, to really look at myself.

I couldn't remember a time when I wasn't willing to pick a fight. There'd been a chip on my shoulder as long as I'd been able to put two thoughts together. First it was being a gypsy in a comparatively stable world, then being a girl who was into cars. Being a stranger in a strange land when we went back to North Carolina, and God help anybody who'd gotten in my face when my pregnancy started to show. All the way through college, all the way through my job at the department, epitomized by my relationship with Morrison.

Mark had refused to fight with me.

I crouched, carefully, and put down my sword and shield, ending with my face in my hands, my stomach twisting. I wasn't accustomed to facing anything without a weapon of some kind in hand. *In hand* didn't even have to be in hand: it could be my tongue or my fist or my power. It didn't matter. It was all something to fight with.

I could see where that reckless confrontation could look like the forerunner of doom, especially when coupled with the sign that the Navajo people had been told to watch for. I wondered if the men and women who'd fallen asleep and awakened again to prepare for the end of the world could ever forgive me for being such a mess.

I wondered, sharply, if Coyote had been one of those people, and knew that he would've forgiven me.

That, of all things, was what gave me the strength to put my hands on my thighs and push myself upward. I'd blown it badly enough. My heart was sick in my throat, but my younger self's distaste and dislike weighed even more heavily than fear. I could do *one thing* right by her at this late date, and I wasn't going to screw that up. Not now. Not when it was the only way I could say thank you to the girl whose childhood I'd managed to take away.

"I'm not the bad guy, Begochidi." My voice broke, nothing more than a little laugh. "I'm just a rank beginner. I'm not the rainbow that lasts all day. I'm a healer. Maybe not a very good one, but it's what I'm supposed to do. And I'm not going to fight you." The laugh came back, more self-deprecating. "I hope you won't take advantage of that by sticking a spear through my head." There wasn't any answer to my brief laugh. Damn. I curled my hands into loose fists, then relaxed them again. "Go back to sleep, Maker. It's not time for you to be here yet. There's gonna be a real rainbow that lasts all day sometime down the line, and your people are going to need you then." I passed my hand over my eyes. "If you don't think it's arrogant of me, I'll do what I can to keep an eye on things until then. I really am trying to do the right thing," I added more quietly.

I was about to give it up as a lost cause when white light flashed and left me blinking and blinded in the dark.

CHAPTER THIRTY-FIVE

Saturday, July 9, 9:39 a.m.

Voices, low and good-natured, mumbled around me in the careful pitch used for sick rooms and hospitals. Once in a while someone broke out of that, a laugh climbing up, or a discussion rising out of polite tones. There were other sounds, too: buzzes and beeps that went on rhythmically. Not the kind of thing I expected to hear in my apartment. It was all muffled, like somebody'd wrapped six or eight scarves around my head. Perhaps they had. That would explain why I didn't seem to be able to open my eyes, either.

Instead of opening them, I yawned so hard tears leaked through my eyelashes. I couldn't quite get a groan out, even though I felt the situation warranted one. I was sure it was too early to be up. The blankets were heavy and my head was weighed down. I yawned again and rolled over, dragging my pillow down to bury my face in it.

I tried, anyway. My wrist ran into something cold and metal. I did groan that time, and pulled my eyelids half open to see what the problem was. The noise around me stopped.

There was a metal railing about ten inches from my nose. Beyond it was a fuzzy green curtain, though the fuzziness was probably due to my lack of contacts. Between the railing and the curtain was somebody's burly arm. The arm was attached to a hand gripping the railing. The hand was in focus, and had pale pink polish on the nails. I chuckled, or croaked, depending on how you wanted to look at it, and said, "Billy?"

The sound came back much louder than before, a cacophony of cheers and yells and general glee while a surprising number of people shoved around the bed and bent over to hug me. Gary appeared, trying to look gruff, and I hung on to his hand. "You saved me in there," I whispered. "You and your crazy totems."

"Weren't nothin'," he said, but his eyes were suspiciously bright and he held on hard when he hugged me. "You been out two days, kid."

"Really." I couldn't rub my eyes and hang on to Gary at the same time, so I only squinted blearily, trying to see past him. Billy and Mel were hovering side by side, Robert poking his head over Mel's shoulder. "I dunno, Billy." He took a step forward, worried, and I shook my head. "You're thinner, but going into a coma for days on end seems like a kind of drastic weight loss plan to me. Maybe you should just avoid The Missing O and all those doughnuts."

He laughed and Mel put an arm around his ribs, hugging him. She looked better, her color back to normal and her dress cut to disguise four months of pregnancy. I could see glimmers of buttercup yellow around her, even without trying. The same kinds of shadings fell away from everyone in my line of sight, in fact, from Gary to Robert to other people from the department. Bruce was there, thin face lit up with happiness as he spoke into his cell phone, telling Elise I'd woken up. "Ask her if I can have some tamales, Bruce." His smile widened and he nodded. I flopped back into the bed, yawning until my eyes teared again. I couldn't be as tired as I felt. I'd just slept for two days. "Everybody's okay?"

A wave of solemness came over the room. "Yeah, pretty much," Billy answered after a moment.

I closed my eyes, tears suddenly having nothing to do with yawning. "Pretty much?"

Billy hesitated too long and my stomach clenched. "Who, Bill?" I sat up, knotting my fingers in the covers. I'd severed Begochidi's link with Morrison. It couldn't be him. Unless Barbara, in the waking world, had reached him somehow. "Billy. Please."

"Mark Bragg still hasn't woken up. I'm sorry, Joanie."

A horrible combination of relief and dismay chilled me right through the gut, color draining from my skin. "What about Barb?"

"Nobody's seen her." Billy said quietly. "They've got an APB out. The captain's been out looking for her himself."

My heart tightened and I nodded, trying to sound indifferent as I asked, "He's okay?"

Half a dozen people said, "He's fine." I got the idea my nonchalance ploy hadn't worked. I nodded again. "Where's Mark?"

"Down the hall," Gary said. "Doctors don't think he's gonna wake up."

I fumbled the bed railing down while he spoke and pulled the oxygen sensor off my finger. "Bring me to him."

The same half dozen people said some variation on "Joanne," and I swung my legs off the bed, wishing I was wearing something more dignified than a hospital gown. Mel, as if on command, dropped a robe around my shoulders, and I looked at Gary. "Yeah," he said after a moment. "Arright. C'mon, sweetheart."

The herd of them—I was touched at how many people were sitting vigil at my bedside—left me outside Mark's room. I went in barefoot and cold to find him alone with the sounds of a hospital room. I wondered what had happened to Barb, if she'd suffered the same unexpected coma Mark had. I didn't think so. I wondered if there was a way for me to find her. The same cool certainty that said she hadn't collapsed in a coma told me I wouldn't be able to find her, either. It wouldn't stop me from looking, but my gut wasn't on my conscience's side this time.

The glimmerings of Sight that were with me when I woke deepened as I sat down at Mark's side. His aura no longer shone with half a spectrum's colors, but lay quiet against his skin, the rusty brown I'd seen before. I had a pretty good idea already of what had happened, but I put my fingers on his shoulder and slipped out of my body to do a diagnostic. It was only later I realized how easy it was to do that, even without the drum bringing me under.

Mark's soul lay unguarded, a desert oasis full of blooming cactus and clear sun-warmed water. But no wind blew, the water lay still and lifeless in its pools, and the sun's warmth faded a little even as I stood there. All around me, the blooms seemed in stasis, not yet dying, but no more living than a shadow. I'd cut off too much, when I'd pulled Begochidi's power from the gentler side of his human host. The bond Mark held on his own soul was fragile now, barely there.

My vehicle metaphors came back to me with a sense of the ridiculous. The easiest way to fix a lot of problems was with duct tape. I just needed to bind his soul and his body together again, wrapping them tight with tape until they grew strong together again.

The power that flowed through me was far less half-assed than tape would've been, though. It had permanence and strength, sticky silver glue binding life to body. I had no sense of how much time it took, but when the ghost of a breeze whispered over me, I knew I'd succeeded. With a small sad smile, I left Mark's desert garden and stepped into another one, a place between souls in the astral realm. It only took a moment to settle down into a coyote-sized hollow in the rocks, though I fit into it no better than I had before. "Coyote?" The word was hardly a whisper, and the second one even fainter: "Cyrano?" I said nothing else, only sat beneath the violent blue sky and stretched my senses, pouring myself out in hopes of a response.

In time, the wind turned acid with sand, heat intensifying by degrees until the sky was white with it, and the horizons bled with rising, burning waves. The sun settled closer to me, hard and merciless, and I felt the stones I lay curled into shift around me. Rock became sand, gritty and white as salt, baking under the light. I knew without looking up that what I leaned on now was a single bleached tree in the midst of desert, as lonely a thing as ever I'd known. Breath ached in my chest, air so hot it felt too thin to keep life in my body. When tears swam in my eyes against the heat, I opened my mouth and said, very softly into the weight of sun, "I honor you, Trickster. You may as well show yourself. I know you're here."

Then he was sitting before me, Big Coyote with his coat made of copper and gold threads, so sharp and vivid I expected to cut myself when I leaned forward to wrap my arms around his bony shoulders. I buried my face in metal-colored wire fur, and poured a lifetime's worth of thanks and sorrows and fears into Big Coyote's heart. I scraped up all the love I knew how to and offered that up, starting with my own mother's hard choice to send me away and my unconscious echo of that decision fifteen years later. I added in everything I'd learned from Gary, and the admission about Morrison I still didn't like to put into words, and Billy and Melinda and their kids and the mistakes I'd made and every scrap of life my memory and my soul could find to share. I was trembling and light-headed under the relentless sun, still searching for essence to give away, when Big Coyote pulled away very gently and licked tears from my face.

Surprised, I laughed and put my hand out. He licked

that, too, solemnly, then stood, his tail wagging slowly at first, then considerably faster. I smiled and tried to pet him one more time, but he turned away with unexpected speed and smacked me in the face with his whipping tail before bounding away into the desert.

The sting was still with me as my eyes popped open and I looked down at Mark Bragg, who gave me a tired, uncertain smile in return. "Do I know you?"

"No," I whispered after a few long seconds. "Not really. You've been sick for a while, but you're going to be okay now." The door opened behind me as I spoke. I looked over my shoulder to see Brad Holliday, who was about the last person I expected. I got up, very aware I was wearing a hospital gown beneath my robe. I desperately wanted to ask what he was doing there, but *helping out* seemed like the obvious answer, so I refrained and said something else obvious instead: "He's awake, Doctor."

"I see that," Holliday said shortly. I cast a rueful smile at the floor and edged toward the door as he came in. He gave Mark a perfunctory look and me a harder one. "Did you do this?"

I slowed and glanced back at him. "Does it matter?"

I saw him struggling with the question, wanting the answer to be yes and not sure it was. After a few seconds he went around the end of Mark's bed, introducing himself and clearly dismissing me. It was as good a start—or finish—as any, and I let myself out as quietly as possible.

Laurie Corvallis, who was as much the last person I expected as Brad Holliday, was sitting on my hospital bed when I padded back into the room. "I missed something," she said.

I hung there in the doorway wondering if I could stage a

retreat through the whole hospital wearing only a robe. Probably not. "Missed something?"

"You promised me the big break on the sleeping sickness story. Yet here we are, the last sleeper awake again and I've got no terrorists, I've got no spooky disease, Project Rainbow is buried and I've got nothing. What'd I miss, Walker?" The *officer* part had been dropped. Apparently I'd slid a few points in her estimation.

I opened my mouth to give her the flippant, if honest, answer, and stopped again. I'd written off my knowledge of things as being magic a couple of times already. Corvallis didn't strike me as the true believer type, but I didn't like to point her along those lines any more than I already had. So I said, "I'm sorry. It didn't work out the way I thought it would," which was true enough. "At least I got you off my back for a couple days."

To my surprise, that got a smile from her. Pointed, faint, but a smile. "It won't work again. I smell smoke, Walker."

"There's no fire, Ms. Corvallis. I'm sorry." I came all the way into the room—it was mine, after all—and looked around for my clothes. Corvallis watched me a good long minute or two, until I thought I might end up doing a strip tease for her, then got off the bed and walked out. I'd gotten myself dressed and down to the front desk to check myself out when Gary reappeared from somewhere.

"Had ta drive your pal Bruce home," he announced. "Guess their Eagle's actin' up again."

I laughed. "I'll fix it. Elise is making me tamales anyway. What happened to Billy and Mel?"

"They headed out, too. Mel says she's makin' dinner for everybody tonight and you're comin' over. And Rob says—"

"Robert. He doesn't like nicknames."

"Robert," Gary said with the patience of an old man humoring a young one, which was to say, no patience at all, "says you looked better when you woke up. Not so patchy, he said. He said you'd know what that meant."

I looked down at my hands as if I'd be able to see what Robert saw in them, and smiled again. "Yeah. I know what he means. I think he's right." I knew he was. I couldn't see my patchwork the way Robert seemed to, but there was no incessant ball of power beneath my breastbone any longer. I couldn't even feel it anymore, not like it was something separate, anyway. It belonged to me, or I belonged to it, as much as my hand or eye did. It took less than a blink to be able to see silver-sheened magic coursing under my skin, and as little to turn that second sight off again. "I really need to practice," I said, "but I think I've kind of got the hang of this thing now. It's…" I looked up at the big gray-eyed old man and smiled. "I guess I'm not fighting it anymore. That's good, right?"

Gary wrapped an arm around my shoulders and pulled me against his chest. "That's great, doll. Now, you take a ride home from an old cab driver?"

"Promise not to drive using only the Force as your guide?"

"No," Gary said cheerfully, and herded me out the door.

I made him leave me alone at home. It was hours till dinnertime and Petite, despite her wrinkled back end, would get me to the Hollidays' home just fine. I also badly needed some time to sit and think and just be me without any magical interference or helpful friends hanging out to make sure I was okay. I took a shower, knowing perfectly well I was going about things backwards, and put on some grubby clothes and my driving shades before getting my toolbox and going down to the parking lot to work on Petite.

Morrison was leaning on the hood of his gold Avalon, arms folded across his chest, studying my Mustang when I got down there. He looked as though he was actively, even aggressively, trying *not* to look like he had when I'd stepped into his garden.

He wore a white short-sleeved T-shirt instead of a button-down suit shirt. It fit snugly, tight around his biceps, and I suddenly realized the suit shirts and jackets he normally wore added a thickness to his waist that wasn't his at all. Either that or he'd had some amazing sculpting surgery in the two days I'd been sleeping. The T-shirt was tucked into dark gray slacks, making his hips and waist look much narrower than I was accustomed to. He wore loafers. I couldn't remember seeing him in anything but shining tied shoes, either, not even at the Fourth of July picnic. His hair was bright with silver in the sunlight, and he was wearing dark sunglasses, which would've seemed like an affectation if they hadn't looked so good. The entire ensemble was completely unlike anything I'd ever seen Morrison in before.

For one brief and rather glorious moment I wondered if my captain had actually dressed to show off for me. Then I got myself under control and came the rest of the way out of the building, putting my toolbox down and leaning against Petite. I wished I was wearing something better than an oil-stained tank top and jeans with the knees already torn out, but that was me, Joanne Walker. You take what you can get. We stood there for a while, both of us leaning on our cars, both of us with our arms crossed over our chests, both of us watching the other through sunglasses that hid our eyes.

Then Morrison said, "Was it real?" and I found I had to look away even with the protective lenses.

"I don't know." I pulled my shades off and pinched the bridge of my nose, setting the glasses on Petite's roof, then looked at him. "Yeah." I didn't like how low my voice was, but I couldn't get it any louder. My heart hurt, and so did breathing. Morrison might have let me get off with the *I don't know*, but I owed a lot of people better than that, not least him. "It was real for me. This is my reality. Waking or not."

Morrison took his own shades off and pushed away from the Toyota. I straightened up automatically to just his height, and there he was, close enough to kiss again, his eyebrows drawn down a little over very blue eyes.

"This is going to keep happening with you, isn't it. Things that can't be explained sensibly. Whether I try to keep my precinct running smoothly and without—" His mouth worked and he grated, "Paranormal incidents," before resuming something of a more natural tone. "They're just going to keep following you around, aren't they."

"Yeah, probably." I sighed, knowing there was no probably about it. "Yes."

"You and goddamned Holliday," Morrison said, exhaled, looked away, and looked back again. "Would you take a promotion?"

"What?" My ears were suddenly ringing, disbelief sharp and tinny in my blood.

"To detective. I'd partner you with Holliday. He knows the ropes, and you two work well together. And there are things you'd work on better together than anybody else I've got." The last words were spoken almost through his teeth, dislike of the truth colored with growing resignation. I knew exactly how he felt. That he could stand there and offer me a detective position, knowing what he was letting himself in for, was a measure of the man.

And I wanted it. To my shock I wanted it so badly I could just about taste it. It meant having license to follow the weird events that my life was becoming a part of. It meant, with any luck, being proactive enough to stop nasty, dark things from happening in my city. It meant working with somebody who believed in what I could do, with tacit understanding from our boss, whether he liked it or not. I had never thought of myself as ambitious, particularly with ambitions to be a cop, but Morrison had pulled me into it and I was starting to realize that I liked helping people.

But there was a huge chasm on the other side of that question. Two questions. He'd asked me two questions, and no matter what I said, answering the one precluded the other. *Was it real* did not, would not, *could* not fit into the same universe as *would you take a promotion*. And Morrison knew it. He hadn't said, "I'm promoting you." That would've closed the door on *was it real*. It would've told me something, and that he left that door open...

...that told me something, too.

Color pounded in my cheeks, so high I knew my tan would never hide it. My throat hurt. My heart hurt. My hands hurt. As if the bracelet and the necklace and the medal all lay tight and piercing those places, maybe trying to build a shield of protection that for the first time, I didn't want and didn't know how to do without. If I'd thought a sword was any good for stabbing myself with, I'd have drawn Cernunnos's blade from its astral sheath at my hip and thrown myself on it, but that kind of behavior required something to prop it on, or someone else to hold it. I didn't want to blink, knowing more of those tears that were coming too easily lately would fall. Regardless of what I said, I was going to lose something.

I knotted my hands into fists until my fingernails cut into my palms, and said, "I'd take the promotion."

Morrison let out a breath like he'd been holding it and inclined his head. "Congratulations, then."

That was all there was to say: he stepped away, turning to his vehicle. I whispered, "Thanks," as he pulled the door open, then raised my voice abruptly to say, "Morrison."

He looked back over the Toyota's door, squinting in the sunlight. "Mel's making dinner for everybody at their place tonight. You want to come?" I heard my own voice with a distant sense of astonishment, wondering what exactly I thought I was doing. Trying, maybe. Trying to tell him something my choice didn't allow for.

There was the faintest hint of expression I couldn't read in Morrison's blue gaze. No: I could read it. All it would take was shifting my sight a little, letting myself see what the colors of his aura told me. I didn't do it, and after a few seconds he said, "I think I'd better not."

I didn't mean to close my eyes. I didn't want to. It was too much of a give-away. Still, my eyelids pressed shut for a moment, my heart lurching like I'd taken a hit. Or, maybe more accurately, a hint. The door on *was it real* had closed. I opened my eyes again and nodded a little, somewhat astonished at my ability to keep breathing. "See you at work, then, sir." One more nail in the coffin. I offered a faint smile that felt like regret, and said, "Captain," very softly.

"Detective," he said, almost as softly, and now that we knew where we stood, he got in his car and drove away. I watched sunlight glitter off his bumper as the Toyota turned out of sight, then put my chin against my chest, eyes closed for a few moments. Making a deliberate choice as to my path didn't feel quite as liberating as I wished it did, but it was a place to begin. I exhaled and scooped up my toolbox, patting Petite's roof as I slid the box into the passenger-side foot well and climbed into my car after it. There were a few hours until dinner. Maybe I'd see how fast and how far I could go, before then. "It's a place to start," I murmured aloud.

Petite rumbled agreement as I turned the ignition. I even found a smile by the time we hit the road.

C.E. (Catie) Murphy holds an utterly impractical degree in English and history, making her unfit for any sort of duty beyond Web design and novel writing. Fortunately, those are precisely the sorts of things she likes to do.

At age six, Catie submitted several poems to an elementary school publication. The teacher producing it chose (inevitably) the one she thought was the worst of the three, but he also stopped her in the hall one day and said two words that made an indelible impression: "Keep writing."

Heady stuff for a six-year-old. It was sound advice, and she's pretty much never looked back.

She lives in Alaska with her husband, Ted, roommate Shaun and a number of pets. More information about Catie and her writing can be found at www.cemurphy.net.

LUNA™

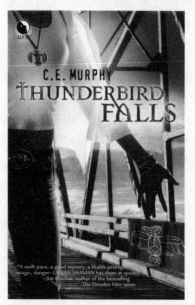